DEAD MAN'S TRUST

Joshua Bane's eyes narrowed into somber slits of fury. "I want to know who put the kill order out, Art."

"It may be buried."

"Dig it up."

"If the information still exists, I'll find it. You have my word on that."

Bane briefly swung his eyes around him. "You left your bodyguards in the lobby, Art. You took quite a chance."

Arthur Jorgenson swallowed hard. "They'd have only gotten in the way. I trust you, Josh, and besides, if you wanted to kill me badly enough, a hundred of them wouldn't have made a difference."

Bane said nothing.

Jorgenson started to stand up. "Then let's go see the President, Josh. It's time to—"

Jorgenson's head snapped backward. He collapsed back into his chair.

"Art!" Bane screamed, grabbing him.

Jorgenson's head slumped to his chest, his eyes open and sightless. A neat hole the size of a nickel had been carved in his forehead. . . .

VORTEX
by Jon Land

ZEBRA BOOKS
KENSINGTON PUBLISHING CORP.

ZEBRA BOOKS

are published by

Kensington Publishing Corp.
475 Park Avenue South
New York, N.Y. 10016

First printing: November 1984

Printed in the United States of America

For Ann, who makes my words the best they can be,
and
For Toni, who made it all happen

ACKNOWLEDGMENTS

Prologue

"CA Twenty-Two, we have you on visual."

Jake Del Gennio glanced up from his console at the 727 sliding toward Kennedy Airport.

"Descend to fifteen hundred. CA Twenty-Two, you are cleared for final approach."

"Roger, Kennedy Tower. Fifteen hundred. See you on the ground."

Del Gennio turned back to the screen and watched the blips flash regularly within the circular grid, flight number and altitude shadowing their lapse into the green void. CA Twenty-Two rested on the right of the screen, just off center, edging closer with each sweep of the line marker across the grid.

The blip of Flight 22 flashed 1,500.

Del Gennio moved his eyes to the window and found the jet as it swung into its final bank, gliding in line with runway two-niner. Everything was normal, strictly routine. Del Gennio held his tired eyes closed for an instant, then opened them to look at the viewing screen.

The blip of Flight 22 was gone.

Del Gennio blinked rapidly and rubbed his eyelids. The line marker swept across the jet's last position on the grid, showing only green as if the void had swallowed it.

Feeling panic rise, Del Gennio struggled from his chair and searched the sky beyond the tower.

Empty. CA Twenty-Two was nowhere to be found.

Del Gennio figured the 727 had already landed. He must have lapsed behind the console, certainly not unheard of in the high-pressured job of an air-traffic controller, lapsed long enough for Flight 22 to find the runway. He looked down.

Runway two-niner was as empty as the sky.

Del Gennio touched his headset to reassure himself it was there.

"CA Twenty-Two, do you read me?"

Nothing.

"CA Twenty-Two, this is Kennedy Tower, do you read me?"

Heads in the control room turned toward Del Gennio's console. No one moved.

"CA Twenty-Two, this is Kennedy Tower, please acknowledge."

Still nothing.

"Oh my God . . ."

Del Gennio hit the red emergency button hard. A siren wailed, earsplitting, seeming to come from the very bowels of the airport itself.

The damn thing went down, Del Gennio thought. *I was looking right at it and it went down. . . .*

Del Gennio steadied the curved microphone beneath his chin. "Kennedy Emergency Control, Flight 22 is down in western sector, mark 17. Repeat, western sector, mark 17."

The area surrounding Kennedy Airport had been divided into a number of squares to promote simple and specific demarcation in the event of an emer-

10

gency. Del Gennio had relayed the area of the jet's last reported position calmly without so much as glancing at the map posted on the wall. He was a pro. Pros didn't have to glance.

"Kennedy Emergency Control, please acknowledge."

The acknowledgment was drowned out by the blasting horns and revving engines of rescue equipment racing toward the scene of the suspected . . . crash. Del Gennio consciously used the word he'd been avoiding and shivered at the horrible thought he might be somehow to blame. Had his lapse behind the console caused this disaster? Guilt chewed at him.

The emergency vehicles streaked off the runway into a field in the western sector toward mark 17 and a downed airliner, the nightmare of everyone connected with the aviation field. Del Gennio imagined the screams, the sickeningly corrosive smells of burned wires, metal . . . and flesh. He shuddered, memories of Vietnam hitting him square in a gut already wrenched with knots.

The emergency vehicles screeched out of sight. Del Gennio strained to see them through the window, standing alone. The rest of the tower team worked frantically to reroute or hold other aircraft. Kennedy Airport was being brought to a total standstill.

Del Gennio expected to see smoke, flames, some evidence of the crash. But there was no sign, no sign at all. Might the pilot have made a successful emergency landing? No. If so, he would have established immediate radio contact, unless the equipment had failed. Even in that case, though, the MAYDAY button would still be operational and no such signal had registered on the screen.

It didn't make sense.

"Kennedy Tower, this is Rescue Boss, please repeat

crash coordinates.''

"Western sector, mark 17," Del Gennio obliged, a bit puzzled. Weren't the rescue personnel there yet? Christ, people were dying!

"Kennedy Tower, western sector, mark 17 is all clear. Repeat, all clear."

"That's . . . impossible."

The Rescue Boss dispensed with the formalities. "Look, Del Gennio, I don't know what the fuck's going on up there but down here I can't find nothing but crab grass."

Del Gennio's eyes darted back to his screen, as though expecting Flight 22 to reappear. It didn't.

"The plane went down," he insisted, a room full of caustic stares cast upon him.

"Well," came the voice of the Rescue Boss, "it didn't go down here."

"Then what the hell happened to it?"

The First Day:

BANE

Well we all have a face
That we hide away forever
And we take them out and show ourselves
When everyone has gone.
Some are satin, some are steel
Some are silk and some are leather;
They're the faces of a stranger
But we love to try them on.

—*Billy Joel*

Chapter One

When Joshua Bane saw the man in the wheelchair, his first thought was to leave the rally because too many memories had already been rekindled. But it had been the hope that the cripple might be in attendance that had drawn him here in the first place, so he swallowed the past down, tucked his hands into the pockets of his windbreaker, and started across the Central Park grass.

It was exceptionally cold for spring, damp and drizzly, and Bane watched his breath misting before him in rhythm with his stride. Perfect atmosphere for a sullen rally of Vietnam veterans the country had done its best to forget. Most came in the uniforms they had worn in the jungles, the pants let out a few inches, the lowermost buttons of the shirts left undone. No one noticed.

Central Park in spring proved a gathering place for just about any group with a cause winter had forced indoors. Some stated theirs better than others, and today's group was having difficulty stating theirs at all. The moist air was playing hell with the makeshift PA set atop a low stage, and the succession of speakers had to battle feedback just to make themselves heard. Some gave up.

Bane reached the man in the wheelchair and tightened his fingers around the rear handgrips.

"Been a long time, Josh," the cripple said without turning.

"A year anyway, Harry," Bane acknowledged lamely.

Harry turned just enough to meet Bane's eyes. "I saw you over there before. I was hoping you'd come over." He looked back at the low stage. "What do you put the crowd at?"

"Five hundred maybe."

"I'd say closer to three. Bad weather shoots the shit out of rallies. In the fall we drew almost two thousand."

"'We'?"

"I belong with these guys, Josh. It doesn't matter that I have to mumble an answer when they ask me what unit I served with."

Bane released his grip, stiffened. "You served with the best, Harry."

The cripple swung his chair around. "We made quite a team, Josh, the Winter Man and the Bat— God, how I still hate that damn nickname. Sounds like something out of a fuckin' comic book." He paused. "We could have won that damn war."

"We weren't supposed to. Politics."

"Fuck politics."

"We did . . . plenty of times."

The two men looked away from each other, lapsing into silence. Sporadic applause filtered around them as another speaker, this one wearing a green beret, rose to take his chances with the microphone. Bane searched for words to comfort Harry, quick and witty ones, but nothing came, maybe because there was nothing to say and even less to hold them together, just memories going back fifteen years that had dried and warped with time.

In his walking days, Harry "the Bat" Bannister stood a shade over six feet and carried 200 evenly

16

layered pounds of muscle on his frame. The exact derivation of his nickname had been lost long before to myth, though the best information put it in 1969 near the Mekong Delta. His platoon had been ambushed and slaughtered by a troop of Vietcong. Harry rolled free of the initial fire burst and lurched to his feet with rifle blasting. When his clip was exhausted, Harry considered running only long enough to reject it. He had long been an expert on knife throwing, so he used the occasion to rocket six razor-sharp blades into the unsuspecting throats or chests of the enemy. And when his knives were gone, he charged the enemy, swinging his rifle like a Louisville Slugger. Maybe the Vietcong were too shocked to respond. Maybe Harry's bat was too fast. Either way, he held them off for an additional thirty seconds which proved long enough for help to respond. Harry spent two months in an army hospital, recovering from wounds he'd never felt being inflicted. He came out with a promotion and a nickname: the Bat.

The Bat saw Joshua Bane for the first time when Bane stared down at him as he lay in his hospital bed. Something impressed Harry immediately, something about his eyes.

"The name's Bane, Captain."

Harry noted his civilian clothes. "You from the USO or something?"

"Something."

Harry was going to smile but he thought better of it. He had placed Bane's eyes, the cold, deep-set stare and the blinks that came with astonishing deliberateness. They were the eyes of a man who walked away from every battle without a scratch, a man you always hesitated to call your friend and feared almost as much as the enemy.

"What can I do for you, Mr. Bane?"

"I'd like you to join my unit."

"Green Berets?"

"Not exactly."

"What then?"

"I had you figured for the kind of man who left asking for later."

"Count me in," Harry said.

Harry stayed in through Nam and longer, when Clandestine Operations found places for both of them in its network. And now Bane looked down at the Bat's withered frame and felt his flesh crawl with guilt. It was his fault Harry was in this chair, and that had kept him from making contact after they'd left the Game.

"So how are things with the Winter Man these days?" the Bat asked. "What have you been up to?"

"Lots of travel. It's different as a tourist, you know. You actually get to *see* the country. No late night escapades, no frantic border crossings, no dark men with guns lurking behind corners." Bane stopped, realizing his words had sounded rehearsed because, in fact, they had been. "Things are quiet, Harry," he said, softer now. "I've grown to like it that way."

"Come off it, Josh, this is the Bat you're talking to," Harry snapped, running his hand through his damp hair as if to hold back the emerging gray. "The Winter Man's no fucking tourist."

"The Winter Man died a long time ago."

The Bat regarded Bane knowingly. "You can bullshit the others, Josh, but you can't bullshit old Harry. Your eyes haven't changed and neither has the way you move. The best stays on top."

Bane shook his head. "I was the best because people thought I was the best. Only it was just a matter of time before they realized they were seeing shadows. I got out just in time. The shadows were everywhere."

"And what about Trench and Scalia? Is that the

way they've managed their lives too?"

Bane flinched. Trench and Scalia were generally regarded as the greatest killers operating in the East or West, now that the Winter Man had taken himself out of the Game. Their allegiances fluctuated from year to year or month to month depending on who was paying the most. These days that usually meant the Arabs.

"Trench and Scalia are probably dead," Bane offered softly.

"Not unless the Winter Man killed them." The Bat glanced down at his useless legs. "Trench put me in this damn chair. I still owe him for that."

"It should have been my assignment. You went in my place. I fucked up and you covered my ass."

"It was Trench who blew my spine apart. A debt's a debt. I'll get him all right."

"Give it up, Harry. It's over. You had your run and it was a damn good one. In the Game you're only better than the man you've got centered in your cross hairs. Everything's relative. Nobody stays on top for long."

"You did, Josh."

"I didn't let it get to me. I got out in time."

The Bat looked at him grimly. "Did you? Did either of us? I lost my legs so they put me behind a computer keyboard. You lost your nerve and your family"—Bane squirmed at that—"so you quit, except you're still held to them by that check you pick up at the Center every other week. We haven't escaped the Game, not by a longshot. We're still playing it, but on their terms instead of our own."

A scuffle broke out just in front of the podium. A leftover sixties radical had gotten too close and said too much. He was being unceremoniously removed. Some of his friends rushed to his rescue. The scuffle grew, closing on Bane and the Bat. Josh watched

19

Harry's eyes come to life as he drew the zipper of his green fatigue jacket down. Clearly, the possibility of violence had charged him.

"I've got four of the goddamn sharpest throwing knives in the world in here," he whispered to Bane, never taking his eyes off the approaching mayhem. "Lord fuck a duck, I'd like nothing better than to hurl a blade at one of those bastards. You carrying, Josh?"

"No."

The Bat's eyes dipped to the fingers Bane held tautly by his sides, coiled springs ready to leap out.

"Then again," he said, "you're always carrying—those damn hands of yours. I've seen what they can do. If my legs weren't dead, I'd've fucked these knives long ago and taken lessons from that bastard friend Conglon of yours. How is the King these days?"

"Never better," Bane said, not bothering to add that he worked out at the King's gym two hours a day on the average. The workouts added discipline to his life, a place to go at a given time, regularly. Without them, Bane often feared one day would swirl unnoticeably into the next. He was pushing forty, just one year down the road now. He had to work the muscles harder and harder just to maintain their present level. The sweat and pain, meanwhile, made the world he had turned his back on seem real and up close again, almost as though it was tapping him on the shoulder.

"Give the King my regards next time you see him. Toughest son of a bitch I've ever met. If we'd had him in Nam, they would've had to let us win the damn war."

"He speaks well of you too, Harry. Always had a lot of respect for what you could do with a knife."

"Yeah, but hands are better. They're always there and they never let you down. If I had it to do all over again, I'd specialize in hands. Lord fuck a duck, legs sure as hell haven't done me much good."

"I came to the rally today because I knew you'd be here," Bane admitted suddenly.

Harry's face brightened.

"And there was something else. Jake Del Gennio left a message with my service this morning."

"The Swan!" Harry beamed. "No shit! You call him back?"

"Not yet."

"But you're gonna, right? I mean, he probably just wants to go over old times."

"Sure," Bane said, but somehow he knew otherwise. Del Gennio, the Swan, was a helicopter pilot who had spent more time behind enemy lines in Nam than anyone else with wings, always stopping just long enough to pick Bane up or drop him off. As the personal chauffeur of the Winter Man, he had to get out of more scrapes and jams than any dozen of his fellows. They hadn't spoken in years, and Del Gennio wasn't the type who liked to sit over a six-pack and rehash the past. He had called because something was up.

"I'm glad I came over, Harry," Bane added. "I really am."

"So am I." A pause. "I didn't mean to make you a backboard for my miseries but there aren't many people left I can spill my guts to."

"What are friends for?"

A smile crossed the Bat's lips. His eyes scanned the perimeter of men who had become soldiers again for the day.

"It wasn't really so bad over there, was it, Josh?"

"It was hell, Harry, but it wasn't so bad."

"Let's have a drink soon . . . for old time's sake."

"There is no old time's sake, but we'll have a drink anyway."

Chapter Two

"What took you so long, Josh?" Jake Del Gennio asked nervously. "I've been waiting by the phone for hours."

Bane's grip tightened around the receiver in the first pay phone he saw after leaving the rally.

"It's been a busy day."

"Well, I've been sweating bullets. You don't know what hell I've been through, Josh, you don't!"

"Easy, Jake, easy. You haven't even said hello to me yet."

"I'll save it till we talk in person. I've got to see you."

"What's up?"

"I can't discuss it over the phone. The world's going crazy and no one wants to listen."

"Okay, but why me? It's been a long time."

"Because I'm desperate, Josh. I need someone who can get answers."

"Jake—"

"How soon can we meet?"

Bane checked his watch, found it was pushing four-thirty. He had planned on going straight to the King's for a workout but that could be put off till evening. Fewer kids around the gym anyway.

"Six o'clock," he said. "Dinner at La Maison on

East Fifty-eighth."

"I'll be there," promised Del Gennio.

Del Gennio was waiting in La Maison at a corner table in clear view of the entrance. They shook hands, Bane detecting a slight tremble in the Swan's grip. Then he noticed the half-empty wine carafe.

"I never knew the Swan to be a drinker," he said, sitting down.

"Well, this is the first time the Swan has been too scared to sleep," Del Gennio retorted abruptly. "And that includes Nam, Josh. At least then you knew what was going on."

"And now?"

Del Gennio leaned forward. "You figure it's safe to talk here?"

"It's clean," Bane assured him. "New York branch of the CIA even has a charge here."

Del Gennio tried to smile and failed. "I need you, Josh. The whole world's gone whacko and you're the only one I know who can set it straight again. . . . It's deep, Josh, real deep."

"*What's* deep?"

Del Gennio ran his hands over his face. "It started two days ago. I . . . lost a plane."

"A crash? Oh God . . . But I haven't heard anything on the news."

"Because it didn't crash. I just . . . lost it. One second it was there and then . . ." Del Gennio went on to relate the events of two days before when Flight 22 appeared to vanish into thin air.

"And what do your superiors say?" Bane asked when he had finished.

"That's just it. They don't say anything. I go to them with my story and all they do is put me off, a

23

first-rate stall."

"But you guys make tapes of everything. They should back you up."

Del Gennio's lips quivered. "I heard the tape for the first time yesterday morning. My voice is the only one on it. Nothing from the cockpit."

"Could be equipment malfunction."

"No way. I checked my terminal inside and out."

"You tell your superiors that?"

"Sure and they kept insisting that I imagined the whole thing. They said Flight 22 came in ninety minutes late due to equipment malfunction and has been dry-docked for repairs."

"You check the hangar?"

Del Gennio nodded. "The 727 in question was present and accounted for. But that doesn't mean shit because I know it disappeared for a while, from visual *and* from the board. A sophisticated *radar* board, Josh. But it's not the machine that's got me losing sleep, it's these." Del Gennio pointed at his eyes. "These never lied to me before. Something happened to that plane and somebody's covering it up. Somebody wants to keep a tight lid on this. They erased the cockpit side of the tape but they can't erase me."

"You call the airline?"

"A dozen times. All unreturned. Nobody wants to talk about it there either."

"Somebody must, Jake. That plane must've been carrying one hundred fifty people. . . ."

"It was undersold. Just sixty-seven passengers."

"All the same, if something happened to the jet, don't you think they would have complained? It'd be all over the papers by this time."

"Now we're on the same wavelength, Josh. I figured I'd check out the passengers on my own, except no one will give me a copy of the manifest. They've stuck me on desk duty and next month I'm up for reevaluation. They're gonna try to can me, Josh, I just know they are. They think I've cracked, gone schizo or something." Del Gennio's voice was frantic, panicked. He seemed short of breath. "It happened, Josh, I know it did. You're the only one I know who can get the real answers, dig them up before somebody buries them altogether."

Bane looked at the fear in his friend's eyes and patted his arm. "You flew into muddy hell to pick my ass up more times than anyone should have asked you to and never once with all the bullets and bombs did I ever see your hand waver on the joystick. You aren't the kind of man to lose your nerve easily or your marbles at all. So when you tell me that something strange happened at Kennedy two days ago, I believe you. *Something* happened, but let's face it, Jake, jets don't disappear."

"This one did."

It was eight-thirty by the time Bane dropped Del Gennio off at his apartment and drove off toward the King's gym in Harlem. He didn't know exactly what to make of the Swan's story but neither did he pass it off. Men like Del Gennio didn't crack under pressure. He agreed to meet the Swan at Kennedy the following morning to obtain more details with which to begin his investigation.

The sky was totally black now, and Bane felt the shadows of the long-gone years creeping up again.

Bane had gone into the army only because he was drafted. He saw no sense in the war and even less in protesting it. He accepted his induction and subsequent assignment to boot camp impassively without enthusiasm or fear, found he enjoyed the rigors of training and excelled in them far above the other recruits. He started noticing men watching him—some in uniforms bearing lines of medals, others in civilian suits. Two weeks later, Bane was transferred to a secret base along with a dozen others from similar boot camps.

They were told simply they had displayed . . . something . . . that warranted a more specialized training. This training went on eighteen hours a day every day, both mental and physical—all torturous. The number of recruits fell quickly until Bane alone was left. He learned all aspects of violence, learned to embrace, even cherish it. He learned to love the physical tests his instructors put him through. Survival training. Subversion. Infiltration. Guerrilla fighting. Killing.

Guns were fine but noisy.

Knives adequate but not always reliable.

Hands were always there, quick and silent.

Bane preferred hands.

He learned to kill a hundred different ways with them. Closed fist or opened hand, it mattered not at all. He could snap a neck in a second, crush a throat in under two. The exercises and drills went on and on, offering him new challenges all the time.

One made him take out three men in sight of each other in less than a minute under cover of darkness, then had him repeat the same exercise in daylight.

Another left him weaponless in a forest with a half dozen heavily armed men in pursuit, his task being to neutralize them all in under an hour. Timing was everything. Success counted on it.

A third forced him to live in the wilds for two weeks with no food, no water, no weapons, not even any clothes.

26

The training continued for six months. Joshua Bane was taught to be a machine whose conceptions of right and wrong never extended beyond his orders. There was work to be done that would take a machine to accomplish. The slightest hesitation would mean failure. Thus, all traces of conscience and morality vanished as the machine's parts were tightened and honed. The weeks passed . . . dragged. The games grew tiresome. Bane craved reality. He felt like a spreading pool of gasoline thirsting for a tossed match.

One night his six instructors were playing cards when the lights went out in their cabin. The sounds of a struggle followed briefly before the lights snapped back on to reveal a grinning Bane hovering over the bound, gagged, and defeated frames of his instructors.

He had passed his final test. A machine was never allowed into the field until he was more than ready. He must, first, have reached a point where he could live *only* in that frame of mind, where that kind of life was the only viable option. And to prove his ascension to that level, he had to go beyond the play book and create his own rules. On the night Bane had raided his instructors' cabin, he'd proved he was all this and more. The student had become the master. He was ready for the field.

Bane spent a good portion of the next five years behind enemy lines. The subject of his missions changed almost daily but the intent never varied: to disrupt the enemy, break down his chain of command and channels of communication through sabotage, espionage or elimination. Mostly elimination.

The machine that had once been Joshua Bane did not require information, just input; not explanations, just orders. He killed as instructed neatly, precisely, and coldly.

Cold as ice.

They called him the Winter Man.

Buried deep within the machine, though, lay something that still thought, reasoned, even felt. While en route to meet the Swan's chopper after a typically successful assignment, the Winter Man came across a burning schoolhouse in a Vietnamese village. Four times he ventured into the flames to emerge with the last of the trapped children, never hesitating or bothering to consider the risk.

A photographer for one of the wire services snapped a whole series of pictures in the midst of the action, some of them close-ups displaying the strangely calm look on Bane's face as he ran to and from the burning building. This, the reporter noted in a tag line, was the work of a true hero. These might have been among the most dramatic pictures of the war, if they had been allowed to run. Army Intelligence and the Pentagon could not have the face of their personal killing machine plastered over the front pages of every daily paper in the U.S. Conveniently, the film proved faulty, the pictures developed into formless blurs. The photographer could do nothing but shrug. The processor smiled and set about recounting the wad of bills his unusual assignment had gained him.

The Winter Man remained in the shadows.

And now Joshua Bane drove past a faded, peeling sign resting over an equally faded building: King Cong's Gym. He swung off 140th Street in search of a space. They were difficult to come by at this time of night in Harlem but Bane knew a place where there were always a few to be found. Cars belonging to the King's patrons were never vandalized, and Bane had been watched often and long enough by hidden eyes to know that included his.

He pulled his stylish and functional Cressida up in front of a boarded storefront two blocks from the gym. The thought of walking through a not-so-friendly section of Harlem in total darkness caused him not the slightest hesitation or concern. He was out of his car and walking before the open hostility of the area struck him.

Fifteen yards and one burned-out building later, he realized he was being followed. Bane didn't pick up his pace here but slowed it, feeling the hackles on the back of his neck rise stiffly. Always the unexpected, that was the key, anything to throw the opposition's timing off. More. Slowing down increased his options while lowering those of his pursuer.

More time passed before he stepped over each dirty sidewalk crack, but Bane felt his tail holding ground, maintaining the gap between them at forty-five feet, maybe forty. Bane swung quickly, in a crouch, found no one behind him, and turned back to the front. His pursuer was good, very good. The advantage belonged to him now. Bane had given himself away, forfeited his element of surprise, and worse, lost track of his pursuer's position. His ears scanned the perimeter about him. He didn't trust eyes. By the time you saw something, it was usually too late to do much about it.

Bane slowed his pace to a crawl.

This was no amateur tailing him, no Harlem hotdog or mugger. Bane would have made one of those in an instant and sent him scurrying home to mama. No, this was the real thing, someone in the Game and a damn good player at that. For the first time, Bane regretted he wasn't carrying a weapon. His confidence in his hands was absolute but there were times when one of the Bat's throwing knives or a cool Browning would feel very good indeed.

His pursuer was almost on top of him now. Bane sensed him all right but had no idea of the man's position. Bane's fingers coiled, ready to spring. He passed into the shadows cast by a streetlight, saw Conglon's battered gym sign just up ahead, and let himself relax briefly.

Too long.

The huge shape rose before him out of the darkness and air, stayed there just long enough for Bane to realize it was gone. Then a massive arm snaked toward his throat, stopped only when Bane got his forearm up in time to act as a wedge. He sidestepped and ducked but his opponent was equal to the task, more than equal, flowing with the move and pummeling Bane's kidney with something that felt like steel.

Suddenly two massive arms joined over his solar plexus, and with great surprise Bane felt his 210 pounds being hoisted effortlessly into the air, just enough pressure being applied to squeeze his breath away and keep it from him as his ribs began to give.

Bane had gone into a counter move he doubted very much would work when a raspy voice slipped into his ear and everything made sense.

"Gotcha," said the King.

Chapter Three

King Cong's 300 pounds might once have been more solid but his six-foot-eight-inch frame had never been more menacing. If anything, the white patches which decorated his thick black afro made him seem even more chilling and monstrous. He slapped Bane on the back, came up barely short of hugging him, and they walked across the street to the giant's gym.

"Been a long time since we played a round of the old game, Josh boy."

"A year at least. You must have been practicing."

King Cong shook his head, stretched his massive arms. "Uh-uh. I'm too old for that sorta shit. Turned fifty last week, you know."

"But you didn't have a party."

"Don't want to go pushin' my luck any now, do I? All those little fuckers runnin' around the street who'd like nothin' better than to do in the King just might take a poke at me if they knew I hit half a century."

"You worried?"

"Hell yeah. I killed enough for one man already. Don't wanna have to kill no more, 'less I do the choosin'."

Bane followed the King into the gym where the air

was stale and thick with sweat. There were two boxing rings, a host of heavy and speed bags, and what could easily have been a thousand barbells. No fancy machines or devices, just cold hard steel dominating the floor. Free weights were the only way to go, Bane knew. The modern stuff didn't even come close. Watchful eyes followed him across the floor. Few acknowledged him, but no one questioned his presence. There was a code in the King's gym that superseded race. When someone needed a spotter, Bane was quick to respond and the favor was always returned. Nonetheless, no other white man was afforded such courtesy mainly because no other white man trained here.

He followed the King into the surprisingly clean locker room.

"So what you plannin' tonight, Josh boy?"

"Some time on the heavy bag, maybe two hours on the upper body."

"You been workin' those legs enough?"

"The usual."

"Gotta work 'em more. That's where quickness comes from. You lose them, just say good-bye." The King made sure the locker room was deserted before continuing. "Like tonight. I'm a fuckin' old man, Josh boy. I got more aches in me than you shot loads, and some days it takes a whole team of horses to pull me outta bed. But I caught ya on the street out there. I had ya." There was no sense of triumph in the King's voice.

"Just a game, King."

"So why don't you fuckin' tell me what isn't? That ain't the point and it don't mean diddley shit. What matters is that back there on the street you was only ready for someone not as good as you. An equal or better coulda fucked ya sideways."

Bane shrugged, opened his locker.

"Don't go spacey on me, Josh boy. It's me that taught ya how to stay alive so some mornin' if I open the paper and read that you got yourself shot or somethin' on a dark street, I'd feel awful bad. Kinda like it was my fault for not teachin' ya good enough. You still got the magic, but that don't mean you rightly remembers how to make it work for ya." King Cong sat down on a bench and turned his mouth into a tooth-filled grin. "Maybe I best give ya some more lessons."

Twenty-three years before as a high school sophomore, Joshua Bane had found himself totally disinterested in traditional sports. Playing basketball and football and all the glory that went with them meant nothing to him. Growing up in the Bronx had taught him to be tough inside but it was time to learn how to be tough outside as well. So Josh threw a fair chunk of his savings into a set of weights and began rising every morning at five A.M. to begin the day with a strenuous one-hour workout. He pushed himself until his muscles throbbed and pounded, and then he pushed himself even harder. He pushed himself unmercifully in a musty cellar scorched by summer heat and unguarded against winter cold, and still looked for more.

Josh knew a number of boys who boxed and a lesser number who had gotten involved with something called Karate. He knew nothing about the latter, other than it was taught mostly by slippery, lithe Japanese men who could move like the wind. He listened almost daily to arguments between boxers and Karate students over which made you a better fighter. These arguments formed the basis of his decision: instead of studying one, he would study both.

He went right from school to a boxing gym for a

workout that on alternate days featured calisthenics, running, heavy bag work, speed bag work, shadow boxing, sparring, and always jumping rope. Then he'd rush home for dinner, which on lucky nights he was able to gobble down in time to make the ninety-minute Karate workout at a *dojo* just down the street from his tenement. His arduous training schedule left him no time for after-school jobs. So instead of paying dues at either the gym or the *dojo*, he worked an hour at one or the other every day to cover his time.

As his senior year began, Josh was near black belt level and a solid golden gloves contender. What's more, following his after-dinner Karate workout, he religiously returned home to study for three hours before going to bed. He had taught himself very early in life to exist on small amounts of sleep, an ability which would become a godsend in later years. His parents had both come from the old country, and his father had learned enough about America quickly to know that if you wanted to get somewhere, specifically out of the Bronx, you had to go to college. He had steered Josh in that direction since birth.

George Bane had married late and come to America with modest dreams that became a candy store, one of five in a two-block radius, but the only one that extended credit to kids. George Bane seldom collected on all his monthly debts but the good will that credit generated was enough to assure him of a reasonably comfortable livelihood and to help him come home with a smile every night at six o'clock.

Then one night the smile disappeared.

Josh couldn't pinpoint exactly when his father's character had changed, though generally it seemed to start near the end of his junior year in high school. For months he heard his parents whispering late into the night in their native language, a language Bane had never bothered to learn. So he lay awake nights trying to pick out vaguely familiar words and string them into something that made sense, failing always to even come close.

Josh spent Saturday afternoons at the candy store, helping his father out. It was the busiest time of the week, a make-or-break period so far as profits were concerned. Rainy days were the worst and it was while cleaning up after one that George Bane finally told his son what was going on.

"There are men who come here wanting money from me, Joshey."

Bane's hands tightened into fists. He had heard enough stories around town to know his father was speaking of a protection racket.

"Did you pay them?"

"At first, no. Then other merchants came to me and said they were approached too, threatened even, and I got to thinking that maybe a little money wasn't so bad to buy a little piece of mind. So I paid . . . for a while."

"You stopped," Josh said proudly, feeling deep love for the man with thin arms and worn features who was standing up to the biggest thugs in the Bronx.

"Yes, Joshey, I stopped. I got to thinking how could I live with myself if I gave even a dollar of my hard-earned money to these crooks? I met with the other merchants and we agreed we would all stick together and refuse to make any more payments."

"And?"

The old man shrugged.

At once Bane knew. "You're the only one holding out."

His father shrugged, managed a slight nod.

"Dad, you've got to go to the police, you've—"

"Achhhhh, you know better than me, Joshey, that the police can do nothing. Calling them will only make things worse. But I can't pay anymore. I came to this country to get away from scoundrels like this. I spent most of my life living in fear and submission. I can't have that again."

"You've told the collectors?"

"I've told them."

"But they still come by."

"Sometimes yes, sometimes no." The old man shifted his weary shoulders. "Maybe someday they'll give up."

It was the beginning of a cold fall on another rainy Saturday when two men in overcoats came in at the store's busiest time and asked to see George Bane outside. Before Josh could object, his father had grabbed his arm, surprising him with a strong grip.

"I can't run away, Joshey. They'll ask me for money like always and I'll refuse and they'll leave."

George Bane walked into the rain without his coat. Seconds later two blasts rang out. Josh ran out into the street in time to see a car screeching away from the curb and his father lying dead in the gutter, blood from the two bullet wounds washing away toward a storm drain.

Josh started screaming and didn't stop until the police arrived.

The thugs knew his father was becoming an example for the other merchants so they made him a different kind of example. The daylight murder in front of dozens of witnesses, virtually all of them children, was a bold stroke undertaken to force the entire neighborhood into utter submission. Instead of fifty dollars a month, the price for protection would now be a hundred. And the neighborhood went along.

The police, meanwhile, were strangely unable to find any trace of George Bane's murderers despite detailed descriptions, which increased Josh's rage and frustration all the more. With nothing else to do, he turned all his thoughts toward revenge, glad in a way that the police weren't trying to catch the killers because now he could deal with them himself. He thirsted for a vengeance only killing the butchers personally could quench. That goal occupied his every waking hour. He planned for it, prepared for it—the knot in his stomach tied tighter each day. He'd get them all right; that certainty was the only way he could live with what had happened.

While Bane was quite aware of his own physical prowess, he was equally aware that even such prowess could not allow him to kill as effectively as he must. And all the bone-crunching workouts in the world couldn't change that. Killing was something new, foreign. He wanted to do it, but he didn't know how. The time had come to seek out a new type of training and a new kind of instructor.

Any kid on the street could tell you that the toughest man in New York was a black hulk named Gus Conglon, better known as King Cong. Bane learned the name of the Harlem bar where the King hung out and went there one afternoon after school.

He started through the door, his guts in his throat. But he swallowed them back down reminding himself of why he was here. A dozen pairs of black eyes turned from the bar and followed his progress, mouths agape in astonishment. Bane never hesitated, just kept walking toward the corner booth where the biggest man he had ever seen sat sipping a beer.

"You lookin' for me, white boy?"

"You the King?"

"That's what my friends call me."

Bane caught his breath. "Can I sit down?"

King Cong laughed in amazement. "Sure, white boy. Sorry I can't offer you a beer but I only got one glass."

Bane sat there, going numb.

"Well, white boy, my time's precious and the clock's runnin'."

Bane saw no other choice but to get to the point. "Two men killed my father ten days ago," he said lamely.

The King looked at him a little closer, nodding. "The candy man over in the Bronx?"

Bane nodded.

"I heard about that. Clock's still runnin', white boy. What you want from me?"

Bane pulled a wad of bills, all his savings, from his pocket and pushed them across the table. "It's not much but I'll get more. I'll pay you whatever you want, everything I have."

That brought a smile to the King's face. "Well, white boy, I been offered all sorts of stuff by people before but I never been offered everything. What you want me to do, ice those two dudes for you?"

"No," Bane said staunchly. "I want you to teach me how to do it myself."

The smile vanished. "Some things can't be taught," the King said and he poured himself another beer, trying hard to look away from the grim, determined boy before him.

Bane's expression didn't waver. Wordlessly, he held his ground.

The King chugged his beer, smacked his lips. "Well, white boy, you already know how to fight; I could tell that much by the way you move. Bet you're damn good too. Trouble is you're used to rules and regulations. Ain't none of those on the streets." The

38

King swept a massive hand across the table and covered Bane's eyes before he could react. "Take away the light and most fighters are near fuckin' helpless." He pulled his hand back. Bane twisted his features. "But the streets are dark and uneven. You got to learn the street way if you want to ice people. Most people get killed after dark. That's the way it'll be for those two dudes who iced your father."

"Then you'll teach me?"

King Cong cracked another smile and pushed the wad of bills back across the table. "What the hell, right? Just get ready to work harder than you ever worked before."

"When do we get started?"

Class began the very next afternoon and Bane learned more about fighting and staying alive in one session with the King than he had in two years of boxing and Karate. Conglon set up an obstacle course in his cellar and tied a blindfold around Bane's eyes.

"Now I don't want you tryin' to dance through this like some ballet faggot," he warned. "Speed's all that matters, speed and balance. If you trip, don't fall. If you bang into somethin', don't let it slow you down."

After two weeks on the obstacle course, the King moved class into a nearby alley and then to the streets themselves, at night mostly. He taught Bane how to use darkness instead of avoiding it, showed him how to focus on an outline or shadow instead of a complete shape. Motion was the key; maintaining yours while you followed your opponent's. Sounds had to be picked up, filtered, analyzed immediately. Attacks came most often from the rear and sounds always preceded them.

In three months Bane was almost able to hold his

own against the King. His senses, all of them, had been improved a thousand percent. He became a skilled night fighter which made him all the more formidable during the day.

"That, white boy, is the point," King Cong told him. "And I'm startin' to think it's time we went to work on those two dudes who made you come round here in the first place."

Bane just nodded. They had spoken barely at all during the months about the motivation behind his coming to the King. He figured the giant had a method and he wasn't about to disrupt it. Patience had to be exercised. Push too hard and the King would push back harder. So Bane waited, though the thought of avenging his father was never far away.

The next day they went to work on guns, specifically a fat snub-nosed revolver with special tape on the trigger and butt that swallowed fingerprints. They only practiced at close range, no more than ten yards and usually less.

"That's the way your hit'll be," the King explained. "And, believe it or not, they's the toughest shots to make."

It took a week before Bane got it down pat.

"Got a line on the hitters who iced your old man," the King said suddenly one night. Later Bane would learn that he had known all along but had held the information back until he was sure his student was ready. "Free-lance muscle for the local strong arms. Not very popular. Won't be missed. That's a break. Anyway, the two of 'em hang out at McGilray's Bar every night. You gotta be waitin' outside for them tomorrow. I'll drive ya. They'll be drunk so you won't have to worry much about them catchin' on but they're still pros so watch your ass."

Josh gnashed his teeth. "I want them to know it's

40

me. I want them to know who's killing them."

The King frowned. "Trouble with that, white boy, is that if they got time to see ya, somebody else might too."

"I'll take that chance."

The King just nodded.

It was raining the next night. Fitting, Bane thought as he huddled on a stoop two doors down from McGilray's. It was one A.M. before the two killers came out of the bar. They were wearing the same overcoats they'd had on that rainy Saturday. He recognized them immediately and realized only one of them was drunk. His heart fluttered but he didn't let himself hesitate.

He moved from the stoop in regular motion, blending with the night. The killers were still standing in front of the bar, inspecting the weather, struggling to light cigarettes in the wind.

Bane stopped six feet away from them.

"This is for George Bane," he said simply and started firing.

The drunk one went fast. The bullets slammed him hard against the building and he slumped down already dead.

The sober one was another matter. He charged forward with two slugs in his gut and kept coming when Bane pumped a third one home. The man was on him before he could get a fourth off and his grasp, born of death and desperation, was the strongest Bane had ever felt. Bane lost his gun, tried to side-step, failed, and felt the man's fingers rising for his throat. The thumbs got there first, and it wasn't until the first of his air had been choked off that all of Bane's night training with the King came back and instinct took over. He shifted his body to the side and broke the choke hold with a wrist lock. When the man tried to regain his grasp, Bane came up and around, grabbing the man's head with a hand on either side and twisting violently. The snap came as loud as any of the gunshots. The man stiffened, crumbled.

A black car screeched to a halt. The passenger door swung open. Bane jumped in.

"Not bad, white boy," the King complimented, tearing away. "Not bad at all. You handled yourself real good."

Bane almost asked the King why he hadn't intervened when things looked bad but didn't because he knew why, knew that this had been his battle to win or lose on his own. That was the way he had wanted it, a code the King understood and wasn't about to break.

Bane sat back in the car and said nothing at all. He felt no guilt, nor did he feel any joy. He felt only an empty sort of relief and a strange certainty from deep within that there would be more killing, much more. Somewhere, someday.

That rainy night, Bane guessed, contained the actual birth of the Winter Man.

And now, more than twenty years later, that memory brought a thin smile to his face as he climbed into his workout gear and looked across at the giant who had started it all.

"What you smilin' at, Josh boy?"

"The old days, King."

"Yeah, remember 'em well. They turned me down for Nam, you know. Said I was too damn old. A couple years past thirty wasn't too old if you ask me, 'specially after the way I laid out those Gooks in Korea. And all I got to show for that is a dishonorable discharge 'cause I knocked out some MP who had no business bein' where he was. I'll tell ya, Josh boy, I coulda had the GI Bill, a nice sweet pension, free doctorin', and a host of other shit. But one punch that broke some shithead's jaw took it all away and I was lucky to stay out of the stockade." The King ran his eyes around the locker room, then cocked his head toward the door. "All I got's this place and only 'cause of you." The King's eyes found Bane again, suddenly warm. "I owe ya, Josh boy."

"Not as much as I owe you."

"Bullshit! I bought this place with your greens."

"Which I made in Vietnam where I stayed alive thanks to what you taught me."

"They paid you well over in that hellhole."

"Money was never the object."

"You know, I mighta even made a pretty fair Winter Man myself, 'cept I ain't exactly got the color for it." The King paused and held Bane's stare. "The Winter Man wouldn'ta let me beat him back there on the street."

"The Winter Man's not around much anymore."

"He's there," the King said surely. "When you need him he'll be there." His hands tightened around his bench. The wood seemed to creak from the pressure. "You and me, Josh boy, we got a lot in common. Both of us in lotsa ways don't belong in this kinda world, me 'specially. Wasn't too long ago a man in these parts could carry himself with his fists. Today twelve-year-old kids are carryin' heaters and ten weeks allowance'll get ya a machine gun. You mind explainin' that to me?"

"Wish I could, King, wish I could."

Chapter Four

Col. Walter Chilgers sat leisurely in the back seat of his limousine as his driver maneuvered through early evening San Diego traffic. As director of COBRA, Control for Operational Ballistic Research and Activation, it was sometimes necessary for him to play the role of politician by meeting with major civic leaders and kowtowing just enough to provide the impression that he gave a shit about what they thought. Such had been the case today, except it had been more ho-hum than usual. Something about the city wanting COBRA to open its doors for a tour by local businessmen. Chilgers hadn't paid much attention.

COBRA sat in a wide expanse of fenced-in land just off the San Diego freeway in virtual spitting distance from the Pacific Ocean. The huge complex of interconnected buildings rose five stories above the ground in some places, four in others. And it would be within these where the tour would take place. Beneath them, meanwhile, in five full underground layers, the real work of COBRA would proceed as usual.

Chilgers checked his watch, found it was 6:10. He had a 6:30 meeting with his two top department heads and he dreaded being late. He prided himself on being punctual and precise and expected the same of any man or woman who served under him. Being late for a meeting was clearly a rebellion against authority, and to Chilgers rebellion in a company that demanded allegiance was grounds for dismissal. Accordingly, employees made doubly sure to reset their standard issue digital watches each and every morning, usually setting them five minutes ahead.

Chilgers leaned forward and looked ahead out the limousine's windshield. An accident up the road had snarled traffic. His flesh started to crawl. He had no tolerance for anyone who couldn't execute a simple right turn without taking someone else's fender with him. People didn't pay attention to anything anymore; that was the problem. But he had weeded them out at COBRA. If the time schedule was strict, the dress code was even stricter. Men were expressly forbidden to work in shirt sleeves even in the confines of their own offices. A woman caught wearing pants to the office would arbitrarily be given two weeks notice if she was fortunate and fired on the spot if she wasn't. Long ago Chilgers had been an officer in the Air Force, and he believed strongly that effectiveness began with discipline.

For himself, Chilgers maintained a stable of three-piece suits he rotated regularly: green on Monday, blue on Tuesday, gray on Wednesday, black on Thursday, and brown on Friday with white and beige saved for weekend duty. The routine never varied. Chilgers wore his suits as stiffly as he'd worn his Air Force uniforms years back, and often when entering the building housing COBRA's facilities he had to fight back an urge to raise his hand in salute to those he passed. His silver hair was trimmed every Friday at 11:45 which left him enough time for a hurried lunch before the start of his weekly staff meetings.

The driver had caught up with the traffic jam. Chilgers' watch told him it was 6:14. No way they could make it at this rate.

"The curb," he said, tapping his driver on the shoulder. "Drive up on the curb, the sidewalk. Get me the hell out of here."

The driver started the wheel to the right. The limousine lurched atop the sidewalk, straddling the curb. Horns honked in protest. Terrified pedestrians dived to the pavement. If any of this bothered Chilgers, he didn't show it. He merely eased his shoulders back and relaxed. He'd make the meeting easily now.

They passed through the front gate of the COBRA complex at 6:26 and moved immediately to Chilgers' private garage bay. Once the door had closed behind them, the floor of the bay began to descend, heading down five stories beneath the earth's surface. Another door slid up at 6:29 and Chilgers hurried from the bay, leaving his chauffeur behind as always. At 6:30 on the dot he swung open the door leading to the conference room which bordered his private office.

"Glad to see you're on time, gentlemen," he said to the two men seated in armchairs off to the right from the conference table. "Let's get started."

The two men rose and waited for the colonel to take his customary black leather chair before being seated again, not noticing him flip on the intercom box resting on the end table next to him. They were a study in contrasts. The larger of the two, Dr. Benjamin Teke, was a composed, confident man whose certainty of his own position on everything bordered on pomposity but never quite crossed over. His head was clean-shaven and round, showcasing his particularly spacious craneal cavity and the—he claimed—

46

particularly large brain contained therein. Though there was no medical evidence to back him up, Teke was undaunted. He had been a COBRA man from the beginning, a damn good researcher who had risen to take over the Confidential Projects section. He was a company man all the way and Chilgers knew he could always count on Teke for support when needed. Teke wasn't nearly as smart as he wanted people to believe, but he was exceptionally good at fooling them. When he failed to do so, there was always the intimidation route at which he was as adept as Chilgers.

Professor Lewis Metzencroy was something else entirely. Slight, balding, and bespectacled, Metzencroy was a genius in every sense of the word but a modest and humble one. Nothing was ever clear-cut for him. He was a scientist in the truest form, believing the purpose of his field was not to pass judgment or even make decisions but simply to discover and explore. He was meticulous in his work and never expounded on any theory or discovery until he had tested it from every conceivable angle. Like Teke, he was a company man, but unlike Teke his relationship with COBRA seldom extended beyond being told what to do and following through. He left the activation part to men like Chilgers who had the stomach for it, because he certainly didn't.

Metzencroy took off his glasses and wiped them with the handkerchief he held perpetually in his right hand.

Colonel Chilgers lit his pipe. "I believe the only item on tonight's agenda is an updated report on the tangent stage of Project Vortex." He met Metzencroy's eyes and already knew there was trouble, a hundred sides about to come to a problem that could have only one. Chilgers liked things neat, clean, and sure. Second-guessing and overexplaining were tantamount to lunacy, curses of the weak. He loathed men like Metzencroy and longed for more like Teke. He realized, however, that Metzencroy, for all his faults, was a brilliant scientist, specifically the scientist who had nursed Project Vortex from its inception. And Project Vortex was the biggest thing COBRA had ever taken on.

Chilgers moved his eyes to Teke. "What is the latest on Flight 22?"

Teke smiled slightly. The bright fluorescent lighting of the underground room bounced off his barren dome. "All computer reports and analyses confirm that we successfully degenerated and then regenerated the jet within all accountable limits of margin for error. In fact, I'm inclined to call the tangent phase a smashing success so far as all practical considerations go."

"I'm inclined to disagree," argued Metzencroy, dabbing nervously at his brow with the ever-present handkerchief. "I studied the readings in detail last night and did some computer enhancements of them this morning. Something's wrong."

Chilgers stroked his pipe. "What?" he asked, trying to sound sincere. Project Vortex was the professor's baby. He couldn't risk aggravating him.

"A bubble," said Metzencroy.

"A bubble?" from Teke.

"In the space/time continuum," the professor continued. "Consider first that the gap in dimensions—the discontinuity—we're talking about isn't much different from a carpet laid over a floor. Sometimes a bubble appears and usually it can be smoothed over . . . unless, of course, the rug was too big to begin with in which case the bubble can be moved but not eliminated."

48

"I'm not a scientist," Chilgers reminded him. "You'll have to speak plainer."

Metzencroy frowned. "The computer grids taken during the tangent stage show a discontinuity, a lapse, probably only a second in duration in which we lost the plane."

"Come now, Professor," the colonel chided. "You know better than I that losing the plane was precisely what we were after."

"To the naked eye, yes. To even the most advanced radar equipment, yes. But not to the computer relays on board. The implications of that are catastrophic."

"But we're only talking about a second, if that," interjected Teke helplessly.

"In the space/time continuum, a second might be an eternity for all we know. Besides, you're missing my point. I'm telling you that for an instant the plane didn't just disappear from sight, it disappeared altogether. It didn't exist anymore anywhere."

"Haven't we experienced similar results before?" asked Chilgers, puffing his pipe.

"Previous tests prior to the tangent stage were conducted at speeds too high for our computers to register accurately. That doesn't mean similar lapses didn't occur."

"I fail to see the enormity of your discovery," snapped Teke.

"Very simply put, Doctor, if the plane, for however long, wasn't where it was supposed to be, then where was it? The computers don't lie. They're telling us that the experiment was out of our control long enough for me to question the feasibility of the project."

Chilgers pulled the pipe from his mouth. "The project?"

"The tangent phase of it at the very least. The new

49

factor might have been more than Project Vortex could endure."

"People," muttered Teke.

"Exactly," echoed Metzencroy. "The whole purpose behind the tangent stage was to test the effects of Vortex on human subjects instead of just machines. I agree with the concept in principle from a scientific standpoint. But from that same standpoint, I must argue in favor of abandoning all tangent phases for the foreseeable future."

"And the rest of the project?" wondered Chilgers.

"I can't say until I reevaluate the findings from this latest experiment. But there's obviously something we haven't considered about Vortex which might change everything. Frankly, the presence of that bubble frightens the hell out of me. I can see no logical explanation for it."

"Professor," interposed Chilgers, "logic had little to do with starting Project Vortex in the first place. Why should it enter in now?" He rested his pipe in an ashtray on a stand by his chair.

Metzencroy was dabbing furiously at his brow. "Because we've entered a new realm here, a realm as far removed from atomic weapons as they are from slingshots. We've got to tread slowly, slowly and cautiously. We can't take extra steps until we're absolutely certain about the ones we've made so far. I'm afraid that certainty no longer exists, if it ever really did."

Chilgers just looked at him.

"I think you're exaggerating," insisted Teke. "This bubble of yours, Professor, could easily be the result of a simple slip in magnetization or a false reading due to movement in the jet stream. Hell, the answer may lie in the charts gathered by some simple weather balloon sitting up there in the general area of Flight 22."

Metzencroy squeezed his handkerchief dry and shook his head. "I've considered those possibilities as well."

"And rejected them out-of-hand?"

"No, but neither am I willing to accept them under the same terms."

"They certainly make as much sense as the postulate you've advanced," Teke continued.

"If not more," Metzencroy agreed. "But in Project Vortex we must be sure at all costs. The slightest doubt cannot be allowed to enter in. The stakes are too high."

"Professor," began Chilgers, choosing carefully the point at which he reentered the conversation, "let me remind you that we are the Control for Operational Ballistic Research and Activation. Finding new weapons to assure our country of world supremacy, or at the very least the avoidance of all-out war, is what COBRA is all about. And that directive, I'm afraid, entails taking chances while we endeavor of course to minimize the risks. I've been around long enough to have heard all the stories out of Los Alamos and the Manhattan Project. That five hundred scientists signed a petition begging the United States not to set off the first bomb because maybe, just maybe, it would set off a chain reaction that would have led to the end of the world. Some well-respected scientists, in fact, put the odds at no better than fifty-fifty. *Fifty-fifty* that the world was going to cease to be, Professor, and they still went ahead with the bomb. Perhaps a hundred have been detonated since and the world has remained in one piece."

"Vortex goes far beyond the atomic bomb," Metzencroy repeated.

51

"Which is all the more reason to go on with all experiments as scheduled. Do you think the Russians are sitting around asking themselves these same questions of conscience and morality? Do you think *they* care about being sure? God, no. They'll be proceeding full speed ahead with their own research and I'd wager they'd laugh at the points you raised."

"So where does it end?" Metzencroy asked in frustration, staring vacantly before him. "We build an atomic bomb, they build an atomic bomb. We have our version of Project Vortex, they undoubtedly are working on theirs. Where does it end?"

"In this case," answered Teke, "with who finishes first."

"Which means," picked up Colonel Chilgers, "that we can't afford to come in second. Your points are well taken, Professor, but not very convincing. I'm a man who believes in the odds and right now the odds you've presented don't require suspension of the project."

"But I can continue to work on the problem."

"Certainly," Chilgers agreed, glad he could placate Metzencroy with something. "But the final stage of Vortex is scheduled for one week from today. I want everything finished up by then."

Metzencroy rose, apparently thankful for a reason to take his leave. "Then I'd better get to work. Be warned, though, Colonel. You might not like what I find."

"It's your project, Professor. My faith in your abilities and judgment is total."

Chilgers bit his lip as Metzencroy passed by him and left the room.

"He may turn into a problem," Teke advised.

"He already has. Unfortunately, replacing him would pose an even greater one."

"All the same, we'd better keep our eyes on him. If he reached the right people in Washington, we'd be finished."

"If he reached anyone in Washington, we'd be finished, Teke. But they'll thank us when it's over."

"If they don't hang us, you mean."

"This is COBRA, Teke. It's our business to take chances."

Teke extracted a set of stapled pages from his jacket. "We certainly took one by initiating the tangent stage of Project Vortex. Nothing good's come out of it at all. I wanted to save my report for when the good professor took his leave."

Chilgers relit his pipe. "I'm waiting."

Teke turned his head slightly and his bald dome caught some stray light and shot it against the wall. The pumped-in, filtered air was strangely cool and fresh, containing the scent of pine.

"To begin with," Teke said, studying his pages, "we picked up the passengers of Flight 22 on schedule, to follow and monitor as outlined in the schema for this stage of Vortex. Trouble is we lost one."

"Impossible!"

"That's what I said. But a report came in from one of our field agents assigned to the original airport detail that reads otherwise."

"Who'd he lose?"

"A fifteen-year-old boy named David Phelps. Claims he was looking right at the boy standing in line at a drinking fountain and then he just wasn't there anymore."

"Must have melted into a crowd and run off. Your man must have gotten clumsy, Teke," Chilgers charged. "Still, we've taken steps in the event of such an occurrence. Tracking him down should have been no problem at all."

"Not exactly. As you know, all passengers on Flight 22 had small tracking nodules placed in their meals. . . ."

"And I suppose you're going to tell me this boy didn't eat," Chilgers interjected.

"The problem is a bit more complicated than that. Tracking the signal the nodules give off has proven virtually impossible thanks to video games."

"Video games, Teke?"

"They operate on the same wavelength as our nodules. Our trackers have been going crazy trying to pin down the boy. Due to interference they've had to limit their search to late nights and even that's been confusing. We've narrowed things down, though. Should have a fix on the boy sometime tomorrow."

"Fine. Now let me have the rest of your report."

Teke sighed. "It gets worse. The delay in degeneration caused some problems at Kennedy Tower. An air traffic controller out there is trying like hell to find out what happened. It appears he witnessed the moment of degeneration."

"You've covered our tracks I assume."

Teke nodded. "All tapes included."

"Then it would appear this controller can be dealt with rather easily."

"Maybe not. I pulled his file this afternoon. The computer spit out the name of a former acquaintance of his who might be of interest to us: Joshua Bane."

"Jesus Christ . . ."

"We have reason now to believe that the controller's already made contact with him."

Chilgers snuffed out his pipe. "What's his connection with Bane?"

"Vietnam."

"That's not good. It implies far more than casual

54

acquaintance which means Bane won't dismiss the controller as crazy."

"Potentially, he might even believe him," added Teke.

"Believe what, that a 727 vanished? Even if he did, he'd have no place to go with it. The trail's already gone ice-cold. Still, we'd be well advised to observe caution here. We don't want Bane becoming too active."

Chilgers started fidgeting in his chair, a clear sign to Teke that it was time for him to leave.

"I'd better see about the professor," he said, rising. "I'll keep you informed on our efforts to locate the missing boy."

Chilgers nodded. Teke walked stiffly from the room.

The colonel leaned back and drew in a heavy breath. "You can come in now," he said into the intercom he had switched on at the meeting's start, piping the conversation into a room across the hall.

The door opened and a tall man entered, an overcoat draped around his shoulders leaving his arms free. His hair was mostly gray and neatly styled. He moved slowly, each step measured and sure, his gaze deliberate to the point of being mechanical. His eyes, a medium gray color, digested everything about them like a computer weighing data for evaluation.

"Well Trench," Chilgers began, "what do you make of Teke's report?"

Still standing, Trench spoke. "I assume you're referring specifically to the parts relating to Bane. The Winter Man's finished. The damage he could do us if left alone is minimal. If we provoke him, his potential rises significantly."

"And what if I said I wanted him taken out?"

Trench smiled, or almost did. "In my profession a

man must know the level of his limitations before those limitations consume him. Bane and I are equals. I don't like the odds of a direct confrontation."

"You said he was finished."

"No, I said the *Winter Man* was finished. Not dead, mind you, just pushed beneath the surface. But push Bane too far and the Winter Man will return. We must avoid that now at all costs."

"In other words, you're not up to the task of eliminating him."

Trench took one step forward. His eyes grew even colder. "Don't bait me, Colonel. I'm too old and smart for the ploy to work. Bane burned himself out because everything became personal with him. I have always been able to remain detached. Success and failure are merely relative states of being, as are life and death. Emotions cannot be allowed to enter in because they are the true killers. At my level, you can only be destroyed by yourself."

"Or the Winter Man . . ."

"Not if I don't give him a reason . . . and you don't."

"Accepted," Chilgers agreed. "But something will still have to be done about that air traffic controller."

"That might spark Bane into action."

"Handle it in a way that it doesn't. A *professional* way, Trench. I'm sure you're capable."

The Second Day:

COBRA

The problem's plain to see:
Too much technology;
Machines to save our lives,
Machines dehumanize.

—Styx

Chapter Five

Davey Phelps crossed his arms to ward off the cold breeze of the early spring morning in New York. He had slept in a rooming house off Forty-second Street in a room shared with five others. He'd paid for it with his last five dollars which didn't matter much, because so long as he had The Chill, money was just a formality.

By rights, he could have stayed in the flop house until noon but he wanted to get out early because the gnarled, angry thoughts of the five men in the room were unnerving, even scary. Davey could hear their thoughts as clearly as if they had spoken them. They came to him as sharp as voices over a radio you couldn't shut off. He thought sleep might bring silence but instead his rest was continually disturbed by the vicious, frustrated dreams of these men, dreams which reached him as loud and strong as bloodcurdling screams in slice-'em-up horror movies. So Davey stayed in his jeans, legs curled up tight, on a bed against the wall, stealing whatever sleep he could.

When morning came, he slipped silently into his sneakers and tiptoed from the room back into the streets. The city felt calm and unforeboding at this time of the day. Davey walked off down the street looking for a place to eat, watching his breath dance before him in a cloud. For now he was safe. But the Men were closing in; he could feel them, so he'd have to stay on his toes.

A corner diner advertising bacon and eggs with toast for $1.99 had just opened. Davey stepped inside and chose a seat at the counter. A waitress took his order and he watched the cook drop his eggs onto a flat grill in full view of the counter. It was comfortably warm inside and Davey realized he'd been shivering with only his rugby shirt for cover. He'd have to get a jacket today, a real nice one, leather maybe. The Chill would take care of everything.

It had all started on the flight back to New York. He remembered the pilot announcing they were beginning their descent toward Kennedy and then there was nothing. He just blacked out. He came to with the terrible realization that he was already in the terminal building and didn't remember getting there. He was standing by a drinking fountain using the wall for support, even though he didn't feel dizzy or weak. In fact, he felt really strange, different. A big man in a suit was standing thirty feet away, looking at him, and Davey looked back.

Why's the kid hanging around? He should've been on his way already. . . .

Davey turned a bit to make sure nobody was whispering in his ear, found he stood alone. The words were in his mind, pulled from the man's head. He didn't know how, but he knew it. He could read the man's thoughts, wished he could tell why the man was thinking about him. He gazed back in the man's direction.

I've got to call headquarters. I've got to report this, I've got to report this right away. . . .

Report what? Davey wondered. Why was the man

60

following him? What had he done?

Davey felt scared. Something was very wrong here and having the man around only made it worse. He had to get rid of him, had to get out of the airport. He thought of running, taking his chances in the open. Then something happened to him. He felt his whole body quiver, the feeling that of a soft feather being dragged up his spine, a chill. He held the big man's eyes and started moving away from the fountain, leaving a little bit of himself behind, and sure enough the big man's eyes stayed glued to it.

That was the first time he had felt The Chill.

Davey left the airport feeling strange, powerful, and a little scared. He didn't know exactly what had happened back there; he just knew that the last time he'd looked, the man's eyes were still glued to the drinking fountain where Davey *had* been. But he knew there'd be more of the Men, lots probably, and he had to stay clear of them. He jumped into the first taxi he saw and told the driver to take him into the city, Times Square area specifically where there were always plenty of kids hanging out. They would provide a perfect camouflage to keep the Men from finding him.

By the time he reached his destination, the taxi meter read $21.90 and Davey realized with a shudder he didn't even have half that in his pocket. So he handed the driver a pair of ones and made The Chill again.

"Keep the change," he said a bit tentatively, waiting for the driver's reaction.

"Thanks, kid," said the driver, pocketing two bills he fully believed added up to twenty-five dollars.

The cab drove away. Davey started walking.

Didn't that beat all?

He didn't know what was happening to him but it

was sort of fun and he wasn't complaining. God knows he had plenty of other things to complain about. His father had run off a month after his mother had given birth to him on a transit authority bus headed for Manhattan. And to complete the circle she'd been beaten and killed in the subway on a gloomy night just before his fifth birthday. He'd drifted in and out of foster homes, some of them good, most not so good, and twice a year he'd flown out to San Diego to visit his grandparents who lived in a retirement community with strict rules against live-in kids. Not that he believed that changed things. His grandparents didn't love him, at least not enough. They tolerated his visits as an interruption of their lifelong dream of easy living, realized in a two-story yellow townhouse set among a zillion other two-story yellow townhouses a good quarter day's ride from the ocean. Davey long ago gave up trying to convince the aged couple to move elsewhere and take him in. He figured he was lucky they remembered who he was, though he often doubted that they cared.

So he had boarded Flight 22 to return to his latest set of foster parents, a nice enough pair who kept house for three others like him—middle teens, unadoptables society was doing its utmost to shove under the rug to be stepped on by the system. Davey had it easier than most. Passing into his middle teens had not robbed him of the boyish good looks that probably made him the only fifteen-year-old in the city who had trouble getting into R-rated movies. His hair was long and brown, stylishly unkempt. People who knew music told him he looked like a young Jim Morrison, the dead lead singer of The Doors. Davey liked his looks because tough-looking boys had much more trouble finding foster homes and then staying in them, so they ended up floating through reform schools and detention centers which hardened them beyond all reasonable bounds. Davey wasn't tough and was often perceived to be too much the opposite by social workers who feared his looks might influence him to drift toward a life in the streets as a male hooker. Davey didn't pay much attention to them because if they thought that about him, it showed they really didn't know him. He was basically as normal as a boy could be, in spite of the circumstances of his upbringing. He liked sports, made friends easily, lived in jeans, and had mastered tucking just enough cuff into his untied sneakers or winter boots.

And now he had The Chill.

The waitress said, "Here you go," and Davey went to work on a steaming plate of eggs decorated by bacon and toast. He had forgotten to order milk but there it was before him anyway, meaning The Chill had been at work again. The waitress never knew what had hit her.

Of course with The Chill came The Vibes, and The Vibes were bad, scary. Davey had felt them first the day before yesterday during rush hour while wandering around Times Square and Forty-second Street. Something had made him stop dead and he'd looked up ahead at a corner and seen a car accident. Well, he hadn't exactly seen it because it hadn't happened yet. The Vibes showed it to him. And, as he stood with his sneakers frozen to the pavement, a tan Ford sped through a red light and bashed into the driver's side of a blue Chevy—just the way he had seen it maybe a half minute before. Of course it could have been coincidence but Davey knew it wasn't. And if he hadn't known, what happened last night would have erased all doubt.

He was coming out of the movies down near Broadway, an old James Bond double feature with Sean Connery—his favorite—when The Vibes struck again. He saw something happening right in front of him, but he knew it wasn't real because the scenery was all wrong, not the street he was on. So he watched the action unfold the same way he had watched celluloid images for four hours on the big screen.

A black man in a long purple coat slapped a white girl dressed in black leather pants hard in the face. The girl's platinum blond hair tumbled over her eyes and she reeled back. Davey caught a glimpse of her features which were as white as her shiny blouse.

"No tramp holds out on me!" the purple shape with the black face shouted. And he moved for the girl with something glimmering in his hand.

Davey knew what was coming next but he watched it anyway, the same way you do in a horror movie, cowering to your seat and digging your fingers into the armrests.

The black man thrust the knife forward. Davey heard it thud into the girl's stomach. She gasped horribly, sliding down the brick wall, her hands clutching the wound as if to hold her insides in place. Her eyes had already glazed over when her leather pants met the sidewalk. Her fingers slipped away, allowing the rest of her life to pour out and make a pool on the cement.

Then the image faded and Davey just stood there looking at the street as it really was, knowing the scene would play itself out again before long, only this time it would be for real. He walked on with no destination in mind, somehow ending up in a darkened section of Forty-fourth Street which looked strangely familiar because it was the setting he had just been shown by The Vibes.

A voice shouting, "No tramp holds out on me!" forced him to shrink back against the chain front of a closed fruit store. He couldn't see much of what was happening down the street a hundred feet away, but he'd already seen it once and that was plenty. There was the sound of the knife parting the girl's flesh and the dying gurgle which followed. Davey waited till he was sure the purple-coated black was gone before approaching because he had to know, had to be sure.

The girl sat propped up by the brick building, head tilted toward the gaping wound in her stomach and blond hair almost reaching it. Davey held his breath and looked down to see the pool of blood that was creeping toward the tips of his sneakers. He bolted off, stealing one last glance back, and somehow made it to the rooming house where he had spent the night and his last five dollars.

But it didn't matter. The Chill would take care of him. He could handle The Chill but The Vibes were something he'd rather be rid of. It was no fun knowing when something awful was about to happen. Still, The Vibes would warn him if the Men were near and that warning was something he desperately needed.

Davey scraped his plate clean and moved to the cash register. The waitress took his check, the register jangled, and she read him the amount rung up.

"That'll be $2.40."

Davey smiled, made The Chill.

The girl handed him a five-dollar bill. "Please come again."

Davey said he would and moved back into the

65

street. It was still cold, freezing for spring, and Davey noticed he was the only one on the street without a jacket. That made him stand out, too easy for the Men to find, and besides he was shivering again. So he had to get a coat to keep the cold out and the Men away. Leather would be nice. He had always wanted a leather jacket. It would mean a walk to Seventh Avenue, but that wouldn't be a problem, especially if he did it later during the lunch-time rush hour. In a million faces, the Men would never be able to spot him. Then he could ditch back to Forty-second Street and Times Square and melt into the scenery of hundreds of kids who looked pretty much alike. They'd never find him. And if they did, there was always The Chill.

What he really wanted to do was go home, especially now after two days on the streets. But The Vibes got scrambled when he just thought about that, as if they were telling him that was the wrong thing to do at this point. Davey listened.

He started to walk. Maybe he'd find a twenty-four hour movie theater to kill some time. Maybe he'd just walk. . . .

Something made him stop suddenly. It was like The Vibes he had felt last night only a hundred times worse, a hot wind that buckled the cold and struck him in the face. His flesh turned to glass, started to break, to shatter. Then the heat nearly swept him off his feet. Woozy, he moved to a stopped bus and leaned against it. The weird feeling in his face was gone. Even if his flesh had turned to glass for an instant, none of it had broken so everything was okay.

But something *was* coming. Davey had felt it pierce the cold air just like the blade had split the girl's stomach the night before. The strongest Vibes he'd felt yet, only this time he couldn't see what they were trying to tell him. It was vague, hazy, distant. It was coming, though, and it was going to be awful. He didn't know how he knew that, he just did; and, boy, he didn't want to be around when it got there.

Shuddering, Davey pushed himself away from the bus and rejoined the flow of people.

Chapter Six

Bane arrived at Kennedy early for his meeting with Jake Del Gennio. Maybe that was why security had not been given word yet to clear him for entry into the tower. No matter. Bane had a way of appearing to belong wherever he wanted to. The guard's resistance melted quickly, and he informed Bane that the briefing room where he was supposed to meet Jake was on the third level. Bane thanked him.

It was eight-fifteen so Del Gennio would surely be up there already. Bane found the briefing room easily and saw a man hovering over a cup of coffee in the corner. The Swan.

"Morning, Jake."

The man turned. It wasn't Del Gennio.

"Sorry, I thought you were Jake Del Gennio," Bane apologized.

"I only wish I was," the man said wearily. "Then I'd be home in bed instead of working two shifts out of three."

"Del Gennio called in sick?"

"That's why I'm here."

The man stood up and passed by Bane without saying excuse me.

Bane felt the familiar prickle of fear on the back of his neck. Something was wrong. That Del Gennio might have taken sick was certainly a possibility, but not calling him to revise their plan was simply unthinkable, not the Swan's style at all. He was a detail man all the way, and the missing jet was too important for him not to make contact.

Bane moved through the narrow corridor toward a pay phone he remembered passing. Del Gennio's number rang once, twice, three times, and after that Bane was sure there was no one home to answer. Still, he gave it another five rings and almost forgot to retrieve the dime in his hurry to get out of the tower.

He could make it to Jake's apartment in thirty minutes tops, but his feelings told him it was already too late.

Jake Del Gennio lived on the twelfth floor of a typical Manhattan high-rise, one that advertised top-notch security and burglar-proof doors. In this case, the latter at least was far from true. The door was good all right but nothing a little patience wouldn't solve. Bane had all three locks picked in under two minutes, and the fact that no chain greeted him when he finally got the door open convinced him beyond all doubt that Jake Del Gennio wasn't home. The Swan took all precautions.

He felt something as soon as he entered, something cold. Passing the feeling off to nerves, he made a quick check of the apartment and found all three rooms were in perfect, lived-in order. A more thorough examination of the closet revealed that its contents had not been disturbed by a rushed packing job and the same held for the drawers. If Del Gennio had left in a hurry, he hadn't taken any luggage.

The next check was the one Bane dreaded the most. Del Gennio might have lost a step and gained an inch over the years, but he was still careful and quick. He couldn't have been taken or killed without a fight. A fight meant blood and blood meant washing and/or disposing of all evidence. Bane moved into the bathroom and pulled a file from his kit. First he carefully scraped the sink drain, found nothing. Then he scraped the underside of the toilet bowl and the drain. Again nothing. Finally he moved into the kitchen and made a similar inspection of the sink and garbage disposal with the same results.

Bane was puzzled. Del Gennio had called in sick, but he wasn't home. If he had been taken forcibly, the principals behind it must have been damn good because they'd left no traceable evidence at all.

Of course Bane realized he might have been jumping to conclusions. There was nothing to indicate foul play, and Jake had indeed been acting strangely last night. He might have bolted.

Bane started to close the door behind him and then opened it suddenly again. He had realized something, something which sent slabs of ice sliding down his stomach. He checked the bedroom once more, and then the den. The evidence was present all right, not in what was there but in what *wasn't*.

On the way out of the building, Bane stopped at the front desk to quiz the doorman. According to the security system coded in red and green lights, Del Gennio was safely upstairs and had been since eight-thirty the preceding night. For Bane, the smell of a professional's work was even stronger.

The Swan was gone and wouldn't be coming back.

Bane was back at the airport twenty minutes later. "Am I to assume that this is a professional inquiry, Mr. Bane?" wondered Burt Cashman, a short, heavy-

70

set man with half-closed eyes and a title that made him Administrative Chief of Air Traffic Control at Kennedy.

"No, just a personal one." Bane could have arranged to meet with a higher official at the airport but under such short notice that would have made his intentions too obvious. The cloak of personal concern would gain him the information he needed. "Frankly, I'm worried about Jake's nerves. He's seemed fidgety lately, under a lot of stress."

"You served together in Vietnam," Cashman stated.

"How did you know?"

"I knew Jake served, and since I was in Korea I can usually pick out one soldier's concern for another. Not hard to put together really."

"I see," Bane said, trying to appear impressed.

"In any case, I'm glad you've come because quite frankly I've had the same fears about Jake for some time myself."

"Really?"

"You know his age."

"Forty. Maybe forty-one."

"Closer to forty-two actually. Most controllers are finished by all practical considerations when they've reached thirty-five. We let Jake stay on, given his status as a veteran and his spotless record, but we lowered the number of his flight responsibilities. Put him on a reduction console. I didn't think that was enough personally."

"Did you speak to Jake about this?"

Cashman hesitated. "To be honest, not in so many words. It's an extremely sensitive topic and one that's not brought up routinely. I think he was expecting it, though. I could tell by his eyes. Deep inside he knew it was time to step down. He has a damn good pen-

71

sion to look forward to."

"Jake isn't the kind of man to look forward to a pension."

Cashman smiled uneasily. "You know him better than I thought."

"He called in sick today."

"I'm aware of that."

"He's not in his apartment."

"I'm not surprised. As I said, Jake knew he was reaching the end of his effectiveness. It was only a matter of time before he went somewhere and thought it all over. I don't have to tell you what kind of job this is. It's harder to get in, but it's even harder to get out. The pressure and strain of the job will drive you crazy, but you can't go without them for more than a week. Take a look at all the vacation time most controllers have stored up. Take a look at the low ratio of sick days they use."

"Del Gennio used one today." That got Cashman's attention. It was time to get to the point. "I didn't come here on a whim, Mr. Cashman. Jake looked me up last night for the first time in a while. He looked like a man on the edge of a tightrope, crazy with strain. Thought somebody was following him." Bane hesitated, saving the best for last. To maintain the façade of his intentions, he had to lay everything out. Hold something back and before long whoever had taken Jake out would be onto him. "He kept babbling something about a jet that disappeared three days ago."

Cashman sighed. "He turned the whole airport upside down that morning, screaming it had gone down and nobody could find it. Then he claimed it disappeared right before his eyes. I gave him the rest of the day off. He used it to go pounding on executive doors, the very top, mind you, of both the airport and

72

the airline. Made a lot of people unhappy. My phone rang steadily until six. What could I tell them? Air traffic controllers have a code too, you know, and I piloted a console for twenty years before I started riding this desk. We don't cover up our mistakes but we don't give the asses of our people away either. If you don't stick together this job will kill you. All you've got is each other because nobody in the real world has any idea of what goes on behind that monitor." Cashman stopped suddenly. "I didn't mean to ramble."

"There's pressure behind a desk too."

"Well, if I could do my job half as good as Jake Del Gennio does his, I'd be happy."

"Did you check the cockpit tapes?" Bane asked him.

"Absolutely. I went over them once things settled down." Cashman shook his head. "Nothing. Just Jake's voice, like he was talking to himself."

Bane felt Cashman was telling the truth which meant that if the Swan really did see a jet vanish, the cover-up started higher.

"So how do you explain what happened to him?" he asked.

"Well, Mr. Bane, a controller spends all his working hours avoiding crashes and all the rest dreading them. Sleep is the worst. On bad nights you keep seeing the same scene over and over again in your dreams. A midair, takeoff, or landing crash you're powerless to prevent, so you just sit there behind your console in the dream and watch it happen. Sometimes a controller lapses behind the board and the dream takes over. His greatest fear comes alive right before him, and because he's right behind the console when he comes out of it, he's convinced it's real. It wasn't real in Jake's case because Flight 22 landed forty minutes later, almost ninety minutes behind schedule."

"Why?"

"First the flight was delayed thirty minutes in San Diego because some extra freight had to be loaded and then the pilot reported engine trouble an hour out of Kennedy, leading he expected to an additional delay of twenty minutes."

Bane calculated. "That still leaves forty minutes unaccounted for."

"The pilot erred."

"When did you next hear from him?"

"When he was ready to make his approach two hours later. It's on tape."

"Nothing in between?"

"By procedure, there wouldn't have to be. Except for standard communications, channels are used almost exclusively when something's wrong."

That made Bane think of something else. "You say Flight 22 was held up in San Diego because of extra freight loading?"

"It arrived late at the airport. Government priority as I recall."

"Government?"

"It's nothing out of the ordinary. Strictly routine."

Cashman was holding nothing back; that much was obvious. There were certainly inconsistencies in his story but nothing to indicate he was part of the cover-up Bane was beginning to strongly believe had taken place. Why else would someone have arranged for Jake Del Gennio to disappear? And now the government had been drawn into the scenario.

They can erase the tapes, Josh, but they can't erase me.

Wrong, Jake, Bane thought.

"Thank you for your time, Mr. Cashman," he

74

said, rising.

It was time to visit the Center.

The Center was once precisely that: a fulcrum around which important government decisions were based and policies were made. It had existed in virtual secrecy since the Kennedy days when the young president, eager to be aware of what all government-funded organizations were doing with their grants, created a watchdog unit to oversee the spending of the hundreds of billions passed out annually.

In the early days, the Center had occupied three floors of a major Washington office building, under an innocuous cover that proved to be just deep enough to hold. Headquarters had been moved to New York during Watergate when things really heated up in the capital and high-level minds felt the Center could accomplish more from outside Washington than from within. These were the years when the organization enjoyed its finest hours, freely interpreting its somewhat ambiguous charter to make sure in all cases that a group using government funds to get from point A to point B took no detours along the way. Center operatives researched, infiltrated, developed a chain of informants, checked, double-checked, and generally rode herd on the hundreds of organizations who regularly cashed rather large treasury checks.

But the Reagan years brought with them a new direction and a new mandate. The Watergate scare was over and somehow fewer checks seemed to mean better balances. The Center was phased out gradually, reorganized so that its responsibilities were subdivided among a number of more traditional Wash-

75

ington organizations all of which could be found in the blue pages of any phone book. America's watchdog lost its bark, then its bite, and was finally sent to lie down and linger cursorily in an old brownstone on Eighty-sixth Street. Four full office floors of activity were reduced to twelve Victorian rooms. A staff of fifty in the office and a hundred in the field was reduced to six and twelve respectively. Instead of an investigative unit, the Center became no more than a clearing house where all government grants were inventoried and occasionally spot-checked. Another faceless element in the great bureaucracy.

Strangely, in a technical sense Joshua Bane was part of this element. He may have retired from the Game officially but the government couldn't let him officially go. When a man knew the kinds of things he knew and had done the kinds of things he'd done, they couldn't let him slip free from their grasp. There was no such thing as retirement, so on paper Bane worked for the Center and arrived there every other week to pick up a rather hefty check amounting to a premature pension. The government could afford to pay him generously because there was no one else of his kind left on the payroll. The life expectancy of someone in the Winter Man's position was usually quite brief. Of course, Trench had outlived three decades of pursuit and no one had any idea of how old Scalia was. It came down to a question of luck: when yours ran out, that was it. Except his never had, not really. The same held for Trench and Scalia, though they still played the field while Bane for better or worse had retired to the sidelines.

But Jake Del Gennio claimed he had seen a jet disappear and subsequently he had disappeared too. It was all too neat, too clean, too . . . professional. And all of it made Bane thirst for the life he'd thought was gone forever, the action and the heightened use of senses he needed now to find out what the hell was going on.

Bane climbed the seven steps leading to the Center's front entrance, knowing his moves were being followed by a camera which broadcast its picture onto a series of television monitors before the desk of the building's one, nearsighted security guard. The elaborate security measures were more token than necessary. There was little in the building worth stealing or even worthy of espionage. Bane rang the buzzer. There was a chime, followed by an earsplitting buzz. The door swung open.

"Good morning, Mr. Bane," greeted Charlie, the nearsighted guard who never loaded his gun.

Bane swung through the alcove into what years before might have been called the sitting room, where a woman who had seen the lighter side of fifty was streaming along on a typewriter.

"Morning, Millie."

"Morning, Mr. Bane. I've got your check right here." Center employees never questioned the checks he received with no apparent services rendered. They were, after all, government employees first and foremost.

"I'll grab it on the way out. Tell Janie I'm here."

"Janie already knows." The voice came from the foyer.

Bane turned toward the main stairway, into the gaze of Janie Finlaw, chief of Center operations. They had met one day while he was picking up his check and had begun a casual affair which had grown and deepened until there was seldom a night when they didn't share each other's company and bed. Bane knew he didn't love her, not in the traditional sense anyway, but at times he found himself bonded to her by something even stronger since she had pulled him from the emotional depths he'd plunged into following the tragic deaths of his wife and stepson. She had brought warmth back into his life at a time when he had all but rejected any hope of feeling it again.

Looking at her descending the staircase, Bane considered himself most fortunate. She was extremely attractive, if not stunningly so. Her dark hair, auburn really, smothered her shoulders and rested upon the upper part of her firmly muscled back. Her eyes were the lightest shade of brown Bane had ever seen and her smile was captivating, subtle enough to allow for both vulnerability and strength. Janie had stayed single because she'd wanted to, and she'd made a rapid rise through government levels until she was now in charge of all Center activities, however curtailed. The future for her was bright, a cabinet-level position in the offing, even though Janie would have preferred something in intelligence. Secretly, she harbored a dream of being the first woman director of the CIA.

"Got a few minutes?" Bane asked her.

Janie feigned disappointment. "And I thought you came here to ask me for lunch."

"At eleven o'clock in the morning?"

"I had an early breakfast, remember? Oh well, I guess you might as well come upstairs."

The staircase was carpeted and Bane followed her up it into a modest office that was more functional than anything else. A computer terminal dominated a desk cluttered with papers and reports, as if it belonged to someone perpetually behind. In fact, Janie was always trying to get ahead, hence the clutter.

"I ever tell you about the helicopter pilot who

helped me in Nam, guy named Jake Del Gennio?"

"Not that I remember."

"Well, until this morning he was an air traffic controller at Kennedy."

"What happened?"

"He's gone."

"Gone?"

"Somebody lifted him."

And Bane proceeded to relate the events of the past sixteen hours since he'd met the Swan at La Maison and first learned about a 727 that vanished.

"That's quite a story," Janie told him at the end, no longer smiling. "But how do you know he's gone for good? He might have panicked, run off."

Bane shook his head. "I was in his apartment. Somebody went to great pains to make sure the place looked normal, somebody very professional . . . There were no imprints in the rugs."

"Imprints?"

"Every footstep makes an imprint in the kind of carpeting Jake had. Not much but there if you know what to look for. Vacuuming lifts them out. The only imprints in Jake's place now are mine because somebody wanted very much to disguise how many people had been there before me."

Janie's eyebrows flickered. "I see the point. But how can I help?"

"Something Jake's boss said this morning stuck with me."

"The connection of the vanishing jet with the government?"

"Right, but which branch of the government? Think you might be able to dig that up for me on those wonderful computers of yours?"

"Shouldn't be much of a problem." Janie hesitated. "You think this branch might be connected to what happened to your friend?"

"At this point, I'm grasping. Which leads me to my next request: the passenger manifest from Flight 22. Think you can round it up?"

Janie frowned, shook her head. "Sorry, Josh, I can't help you there. My computer lines don't have access or clearance to mess with civilian ones. More streamlining of Center operations. I guess I could arrange to tap into I-Com-Tech's lines but—"

"I-Com-Tech?" Bane interrupted.

"That's right. We share occasionally. So?"

"So you just lost your lunch date, sweetie. I-Com-Tech's where the Bat hangs his hat these days."

"Harry Bannister?"

"None other."

"Sounds like old home week for you, Josh."

Bane's face became grim. "Except Jake Del Gennio's gonna be missing the festivities."

Chapter Seven

Many say that the expansive Rockefeller Center is a prime cornerstone of Manhattan, functionally as well as aesthetically, and Bane agreed with them. With almost 200 shops and businesses contained in the complex, not to mention headquarters for a score of major corporations, it was difficult to argue otherwise.

The International Communications Technology building was actually an extension of the Exxon structure, sharing the fountain pool that was a close cousin to the Time & Life version across West Fiftieth Street. Bane took a cab from the Center and had the driver drop him on the Avenue of the Americas, a couple blocks from I-Com-Tech so he could walk the rest of the way and check for tails. Not that he expected any. Couldn't be too careful now, though.

The entrance to I-Com-Tech was off West Fiftieth, and Bane approached it by way of the fountain-pool fronting the Exxon building. He flirted briefly with the notion of tossing a penny in and making a wish, and would have done just that if he hadn't been counting on Harry the Bat to grant his wish instead.

I-Com-Tech housed the largest computer facilities on the East Coast, including many of Washington's most important programs and much data. Noble minds had long ago decided that for strategic reasons New York should be the technological center and storing house for the country, not the capital. So, little which passed before important eyes did so without first passing through New York in general and I-Com-Tech in particular.

The government had stowed Harry Bannister in a cubicle on the ninth floor of the mirrored building after a shattered spine had rendered him unfit for duty in the field. Though Bane had lost personal contact with the Bat, he had maintained close knowledge of Harry's progress in his new career, always stopping short of the phone call or visit he had promised himself.

But today was different. Today he had a reason, and besides, the difficult part of the reunion had happened yesterday at the rally.

"Well Lord fuck a duck, if it isn't Joshua Bane," Harry roared when Bane appeared outside the six-foot, enclosed square he worked out of. "Twice in two days. Pinch me, I must be dreaming. Or maybe I just died and went to heaven."

"When you die, Harry, it won't be heaven."

The Bat laughed and wheeled himself toward Bane, who reached down and took his extended hand. Then Harry noticed the grim look etched over his features.

"What's wrong, Josh?" he wondered.

"Jake Del Gennio's dead."

The Bat went white. "Dead? Shit, how?"

"I don't know. That's the problem. Somebody very professional lifted him. He won't be coming back."

"Any idea who the bastards are?"

"Not yet, but I've got some leads."

The Bat's features tightened. "I got a couple weeks vacation coming to me. How 'bout I put in my

82

voucher and we track the bastards down together?"

Bane shook his head. "No, Harry, it's too early for that. Somebody offed Jake because of something he saw three days ago. And whoever it was, they were damned efficient."

"What did Jake see three days ago?"

"He claimed a 727 vanished into thin air. That's what he wanted to see me about yesterday."

"And did it?"

"Maybe. Nobody's talking."

"Except Jake. . . ."

"Not anymore," corrected Bane.

"Jesus Christ, this feels like the old days, Josh." The Bat cracked his knuckles. "So what do you need? What can my magic keyboard obtain for you?" Harry smiled. Bane hadn't made the request yet but there were some things that didn't need saying.

He didn't hesitate. "The passenger manifest from Central Airlines Flight 22 of three days ago."

"It would seem a whole lot easier to obtain from the airline."

"I want to keep this in the family, Harry. If I get the manifest from the airline, whoever offed Jake would know I was interested."

"It may be dangerous, then."

"It already is."

The Bat slapped his dead thighs. "Well Lord fuck a duck, I was hoping you'd say that." His face glowed, vital and alive. The bitterness Bane had sensed the day before was gone. "Of course, in view of the danger I feel entitled to ask for something in return."

"Just name it."

Harry wasn't quite ready to yet. "Funny thing about this computer of mine. I can get you information on just about anything. I've got access to almost every tape that travels on commercial or government lines . . . except one: intelligence, the one I need the most."

"So?"

"So the Center can get access, at least eavesdrop, on all the tapes I can't reach." Now he was ready. "I want you to get me the latest on Trench."

"Harry—"

"Lay any shit on me, Josh, and I'll kick your balls with one of my dead feet. I want Trench and you want the passenger manifest from Flight 22. Fair trade, I'd say."

"Leave it alone, Harry."

"I can't, Josh, don't you see that I can't? I think about the bastard every day when I've got to sweat buckets just to make it out of bed. Christ, Josh, you ever try to ease yourself into shitting position without legs? That bastard even took a normal squat away from me."

Bane was about to argue more until he remembered be was as much to blame for what had happened to the Bat as Trench was.

"I'll see what I can do," he said softly.

The Bat's eyes were cold. "Tomorrow morning, Josh. I give you the manifest, you give me the latest on Trench. Deal?"

"Deal," Bane managed reluctantly.

"So are you gonna tell me what you want the manifest for?" the Bat asked after a pause that seemed longer than it was.

"If something really did happen to that plane, I figure the passengers will be able to tell me what. Whoever's behind it couldn't cover up something that includes sixty-seven people."

"Jake could've cracked, Josh. It happens."

"If he cracked, he'd be home safe now."

The Bat smiled knowingly. "Well, if this don't sound like the old days, I don't know what does."

Bane looked away, something tugging at him. "I handled it all wrong last night," he confessed. "I knew Jake was telling the truth but I didn't cover him, didn't take the right precautions."

"You know what they say about hindsight."

"Doesn't matter. I don't plan on making the same mistake twice. You carrying, Harry?"

The Bat winked and tapped a pouch concealed beneath his sweater. Metal clanged lightly against metal. "Never wheel myself an inch without my knives," he assured him.

"That's good," Bane said.

Davey was looking at the fountain fronting the Exxon building when The Vibes struck stronger than ever.

He had walked here directly from a Seventh Avenue clothing store which featured an assortment of leather jackets in the window. Davey chose the one he liked best, a bomber style, used The Chill, and walked out with it hugging his shoulders tight. He loved the smell of the fresh leather and decided to challenge the unusually cold spring by hiking across town. This part of the city was fun, what with all the interesting thoughts he was able to tune in on. Davey wondered how all the problems he glimpsed were going to be worked out. Would the blue-suited executive make the switch to another company? Would the man with the striped tie and sunglasses keep his appointment with a high-class hooker instead of taking his wife to dinner? Would the repair shop have the nervous-looking woman in white's car back to her today, or would she have to brave another day of public transportation? The questions went on and on. After a while Davey got bored considering them and stopped peeking into people's heads.

He was staring thoughtlessly at the pool when The Vibes came, driving him off the bench to his feet. He didn't see anything, not yet, but he knew it was coming. Then something scraped his spine like fingernails down a blackboard and he shuddered, dragging his hands to his ears. His knees started to wobble and after a few seconds his whole body joined in, his eyes bulging at the sight The Vibes showed him.

The pool erupted in a burst of steam, its cement mold cracking, splitting, shattering. He saw people running about screaming and gagging for breath. Their fingers scraped the air, gave up, and then held their bodies as if to hold themselves together, but it was no use, because suddenly their flesh was being peeled back like an orange rind. Davey saw knobby skeletons for just an instant before the bones went up with a quick *poof*! . . . and then there was nothing, nothing at all except blackness. Davey wanted to scream but suddenly he was alone, no one to hear him. Everything was gone, over. He tried to catch his breath, but there was no air to draw in.

Then The Vibes faded. The fingernails scraped back up his spine and left him cold. The shuddering ceased but he was frozen, his feet held to the cement by some cosmic glue. He looked at the fountain-pool, through it, glad it was back.

And then not so glad.

Because a man stood on the other side watching him, a big man with thick brown hair just starting to creep back over his scalp. Davey regained his thoughts and the shudders started all over again, for the thoughts were jumbled like broken pieces of china and Davey couldn't put them together. This was not one of the Men but whatever he was scared Davey just as much. Suddenly the man was moving forward, his pace rising to a trot, and all Davey could do was try to dig his feet out of the cement before the big man reached him.

Bane left I-Com-Tech feeling hungry and realized for the first time he had skipped breakfast. The lunch-hour rush would make most places totally intolerable. People squeezing against each other, shouting orders, and sweating out a frenzied rush back to the office played hell with the defenses. Too easy for someone in the crowd to jam a gun against your ribs, or drive a blade between them.

Bane couldn't stomach such crowds. That part of the Winter Man had never died. And if he was being followed, a crowded lunch room was hardly the ideal location to spot a tail.

So Bane opted against Lindy's or a similar establishment in favor of the relative quiet of Charley O's Irish Pub on West Forty-eighth. He'd lunched there before and the food never failed to satisfy.

The perimeter of the fountain-pool before the Exxon building was crowded now with people brown-bag lunching and drinking soda from cans. Bane cut between them, close to the fountain's edge, and froze all at once. Standing forty yards before him near the right outer rim of the pool was a boy in a leather jacket and jeans, long shaggy hair covering his forehead.

It can't be . . .

Bane took one step forward, then another. The ghost from his past didn't change form or vanish. His eyes weren't playing tricks on him, though he wished they had been.

He was staring at an older version of his stepson, a vision of what the boy would have looked like now if he had lived!

Bane's thoughts scrambled. The past mixed with the present, and he forgot where he was. But the boy was still there, standing motionless in his tracks. Their eyes finally met and Bane felt something reach into his head. A dull throb rose behind his eyes, followed by a brief flash of spectral color. Then Bane found himself in motion, incredibly quick and sure. The boy was moving too now, though, stealing a glance behind him into the crowd and locking immediately on Bane.

Bane skirted close enough to the fountain pool to feel the cold spray lifting off. Nothing else mattered: not his hunger, or the missing jet, or Jake Del Gennio, or the passenger manifest. There was only the boy and he had to catch him, had to know if . . .

If what?

Bane picked up his pace, pushing by those bodies he couldn't slither through. He saw the gap closing and that was the final fuel he needed for the burst that would close it altogether.

Davey knew the big man was after him and slowed his pace twice to use The Chill. But the man was too much for it, or maybe he needed total concentration to make it work. Davey felt the thoughts exploding from his pursuer's head but pushed them aside because they frightened him in a way different from any others he'd tuned in on yet. He tried to read the big man and had read enough to know that he was like no other person in the city, not even close.

Davey leaped to the sidewalk and collided with two men in expensive coats. They shoved him aside, and he lurched across the Avenue of the Americas in a diagonal, leaving a symphony of screeching tires and enraged horns behind him. He reached West Fiftieth Street, swung by a line of people waiting at the Radio City Music Hall box office, and headed for construction sounds. Steam rose from a new underground furrow and hissed at the cool air. Davey darted by two men with jackhammers, felt cement chips spit into him, and slid between a section of scaffolding reducing his pace only slightly.

He cut across Rockefeller Plaza till it became West Forty-ninth Street and chanced a rush across against a DON'T WALK sign, coming close enough to a few screaming fenders to smell heated metal. He made it across with a last leap to the sidewalk, ignoring the thoughts people nearby turned on him.

Davey looked back long enough to see the big man following almost directly in his wake, zigzagging between cars without slowing. One car skidded to a halt in his path and it looked to Davey as if the big man hurdled over its hood in a single bound, actually *hurdled*, and landed on the same West Forty-ninth Street sidewalk Davey had crossed just seconds before, hotter on his trail than ever.

Davey slowed. His wind was gone and his legs felt like somebody had wrapped tight tape around them. His new jacket was sweat-glued to his shirt, and he noticed small gray specks marking spots where the cement chips had found their mark.

The big man was still coming, thirty yards away now, tops. Davey turned and faced him, trying for The Chill.

Bane felt as if he had crashed through a glass door placed in his path but he kept going.

Then Davey saw the legless man pushing himself across the sidewalk on a skate-wheel platform. He found his mind, made The Chill, felt the now familiar quiver roll up his spine.

The legless man suddenly altered the route of his platform, picking up speed in an incredibly brief period of time.

Bane thundered forward.

The skate-wheel platform sped into his path too late to be avoided. His legs were pulled from under him and he was airborne, tumbling over on his way to the ground, landing hard.

Bane lifted himself back to his feet with the help of a few surprisingly concerned bystanders. He brushed himself off, shrugged off further assistance, and noted the patches of his flesh that were scraped, raw, or bleeding. He gazed up the street at where he had last seen the boy, where the hot blast had come from an instant before the legless man had sent him sprawling.

The boy was gone.

Chapter Eight

"We got a fix on the boy this morning and traced him to this area," the COBRA operations chief was saying as Trench closed the door to the car behind him. "It took a few hours but we finally pinned him down to that clothing store across the street."

The operations chief led Trench across Seventh Avenue to a nest of stores tucked neatly into a single building, their fronts all but obscured by scaffolding which enclosed the entire sidewalk.

"I thought you'd like to talk to the clerk yourself," the COBRA man continued. "Something strange came up." The man's attention shifted back and forth from Trench to a pair of hulking giants who stayed right in his shadow.

Onlookers first thought they were seeing double and then cringed at the sight. Trench had worked with Twin Bears before. Huge, fantastically strong, loyal men who were, in fact, biological twins, each with a shock of flaming red hair which sat atop heads nearly seven feet from the ground. One twin, though, had brown eyes while the other's were, incredibly, blue. Their names were Pugh and Soam and even Trench couldn't keep them straight in spite of the eyes. Not that it mattered. One was very much like the other with respect to duties. They seldom spoke and obeyed his every word. Trench had insisted that they accompany him east after Colonel Chilgers had issued his assignment. Having the Twin Bears around heightened his sense of security. He liked moving between two men who could just as easily rip a door from its hinges as pass through it.

The clothing store, featuring leather jackets, was called Looking Good. Trench left the Twin Bears at the front door and followed the COBRA operations chief inside.

"This the guy you told me could straighten things out?" a sales clerk charged, accosting them.

"Say hello to Mr. Trench," the COBRA man said.

The salesman eyed Trench only briefly before launching into another tirade. "I could lose my job for this you know. I hope you're gonna put that little bastard where he belongs. The son of a bitch tricked me somehow."

"Tricked you?"

"Shortchanged me. Played some kind of game with the bills."

"Tell him everything you told me," the COBRA man instructed.

"Well," the salesman began, "the leather jacket the kid bought cost $99.99. So he hands me a hundred-dollar bill to pay for it, right? And I check it like I check all the others and put it under the cash drawer with the rest of the big bills. It was the only hundred I got today so I couldn't have missed it. But when I lifted the drawer to get the deposit ready for the bank, the hundred was gone and a five was in its place. I figure the kid must've been some kind of magician or something. Hey, I'll bet that's why you're looking for him. He's pulled this stunt before."

"Something like that," Trench said.

"Well, do me a favor. When you find the little

fucker, nail his ass to a cross. I've had my fill of kids like him."

Trench forced a shrug. "By the way, do you still have the bill?"

"The five the kid left me? Sure. I stuck it right on top. I was just on my way to the bank to make the afternoon deposit when your friends came in."

The salesman hit a combination of buttons on the electronic cash register and the drawer slid open. He passed a well-worn five dollar bill to Trench.

"The little shit cheated me out of ninety-five bucks," he lamented.

But Trench didn't hear him. His eyes swept across the bill and focused on Franklin's face instead of Lincoln's. He blinked rapidly and focused on the bill again. Lincoln was back in the center as he must have been the whole time. Except Trench was sure he had seen Franklin, almost like someone was forcing that impression upon him. Just for an instant. The bill trembled in his hand. He shook himself from the spell and handed the salesman a fifty in its place.

"Now you're only short fifty," he managed, tucking the mysterious five into his pocket.

"Hey, thanks. You're a real gentleman. Too bad there aren't more classy guys like you around. World would be a helluva lot better place."

Ordinarily Trench would have smiled at such a remark, but today he just wanted to get out. He left Looking Good and moved his still-agile frame between the Twin Bears, allowing them to hover over him like a pair of umbrellas warding off a rainstorm. He had hit fifty longer ago than he admitted to anyone and now left the physical demands of his trade to people like the Twins, men not unlike he had been a generation or so before and men who would be lucky to see their thirtieth birthdays. Trench was still

93

in the Game because his nerve strings frayed evenly instead of just in the center as the Winter Man's had. The key to maintaining your level of proficiency, he was convinced, lay in not expecting to. In fact, he lived by this credo. Thus, the Twin Bears. They had killed often and well for him. Simple-minded, tight-lipped, and steel-spined, the brothers were his equalizer against any and all threats. Their abilities were seldom wasted. They had been put to good use most recently in disposing of the Del Gennio problem, and now Trench was struck by the distinct feeling they would be seeing more action before this was over.

Trench was still a crack shot himself and remained almost as good with his hands as he'd ever been. It was the mental edge he'd lost, stealing a step from his quickness and an inch from his aim. The enjoyment he got from killing—the fulfillment—was gone. Retirement he did not even consider. Trench had nothing to retire to. So he lingered, not comfortable with his profession anymore but even less comfortable with the alternatives to it.

He climbed into the back seat of his car, the Twin Bears into the front. The COBRA operations chief went back to his duties. One of the Bears, the blue-eyed one, took the wheel. Trench picked up the phone which connected him directly to COBRA in San Diego.

"Yes." Chilgers' voice.

"This is Trench."

"You have a report for me?"

"The Del Gennio matter has been handled. No further problems from that end."

"Splendid. And the boy?"

"No pickup yet."

Chilgers' hesitation signaled disappointment. "I was told he'd been tracked down."

94

"We're close on his tail now, but the homing device went haywire again before we could pin him down."

"Damn . . ."

"The equipment should become effective again tonight. We'll have him by morning."

"You'd better, Trench. His homing beacon is only good for another sixteen hours or so. After that, we're on our own. Tomorrow morning you say?"

"Yes," Trench acknowledged, and he almost told Chilgers about Lincoln's face becoming Franklin's but thought better of it.

"There's something else," the colonel told him.

"I'm listening."

"Bane was at the airport this morning asking questions."

"What kind?"

"About Flight 22. It was obvious Del Gennio told him everything, and equally obvious Bane's suspicions stemmed purely from a personal angle."

"Explain."

"He didn't hold anything back. He divulged everything he knew."

Trench couldn't help but laugh. "He's a professional, Colonel. A professional often gives too much away to disguise his true intentions. If he already knows everything and spills it, you assume he's not looking for more."

"Well . . ."

"Don't be fooled by him, Colonel. He's onto something and he won't stop till he digs the rest out."

"Then take him out, take him out as I suggested when we first learned of his involvement."

Trench considered the Twin Bears sitting before him. "That might turn out to be superfluous, even counter productive. With Del Gennio out of the way, there's nowhere left for him to dig. Leave him alone."

"You talk like he's still the Winter Man."

"Push him too far and that's exactly what he'll become. Right now he's only a minor threat to us. Leave it at that, Colonel."

"I'm not sure I agree," Chilgers said, uncomfortable with being told what to do.

"Colonel, he knows Del Gennio has been erased, and he suspects it has something to do with Flight 22. The trail stops there . . . unless we leave more in his path."

Chilgers sighed. "Then we'll do it your way, Trench," he said, contemplating alternatives of his own. "For now, I want you to concentrate your efforts on bringing in the boy."

"By tomorrow morning, Colonel."

Chilgers held the empty receiver by his ear for a second before returning it to its hook. He was unconvinced by Trench's report; Bane *was* too much of a threat. He had to be sanctioned or the whole operation would be threatened. The Winter Man was a worry Chilgers didn't need, and if Trench wasn't up to the task of taking him out . . .

The colonel retrieved the receiver and dialed an overseas exchange. After two rings a beep sounded, and Chilgers waited until he was sure the tape was working before he left his message:

"Tell Scalia I require his services."

Chapter Nine

How could they look so much alike?
Am I losing my mind?

"You say something, Josh?" Janie asked him.

"Huh? No, I guess I was just thinking out loud."

Beyond the living-room window, night had entrenched itself on the New York skyline, buildings still lit by individual offices instead of floors casting an eerie glow on the streets beneath. Janie's apartment was a four-room modern, counting a galley-style kitchen which rested against the near wall closest to the door.

"How 'bout dinner?" she asked.

"I'm not hungry," Bane said. "Later."

She moved behind him and began massaging his shoulders, her surprisingly strong fingers digging deep into the flesh, finding the root of his soreness immediately. Bane had gone to the King's gym for a workout, direct from Rockefeller Center. Seeing that boy had shorted out his emotions. His failure to catch the kid wasn't so much what bothered him as why he'd made the attempt in the first place. He went to the King's to lose his anxiety in two hours of heavy pumping with the cold steel. But that had served only to make things worse, the realization he would probably never see the boy again clawing at him.

"God, you're tense," Janie told him.

"I think I'm going crazy," Bane said distantly. "How could that boy have looked so much like Peter?"

"You said he was older than Peter."

"By five years or so. And it was five years ago that . . ." Bane let the statement trail off. "When I was chasing him, I felt invincible, like nothing could stop me. But something was trying—I could feel it."

"Then it took a man with no legs to finally bring you down." Janie dug her fingers in deeper. "You're chasing shadows, Josh."

"Or ghosts."

"Coincidence, love, nothing more."

"I suppose."

Bane sighed uneasily. His mind drifted back first five years and then beyond, to his return from the rice paddies and forests of Nam. The war was over, but there was still plenty of work for the Winter Man in the form of a hundred other Vietnams at various levels, each with its own independent importance to the concerns of the United States. Good intelligence services located threats before they could develop fully. And the greatest threats to American security were clever generals, socialist agitators, and men who knew too much and sold their allegiance for too little. These became the Winter Man's new targets. He moved through more than a score of countries, forgetting the name of one as soon as he passed into the next. Some were frigid, most steaming.

Officially in these years Bane served under the powerful Arthur Jorgenson, director of the Pentagon's top-secret Clandestine Operations, the same branch that had determined his assignments in Nam. Bane had long lost count of the number of men he had killed under orders from Jorgenson, nor was he bothered by what he'd done. Killing was a skill to be used like any other. He looked at his chosen victims no differently than a pathologist views a corpse, detached and cold.

Bane traveled to El Salvador during the late seventies in what was to become his final deep-cover mission for Clandestine Operations. His appointed task was to eliminate two rebel leaders responsible for the rising revolutionary movement with the help of a third rebel leader who had apparently come to see the American side of things.

Bane went to work methodically as always, living in the jungles, pinning down the men destined for his cross hairs. He picked a spot and time for both, within forty minutes of each other to maximize confusion. He learned too late that the whole episode was an elaborate setup put into operation by all three rebel leaders with the help of their Russian friends who very much wanted this Winter Man, who had caused them much hardship over the years, out of the way. Bane walked into an ambush of a dozen men.

They sprang from nowhere, one with the trees, rifles blasting. Bane felt the heat of the bullets ripping into his side and back but maintained his calm. The ambushers had expected to take him with the first burst. The need for a second gave Bane an advantage he was not about to squander. He cut down four as they stood, and another three while they reloaded. Two others rushed him with bayonets leveled. Thanks primarily to King Cong, though, that was hardly the way to take out the Winter Man, even from the front and rear simultaneously. Bane averted their charge with a deft move to the side once their move was made. He slit their throats with a single thrust of his knife, never taking his eyes from the clearing in case the other three soldiers who had fled reappeared.

How he'd then dragged himself five miles through dense jungle despite a half-dozen bullet wounds, Bane never remembered. Only figments and fragments of what had transpired remained in his memory. He couldn't reach most of the wounds to stitch them as he'd been taught, so he left the bleeding alone, to stop on its own. When he wandered out of the trees white and dazed, children ran thinking he was some kind of ghost. They were not far off. There was no clinical reason for him to be alive.

Three weeks later Bane was transferred to a Washington military hospital where he lay supine all day and ate out of tubes. His nurse was a brown-haired beauty named Nadine, and what followed was a storybook romance. Bane fell in love with her, deeply and hopelessly. He had never considered himself capable of feeling any emotion so strongly. But necessity had forced him to expose himself to Nadine, both physically and emotionally. She was his physical therapist as well, and they shared the long, painful hours during which he struggled to regain his strength and mobility. Each session would end with her rubbing out his tired muscles, inevitably tracing the lines of his many scars both new and old. Her smile was alive and warm, and she had a peculiar laugh which Bane always focused on in the moments before sleep, hoping to dream of her.

He learned that her last name was Fisk and that her husband had been a paratrooper killed in Vietnam. She had a son named Peter, nearly ten, who took an immediate liking to Bane when Nadine brought him to the hospital one afternoon after school. The boy was painfully shy but flashed his mother's smile often enough to tie Bane's emotions in knots. Soon Bane was walking with a cane and then without, his recovery miraculous even by the most liberal standards. The months had passed, slow and long, and during them a bond had formed between him and Nadine that Bane could never imagine himself breaking. She was closer to him than any other person he had ever known and he didn't want to lose that feeling, once avoided but now sorely required. He moved Nadine and Peter into a Washington brownstone with him two weeks after being discharged from the hospital. He married her before the month was out, in a simple ceremony with Arthur Jorgenson serving as the best man.

Bane laid the Winter Man to rest.

But it didn't last. He moved his new family to New York after a few months to escape the governmental overtones of Washington. Once away from them, he hoped the urge to get back into the Game would diminish. It didn't, despite the long workouts he started at the gym the King had opened with Bane's money, or the love of the family he had found. Finally, after lying in bed three nights in a row in a cold sweat, he flew to Washington for a meeting with Arthur Jorgenson. He wanted to be the Winter Man again, on different terms now and not all the time.

Jorgenson was skeptical but relented and in the end his greatest fears were realized. Bane had something to lose now and he uncharacteristically bungled assignments and botched up standard procedures. What's more, in the months he had been out of the Game more had changed than just his attitude. There were more codes, different ones, and worse, additional accounts to be made for all unsanctioned actions. Bane was confused, bothered. He missed his contact code once, and Harry the Bat flew to Berlin in his place to track down Trench and ended up getting his spine blown apart. Bane flew out after him to pick up the pieces.

He was walking through Kennedy Airport after his return flight when a New York state trooper approached him with the tragic news that his wife and stepson had been killed by a drunk driver on the interstate. Bane took the news with silence instead of tears, while inside he was ripping at the seams. His gut shook with fear. Death had struck him close to home and all at once his own mortality was obvious. He had, briefly, had something to lose, had lost it and all motivation as well. He wasn't invincible; no one was. Death wasn't pretty. He had caused enough, seen enough.

Bane mourned Nadine, Peter, and most of all himself. He grew tired, alone, and for the first time being alone bothered him. He spent long nights going to movies by himself, sitting through the same feature three, maybe four times. The only similar period of his life had followed the murder of his father. Then, though, he had thrown himself into his desire for revenge. Now there was nothing to revenge, nothing to throw himself into. He had exhausted everything. He withdrew into a shell, went to Arthur Jorgenson to be let out all the way, and was told in so many words that in his line of work that was impossible. They had to keep hold. It was the price you paid. Bane didn't care, just plunged into his workouts at the King's and picked up his check every other week at the Center.

Then Janie came into his life. Their relationship was slow to develop, with Janie having to pick and choose the moments to delve into Bane's mind and his hurt. She was sympathetic, understanding, and above all patient. And Bane accepted her because she knew when to leave him alone. He didn't love her and wondered seriously if he would ever be capable of loving anyone again. Janie understood and accepted this, hoping to heal the emotional wounds that had lingered long after the physical ones had closed.

Of course, fuller minds in Washington regarded Bane's plight in a different way. His file described him as "traumatized and nerve shattered. Severe emotional handicaps brought on by overexposure to violence and acceptance thereof. Unsalvageable for field." The file went on to say that the deaths of his wife and stepson had only speeded up an inevitable process.

The machine had become obsolete.

Until this morning.

Somebody had killed Jake Del Gennio and all of a sudden Harry the Bat was a part of his life again. Then seeing that boy at Rockefeller Center . . . Peter at fifteen . . .

The past might not be catching up but it was certainly making a determined surge. Bane felt different, changed, and it took him a while to realize he was moving forward in reverse, growing by going backward.

So as Janie rubbed his shoulders, he felt the old strength, the old senses coming back and he knew they hadn't been dead at all—just dormant, in need of rest to recharge. They stirred slowly and Bane felt himself coming alive again.

"Any luck in pinning down the government group responsible for delaying Flight 22?"

Janie hesitated. "I was hoping you wouldn't ask that."

"I did."

"What do you know about COBRA, Josh?"

Bane felt Janie release his shoulders. He turned to face her. "Not much, besides the fact that their stamp goes on half the sophisticated hardware that makes up our defense system."

"Half is a conservative estimate," Janie corrected. "To begin with COBRA's letters stand for Control for Operational Ballistic Research and Activation. And let me tell you, every bit of ballistic research worth a damn for this country has come out of their base in San Diego."

"Where Flight 22 originated . . ."

"Anyway, COBRA may technically be a government-funded installation but that funding is strictly blank check. The organization's become more powerful than even NASA was during the peak of the space program. The Joint Chiefs lap up everything Col. Walter Chilgers has to say."

"Chilgers?"

"Korean war hero who built COBRA from the foundation up. Well, more accurately he started from the top down with some of the greatest scientific minds in the world. Even Einstein was there in the very beginning I've heard."

"Any idea what COBRA's working on now?"

"Probably a hundred different projects, and it wouldn't be hard for them to keep any number secret from even the White House."

"A blank check," Bane muttered. "What else can you tell me about them?"

"Not an awful lot. They're way out of the Center's jurisdiction and even farther out of our league."

He held her eyes briefly. "There's something else I need—the latest intelligence file on a free-lance agent named Trench."

"I haven't got clearance."

"Get it."

Janie considered the problem, then nodded. "It'll mean a bit of eavesdropping off government discs, but what the hell. Why do you need it?"

"To give Harry in trade for the passenger manifest of Flight 22."

"Trench was the man in Berlin," she remembered. Bane just looked at her.

"What happens when you get the manifest?"

"I start checking. The passengers must've seen or felt something. . . ."

"If there's anything to all this, that is."

"You don't believe Jake's story."

"It is a bit much."

She was right, of course, and Bane didn't bother pressing the issue. He sensed a separation, a gulf, between them that was more his doing than hers. He knew she could never understand that part of him that was the Winter Man, that part which had become active again. It had been a different man she had pulled from the emotional depths two years before. Their relationship had been built on factors which suddenly no longer seemed to exist. He still loved her in his own way, would be eternally grateful for all she had done for him, but at the same time he no longer felt he needed her. And without need, could there be love? Worse, he was using Janie, using her for the access she provided. That made him feel dirty, and yet he found it easy to rationalize his decision.

They made love that night, Bane playing his role mechanically, half as payment for services rendered and half as a mask for the emerging thoughts within him. But Janie was no fool. Bane could feel her detachment and sense of loss, the certainty of it, and he avoided her eyes so as not to see the empty glaze that filled them.

He squeezed her to him, trying to lose himself in her beauty. His pace was measured and even, his hands teasing and surgical. She clung to him tightly, digging her fingers into his back as her pleasure surged. Bane felt his peak as well, but when it was over there was nothing soothing or even comforting about the act. It was simply another task completed, lost among the many others which remained to be done.

Eventually they slipped off to sleep, grateful for the peace it might bring, while only a few miles away Davey Phelps shivered in a cold hotel room, the covers pulled over his face to shut out the presence of the Men who were drawing closer.

The Third Day:

DAVEY

Slow down, you crazy child
You're so ambitious for a juvenile
But then if you're so smart
Tell me why are you still so afraid?
Where's the fire, what's the hurry about?
You better cool it off before you burn it out
You got so much to do
And only so many hours in a day.

—Billy Joel

Chapter Ten

"We've got him, sir," the COBRA operations chief said, holding the car door open for Trench.

Trench climbed out flanked by the Twin Bears. He was facing a broken-down hotel called the Shangri-La on West Forty-third Street near the Avenue of the Americas. He should have known the boy would have run to this area to seek the camouflage of other youths.

"The homing device fizzled out three hours ago but not before leading us to the general area," the COBRA man continued. "The hotel clerk remembers renting a room to a boy meeting his description last night. Room 626."

Trench looked around him, checked his watch: 9:20. The work-day was just beginning.

"How many men have you got?"

"A dozen. I ordered four more just to be on the safe side."

"Good," Trench said without enthusiasm, leery somehow of the task they were about to undertake. Something didn't feel right. He couldn't get thoughts of the strange five dollar bill from yesterday out of his mind. He pulled off his overcoat and tossed it into the back seat of the car, surveying the scene. "We'll move in on my signal," he told the COBRA operations chief. "Deploy your men to ensure all exits are covered. I'll handle the recovery myself."

"Yes, sir."

The COBRA operations chief took his leave, spitting orders into a walkie-talkie. Trench nodded to the Twin Bears and started moving toward the Shangri-La.

Davey Phelps watched the tall, well-dressed man approaching the entrance from the slit in the drawn blinds over his window. At first glance the man looked old, but closer inspection revealed this to be a false impression based only on his thinning, gray hair. The tall man stepped lightly with the spring of an athlete, gliding across the pavement in an evenly measured pace. That he was coming for him, Davey did not doubt. Nor did he doubt that the ten or so other well-dressed men were converging on the area for the same reason.

It had been a restless night that ended about an hour ago when The Vibes drove him from the bed. The feeling of the Men was stronger than ever, so Davey dressed and inched his way toward the steps only to find one of them perched in the lobby and two more outside the thick glass of the hotel's front door. Cautiously, he made his way back to his room. He considered the fire escape only long enough for The Vibes to tell him the Men had that covered too.

They had found him.

And this tall one was different from the others. Davey couldn't get into his mind, just as he hadn't been able to get into the mind of the big man who had chased him in Rockefeller Center the day before. The blue-suited figure radiated dark coldness and the two red-headed giants walking by his side radiated

110

nothing at all.

Davey felt the tug of desperation inside him. It had been fun for a while, adventurous. But now he missed his foster parents and the home they had made for him. He wanted to go back to them, wanted to take a shower where he didn't have to keep his eyes trained on the bathroom doorknob. His clothes felt dirty and moist now, stuck to his skin by the sweat of fear.

Davey moved away from the window and pulled on his leather jacket.

Outside, the Men grouped, moved in. The tall cold one stood on the sidewalk below, looking up.

Davey's eyes grew wet. His knees and fingers trembled. He tried to make The Vibes show him what they had in store for him once he was captured. They wouldn't show him anything, though, when he tried too hard. They came when they wanted to and right now they were nowhere to be found.

The Men had him and there was no escape.

Out of the hopelessness came his way out. He felt The Chill rising up his spine, the strongest he'd felt, the sensation driving him to moan and close his eyes. He saw what he had to do, and somehow he knew he had the power to do it.

The Chill swelled in him, a rising tide of water seeking escape from the dam that pins it.

Davey squeezed his eyes shut and focused his mind on the whole surrounding block. The veins near his temples began to pulsate.

Outside, the air seemed to buckle.

Davey squeezed his eyes still tighter, reached out with The Chill as far as his mind would let him. A jackhammer went off in his head as he let it go. It poured out of him with enough force to slam him back against the wall, and Davey thought if he looked in the mirror he would see his head expanded

111

to maybe three times its normal size. Then his ears were gripped by a dreadful ringing, and it took an instant for him to realize it was coming from outside, not in.

Every fire alarm on the block had been triggered, on every floor and in every room. Then burglar alarms joined the crazed chorus and continued despite the determined attempts of their befuddled owners to shut them off.

People spilled into the street, hordes of them, mixing with the already busy pedestrian traffic to form a mass so tight those in it had difficulty breathing.

Trench, who had started into the hotel when the alarms sounded, now found himself shoved back by an escaping throng, and he became separated from the Twin Bears. COBRA personnel screamed futilely into their walkie-talkies, hearing nothing through the wailing alarms and knowing that their words similarly reached no one. Cut off from a central command, they had no idea how to proceed, so they held their ground in the mindless hope that the boy whose photograph they held might walk right into them.

Davey Phelps joined the flow of people leaving the hotel, passing close enough to the cold man to smell his after-shave. The throng pushed into the street amid halted traffic, and then across it to better view the screaming fire engines drawing closer with each blast of their horns.

By this time Davey had stripped off his jacket, because most of the people forced from the surrounding buildings hadn't bothered to grab theirs. Mixing with the crowd, he eventually slid behind a fire engine that had just screeched to a halt, and joined a large mass of high school students taking in the festivities, his escape virtually complete.

A bus squealed to a halt just across the block. Davey rushed to it, dodging between the snarled traffic, knowing once he was on board he was as good as gone. He had climbed three of the bus's steps and was digging in his jeans for the right change when his balance wavered. He grabbed the handrail.

"Hey, kid," the driver blurted, "in or out, okay?"

But Davey didn't hear him. The Vibes had struck.

The bus felt hot to him, hot with panic and desperation. He heard screams, saw twisted metal, smelled something burning, saw . . . blood.

"Kid?"

Davey pushed himself backward, found the cement but didn't feel it.

"Jesus Christ," from the bus driver and the door hissed closed.

Davey's legs felt wobbly. He leaned against a No-Parking sign to steady himself and followed the bus's progress.

The driver sped up to make it through a yellow light across Avenue of the Americas. There were so many alarms and sirens still blaring that he never heard the one meant to warn him.

The ladder truck struck the bus broadside at forty miles per hour, shoving it across the road with a maddening shriek. The bus buckled, spun, and toppled over on its side, sliding onto the sidewalk and crushing two unfortunate bystanders against a building.

Davey's ears were filled with screams now, instead of sirens. The relief the crowd felt upon realizing there were no fires was soon replaced by true panic. Just as hundreds of alarms were finally turned off, the screams reached a crescendo to take their place.

Davey staggered away. His head felt crunched on

113

the inside, as if somebody were tightening a vise on his brain. But he swallowed the pain down and kept walking, pressing ahead.

Sometime later he found himself on Seventh Avenue with no memory of how he got there. He was sweating cold bullets under his leather jacket, and could still feel his fingers trembling and teeth clicking together.

Davey passed a sidewalk fortuneteller, a minor crowd enclosing him.

"The future lies in the cards," the fortuneteller announced, pulling a deck from his baggy jacket pocket. "Who is brave enough to learn what the cards hold for him, what the *future* holds?" Deftly he separated the deck before him.

Davey joined the crowd.

"Need a volunteer, need a volunteer." His eyes locked with Davey's. He spread the cards out in a fan shape. "How 'bout you, young—"

The fortuneteller's face went white. The fan of cards started to collapse, then broke apart flying everywhere. People booed, laughed, applauded. The fortuneteller staggered backward against a building.

Davey turned away and then glanced behind him. What had happened? What had the fortuneteller seen in his eyes? He continued on.

"The time has come for all God's children to be saved! You hear me, brothers, the time has come to be saved!"

The blaring voice froze Davey in his tracks. For an instant he thought it was directed only at him. Then he saw a black man with white hair holding a cheap wireless microphone as he stood over a yard-high amplifier.

"Give yourself up to God, brothers!" he droned on.

114

"Rebirth! I'm offering you a chance to give in to the power of the Lord!"

Davey moved closer, stopped.

"You won't worry about your boss or your wife or your husband. All your problems will vanish before the Lord because He is all that matters and He will take care of you. Learn a new and better life. Give yourself up to Him, be reborn, let yourself go into His court and see the only truth, the only love!"

Davey moved a bit closer.

"Brothers, I—"

The amplifier whined crazily—feedback. The black preacher threw his hands over his ears.

"Brothers—"

There was more feedback, worse this time. The crowd backed away. The black preacher tossed the cheap microphone dramatically aside.

"This is the work of the devil, brothers. He is among us even now." The black man's eyes scanned the crowd. "He walks the streets in clothes hiding his scales in the guise of a man"—his eyes stopped at Davey—". . . or a boy." The preacher's mouth dropped. His lips trembled. "Lord have mercy, the devil is here among us! It's you, boy, you're the devil!" He thrust a stubby finger forward, started toward Davey, and stopped suddenly as though blocked by a brick wall. *The devil! That boy is Satan himself!* God help us, help us all!"

The black preacher collapsed to his knees. A number of eyes turned curiously toward the boy.

Davey had already moved away, across the street.

First the fortuneteller, then the preacher.

What had they seen? What did they know? What had they felt? . . .

Davey quickened his pace although he had

nowhere to go. He wondered if he had something even worse than the Men to fear.

"Have you got the boy, Trench?" Colonel Chilgers' voice filled the car.

"I'm afraid not."

"What?"

Chilgers listened in somber silence to Trench's report, a part of him clearly excited. "I find much of that difficult to believe," he said at the end.

"So did I. But this makes three separate incidents. First, your man in the airport claimed the boy just wasn't there anymore; then, the matter of the five dollar bill yesterday; and now this. I should have suspected something earlier."

"You should have reported the bill incident to me last night."

"Perhaps."

"In any case, if your suspicions are correct, this boy seems to have picked up some rather interesting abilities which he didn't possess until Flight 22 landed in New York. Most interesting. . . ."

"It will no longer be a simple task to recover him," Trench said.

"But it's all the more important now that we do. The homing beacon's worn out, you say?"

"Yes."

"Then you'll have to find an alternate means of tracking him down."

"I've got a few ideas. I'll need the full resources of your computers, though."

"They're yours."

"And I'm going to require more men."

"How many?"

"Thirty."

116

"You can have as many as you want if they'll help bring in that boy. I want him, Trench, I want him."

The phone clicked off.

Trench leaned back, his face blank and emotionless. He would obey the colonel's orders only up to a point: he would find the boy, but could not risk capturing him. Even if he were successful, how long could he hold Davey Phelps before the boy's yet uncomprehended powers went to work? Furthermore, he knew he wouldn't be working for Chilgers much longer and didn't want to put a weapon of the boy's potential in the colonel's hands. Either way, his own survival was at stake.

So he would find the boy.

And he would kill him.

Chilgers looked up from his desk into the curious stares of Dr. Teke and Professor Metzencroy. The colonel had suspected there might be something in Trench's report he'd want the two men to hear firsthand and his intuition had paid off. Of the two, Metzencroy appeared more affected by the conversation just piped in through an amplifier. His hands were so jittery that he nearly missed his brow with his handkerchief on at least two occasions. Teke took it all in pensively, at most a glimmer of perspiration appearing on his bald dome.

"All right, gentlemen," Chilgers opened. "I want to know what you make of all this."

"Well," Teke responded, "earlier experiments in secondary stages of Vortex have indicated the possible effect of the energy fields we're dealing with—high frequency electromagnetization—on the human organism. We have, in fact, noted a number of possible—and I emphasize possible—changes in brain

117

function and body chemistry, up to and including severe neurological imbalances. But to say that this boy's participation in the tangent stage of Vortex in any way relates to whatever ... power he may possess is clearly unfounded.''

Metzencroy cleared his throat.

"You take issue with that, Professor?" Chilgers prodded, hoping he would.

Metzencroy leaned forward and tried to pocket his handkerchief. His trembling fingers almost precluded the effort. "The mind, Colonel, consists mostly of vastly unexplored territory. Some men of science have even suggested that we know more about the outer reaches of space than we do about the gray matter which inhabits our own heads. An exaggeration perhaps, but there is something to be said for the position. If conservatively we understand, say, five percent of the brain's operating process, its capabilities, what about the other ninety-five? Similarly, many in our field believe we only utilize that same five percent of our brain's capacity. Again, what about the remaining ninety-five?" Metzencroy pulled his handkerchief from his pocket again and closed his hand around it. "It is quite conceivable, Colonel, that exposure to the Vortex fields has given life to a previously dormant part of this boy's brain which may explain this strange power he has developed.''

Teke's round face was drawn into a frown. "It sounds to me, Professor, as if you're abandoning logic and scientific principle in favor of spirits and poltergeists.''

Chilgers leaned forward. "If spirits and poltergeists could help us destroy the Russians, then I'd be all for them, Teke.''

"There's something else we must consider," Metzencroy said hesitantly. "Once any previously unex-

118

plored territory is uncovered, in the mind or anywhere else, it tends to expand—that is, grow—as we look for more."

"The point?" from Chilgers.

"Is that the power this boy possesses is almost certain to grow stronger as more of his brain opens up. He is exploring it now tentatively, unsurely. Once he gains confidence, there is no telling the extent to which he might develop it."

Intrigued, Chilgers had to bury a smile. "Speculate further."

"I'm afraid I can't . . . not on this anyway." Metzencroy's handkerchief found its way back to his brow; then it slipped from his fingers. He was barely able to retrieve it, his hands were trembling so much.

"What else is bothering you, Professor?" Chilgers wondered.

Metzencroy steadied himself. "To continue my analogy of the mind to the universe, several problems are raised. Something has happened to David Phelps which we in no way expected or could have predicted. The mind of one boy is one thing, the entire universe something else again. But in this case they are very much the same, and we must consider the potential ramifications of any future actions we undertake."

"By actions," Chilgers concluded, "you mean Vortex."

"I mean we are dealing in areas we don't fully understand, areas whose mysteries are not even close to being entirely revealed to us. Ancient man discovered fire only to have it consume many of the trees from which his food came until he learned to harness it."

"You would've preferred that he just left it alone and stayed cold, I suppose," Teke chided.

119

Metzencroy held his stare. "The consequences are considerably more than a few trees with Vortex."

"It was necessity that brought man down from the trees to begin with," put forth Chilgers.

"And fear drove him back up on more than one occasion," added Metzencroy.

"I hope all this is getting you somewhere," snapped Teke.

Metzencroy hesitated. "I want to know what has given David Phelps his new power . . . and I want to know what caused the bubble on Flight 22 five days ago."

"Not that again," muttered Teke. "It was computer flutter, nothing more."

"Then explain how the computers don't remember it. Explain how the entire energy-matter field surrounding the jet seemed to blink for a brief instant without cause or explanation. Answer me that, Doctor!"

Teke didn't.

"The fabric of our universe does not function all that differently from the fabric of David Phelps's brain. Something has altered the boy's brain now and if Vortex is moved into final activation, the fabric of our universe might be similarly altered."

"So we'll all be running around changing five-dollar bills into hundreds." Teke chuckled. "Beats the hell out of inflation."

Metzencroy wasn't amused. His fist clenched over his moist handkerchief. "The time-space continuum is nothing to joke about, Doctor. We are dealing with forces here that—"

"Will assure us of world supremacy for hundreds of years to come," cut in Chilgers. "Are you suggesting we abandon Vortex in the face of that, Professor?"

"Postpone it perhaps."

"Considering the timetable, that amounts to much the same thing, doesn't it?" Chilgers leaned back in his leather chair, looked at Metzencroy and through him. "I've already watched us squander one advantage with the atom bomb and I'm not about to allow the same mistake to be repeated. We've been caught in a loop since the Cold War, Professor. We design and design, build and build, revamp and revise. But it doesn't matter, none of it does, because up till now it's all been a stalemate. The term *first strike* really doesn't exist because the best either side has ever been able to hope for is a simultaneous strike. But Vortex has changed all that. We have a means to break the loop, Professor, and break the stalemate. We've been given a second chance to do what we should have done twenty-five years ago but lacked the decisiveness to do. We will activate Vortex on our own in five days to avoid a similar debacle. There's only room for one superpower in this nuclear world we've created where high school students can build bombs out of chemistry sets."

Metzencroy felt the heat rising behind his cheeks, and was aware that his face was reddening.

"And I'll tell you something else, Professor," Chilgers went on. "We're going to find out where this Phelps boy gets his power from, we're going to find out if we have to pick his brain apart piece by piece. Because the Russians don't have him, the Chinese don't have him, nobody has him except us. The boy is ours."

Chapter Eleven

Bane arrived at the Center at ten o'clock sharp and went straight to Janie's office.

"Close the door behind you," she said, after he had stepped inside.

"Sounds serious." He moved toward one of the vinyl chairs before her desk.

"Stealing information from government computers usually is."

"Just borrowing, Janie, and for a good cause." He forced a smile, hoping to get one back from her.

None came.

"You're not gonna like it, Josh."

Bane sat down. "What's the latest on Trench?"

"There is none."

"What?"

"U.S. Intelligence's file on him has been removed from the active list. Maybe he's dead."

"Then his file would be cross-referenced for contacts, not deactivated."

"He might have retired," Janie said, grasping.

Bane shook his head. "Not Trench."

"That doesn't leave many alternatives."

"Just one by my count," Bane told her. "He's working for us now, some branch of our government."

"Could that be?"

"Uncle Sam doesn't hold grudges, Janie. Trench is a professional. If some agency of this government had need for his services, they'd get them."

"Then why deactivate his file?"

"Because if he's working for us, they'd want to keep a tight lid on it. Those files exist to keep regular track of all opposing agents' movements. That would be superfluous if Trench was one of ours now. They also wouldn't want any free-lancers sniffing out his trail, or people who *do* hold grudges."

"Like Harry?"

"Like Harry."

"What are you going to tell him?"

"The truth."

"Do you think that's smart?"

"Probably not, but when you start lying to your friends it doesn't leave you with much." Bane hesitated, eager to change the subject. "Any way of figuring out which branch Trench is working out of?"

"Possibly, but it'll take some time."

"Then don't bother. Harry's got a lot of favors owed him in the network. It's about time he called some of them in."

"You're not talking like a friend of his, Josh," Janie scolded, her eyes angry. "That poor guy's probably gonna walk off—excuse me—*wheel* off to get himself killed and you're just going to stand there."

"If I stand anywhere, it'll be by his side. I owe Harry that much."

"Then you want him to go after Trench so you can go too and get rid of some of that guilt you carry around with you."

"Maybe," Bane conceded because there was no

123

sense trying to explain further. There was no way he could expect Janie to understand men like himself and the Bat, the way they lived and died. The rules were different and so were the values. There was a code to consider.

"Well you know something, Josh? Harry may move around with no legs but sometimes you move around with no heart. Chalk them both up as war wounds, I suppose, and make sure the government keeps the checks coming. But what's different about the two of you is that the wounds don't seem to matter. Even if they don't heal, you keep on going. I guess scar tissue doesn't bleed."

Janie could have gone on but chose not to. This was a different man before her now, more stranger than lover. She could fight to reach him, get him back, but the futility of trying stifled the attempt before she even made it. She had always known this part of Joshua Bane existed, lurking below the surface, beyond her control and her love. Nonetheless, seeing it now unnerved her; the clarity of its intentions and resolve were so chilling—foreign. The part of Joshua Bane she loved might return someday but she wasn't counting on it.

Bane called Harry Bannister at I-Com-Tech from an open office across the hall.

"I've got the list you asked for, Josh," the Bat announced.

"I'd like you to add something to it. Reference profiles: age, occupation, residence—all the usual material."

"Looking for something that links them together, eh?"

"You read my mind, Harry."

124

"Well Lord fuck a duck, Josh, you've always been an open book to me." The Bat hesitated. "And what about your part of the bargain?"

"You sure you want it, Harry?"

"I'm sure."

"Trench is in America."

"No shit! That fucker's come over to our side now?"

"Apparently."

"All the easier for me to burn him. I'm not much of a traveler."

"He might be protected."

"My ass. The man ain't been born yet, Josh, who can protect Trench from one of my knives. That fucker stole my legs and now I'm gonna get even."

"You'll still have to find out what branch he's working out of."

"No sweat. I'll make a few calls. I'll get to that as soon as I run a check on these sixty-seven names on your passenger manifest. Give me about an hour."

Bane checked his watch. "I'll be there at eleven."

Harry the Bat peeked out from his I-Com-Tech cubicle as Bane glided across the carpet toward him.

"Good morning, Josh, and this is a good morning if ever they made one."

From the neck up, this was the same man who had almost died with him ten times over in Vietnam, the same man who'd taken a blast of double-aught shot meant for him in Berlin five years ago.

"Looking quite chipper today, Harry."

"Lord fuck a duck, Josh, do you blame me? I've finally got my chance to nail Trench."

"Your contacts come through?"

"Not yet. But they will."

"Keep me informed."

"Like the old days, Winter Man, just like the old days. I'm packing a set of extra knives today."

"I'll remember to keep my distance."

The Bat opened the top drawer of his desk and withdrew two sets of green and white computer paper.

"The fatter one's got the profiles on it too," he explained.

Bane took the pile and sat in the chair squeezed against the side of the white cubicle. The other cubicles hadn't been provided with such a luxury but then Harry didn't have any use for the seat ordinarily placed behind the desk, hence the spare. Bane scanned the passenger manifest for possible familiarity, found none, and then turned his attention to skimming the reference profiles.

"These weren't easy to cop, Josh. Tough little fuckers, they were."

Bane looked up. "What do you mean?"

"The airline had put a lock on the manifest for starters. I had to use my key."

"Problems?"

"Not directly. Except it won't be hard for whoever turned the lock to trace the lifting back to me."

"I don't like that, Harry. You should have checked with me on it first."

"Have no fear, the Bat is back."

"Take it easy. We don't know what we're facing here yet."

"I'm facing Trench and that dumb fucker's gonna regret the day he back-doored me before I'm finished with him."

Bane felt eager to change the subject. "You dig up anything on the pilot?"

"Yeah. Whole cockpit crew's been reassigned to European routes. You can forget about talking to

126

them for at least a month. Dug up something else interesting, though."

"What?"

"One of the people on the passenger manifest is missing. Report was filed with the police three days ago."

"Which one?"

"Kid by the name of David Phelps, goes by the name of Davey."

Bane found his brief profile. *David Phelps. Age 15. Address . . .*

A numbness grabbed Bane's spine and a dull throb found his temples. The senses lying on the very edge on his brain, senses that had kept him alive in a hundred steaming jungles and a hundred more impossible situations, snapped on, alerting him.

Alerting him to what?

"Missing persons report says the kid never made it home after the plane landed," Harry was saying. "That stuck out. I figured you'd want to know."

"Thanks," Bane said distantly. "It's as good a place to start my check as any."

"I figured there might be a connection," Harry said, studying Bane closely.

Connection . . . The word stuck in Bane's head. Everything was connected here, tied up tighter than a drum. The Bat had given him a list of people on board a plane Jake Del Gennio claimed had disappeared. Then Jake had disappeared, and now the Bat had stolen a computer program locked away quite possibly by the people behind it all. Bane could smell danger here thick as barbecue smoke, and all at once he regretted dragging the Bat into the whole mess.

"Watch your back, Harry," he offered lamely, rising with the computer print-outs tucked under his arm.

"Watch yours too, Winter Man," the Bat told him.

Chapter Twelve

Colonel Chilgers left for Washington by private jet as soon as his meeting with Teke and Metzencroy was completed. He had an appointment to see the President and two of his advisers to discuss, unbeknownst to them, the final stage of Vortex. The discussion, Chilgers felt certain, was merely a formality. He knew the way they thought. They would accept his proposal, perhaps even embrace it.

Everything seemed to be falling into place. Trench would have Davey Phelps delivered by tomorrow, and he was bringing Scalia in to deal with Joshua Bane. Still, there was Metzencroy to worry about, but Chilgers felt confident he could handle the professor.

The limousine deposited him at a side entrance to the White House so he could avoid the press—Chilgers loathed publicity—and he was ushered immediately through the long, wide corridors into the reception area where he waited briefly while the President was informed of his arrival. When the President's chief aide finally led him into the Oval Office, Chilgers noted the presence of the other two men he had been expecting: Secretary of Defense, George Brandenberg; and director of the Pentagon's Department for Clandestine Operations (DCO), Arthur Jorgenson.

"Sorry to keep you waiting, Colonel," the President said, rising behind his desk. Chilgers noticed a velvet chair had been placed between Brandenberg's and Jorgenson's. "I appreciate your promptness."

Chilgers took the President's outstretched hand. "A way of life for me, Mr. President." And he sat down gracefully, eyes darting between Jorgenson and Brandenberg, sizing them up. Brandenberg was a military man all the way—no problem there. Jorgenson, though, was another matter. DCO was a nonpolitical branch, so its director could address the President any way he saw fit. In fact, Chilgers knew this was the reason the president often turned to Jorgenson. It would not be so easy to convince him of the necessity of the project he called Placebo.

"I've read your report," the President began. "In fact, we all have."

"Just a summary, Mr. President," Chilgers offered, "of ongoing discussions that have been taking place for some time."

"I must say the results are rather distressing."

"Unfortunately."

"That hardly speaks well of our multibillion dollar defense and retaliatory systems."

"The systems are fine, sir. The problems, potentially, lie with the people manning them."

"So I read," the President said grimly.

Chilgers shrugged, burying a smile inside. Brandenberg and Jorgenson exchanged nods as they took the discussion in passively. They were here for later counsel, not direct participation, Chilgers realized, and thus would not stand as immediate obstacles in his path. He had only the President to convince. Still, Jorgenson worried him. The short, stout, silver-haired man ran DCO as neatly as Chilgers ran COBRA. Jorgenson was a detail man who explored all tangents before proceeding with anything. A committed skeptic, and worse, an incorruptible, nonpartisan one.

Chilgers met Jorgenson's eyes. No reaction. The man was a pro.

"We can deal with the people," Chilgers told the President, grabbing the offensive. "There are ways of exploring exactly how deep the problem extends."

"I read that too," the President commented. Then his features grew taut. "But I'm not convinced Project Placebo is the way to proceed. The measures are quite drastic."

"So is the problem."

"We're all in agreement on that point, Colonel."

"But at different levels, I'm afraid. I'm strictly a systems man, Mr. President. I know how to make weapons work and how to stop them." Here, Chilgers almost turned his attention to Jorgenson and Brandenberg but there was no reason to drag them into the discussion or to antagonize them. "COBRA began developing the present Red Flag alert system a dozen years and three administrations ago. We have studied all potential problems relating to it and our fears have been made known to you."

"Concerns, you mean," from Brandenberg.

Chilgers held back another smile. "No, I mean fears and that's what I meant by levels of agreement. We all agree on the problem. The issue is how far do we go to correct it."

"And I say Project Placebo might be going too far," insisted Jorgenson, taking the President's side.

"Perhaps." Chilgers shifted in his chair. Jorgenson was pressuring him. The colonel worked best under pressure. "But let us consider the fact that of all our land-based retaliatory and defense systems, only *one percent* have ever been proven effective in a real and clear sense of activation. That leaves ninety-nine as an uncertain commodity."

"There are tests—"

Chilgers cut Brandenberg off. "Which prove nothing, nor do drills. Games, gentlemen," he said, speaking to all three of them. "Nothing but games. The simple fact is that our procedures remain untested in a true high pressure situation. We have no way of knowing if our people will respond totally and unequivocally to orders, or if they'll follow procedures precisely and surely." Now, back to the President. "Project Placebo will give us our first accurate answers to these questions."

The President nodded slowly, tracing the line of his jaw and chin with his fingers. "Colonel Chilgers, I want you to briefly sum up the essence of Project Placebo."

Chilgers hesitated just for an instant. "Basically, that we 'create' the impression of all-out war for one of our missile installations and carefully chart their performance and reaction up to and including the point at which they are given the launch code. The human factor, Mr. President, is the one unknown present in an otherwise flawless sytem. And until we've tested it fully, under no circumstances can we maintain total confidence in our abilities."

"It's all computerized, though," advanced the President.

"Only up to a point, sir. The buttons still have to be pressed, a whole series of them, and the slightest foul-up triggers the abort feature and we'll have to start all over again. We're talking about seconds here, but in the event of a Soviet strike, seconds might be all we have."

"I still don't see what you expect to gain from an exercise at just one of our silos."

131

Chilgers leaned forward. "Each silo, especially each primary one, functions as a microcosm of the entire system. The stress factors and problems encountered within it are almost certain to provide more than adequate analysis of the concerns we're talking about."

"I assume you've worked out all the details of this Project Placebo of yours by now."

Chilgers nodded. "The reports and procedures, down to the second, are in my briefcase. For security reasons the only copy is locked in my safe."

"Well, we certainly wouldn't want word leaking out if we do decide to go ahead with this." The President rapped his knuckles on the desk surface. "I assume, Colonel, you've already got a test site chosen as well."

"Bunker 17."

The President turned to Secretary of Defense Brandenberg. "George?"

"A wise choice," Brandenberg acknowledged. "Bunker 17 is one of our primary installations, constructed along with five sister stations as a kind of compromise for Dense-Pack. It has the capacity to fire thirty-six MX missiles, each loaded with ten high-yield hydrogen warheads, into Russia with a twenty-one-minute time lag."

"Targets?"

"They're changed at regular intervals for security reasons. A fair estimate would be the Soviets' primary attack centers in addition to major areas of population and government."

"I didn't realize we put so many eggs in one basket," the President said uneasily.

"There's a reason for it, sir," Brandenberg explained. "Our latest intelligence information indicates that the Russians are still in the dark about the existence of Bunker 17 and its five sister stations."

Here Brandenberg swung toward Chilgers. "As you know, Colonel, we spread the six units out over the most isolated parts of the West and Midwest: Wyoming, Montana, Utah, the Dakotas, Nevada. Mostly desert country. The installations are contained almost entirely underground with U.S. Agriculture cover buildings constructed over them. The firing silos themselves are spread out in a circle around the installations, under camouflage that makes them undetectable to even the latest Russian spy satellites."

"The point," Chilgers interjected, "is that Bunker 17 and her sister stations represent the strongest leg of the system rebuilt by your administration, Mr. President. Yet with all the hardware and computer simulations, we still don't know if things will function as they must in a crisis. A million hours go into testing the machines. Project Placebo will test the people."

"You've raised some interesting points," the President said, "certainly worthy of serious consideration."

"I'm afraid, sir, that the consideration must come rather fast. As my report indicates, three days from today would be the ideal time to activate Project Placebo."

"Why?"

"Because in four days COBRA will be set to deliver to Bunker 17 thirty-six of the new MX Track One missiles with increased yield to their ten individual warheads."

"I don't follow your point."

"Simply, sir, that the timing would allow us to substitute dummy warheads in the rebuilt Track Ones."

"Which would be superfluous unless . . ." The President's eyes sharpened. His cheeks puckered. "Good God, Colonel, you're not suggesting we follow Project Placebo through to the point of actually *firing* the missiles?"

"Yes, I am," Chilgers said without any hesitation whatsoever. "I left that factor out of my initial report purposely because I felt it was better expressed in person. For Placebo to have any tangible effect, it must be carried through to total completion—up to and including launch—to enable us to study the aftereffects of the stress involved. In a shooting war, Mr. President, we'll hopefully get a chance to reload."

"But we'd be taking an awful chance of alerting the Russians to the presence of Bunker 17."

"Let's not be naïve, sir. They already know about the existence of Bunker 17 and her sister stations, just as we know about all their *secret* installations. What we don't know is how well our hundred billion dollar investment will function if actually called upon." Chilgers paused briefly. "And the whole point of Project Placebo is to make a detailed study of the most important component of our entire defense system: the men who man it."

"Then the missiles used for the project will be little more than drones," the President concluded.

"Easily destructed once they pass into the atmosphere," Chilgers added.

"So for part of this exercise Bunker 17 will be carrying blanks in all thirty-six cylinders."

"My report outlines the exact scenario of Placebo," Chilgers explained. "For optimum effect, the base should be at Yellow Flag status for a minimum of seventy-two hours before we trigger Red Flag. I've proposed we bring the bunker's status up to that level in three days' time, one day before the shipment of the new Track Ones is due. That way the dummy warheads will only have to be in the silos for forty-eight hours prior to final activation, so as not to weaken this crucial leg of our defense system for any prolonged period."

"And leaving us hardly enough time for proper advance study."

"There won't be time for proper study if the Russians launch first either, sir."

The President's eyebrows flickered. "This office seldom affords me the luxury of making an immediate decision. Today is one of those times. Your proposal is tentatively accepted, Colonel, pending study of the detailed schema submitted today."

This time Chilgers let his smile out.

The President held his gaze out the window after Chilgers had gone. "I'm not sure I like it, gentlemen, I'm not sure I like it at all."

"On the surface," said George Brandenberg, "the son of a bitch makes a hell of a lot of sense."

"Except with Chilgers we never seem to know what's going on *beneath* the surface."

"But he gets results," reminded Brandenberg. "He always has. Hell, COBRA has almost single-handedly kept us in step with the Russians militarily."

"I suppose."

"Then you're serious about accepting Project Placebo," from Arthur Jorgenson.

"George has been on my back to run a similar test for more than a year but the right circumstances never presented themselves. They have now."

"Besides," added Brandenberg. "How can we go wrong? Let's take the situation to its worst possible extreme: that Chilgers intends to leave the warheads armed in hopes of starting up with the Russians so we'll have to use all the marvelous equipment COBRA has developed in the last five years."

"Then our fail-safe systems," picked up the President, "would make it impossible for the missiles to ever leave our airspace. There are a dozen ways we could circumvent or abort the mission."

Jorgenson scowled. "And what stops Chilgers from restructuring the missiles to override them? I mean, just about every piece of equipment at Bunker 17 probably contains component parts constructed by COBRA."

"Doesn't matter," said Brandenberg. "With that concern precisely in mind, all missiles go through a safety check on a regular daily basis, four times a day actually, to make sure all fail-safe systems are functioning. Even if half the systems somehow failed, that would still leave six operational."

Jorgenson shook his head. "Once the missiles are actually launched, there are only four fail-safe systems available to us."

"And even if all of them failed—a billion to one shot—we'd still be able to shoot them down with relative ease. Let's say we give Chilgers' dummy missiles a one-mile altitude before they self-destruct as laid out in Project Placebo. Even if they aren't dummies and they don't self-destruct, we use our own fail-safe destruct systems or just shoot the suckers down. There's no way even COBRA can get around that."

"Your point's well taken," Jorgenson conceded. "I don't particularly like Chilgers. Maybe that's the problem."

The President nodded faintly in agreement. "None of us like him, Arthur. But he gets the job done extremely well with no leaks whatsoever. He's survived five administrations before mine and has outlived them all. That's a tenure unheard of in government circles. I'd wager that all my predecessors had their suspicions of him too. But if any of them were warranted he couldn't possibly have lasted this long."

"It never hurts to be careful," Jorgenson advised.

"Strangely, Arthur," the President said ironically, "that might be the strongest argument in favor of Project Placebo."

Jorgenson's eyebrows fluttered. "Then I just hope we've got a good man in command of Bunker 17."

"In fact," Brandenberg noted, "we do: Major Christian Teare."

"*Christian* Teare? I hope he lives up to his name."

"And then some, Arthur. Teare's six-and-a-half feet tall and carries enough weight for us to have to make up his commander's uniforms special. Also gives us a helluva time regularly for refusing to shave one of the scraggliest beards I've ever seen."

"You've met Teare, then."

"I *recruited* him and with good reason. He comes from redneck county, Georgia. But don't let that fool you because before he joined up with us he once spent an evening saving fifteen blacks from a KKK raid. There were twenty klansmen and one of him. Teare won." Brandenberg paused to let his point sink in. "He's not a man you want as your enemy, but he's a man who scored the highest leadership quotient in his class as well as exhibiting a constant *negative* stress factor."

"Tough combination to beat," acknowledged Jorgenson.

"Which is precisely why I placed him in command of one of this country's most sensitive installations."

"Sounds like the right man to have between us and Project Placebo," noted the President.

"Let me put it this way, sir. If you're looking for a man to keep a rock from pinning you to a hard place, you need look no further."

"I'll sleep easier tonight," said Jorgenson.

Chapter Thirteen

Bane went straight from I-Com-Tech to Brooklyn
Heights and the residence of Mr. and Mrs. Joseph
Martini, the foster parents of Davey Phelps. The fact
that the boy had disappeared after Flight 22 had
landed intrigued Bane. Had he, like Jake Del
Gennio, seen or known something that had necessi-
tated his removal? The way to finding out began
with the Martinis and he'd already decided on his
cover for them: he would pose as a field agent for
Child-Find, the national center for locating missing
children.

The Martinis lived on the western edge of
Brooklyn Heights, in a neighborhood far enough
from the East River to be spared the massive renova-
tion and conversion efforts that had turned much of
the Heights into a prime—and exclusively priced—
area. Their home was the larger half of a two-family
which reminded Bane somewhat of the Bronx house
he'd grown up in. It was homey enough from the
outside with soft, well-kept brick and a clean sidewalk, the city sounds just far enough away to ignore.

Bane climbed a set of comfortably aged cement
steps and gave the bell one long ring. Feet shuffled
toward the door and he felt himself being scrutinized
through the peephole. Locks jangled and the door

opened just wide enough for a pair of eyes to poke out over a fastened chain.

"Mrs. Martini?"

"You must be Mr. Bane." Bane nodded and she shut the door again in order to undo the chain. "Yours was the first hopeful call we've had in days," she said, holding the door open for him. "It's good to see you important types taking an interest in the problems of people like us. My husband's at work. Always gets home by four so he can spend some time with the kids."

Bane watched Clair Martini close the door behind him and ran her features through his mind. Her pale face was creased by lines and dominated by a pair of tired eyes. Her hair fell unevenly across her face and neck. Her dress clung to areas where she had started to bulge. She had the appearance of a woman who had given up trying to look young, but inside Bane felt warmth and honest caring.

She tried to smile and failed. "We can talk in the living room."

They sat down next to each other on a simple cloth couch. The rest of the furniture was also plain: a stained throw rug, a pair of matching chairs, a television set missing a knob or two. The shades were half drawn, casting the room into dark and somber silence. Bane's uneasiness increased.

"You know," Mrs. Martini began, "we got four kids with us right now, including Davey, and we wouldn't mind keeping them for good. Davey's the oldest, one of the nicest kids we ever had stay with us. Been here for almost six months now." Mrs. Martini sighed and pushed back tears. "I remember the first time the city brought him over. We got taken with him from the start. He had these real wide eyes and shaggy hair, see, that made him look so innocent and

139

lonely you just wanted to cry."

Bane's flesh prickled. She might have been describing his late stepson. "Would you happen to have a picture of Davey around?" he asked, not fully knowing why, something tugging at his gut.

"What for?"

"To put on the national wire. If Davey's a runaway, it'll help turn him up."

"He had a set taken in school. I'll get you one."

Mrs. Martini returned to the room holding a dogeared snapshot. "Best I can do," she said, handing it to him.

Bane's eyes found the face and froze. The snapshot quivered.

Davey Phelps was the boy from Rockefeller Center!

The snapshot wasn't a great likeness, but it was close enough, especially the long, scraggly hair and deep-set, haunting eyes. There was no mistaking those. Incredible . . .

"When was the last time you saw him?" Bane asked Clair Martini.

"Before he went to the airport to visit his grandparents in San Diego. Ten days ago now. He should have been home before noon on Saturday. I guess I should have met him at the airport but I had the other three kids to watch, see. When he didn't show up by two, I called his grandparents and they told me they had watched him get on the plane which means if something happened, it was after he got to New York." Her stare became cold, sure. "He wouldn't have run away, Mr. Bane. He wasn't the type. I wish he was, then I wouldn't be so God-awful worried. Something's happened to him, I just know it has!" Mrs. Martini was on the verge of tears.

"And you haven't heard from him at all these past

140

five days? A phone call even?" Bane asked, his mind moving in another direction.

"Not a whisper, Mr. Bane. My husband Big Joe's been spending a couple of hours at night on the streets asking around and checking with Davey's friends. We've gotta do something or we'll just go crazy. But something happened to Davey. It's like I told that other man. But he didn't listen like you are. He didn't care."

"What other man?"

"I don't remember his name. Said he was from some kind of special bureau. Tall and well dressed, with real funny eyes."

Bane felt something cold grip his insides. "What kind of eyes?"

"Light colored, kind of gray. I never seen anything like them."

Bane's heart skipped a beat. Mrs. Martini was describing Trench! *Here, in New York!* The whole thing was starting to come together but it made no sense.

"When was he here?"

"Yesterday afternoon. Late."

"What did he want?"

"He asked to see Davey's picture like you, but I didn't want to let him keep it. Then he put it in his pocket and gave me a funny look, and I was afraid to ask him for it back. I didn't like looking at his eyes. But he was polite and he had the right credentials. Asked the same questions as you. You know him, Mr. Bane?"

"I might."

"Well, it's good to have important people looking out for you." Mrs. Martini hesitated and then took a deep breath. "You'll find Davey for me, won't you, Mr. Bane?"

Bane nodded slowly, and Mrs. Martini seemed to relax for the first time but only briefly.

"You know, Mr. Bane," she said softly, "the city tells you to love them—but not too much. And to care for them—but not to get too close. Well, me and my husband, Big Joe, can't abide that, especially with a boy like Davey. He's something special. His grandparents ought to have their heads examined for not taking him in permanent, if you know what I mean."

"Can I keep this picture?" Bane asked her, still gazing at it.

"If it'll help you bring him back." Mrs. Martini's lips quivered. Her eyes grew watery. "Bring him back to me, Mr. Bane, just bring him back to me," she pleaded.

But Bane barely heard her because his mind was elsewhere working together all the variables. Davey Phelps, the boy from Rockefeller Center who reminded him so much of his stepson, had been a passenger on the disappearing 727 and now he was running from something. Why else wouldn't he have come home? Trench was in New York, as an operative for some government group, looking for him. Of course, it would have taken a pro like Trench to dispose of Jake Del Gennio so cleanly. But why was he now searching for a fifteen-year-old boy? And who was he working for?

COBRA, Bane thought, it had to be. Everything came back to them. They had delayed Flight 22 in San Diego and certainly qualified as a government agency with enough clout to have Trench's name removed from the active list if he was working for them. And if that were so, then COBRA was behind Jake's death and now they were after Davey Phelps.

Bane figured Trench was still looking for the boy; otherwise he wouldn't have bothered with a visit to the Martinis, a move hardly in keeping with his style. The problem was to get to Davey Phelps first and Bane thought he might have a lead. Davey hadn't called home in five days. A fifteen-year-old boy, scared and alone, would sooner or later use a phone, which was exactly what Bane did in a booth just down the street from the Martinis'.

"Manhattan South," a receptionist's voice told him.

"Lieutenant Dirkin please."

"One minute."

"Dirkin," a raspy voice announced twenty seconds later.

"Lou—Joshua Bane."

"Hey Bane," Dirkin shot out, "long time no hear. How goes the battle?"

"Surviving, I guess."

"Well, that's more than I can say for most. What can I do for you?"

"I need a favor. How soon can I see you?"

"An hour from now at the Bagel Nosh near the precinct. You're buying."

"Deal."

Lou Dirkin was a barrel-chested man who stood barely five-and-a-half feet tall. He had done two tours in Nam and still limped a little on rainy days. Bane had worked with him once in the jungles and somehow had stayed in contact.

Dirkin was already seated at a center table when Bane arrived. A plate containing a bagel and cream cheese had just been placed in front of him.

"Love these things," he said, rising to take Bane's hand. "What can I do for you, Josh?" Dirkin sat back down. "Damnit, they put butter on this thing." And he went to work with a napkin swabbing the bagel clean.

"I need a trace put on a line. Think you can handle it?"

Dirkin regarded him with interest. "Depends. Where's the line?"

"Brooklyn Heights."

"No problem. Should be able to ease it right through."

"Time's a factor."

"That's a problem. How soon?"

"Immediately."

Dirkin frowned, started painting his bagel with cream cheese. "The impossible takes a little longer than that, buddy boy."

"I've got faith in you, Lou."

"I figure you wouldn't be here if it wasn't important. You must be active again which means the streets are gonna be even less safe than usual. You working for Uncle Sam?"

"Right now I'm working for myself. Personal, not business."

"Yeah, well this ain't Nam, Josh. If you're gonna litter the streets with bodies, do it in somebody else's precinct." Dirkin paused. "So what's the machine?"

"I need a trace on all incomings and lots of updates."

"You're asking a lot of the old computer, Josh."

"Think you can swing it?"

Dirkin took a bite of his bagel. "Hell, with the new equipment we've got, we can have a line traced in five seconds. I'll just have to keep it secret from the captain or he'll have my ass."

"Not if you're still running the precinct, he won't."

Dirkin winked, started another mouthful. "What

he don't know, won't hurt him. What number you want watched, Josh?"

Bane gave it to him.

Chilgers made the phone call from his private jet en route back to San Diego.

"I'll be arriving in New York tomorrow evening," Scalia told him.

"Your work will begin immediately. There's some cleaning up to do."

"How many targets?"

"One primarily."

"My price is a half million. Usual procedures. Who is the primary target?"

"Joshua Bane."

Scalia paused. "The price for that will be a million and a half."

Chilgers knew there was no sense in arguing. "Very well," he said. "Other services may be required."

"We'll negotiate when the time comes. You know where to reach me."

"Things might get messy."

"You've come to the right place."

Harry Bannister lived in a nice enough building on East Sixty-ninth Street refurbished by a compassionate architect with the handicapped in mind. The halls were wide and the elevators deep. And the main front entrance wasn't through a revolving door.

"Welcome to my humble abode, Winter Man," Harry greeted and wheeled himself forward.

Josh closed the door behind him. Everything in the apartment seemed to be made of wood. Harry

145

prided himself on traditional furniture, loathing modern plastics, metals, and glass that laid to waste aesthetic design.

"Pour yourself a drink, Josh. This is a day for celebration. I've finally got the bastard. After all these years, I've finally got him."

Bane stopped halfway to the wood-finished wet bar. "You found out who Trench was working for?"

"It took some arm twisting."

"Mind if I venture a guess?"

"Be my guest."

"COBRA."

The Bat's features sank a bit. "Shit, Josh, you really know how to spoil a poor cripple's surprise. How'd you figure it out?"

"You go first."

"Lots of people owe me favors, Josh, but not nearly as many anymore. They didn't want to talk, but living in this chair does have its advantages. People don't refuse you much if you know how to ask for what you want."

"You could have asked before. Anytime."

"Except I never had the specifics before. You gave them to me this morning. Besides, running into you in the park the other day made me realize maybe I haven't changed so much after all."

"Neither has Trench."

"Your turn," Harry said simply.

Bane told him how COBRA seemed to fit into everything that was going on, and had been, since Flight 22 had been delayed out of San Diego.

"So you figure COBRA sent the tall bastard out here to ice Jake," the Bat said bitterly.

Bane nodded. "And now he's after a fifteen-year-old kid."

"Seems a bit low for him."

146

"The kid was on the plane."

"So were sixty-six other people."

"The boy must be different," Bane said. "COBRA seems to want him awfully bad."

"Sounds to me like you do too."

"Once we've got him, the rest will fall into place. I've got this feeling he's the key to the whole thing."

The Bat regarded him with a knowing grin. "There's more, Josh, I know there is. What is it with this kid and you?" When Bane stayed silent, Harry continued. "Got a plan to find him?"

Bane told him about the phone tap he had arranged through Lou Dirkin.

"Sounds promising, Josh. Except if you figured it out, it's a cinch Trench did too."

"The thought had crossed my mind."

The Bat started to wheel himself past Bane, to the wall bar dominated by mirror-backed shelves. "Sounds like you're goin' hunting tonight, Josh, so I figure you could use some artillery. Hands are fine but not against Trench and his army."

"Any suggestions?"

"Let's see . . ." Harry hit a switch concealed under the counter. The mirror backing rotated, the shelves disappeared, and Bane found himself looking at a wide assortment of every handgun imaginable. "I keep the rifles in my bedroom closet. You can't be too careful these days."

"So I see."

Harry was fingering a sleek automatic resting on the first row. "How about a Walther PPK? You've already got James Bond's initials. You might as well take his gun."

"I'd prefer something with more stopping power."

The Bat winked at him. "Got just what ya need." He pulled a somewhat larger, but just as sleek, pistol from the row above the Walther, stretching his fingers to reach it. "The latest from Browning. An FN highpower, self-loading, semiautomatic with a thirteen shot clip. And, as a special added extra, a couple clips packed with silver bullets, just like the Lone Ranger used to use. Bet you never heard Tonto say that getting shot with one of these bastards is like swallowing a grenade. Tear your head off at sixty yards."

"Hollow points?"

"Standard equipment."

Bane reached out and Harry handed the Browning over. "I'll take it on approval."

"Happy hunting, *kemosabe*."

Chapter Fourteen

Davey Phelps huddled in a corner of the couch, arms wrapped around his knees. He didn't know what time it was, though he guessed ten o'clock had already come and gone. He hadn't turned the lights on because he knew the Men were close and might discount a dark apartment.

He had almost gone home; in fact, he was on his way there when The Vibes warned him not to. Maybe the Men were watching his house. Maybe going home would mean danger for his foster family. In any case, he ended up in Queens halfway between the Brooklyn-Queens Expressway and the East River, just off Nassau Avenue and near a renovated apartment building named the Ferdinand. He pushed hard for The Chill with the doorman and ended up in a seventh floor apartment vacated by a tenant on a month-long vacation.

Davey's head pounded the whole time the doorman led him up to the seventh floor and opened the apartment for him. He felt The Chill slip a few times and had to fight to get it back. It didn't seem to be working right anymore. Since that morning, when he'd escaped from the hotel, his head had been filled with an awful thumping that threatened to split it apart. Once inside the apartment, he had pressed both temples hard for twenty minutes to block the pain but it came back every time he pulled his fingers away.

He was lonely and scared. He couldn't go home but at least he could call, talk for a while, tell his foster parents he was okay—even though he wasn't he owed them that much.

An hour before he had dialed the number.

"Hello," said his foster mother on the other end. "Hello?"

Davey couldn't speak. What could he tell her? Talking would only make things worse. He hung up, only to call twice more in the next twenty minutes, always with the same results.

His head hurt worse than ever.

His nose suddenly felt stuffy and he realized he was sobbing. He swiped at the tears with a sleeve of his jacket.

The Men were coming for him; he knew that now. Somehow they had found out where he was and they were coming. He couldn't run anymore. His head hurt too much and he didn't have the strength.

He relaxed a bit, almost fell asleep, until a succession of car doors slamming on the street below told him it was over.

"Hey, Josh," said Lou Dirkin, "glad you called."

"Got anything for me?"

"Yeah, the bag of shit the captain gave me for running an unauthorized tap. He made me pull it."

"Shit . . ."

"Don't fret, buddy boy, that bagel you bought me was still a good investment. I ran down all the calls that came in since this afternoon. One series stands out: three calls in maybe a twenty-minute period

150

ending fifteen minutes ago, all from the same location, all thirty seconds in duration with, get this, no dialogue exchanged. Weird, huh? Think that's what you're looking for?"

"Give me the address," Bane told him.

Trench addressed himself to the five COBRA operations men in charge, respectively, of seven men each. "I want this building surrounded. Front and back. Three men minimum on each exit. No slip-ups this time." He felt the sweat forming inside his gloves in spite of the cold. The temperature had dipped below the freezing mark, and his breath made clouds of mist in the air. "My men and I will bring the subject out personally. None of you makes a move unless I authorize it. Understood?"

The five men nodded and moved away to relay the instructions to their specific groups. Trench started back toward the Twin Bears. Chilgers had tapped directly into the local telephone system to get a fix on all calls terminating at the Martinis' residence. Trench cared only about those originating within a twenty-mile radius. The boy was still close; he knew it. It was just a question of getting a break, and that came with those three strange phone calls which had come less than an hour before, all originating from a seventh-floor apartment in the Ferdinand.

Davey Phelps undoubtedly.

There would be no escape for the boy this time. Trench had thought everything out, up to having one of his men atop a nearby utility pole cut off all juice to the street in the event the boy tried a repeat of that morning's performance. It would end for him here and now.

His confidence in the red-headed Twin Bears,

Pugh and Soam, was total. He would leave one on the first floor as insurance against one of COBRA's soldiers interfering or the boy escaping him on the floors above. Trench would go upstairs with the second Twin Bear and would enter the boy's apartment after Soam, only when he was sure it was safe. That way, if the boy turned his unusual powers on the giant, Trench would be free to burst in and empty an entire clip into him, though he fully expected the giant to take the boy without a struggle, after which Trench would follow them to the cellar, execute Davey Phelps, and report that he had escaped once again.

Trench nodded at the Twin Bears and the three of them started across the street toward the building.

Bane was approaching the apartment building by car when he saw the tall man in the beige overcoat. The man turned enough for him to realize it was Trench flanked by two of the biggest brutes he had ever seen. The killer seemed to be speaking to them, issuing instructions. That was all Bane could pick up before his car passed out of range; enough, though, for him to realize there was no way he could gain access to the building from the outside—Trench would have all entrances covered. That the killer was here surprised Bane not at all. The important thing was that it appeared Trench was about to enter the building for the first time, which meant there was still a chance to save the boy. But how to get inside?

There had to be a way. He could rush one door perhaps and hope for the best, a small number of men to encounter and defeat. No, that was too chancy, long odds surely with a virtual army to defeat before he was finished. Then he remembered something.

These buildings had all been constructed long ago between the two world wars. For safety and security reasons, they shared a common cellar. That was the answer!

Entry into a neighboring building would assure him of passage into the one he sought. Bane left his car around the corner in a towaway zone and headed back to Davey Phelps.

Trench entered the lobby of the building with a Twin Bear on either side of him, confident that COBRA's men had the outside sufficiently surrounded. Those residents returning or leaving, if they asked, were informed that a joint police-federal operation was in progress and were told not so politely to stay out of the way.

Trench nodded to the blue-eyed Bear, Pugh, signaling him to remain in the lobby while his brother led the way upstairs. Pugh crossed his arms and stood directly between the door and the stairs. No one would be getting by him. His brown-eyed brother, Soam, started up the steps with Trench close behind. The killer didn't trust the elevator, not with a boy who could turn fire alarms crazy seven floors above.

By the fifth floor, the two men had slowed their pace to a crawl, gliding across the steps with no hint of any noise that might forfeit their presence. Halfway up the sixth, Soam withdrew a thick, razor-sharp hunting knife from a sheath on his belt. Trench worked his gun free of its holster.

They crept to the designated room on the seventh floor, Trench making sure it was the correct one, and stood on opposite sides of the door.

Inside, The Vibes told Davey Phelps they were

there and he lurched to his feet, pressing himself into the room's far corner. If only The Chill could make him invisible, part of the wall. But his head was still splitting and The Chill continued to elude him. So he would give himself up, hold his hands up in the air just like criminals did when cornered in the movies.

Then The Vibes screeched through Davey's head and he knew at once these men had come to kill him, not take him. He had started to push himself away from the wall when the door exploded off its hinges revealing a man as wide and tall as the frame.

Soam showed his knife.

The dark cellar stairs came to an end in the Ferdinand's lobby. Bane opened the door just a crack, enough to catch sight of the giant hovering in the hallway. His back was to Bane, an easy enough shot for the Browning and Bane cursed himself for not bringing a silencer. He'd have to take the giant with his bare hands which promised to be no simple task, at the very least time consuming. He had surprise on his side, though, and could be across the floor before the monster knew what hit him.

He was almost right.

Pugh turned at the last instant before Bane's arm closed around his throat. The Bear lashed out with a forearm that landed with the impact of an oak tree, cheating Bane of his balance. The giant followed the blow up immediately, but Bane was in motion again, ducking under the giant's outstretched arms and ramming his kidney hard with an elbow. Pugh felt the blow, wincing, and staggered to turn. Bane closed again but the Bear caught him with a glancing blow to the head. He lurched back, stunned, his senses clearing in time to realize the giant was stalking him, closing for the kill, a huge knife glinting in his hand.

Bane backpedaled, holding his distance. The giant shifted the knife agilely from his right hand to his left, smiling, red hair flaming in the light. A sudden shift and he was closing Bane into a corner, sensing the end.

Bane felt his shoulders graze wood.

The Bear took the bait.

The knife came forward at the same instant Bane did, but the giant was totally unprepared for a frontal assault. Bane deflected the knife hand easily, simultaneously jabbing a set of strong, rigid fingers up toward the eyes. They mashed home, the giant howling in pain and raising his hands to comfort his torn sockets.

The knife slipped to the floor.

The Bear staggered backward, fighting to see Bane who was on him before he could blink. First to the groin and then the throat. He smashed the giant's windpipe with tight, gnarled fingers till he felt cartilage crack and withdraw. The Bear toppled over like a felled tree, clawing the floor madly as the last of life bottlenecked in his crushed throat.

Bane bolted for the steps.

The red-haired monster hesitated before entering Davey's apartment, as though unsure, expecting something to happen. When it didn't, he crossed into the darkness, slicing the air with the shining blade that marked his path.

The giant moved toward him like a cat and Davey wanted to say, "It's okay. I give up." But no words came because he knew they wouldn't matter. Davey could read the giant's eyes too well, his intentions as

155

plain as his pupils. A shadow flickered in the hallway, so there must be another of them waiting beyond the door, and Davey knew suddenly it was the tall man he had seen that morning on the sidewalk, the real cold one whose thoughts were buried deeper than the others'.

The giant was drawing closer, almost upon him, the knife just out of range. Davey watched his eyes shimmer eagerly and then saw the knife plunging toward his stomach, felt the horrible moment of pain and the sick feeling of warm blood pulsing out. He felt himself sliding down the wall, already dead, but his eyes, strangely, still seeing until the giant stuck the knife in deeper and yanked up, splitting his whole abdomen in two and spilling its contents all over the floor.

Davey's hands went to his stomach and found it whole. He looked up to see the giant still approaching, a final lunge away. It had been The Vibes, Davey realized. The Vibes had shown him what was about to happen and the reality of his own death sent a quiver up his spine and Davey knew he had The Chill again.

The red-haired monster drew his knife back.

Davey pushed for The Chill, ignoring the blasting in his head, pushed for The Chill with everything he had.

The red-haired monster stopped in his tracks, as though an invisible door were suddenly before him. His face grew puzzled, uncertain. Then Soam's eyes bulged in agonizing fear as he realized his knife hand was headed for his own midsection. He couldn't control it. Desperately, he latched his other massive hand onto the trembling wrist, slowing the blade's progress but not halting it.

Davey made The Chill stronger.

Soam's knife hand was trembling horribly now but still the blade snailed on. He tightened his grip with his other fingers, trying to shut off the blood flow. The razor-sharp edge neared his stomach.

It was taking too long, Trench realized, and decided to check the room. His eyes first caught the frozen Twin Bear and the knife ready to pass into his midsection by his own hand. The boy's attention was riveted upon him. Trench couldn't believe his eyes. He was aware only partially that his strategy had paid off. He withdrew his gun slowly, careful not to draw the boy's eye, and leveled it for a head shot. A simple squeeze of the trigger and the boy's brains would be coating the wallpaper and with them, his power.

Soam felt the tip of the blade pierce his flesh, then sink steadily deeper.

Trench took final aim.

Soam retched as the blade plunged in to the hilt and started its move upward.

Trench was curling the trigger now.

Bane crashed into him from behind, forcing the killer off balance and his shot into the wall. Trench tried to turn the gun on him, but Bane drove the killer's arm against the wall and the pistol went flying into the darkness.

Davey saw all this transpire deep in his consciousness as he pushed The Chill one last time. Soam gurgled blood as the blade split the bone and gristle of his thorax and his hot insides poured out in a flood.

Trench came up with a knee, Bane deflected it easily. The killer was breathing hard—too old for hand-to-hand—and Bane had only to hold out to assure himself of victory. That underestimation almost cost him his life, because suddenly there was a knife in Trench's left hand, literally pulled from his sleeve. The blade was moving toward Bane's throat too fast to duck so he brought his right arm up to ward off the blow and the blade cut through fabric and found flesh.

Bane screamed in agony and jammed Trench's body hard against the plaster, pummeling him once, twice, three times with the knife pinned against the wall. The killer went limp. Bane released him and let his unconscious frame slip down the wall leaving a thin trail of blood behind his head. Trench flopped to the floor weightlessly, a scarecrow without ties.

Bane started to go for his gun, intent on finishing Trench, but stopped. Something held him back. It might have been the fact that he had never fancied the idea of killing someone in an utterly helpless state. Or it might have been that he was standing over a man who was one of the few who had survived the Game long enough to be considered a legend. You didn't kill a legend while he lay slumped against a wall. Bane turned toward the boy.

Davey released Soam from The Chill and the Twin Bear keeled over into his own blood and innards.

Bane saw the body fall. Then his eyes met Davey's. He had started forward when a blast of scorching wind met him head-on, jabbing his flesh with hot needles. He almost felt he was melting and was powerless to do anything about it when Davey slid slowly down the far wall and curled his arms about his knees, his whole body trembling awfully.

Released from whatever had held him, Bane moved tentatively forward, aware that he had little time but not wanting to frighten the boy further. He shoved what he had just seen and felt aside for the time being and knelt by the boy.

"Davey . . ."

Nothing.

"Davey?"

Still nothing. The boy looked blankly ahead past Bane, past everything, teeth chattering and hair curled at the tips by sweat.

"We've got to get out of here," Bane told him. He helped the boy to his feet and steadied him, supporting his frame with an arm around his shoulders. "We've got to get out of here," he repeated. "I'll help you but you've got to walk. Try now, come on."

Bane was still holding onto the boy when they moved into the corridor, palming the gun in his free hand. The forces outside might have heard Trench's shot, and even if they hadn't there was certainly a time factor here that might well have been exceeded. The rest of Trench's men, or some of them, would be following him in.

Bane chose the elevator this time and hit the lobby button. He eased Davey gently away from him to check the Browning. The boy's eyes seemed to be coming back to life. They looked up into Bane's full and trusting.

The elevator ground to a halt. Bane pushed the boy behind him.

The doors opened across the lobby in full view of the front door. Three figures were entering hesitantly, perhaps even fearfully, seeing Bane too late to respond. Their hands never touched their guns or their walkie-talkies before he took them out with one bullet each. The spent shells danced hot in the air as the chamber continued to clear itself, barrel spitting smoke.

"Come on!" he shouted at Davey, pulling him by the arm toward the door leading into the cellar. The shots would bring reinforcements and lots of them.

There was no more time to waste. Bane took the cellar stairs quickly, never losing his grip on Davey who dragged behind him like a dead weight.

Then footsteps pounded the floor above them, unsure and without direction until they realized the only possible route of escape. Davey must have heard them too, because suddenly he sprang to life and began moving on his own in Bane's shadow just as both of them heard the cellar door shatter open and the sounds of men clearing the steps.

The cellar was dank and dimly lit, cluttered with storage and old plumbing, which didn't stop Bane from rushing through it on a sure path Davey followed. The men were closing on them, though now the clutter was working in Bane's favor by effectively screening him and the boy from sight and, thus, bullets.

Their pursuers had come dangerously near when Bane spotted the staircase that had been his passage in and bolted toward it, pulling Davey along so hard that he was nearly carrying him. The boy struggled to keep up and not lose his footing.

They took the stairs quickly and emerged in the lobby of the second building from the Ferdinand. Screening the boy's body with his, Bane slithered down a hallway and crashed through a side exit just as a horde of men rushed the front door and blanketed that half of the building.

They had escaped the dragnet by seconds but steps still pounded the sidewalk not far behind. Bane didn't even think of using his gun; even silver bullets were good only one to a customer. He just kept pulling a winded Davey along toward his parked car and God help them if Trench's people had found it.

The car seemed clear up ahead, a narrowing distance away. They reached it and Bane pushed Davey into the front seat. He jammed the key home before he'd even got the door closed.

The car roared to life. Bane gunned the engine, spun the wheel, floored the gas pedal. The car rushed away, tires screeching.

Bane stole a glance at the quivering boy beside him and headed the car toward traffic.

Chapter Fifteen

Bane carried Davey up to Janie's apartment.

"My God!" she managed after opening the door. "What happened? Who is he?"

"Long story," Bane said, kicking the door shut. "I think he might be going into shock. I'll put him on the couch. Grab a blanket."

Janie returned with it just as Bane was lifting Davey's legs onto the fabric. "Who is he?" she repeated.

Wordlessly, Bane covered him up to the neck and smoothed his hair. The boy's eyelids fluttered.

"He's the boy you chased at Rockefeller Center, isn't he?" Janie demanded.

"He's a hell of a lot more than that."

She hesitated. "Why'd you bring him here?"

"Because they'll already be watching my place. We won't be able to keep him here long. They'll make the connection soon enough."

"Who?" Janie grabbed him by the shoulders. Bane winced and she saw the blood seeping down his right arm. "Josh, you're hurt!"

"Just a scratch."

She regarded him fearfully. "What's going on?"

"It's like I feared, only worse. COBRA's behind all of it and they've got Trench in their corner. I slowed them up tonight but it'll only be temporary."

"Then it was Trench who killed your friend Jake."

"And he was about to kill the boy."

"When you arrived to save the day? . . ."

"Not exactly. I only handled Trench. The boy did a pretty good job on one of Trench's giant henchmen."

"But that's not possible."

"It happened. I saw it. I don't know how, but it looked like the boy made the giant split his own stomach open."

Janie pulled back, her face wrinkling in disgust. "But you're not sure. You're not sure what you saw."

Bane pulled her back around to face him. "But I'm sure of what I felt," he said, remembering the numbing heat that had surged into him in the death-filled apartment. "This boy's got some crazy power. Maybe COBRA gave it to him and wants it back, I just don't know." But suddenly he did. "Or maybe it all has something to do with the disappearing plane that cost Jake Del Gennio his life. Maybe that's—"

"You're not making sense," Janie broke in anxiously.

"That's the point. None of this makes sense. Forty men in New York looking for one boy. A contract assassin hired to bring him in. No, none of it makes sense, and it all started when Davey Phelps didn't come home after getting off Flight 22."

"Didn't come home? What are you talking about?"

Bane explained that part of it to her.

"So is that where you'll take him from here?" Janie wondered. "Back to the Martinis?"

"It won't be safe for him there either. COBRA won't be giving up the chase so fast."

"Then what do we do?"

"First, we get you out of here."

Janie shook her head, slow but sure. "Uh-uh. There won't be any running for me. This is my home and that's the way it's gonna stay."

"That's probably the same way Jake Del Gennio felt. If they made him disappear, they can do the same for you." Bane sighed. "At least let me call Harry and have him come over and watch the place while I take the kid to a safer lodging."

"Wouldn't make a difference if I said no, would it?" she asked.

"You need protection."

Janie moved away from him, eyes cold. "And you need a bandage on that shoulder. Let me see what I can dig out of the medicine cabinet."

Bane pulled a Coke from the fridge before waking Davey up at three A.M. Janie had fallen asleep in front of the television in her bedroom, leaving them alone in the den.

On the first touch to his shoulder, Davey sprang to a sitting position, eyes flashing madly, trying to accustom himself to his new surroundings.

"Wh-wh-where am I?" he stammered. "Who are you?"

Bane handed him the can. "Drink this and relax. You've been through an awful lot tonight. Let it come back slowly."

Davey took the Coke hesitantly and gulped a third of it down. The blanket had slipped down beneath his waist; his shivering was apparently over. Then Bane saw him shudder beneath his leather jacket.

"The apartment! It all happened at the apartment!" Davey's deep-set eyes sought out Bane's. "You were there. I remember now. Those men wanted to kill me and you stopped one. Hey, your shirt's got blood on it."

"I got a little careless." Bane sat down next to him on the couch. "Well, Davey, we better figure out what to do with you."

"How did you know my name? I never told you my name," the boy snapped defensively, shrinking away.

"My name's Josh. I'm sorry we haven't been formally introduced. I got your name from the Martinis."

"You knew where to look for me?"

"So did the men who found you at the apartment."

Davey shrugged and curled his lips. "They've been after me since it all started." He looked at Bane suddenly and recognition flashed in his eyes. "Say, wait a minute, I do know you. You were the man I saw at Rockefeller Center yesterday. You chased me a couple blocks. Why'd you do that?"

"You looked like someone I used to know," Bane said distantly.

"I hope I didn't hurt you."

"Hurt me?"

"The fall. It looked like you might've broken something."

"Because of some cripple on a skate-wheel platform, not you."

"I made him do it," Davey said simply. "I put the thought in his head."

Bane was speechless. The pieces of the puzzle were starting to fall together.

"I tried to make The Chill work on you first," the boy went on, "but I couldn't. Something blocked it."

"The . . . *Chill?*" Bane asked, recalling the feeling of having something push back against him suddenly as he had run.

Davey nodded. "That's what I call it 'cause that's

what it feels like when I make it. 'Cept it didn't work for a while tonight and it really hurts my head now."

"That's how you killed the giant in the apartment. . . ."

"But he was going to kill *me*! I know it! I *saw* it!" Davey roared. "I only did exactly to him what he was planning to do to me. Sort of like a mirror. I gave the reflection back to him. The Vibes showed it to me. They've showed me lots of things the last couple days."

"The Vibes?"

"That's what I call them anyway. They're what told me you were looking at me by the fountain and most of the time they warned me when the Men were close. Other times, they showed me things I didn't want to see but it doesn't help to close my eyes 'cause I guess The Vibes come from the inside, kinda like a movie projector in my head."

"And you can use The Chill as much as you want?"

Davey looked down. "For a while I could. Then it started to hurt my head, so the last couple times I've only been able to make it work when I really needed it. Like tonight."

"You disappeared from the airport after your flight came in."

"'Cause they were watching me."

"But you never went home."

"'Cause I knew they were watching it too."

"But you called tonight."

"I got . . . lonely." Davey eyed Bane curiously. "You said I reminded you of somebody. Who?"

"A boy who would've been about your age. He was killed in a car accident five years ago. He was my stepson."

Davey looked away. "My parents are both dead too."

Bane squeezed his shoulder tenderly. "I know."

"How come you know so much about me?"

Bane pulled his hand back. "Something happened on the flight you took back to New York. You remember anything about it?"

"Nah. I slept most of the way. Had this funny nightmare where I thought I woke up, only everything was funny colored. The light was gone, but it wasn't dark either. And where all the other people had been sitting, all I could see were traces of them like they weren't really there anymore. I could see right through them."

"That's all you remember about the nightmare?"

"The weird thing is I don't remember waking up, or the plane landing, or getting off it. Next thing I knew I was standing in the terminal. I must've been in a trance or something." Davey regarded Bane hopefully. "Are you gonna take me home now?"

Bane shook his head slowly. "It's not safe yet."

"Shit," Davey muttered; then quickly he raised his hand to his mouth. "Sorry, I didn't mean to say that."

Bane smiled. "That's okay. You deserve it."

Davey smiled back and the bond between them tightened. Then Davey's smile disappeared. "There's something I want to tell you."

"I'm listening."

"I don't exactly know how to say it. It's . . . The Vibes. A couple times I've felt them real strong, different from the other times, stronger but farther off."

"Like what you're seeing might be coming more in the future?"

"I guess. . . . But these Vibes have been the worst of all. I don't see anything specific, just lots of things

167

melting, breaking apart, and people—" He looked suddenly at Bane. "Something awful's gonna happen. Lots of people are gonna die."

"For now I'm just worried about you."

Davey toyed with the seams of his jeans. "I'm scared, Josh, real scared. I don't know what I did, I don't know why these guys are after me. Why do they want to kill me? What did I do?" He paused, swiped at his watery eyes. "Can I . . . go home now?"

Bane's hand found Davey's shoulder again, stayed there. "They'll still be watching your house. It's not safe," he repeated.

"When will it be safe?"

Before Bane could manage an answer, the doorbell rang. He had the Browning out before he was halfway over.

"Who's there?" he asked, back pressed against the adjacent wall, out of range of a shotgun blast from the outside.

"Santa Claus," snapped the voice of Harry the Bat, "but I couldn't wheel this goddamn thing down the chimney."

Bane unchained the door and swung it open. The Bat wheeled himself in.

"Don't bother to thank me for coming over here at three in the morning. After all, what are friends for?"

"Took the words right out of my mouth."

"I won't ask you if it's important because it better be."

"And then some."

"Lord fuck a duck, Winter Man, I never realized how much I missed your company," Harry said, voice laced with sarcasm. There was a shuffling noise from the den of the apartment and he swung toward it. "Well Lord fuck a—er—sorry . . ."

"Davey," Bane announced, "I want you to meet Harry Bannister, the Bat to his friends."

"And some of my enemies. Nice to meet ya, kid. Excuse the language." Then, to Bane, "Is that the kid you—"

"That's the kid and I don't think you have to worry much about your language around him after what he's been through."

"Lord fu—er-frig a duck, Josh, he does look a bit like Peter. I see sure in hell what you meant. Well, him being here means you must've had a successful hunt tonight."

"I'll fill you in on everything later. Right now I've gotta get the kid stashed somewhere safe."

"The King's?"

"The King's." Bane's eyes shifted toward the bedroom where the television was still whispering. "Janie's not going to be too pleased when she wakes up and finds you here. . . ."

"Terrific . . ."

"So go easy, Harry. Just be your regular charming self."

"I left him back in bed at my place, Josh."

Bane smiled, though he didn't feel much like it. "You're carrying I assume."

"A fuckin' . . ." Then, with an eye on Davey, ". . . I mean a friggin' arsenal. I figured the elevator might not make it up 'cause I'm packed so tight."

"Watch the door, Harry," Bane said, motioning Davey toward him.

"Anything that comes through there, Winter Man, better be ready to spend the rest of its life in a thousand pieces."

"This your car?" Davey asked when they were inside a Cutlass parked in the garage beneath the building.

"No, it's Janie's. They'll be watching for mine."

Davey looked down, a habit apparently. "Oh." His eyes came back up again. "She your girl?"

"She used to be. Right now, I'm not quite sure."

"Is that 'cause you brought me to her place?"

"It's because of a lot of things."

Bane pulled the Cutlass onto the street, careful to watch for sudden movement in the area.

"So where we going?" Davey asked.

"To get you a baby-sitter."

"What?"

Bane's eyes rotated between the road and the rear-view mirror. "Not some old lady who passes the time away with knitting needles," he assured jokingly. "This guy happens to stand about seven feet tall and bends steel bars for fun."

"Who is he?"

"His name's King Cong."

"Come on. . . ."

"You'll see."

"Hey, we're in Harlem," Davey realized as they drew near the gym.

"The King's home turf," Bane explained. "He doesn't leave it much and most people with brains stay clear."

"I thought you had brains, Josh."

"I'm different." Bane's eyes checked the rearview mirror yet again. "How many of the men after you were black?"

"None that I saw."

"That's the point. The King doesn't take a fancy to most white folks and around these parts they'll stick out long before they get a chance to use their guns."

"Right on, brother," Davey quipped, flashing his smile.

The King was waiting for them at the door to his gym.

"You keep funny hours, Josh boy," he greeted, locking it behind them. He looked bigger and more menacing than ever. Bane noticed a pistol the size of a cannon tucked into his belt.

"Sorry if I woke you up, King."

"No sweat, Josh boy, the King don't ever sleep at night. Too many better things to do." The King paused and checked Bane over, stopping at the eyes and holding onto them, nodding with apparent satisfaction at what he saw. "You's a different man, Josh boy, than you was the last time I saw ya."

"Two days can make a big difference, King, a world of difference."

"Yeah." Conglon grinned. "Winter's stayin' late this year." His huge eyes focused on Davey who felt his knees buckle from the stare. "Don't pay me no fear, boy. I'm a lot meaner than I seem."

Davey just looked at him.

"He's all yours, King," Bane said.

"I ain't never been much at baby-sittin'."

"Keeping him safe and sound will more than suffice."

King Cong took a menacing step forward. "Treat me nice for the next decade or so, Josh boy, and I just might forget you said that. When the King says he'll do ya a favor, you can bet your white prick it'll get done right. I got ten guys on call already. Your boy here won't take a step without one of 'em on either side every fuckin' minute."

"You trust them?"

"I trained 'em, you mother."

"That's all I wanted to know."

Bane started back for the door, turned, and held Davey's shoulder briefly. "I'll be back for you when

171

it's safe." Then, with his eyes on the King, "You're in good hands, the best." He squeezed Davey's shoulder one last time and moved for the door again.

King Cong sensed the boy's fear and uneasiness, so he thought fast and yanked the pistol cannon from his belt.

"Ever shoot a gun, boy?"

Davey looked at him with awe. "No. I mean, not really."

"Well, next couple days should be as good a time as any to learn. Here, heft this." The King handed his magnum over and its weight sunk Davey's hands past his belt. The boy looked at it mesmerized. "Might even get in a little boxin', and I'll teach ya a thing or two 'bout weights," the King continued but Davey's attention stayed locked on the gun.

"Thanks, King," Bane said gratefully from the door.

"A pleasure, Josh boy. I ain't even come close to evenin' up our debt chart."

"This makes it paid in full."

Bane was halfway out when the King's voice made him turn.

"Know somethin', Josh boy? I got me a funny feelin' that if I had tried to play the Game on ya in the street tonight, you just mighta won."

172

The Fourth Day:

PROJECT PLACEBO

Tell us Commander, what do you think?
'Cause we know that you love all that power
Is it on then, are we on the brink?
We wish you'd all throw in the towel
We'll not fade out too soon
Not in this finest hour
Whistle your fav'rite tune
We'll send a card and flower saying,
It's a mistake

—Men at Work

Chapter Sixteen

"Round up the usual suspects."

Claude Rains finished speaking, his eyes still on Humphrey Bogart, in the climax of *Casablanca* when Bunker 17's emergency alarm began to screech.

"Goddammit," moaned a private seated in the middle of the darkened room. "You'd think the big bastard could at least wait till the movie was over."

"I'll let you in on what happens from this point on, boy," drawled a heavy voice from just behind him. "Now get to your station 'fore I plant your ass in the ground and grow shit stalks."

The private gulped down some air and saluted Maj. Christian Teare with a trembling hand before rushing from the room.

Teare rose, his massive frame effectively blocking projection of the rest of *Casablanca* and replacing it with his silhouette on the screen. The room was empty now, save for the projectionist.

"Private," Teare addressed him, "I want a note on my desk tomorrow requesting more first-run movies. These old black-and-whites are startin' to get on my nerves."

The private started rewinding. "*Casablanca*'s a classic, sir."

"Yeah, well I ain't never been there and I don't take

much of a fancy to a guy who talks out of the side of his mouth like he has marbles inside."

The private shrugged.

Capt. Jared Heath, operations chief for Bunker 17, appeared in the small auditorium's doorway and made a quick salute.

"Be with ya in a minute, Cap," Teare told him. "How 'bout we get *The Sting* again?" he asked the projectionist.

"We've had that eight times in the last nine months, sir."

"Just what I thought. We're overdue for another showing."

"Yes, sir," the projectionist agreed reluctantly.

Teare turned to Captain Heath. "Let's get to it, Cap."

The two men moved into the brightly lit but antiseptic corridors sixty feet below ground level in the foothills of Montana. The flashing red lights would have stung almost any normal set of eyes. But the men—and three women—of Bunker 17 had grown accustomed to them.

"Let's have the operations report," Teare requested.

Heath gazed down at his clipboard. He was a medium-size, well-built black man, still a dwarf next to Teare, with a tightly sculptured afro. As operations chief of the bunker, he served as second in command to the major, with responsibilities in the area of organizing all Red Flag procedures. Eyebrows had been raised when Heath had been assigned here as exec—a former civil rights protester linked with a southern redneck—but they hadn't stayed up for long. Heath and Teare had become fast friends and Bunker 17's consistent drill proficiency reflected that.

"All systems are running green, Major," Heath

informed him, as they continued down the wide, circling corridors which might have been lifted right off the Starship Enterprise. "Tracking, weapons, com-link, security systems—everything is go."

"Launching sequence will commence in one minute," a dull, preprogramed voice droned over the loud speaker.

Captain Heath checked his watch. "Right on schedule," he informed Teare.

Sixty feet above them, four-feet thick steel doors had slid across all access areas within the agricultural station that served as their ground cover, denying unwarranted entry into the base. Once on Red Flag alert, the bunker was effectively sealed from the outside world. Even all air terminals were closed tight to prevent possible chemical contamination by enemy forces. Bunker personnel were now getting their air from huge tanks located at the core of the complex. The supply would last seven days. As an added precaution, armed guards were posted at all possible routes of escape and exit. Teare had chosen the commandos himself, all men he could look right in the eye.

"Launching sequence will commence in fifty-five seconds. . . ."

Captain Heath and Maj. Christian Teare had passed three guards standing at attention at their posts before they turned into the first silo to make a spot check.

"Warhead armed and ready, Major," the sergeant in the terminal room reported. "All systems go. All board lights green."

"Launching sequence will commence in fifty seconds. . . ."

Bunker 17 contained thirty-six silos in all, spread out over a nearly half-mile radius. Once the final

177

launch sequence commenced, these too would be sealed with triple-plated lead and steel, but not so much for security as protection. The heat of the missiles' initial ignition and blast-off stretched into the millions of degrees. Without the blast shields, irreparable damage might be done to the base proper, thus throwing off continued launchings. It was a matter of microinches and milliseconds. The men—and three women—of Bunker 17 could afford nothing else but total accuracy. Hence, the drills, which came in various forms and levels, sometimes occurred as frequently as four times a day. If nothing else this served to break the often maddening routine. Living in a nuclear installations bunker was, at best, a waiting game. Personnel were rotated on a basis similar to that used for the crews of submarines and the effects of long duty were not dissimilar.

Uniformed figures rushed by Teare and Heath the whole length of the station.

"Launching sequence will commence in forty-five seconds. . . ."

"Well, Cap," said Teare, "let's make our way to the Disco."

The Disco was Maj. Christian Teare's term for Launch Control, the very heart of Bunker 17 where any or all missiles were sent from their silos. Teare called it that because all the flashing lights and different colored knobs and consoles reminded him of the discos he had always done his best to avoid.

They paused at the entrance to Launch Control while a hazy blue light scanned them. The bulb atop the steel-plate doors flashed green but entry was still refused until Teare inserted his command ID into the proper slot. In the event of an actual Red Flag alert, the Disco would be totally sealed inside and out. All intercom and voice contact would be broken off to prevent any chance of electronic jamming, subliminal suggestion, panic by someone at the base, or contact from a possible saboteur or spy. Even Teare, command card and all, would be unable to gain entry or achieve voice contact. During a drill, though, observation was mandated so a slight exception in the actual procedure was made. Actual procedure also dictated that once the base went to Yellow Flag, all direct line contact with the outside world would be terminated, replaced entirely by a computer relay into the SAFE (Systems Attack Fail-safe Evaluator) Interceptor, which for all intents and purposes became commander.

The Interceptor was a direct communications link with NORAD in Colorado and the President in Washington. Its purpose was to guard against someone outside the system ordering a nuclear strike. It accomplished this by analyzing the coded sequence a hundred different ways to insure it was genuine. It worked on a binary system with codes that were changed, incredibly, every quarter hour.

In addition to guarding against accidental nuclear attack, the SAFE system took the uncertainties out of the loop by eliminating as much of the human element as was possible. People would still launch the missiles but the order to go to Red Flag could come only from the computer through the Interceptor, and once it came everything on the base became automatic, the chance of human error being substantially reduced by obviating the need to make decisions. Men like Teare had been against the change from the start, but no one was really asking them. Other heads, saner it was thought, had prevailed, deciding that the best American defense was one which let computers do as much of the work as possible down the line, thereby reducing error

179

potential along the way. Teare knew, then, that he would be powerless to act at a time when his decision-making skills would be needed more than ever. Strange how the high command thought.

The slot swallowed Teare's command card and spit it back out. The heavy, blast-proof door slid open. Major Teare led Captain Heath inside.

The Disco was lit in a dull shade of red, color code for the sequence. It wasn't a tremendously large room. Longer than it was wide, its windowless dolor contributed to its apparent vastness. The far wall contained a grid design of the bunker's outer rim on which computers could monitor the constant status of all thirty-six silos. So long as the lights denoting each silo flashed green, the missiles were tied into central launch control in the Disco. If the light showed yellow or red, the line was rerouted and the fail-safe system activated to make it impossible for that missile to be launched.

"Launching sequence will begin in thirty-five seconds. . . ."

Once a missile was launched, and there were roughly 400 possible sequences for this under Red Flag at Bunker 17, its progress was charted on the world-overview chart on the right side wall. Since all of Bunker 17's targets inevitably lay inside Russia, its chart was missing those corners of the world which didn't figure into the attack pattern. After launch, a a missile's coded identity sequence would flash on the path it rode through the sky en route to its target.

In the middle of all this, nine bunker personnel moved about checking keyboards and running final test sequences prior to launch. There were thirty-six separate red abort switches in addition to the one which aborted all missiles at once, forming the last of many safeguards in the fail-safe system. If it went that far, Teare had often chided, there wouldn't be a dry pair of pants in the room.

"Launching sequence will commence in twenty seconds. . . ."

Teare and Heath stepped farther into the Disco. Six men were at work behind the most advanced computer terminals on Earth checking all of thirty-two safety features incorporated into the launching procedure and the missiles themselves. If any one was out of sync, and the computers somehow missed it, their monitoring boards would catch it and manually they'd switch the light to yellow or red on the Disco's Big Board. The final three members of the Disco team sat entrenched behind the largest console of all. It contained Bunker 17's launch command system and primary abort and destruct functions. Once Red Flag was signaled, procedure dictated that the three handcuff themselves to the steel-based console and to each other. All three possessed firing codes and keys worn around their necks that had to be inserted into the launch terminal to trigger the firing mode. Each would insert his key, punch in his code, and when the center, board light flashed green, the Disco king for the day would press the final trigger button, which, strangely, was the smallest and dullest colored of all. Something to do with psychological stress, Christian Teare remembered reading in a report.

Today was unique in that the Disco king was a queen. Kate Tullman wore her olive drab one-piece uniform as fashionably as a pair of designer jeans, and Red Flag alerts were probably the only times the eyes of the bunker's men weren't drawn to her. Her hair was blond and stylishly short, her eyes as green as the code lights flashing on the Big Board. Her buttocks filled out the contours of her console chair

181

neatly enough for it to appear tailored for her. As she leaned over toward the terminal, though, part of her cheeks wedged themselves out the chair's back.

Maj. Christian Teare winked at Captain Heath.

"Launching sequence will commence in ten seconds, nine, eight, seven . . ."

"Final systems check," barked Kate Tullman, queen of the Disco.

". . . six, five, four . . .

"Board shows all systems go, all lights green," announced the man seated to her right.

". . . three, two, one . . .

"Terminal shows all systems go, all lights green," from the man on her left.

"Launching sequence has commenced. . . ."

Six voices from behind Kate Tullman chimed in.

"Silos one to six, all systems check."

"Silos seven to twelve, all systems check."

"Silos thirteen to eighteen, all systems check."

"Silos nineteen to twenty-four, all systems check."

"Silos twenty-five to thirty, all systems check."

"Silos thirty-one to thirty-six, all systems check."

Kate Tullman spoke again, eyes never leaving the console. "Computer attack sequence Plan R for Roger, W for William, D for David."

"Confirmed," from the man on her right.

"Confirmed," from the man on her left.

"Commence final launch procedures," she instructed and jammed her own key into the console, punching in her personal code for the day as soon as it turned. The codes changed with each shift and sometimes even during the shift. If the wrong code was entered and not corrected within five seconds, the fail-safe system would cause an immediate shutdown of all procedures and a toner alarm would summon security to the Disco. Though at this stage they wouldn't be able to gain access, they would be there to deal with the person or persons inside once the doors opened.

But today the center light on Kate Tullman's console flashed green.

She moved her hand ever so slowly toward the button that would trigger the launch and pressed it without hesitation.

At that instant, Red Flag came to an end. All lights returned to stable white and Bunker 17 was officially off alert. If it hadn't been a drill, however, none of this would be the case and thirty-six MX missiles carrying ten warheads each would be on their courses toward the Soviet Union. The Target Board would already be tracing the beginning of speeding red arcs drawn across the world.

But the Board was quiet. No arcs because no bombs had actually been launched.

Kate Tullman, queen of the Disco, sighed.

Captain Heath, who had hit his stopwatch at the very instant she had pressed the final button, turned to Major Teare.

"One minute, twenty-nine seconds."

"What's prime according to the Pentagon, Cap?"

"One-forty-five."

"Good. Then I want us at one-twenty inside the next month."

"Nine seconds is a lot to chop at this stage, Major."

"Well it was a lot when we was battlin' the one-forty-five mark too. I want it done, Cap. If there are any slow spots in the drill, I want them found and eliminated."

"Nine seconds is still a lot of time to cut, Major."

"That's what they said about the record at the frog jumpin' contest back home when I was twelve. I broke that one too," Christian Teare said with a wink. Then he moved toward the Disco's main console and Kate Tullman. "Well executed, Sergeant," he complimented.

She rose quickly to attention and saluted. "Thank you, sir."

"Kate T. What does the *T* stand for, Sergeant?"

"Trouble, sir. Kate *T* for trouble." The Disco queen didn't bother to hold her smile back.

"*T* for tits," Teare whispered to Heath and didn't bother to hold his back either. "At ease there, Sergeant," he continued to Kate Tullman. "Stand that straight too long and you'll give yourself a back 'bout as bad as a plow horse in a field of shit."

There was a brief pause, after which the entire Disco broke into laughter. Teare joined in.

"Just somethin' to break the tension, people. Rest easy."

And then he was gone with Captain Heath right behind.

Teare closed the door of his private quarters behind Heath. The bare, metallic walls were adorned with posters and pictures of Teare's movie favorites including Burt Lancaster, John Wayne, Clint Eastwood, and Obi-Wan Kenobi.

"Care for a couple fingers of happy juice, Cap?" he asked, reaching into the cabinet beneath his sink.

The captain shook his head with a smile. "For a man determined to break the minute-twenty Red Flag barrier, you sure don't pay much attention to rules."

"That don't answer my question, Cap. One finger or two?"

"One." Heath relented and watched Teare pour

three times that into a glass for himself.

"Anyway," the major said, "I don't use ice. Happy juice ain't really nothin' without ice."

Heath took a sip and felt the whiskey burn his insides all the way down. "That's not how the Pentagon sees it."

"Fuck 'em's what I say. Hell, Cap, isn't givin' up sex good enough for them during our six-week shift? A man's gotta have his booze. And that's hundred-proof pure sour mash you're drinkin' there, Cap. Hot enough to scorch the insides of a corpse and make it fall from heaven. My daddy used to make this himself."

"He hand you down the recipe?"

Teare winked. "I could put together a batch in the 'fridgeration system that would pop your eyes out." The major sat down on his freshly made bed and gulped down half his glass. "Ya know, Cap, it's funny. We got rules and regulations 'bout ever'thin' in here. Shit, there must be three pages on the evils of booze alone. But there ain't no words mentioned 'bout sex. Know why?"

Heath shook his head.

"'Cause, buddy boy, when the damn rule books were written, there weren't any women in NORAD and I suppose the noble minds in DC didn't pay much worry to cornholin'. But now there's quite a few women in the loop and the rule book ain't been changed one damn bit. Check the title page, though, Cap, and you'll find that the thing is supposedly updated every month."

"What are you getting at, Major?"

Christian Teare drained the rest of his whiskey and leaned his massive frame back. "What am I getting at? I'll tell ya what I'm getting at. If those boys who

185

send down our orders are behind in the rule book, what else might they be behind in? Hell, Cap, you think the Ruskies would make the same mistake?"

"I never thought about it much, Major."

"Yeah, well I got this feelin' the boys in Washington ain't neither."

Chapter Seventeen

When Janie walked into the kitchen at seven A.M., she found Bane placing a platter of steaming scrambled eggs on the table. A glass of fresh squeezed orange juice was waiting on her plate and Bane had gone back to buttering what looked like a whole loaf of toast.

"I don't know about you but I'm starved," he told her. He had relieved Harry just before five A.M.

"You get any sleep?"

"A wink here and there. You?"

"Like a log for a while. Got up around four and found Harry eating Fritos in the living room."

"He likes junk food," Bane said and brought over the basket of toast, helping himself immediately to a huge portion of eggs.

"He also left guns all over my apartment."

"Harry likes to be careful. You never know where you'll be when you need one."

"One in the belt should be sufficient."

"Not for Harry."

Janie went to work on her eggs, hoping to swallow the tension between her and Josh down with them. But all the banner breakfasts in the world couldn't change what had passed recently between them. Truth was she had stayed up most of the night searching for a way to make their relationship right again, and had come to the conclusion that Bane had learned to live without love well enough to prefer life that way. Their relationship had been merely an interlude between violent episodes in what he liked to call the Game. She knew that now, probably had all along, but she'd always clung to the hope that this time the interlude might last.

Bane, meanwhile, felt himself losing her and loathed the emptiness that brought on. He wanted, needed, even loved her. There was no room in his life—the Winter Man's life—though, for love and dependence. It was an either/or situation and Bane had made his choice, survival having determined it. He told himself when this was over he would make it up to her, might have promised her as much if he'd really believed it. There were no words that might express what he was feeling because he didn't know himself. There was only a certainty of task, a singularity of purpose—the icy cornerstones of the Winter Man.

"Isn't it about time you brought all this to the attention of someone in the government?" Janie asked him.

"Possibly, except I have no way of knowing how deep it goes. Conceivably, all of COBRA's actions could be under government direction."

"What about your former boss?"

"Arthur Jorgenson? He's a good man, definitely the first one I'll go to when the time's right. He never approved of men like Chilgers. I can't believe he'd be in on this. Trouble is, I haven't got enough to take to him yet. I want a strong case, Janie, proof positive."

"That boy the King's baby-sitting seems like pretty good proof to me."

"Not enough to nail COBRA and that's what I'm

after." Bane gobbled up a heap of the eggs on his plate, took a swallow of coffee. "Which reminds me, I need your computers again."

Janie toyed with her plate. "I figured there was something else behind this breakfast. . . ."

"We've got to find out what project of COBRA's we've stumbled upon here. Whatever we're onto, whatever Jake Del Gennio uncovered and Davey Phelps has become involved in, must be related to some project they're working on, or to a weapon they're developing. Maybe both."

"If that's the case, you can be damn sure the information won't be present on my computer or Harry's."

"But the names of COBRA's top research personnel will, and that might give us a clue. What kind of scientists have they been going after lately? Who has joined their payroll and where did they come from? What's their specialty?"

Janie frowned. "With those kinds of questions, I can get you enough material to keep you reading all weekend. Trouble is I'm not sure if there'll be anything worth your time."

"It'll be there," he assured her. "We just have to find it."

The pounding in Trench's head had been reduced to a dull throb thanks to an hourly dose of Percodan. He wasn't at his best to begin with and the drugs, along with the absence of the Twin Bears, had him feeling very uneasy indeed. He was due to make another report to Chilgers in a few minutes and he was damned if he knew what to say.

They had found him slumped in Davey Phelp's apartment, just coming around. They helped revive

189

him and watched as he made a thorough inspection of the damage.

Both Bears were dead, the one in the lobby of a shattered windpipe at the hands of Bane and the one in the apartment of a stomach ripped open by his own knife. Trench had seen what the boy was doing to the Bear, had seen it but still couldn't make himself believe it.

He had reached the street last night only to learn that Bane and the boy had escaped from the area. The trail went cold from there. The Winter Man was obviously hiding the boy someplace where Trench would never think to look. A clue, even the exact answer, might be found in precise scrutiny of Bane's file. But Trench had neither the time or the head for such reading. He would leave it for COBRA's administrative personnel, and of course, they would miss it because only a fellow professional would know what minor bit of information was the key.

Not that it mattered. Trench wasn't sure he wanted to find the Winter Man anyway because then he'd have to decide what to do. Bane could have killed him last night and didn't, a blunder unbefitting a professional of his caliber. And yet Trench had to admit that if the roles had been reversed, he probably would have responded in the same manner. That bothered him because it revealed what he had always considered to be weakness. Now he wasn't sure anymore. Doubt had entered in. Trench pushed these thoughts back, seeing them as a sign of hesitance and thus danger. He was too old to change, but similarly too old to stop change from happening.

The report from COBRA field operatives told him that Bane had ended up at his girl friend's apartment early that morning but there was no trace of the boy. Although COBRA's people would now be following Bane's every move, Trench harbored only the slightest hope that those moves would lead them to the boy. Bane could lose as many men as Trench put on his tail at will. The Game might have been cat and mouse; it was just difficult to tell which was which.

Trench dreaded calling Chilgers but knew he must. He sat in the back seat of his car and felt himself dozing again before he reached for the phone. He'd have to find replacements for the Twin Bears as soon as possible. It wouldn't be easy. They were rare finds.

"Any luck, Trench?" Chilgers asked in a typically cold voice.

"No. No leads at all."

"I want that boy, Trench. I'd have him now if not for your bungled operation."

"The operation was well conceived. Bane's presence wasn't considered."

"I considered it. It's why I suggested we eliminate him."

"I don't understand why he was tracking the boy. He couldn't have known about his powers."

"Apparently, he knows more than we think. Worse now he's got the boy and we don't. This whole matter has become immensely complicated. It's not a simple recovery operation anymore. Holes must be filled, eliminated. I've sent for Scalia."

Trench bit his lip, felt a sudden rush of pain to his head. "You didn't need him."

"I needed an equalizer. Scalia makes up his own rules and God knows we need that approach before things get any more out of hand. I'll brief you on the details when the time is right. We'll have this all wrapped up tomorrow," Chilgers said confidently.

The phone clicked off. Trench reached into his pocket for another Percodan.

*   *   *

Colonel Chilgers felt strangely calm. The events of the preceding evening should have frustrated, even enraged him. But they hadn't. He had accepted the report with cool detachment. It was a victory for him, not a loss.

Because the strange power of Davey Phelps was being confirmed more and more with each step. And the power was getting stronger.

The boy hadn't been born with these intense telekinetic abilities; Chilgers felt certain of that. Something about the tangent phase of Vortex had given them to him. The colonel wanted to find out what.

He leaned back in his chair and let his mind drift.

Imagine understanding and harnessing the boy's powers . . .

Imagine training men to use them to their fullest . . .

Imagine an army of Davey Phelpses . . .

The power was there to be exploited.

Chilgers was equally certain that the boy was still unsure and frightened of his newfound abilities, which could serve only to hold him back. Nothing would hold back the army Chilgers envisioned.

The Russians wouldn't have this weapon and neither would the Chinese. Nobody would have one except—

Chilgers leaned forward again, drew his mind back to the present. For now there were other matters to deal with, equally pressing. An obstacle existed that had to be dealt with before any further progress could take place. The Colonel touched his intercom switch.

"Please tell Professor Metzencroy I'm ready to see him."

"You've read my report?" Metzencroy asked before

he even sat down, dabbing furiously at his brow.

Chilgers regarded him sternly. "Please take a chair, Professor, and let's sort this thing out."

Metzencroy stayed on his feet. "There's nothing to sort out this time, Colonel. My fears have been confirmed."

"Since they're your fears, you're hardly the right man to handle the confirmation end."

"Then by all means, retain a second opinion."

"I already have."

More dabbing. "When?"

"That is of no concern to you."

Metzencroy placed a set of trembling hands on Chilgers' desk top. Beads of sweat glistened on his forehead. "Isn't it? I developed Vortex from the very start. Always I had fears, reservations, but nothing firm. That has changed. The bubble on Flight 22 opened the door to a new and problematical area. I ran tests, I did experiments, and the results confirm what we'll be condemning the world to if Vortex is moved into its final stage. There is simply no doubt."

"There is always doubt, Professor."

"Not in this case, Colonel."

Chilgers rose and looked Metzencroy square in the eyes. The Professor shrank back from the desk and drew his handkerchief to his brow.

"I read your report, Professor. You're dealing in theoretical concepts that have never been tested. Yet you remain surprisingly confident of your results."

"Call it a feeling, if you choose."

"I *do* choose, indeed I do. And if you expect me to abort Vortex based on one man's feeling, well . . . I have the greatest respect for you, Professor. If I hadn't I never would have put you at the helm of the most expansive project COBRA has ever undertaken. But please don't ask me to toss it all away now. We are on the verge of something great here, something fantastic."

Metzencroy nodded uneasily. "That's the point, Colonel, we *are* on the verge. We have yet to cross over into an acceptable margin of certainty. I've spent twenty years of my life developing Vortex. I'm closer to it than anyone, and in no way would I want to see it abandoned. I am merely recommending further study and scrutiny."

"For how long? A month? A year? More perhaps?" Chilgers shook his head deliberately. "Project Placebo is only days away now, Professor, and you will have the missiles ready by that time."

"Please, Colonel, all I'm asking for is a month to work out the new formulas. At least give me a chance."

"You've had twenty years."

"I had no means to predict how Vortex would react in bent space in jet-power acceleration. None of our experiments showed any trace of a flutter until the airplane last week."

"Then you're basing your entire study on one incident over the course of twenty years."

Metzencroy nodded. "In science, Colonel, one incident is very often the catalyst regardless of time . . . for better or worse."

"You know that Dr. Teke has an entirely different interpretation of your data."

"Teke is hardly an expert in quantum mechanics and gravitational fields."

Chilgers leaned forward. "But we have five scientists on our staff who are and they also have all reached different interpretations of your data. Independently, I might add."

Metzencroy's lips quivered. "That's impossible. If I could talk to them. . . ."

"I already have, Professor, and on this issue I am forced to accept their conclusions."

"Then you plan on proceeding with Vortex as scheduled."

"Absolutely."

Metzencroy started pacing madly before Chilgers's desk. His face flushed and his entire body all at once seemed to be trembling. He looked to the colonel like a man on the verge of a nervous breakdown. He spoke finally through lips that seemed determined to deny the words passage.

"Colonel, we are not speaking of simple bubbles, flutters, or blinks here. We are speaking of the potential of a high-energy mix within the time-space continuum. We are speaking of a bubble a hundred trillion times the intensity of the one recorded on board Flight 22. And a bubble that size could rip a hole in the fabric of our universe that would change every law of physics we've come to accept. We are speaking potentially of *total* destruction. Nothing left, Colonel. Our world hangs in a surprisingly delicate gravitational and magnetic balance, like living inside a balloon. We are speaking theoretically of sticking a pin in that balloon, Colonel."

Chilgers just looked at him. "You're tired, Professor, take some time off. I'll have your car brought around."

"Colonel, I beg you—"

"It's over, Professor, finished."

Metzencroy's stare was distant. "It may well be."

Chilgers knew Metzencroy had reached the end of his rope. The steps the professor would take now were as unavoidable as they were unfortunate. He was a scientist, not a soldier, with no understanding

195

of loyalty or discipline. He would reveal his fears to Washington, perhaps even make them public. He wouldn't care about destroying Chilgers or Vortex. His stubborn scientific principle clouded everything. Scientists couldn't be told they were wrong; that was the problem with them. You used them as long as you could and then discarded them rapidly, sometimes permanently.

Such would have to be the case with Metzencroy.

Chilgers considered himself above all else to be an excellent judge of character, capable of understanding when a man under him changed from an asset to a liability. The key was to ferret such men out just as the transition was beginning. There were no board-room politics at COBRA. A man contributed as much as he could for as long as he could and then was released. Chilgers thrived on a world of such clarity.

Of course, few who reached their limit—none actually—had ever had the potential to do as much damage as Metzencroy. A drastic situation called for a drastic response. The professor was valuable to him; his knowledge in the field of weaponry physics was unsurpassed. It would be a great loss to COBRA and the entire country. But an even greater loss was possible, even probable, if he was left operable. The risk was too great, and risks had to be staunchly regarded, whatever the cost.

Too bad. Chilgers especially would have liked to have had Metzencroy around for analysis of Davey Phelps when the boy was ultimately brought in. Teke was a good man but he was no Metzencroy, and to understand the boy's power to its fullest the colonel believed he would need a Metzencroy.

But the professor had made his decision.

Now Chilgers would make his.

Chapter Eighteen

"Yo, Josh boy, those dudes still on your tail?"

Bane glanced out from the phone booth at the blue sedan which had pulled up across the street. "Closer than ever, King. How's the boy?"

"Doin' fine. I got him shootin' well enough already to split hairs. Wait till ya see."

"I'll look forward to it. No company?"

"Ain't been a white man within five blocks."

"They might not be white."

"I'll know 'em no matter what color they paint themselves."

"I figured that much," Bane told King Cong and hung up the receiver.

It was closing on eleven A.M. and Bane planned on spending the rest of the day tracking down other passengers from Flight 22. He knew that Davey could not have been the only one affected by whatever had happened on the plane. If some of the others were able to tell him more, be more specific about those foggy moments before the jet landed, he'd be able to take the information to Washington. His proof that something had indeed happened to Flight 22 had to be irrefutable; otherwise the risk was too great.

Bane pulled his Cressida into traffic and watched the blue sedan lag comfortably back. Within a few blocks, another car would take its place, and then another . . . and another. Bane could lose them at any point if he chose to but he did not. He felt more comfortable knowing where they were. Besides, it wouldn't be hard for them in any case to figure out his afternoon strategy. It was the next logical step for him to take, and Trench certainly would have expected it, professional that he was. So for now an uneasy stalemate existed, a truce of sorts. The men in the cars could receive orders to move in and take him at any time. But Trench wouldn't want to chance a bloody showdown and risk coming away empty again. That wasn't his style at all. He'd choose his time more appropriately and on his terms. What's more, Trench would cling to the hope that Bane might slip up somehow and lead him to Davey. Take him out now, Trench would think, and the boy's location might remain a mystery indefinitely. COBRA couldn't have that.

Bane's first stop was a fashionable high-rise on Central Park South and a man named William Renshaw. He had no way of knowing who on his passenger manifest would be home or not, so he elected to start at random with one who lived relatively close by in the city. He squeezed his car into a no-parking zone and learned from the doorman that Renshaw lived on the eighteenth floor. The man insisted on calling first and Bane was surprised when a raspy, male voice shot back over the intercom to send him up immediately.

Inside of a minute later, Bane found himself ringing the bell of Renshaw's apartment. The door opened just a crack. A pair of bulging eyes inspected him up and down.

"About time you showed up," the mouth below them charged.

"Mr. Renshaw?"

"Damn right. They're everywhere and I'm running out of ammo."

"What?"

Renshaw's answer was to unhitch the chain and open the door only long enough to drag Bane inside. The plush, richly furnished apartment lay drenched in darkness, all sunlight held back by drawn shades. Only one lamp was on, casting eerie shadows on the walls as Bane followed Renshaw into the living-room section.

"They're hiding because they know you've come," Renshaw said with a wink. He was wearing a blue bathrobe over a white T-shirt and floppy bedroom slippers. His thin gray hair hung wildly about his head and he smelled of stale sweat. "If we wait long enough they'll come back. Come on out, you bastards!" he shouted at the bare walls. "We know you're there. No sense hiding."

Bane realized Renshaw was quite mad. He had seen enough men crack in combat to know the symptoms. The issue here was the cause.

"What'd you say your name was?" Renshaw shot at him.

"Bane."

"Well, Bane, I hope you've had experience in these matters before. They're too big for a rookie to handle. Some the size of rats, I tell you, rats!"

"What are *they*?"

"Don't be an ass, Bane. I've called the exterminators a dozen times now. They haven't changed since the first. Cockroaches. Big ones, big as rats."

"I see."

"You haven't yet but you will." Renshaw gazed back toward the door. "So where is it?"

"Where's what?"

199

"Your equipment, dammit! Whatever it is you plan to use to kill these mothers! Vacuum them up, isn't that what you boys do?"

"Depends."

"Well, I haven't slept in five nights now. Just get rid of the bastards quick. Big as rats, I tell you."

Five nights went back to the day Flight 22 touched down, Bane thought.

"There!" Renshaw screamed suddenly. "There's one!"

Then, from inside his bathrobe, he whipped out a pistol that might have been a twin of King Cong's cannon.

"On the wall! On the wall! See it! Here it comes! Oh God, oh God . . . See it!"

Bane looked at the wall and imagined a giant cockroach sliding down. No wonder Renshaw hadn't been sleeping.

"Bang!" Renshaw shouted, pulling the trigger to an empty click. "Got the bastard. See that, I got him."

"Good shot."

"But I'm running out of ammo and they just keep coming back no matter how many I kill. You'd think they'd get the message after a while. What do you think made them grow so big?"

"I'll take one down to the lab and have it analyzed."

"Good idea. Hadn't thought of that. They could overrun the city if they wanted to."

"I'll need some information first," Bane told him. "You'll answer some questions, Mr. Renshaw?"

"Questions? Sure. Of course. Ask away." His eyes wandered to the spot where his imaginary bullet had downed the imaginary giant cockroach. "You think they might be too big for your equipment? Big as rats, they are. You saw."

"I'll use a special adapter," Bane assured him. "Can we sit down?"

"On the furniture, you mean? Well, I guess so but we'll have to be careful. Caught a whole swarm under the couch last night trying to climb up my legs. I'll watch yours if you'll watch mine."

"Legs? Of course."

"And behind. They love to sneak up on you from behind. It's not safe to have your back anywhere but against a wall. Big as rats, they are."

Finally Renshaw sat uneasily on the couch. Bane took a chair directly before him, eyeing the magnum clutched in his fingers. Was there any way he could be sure the other chambers were empty as well?

"Mr. Renshaw, when did you first notice the bugs?"

"Notice them? While on the plane, of course. They came in through the windows. Smaller then. They've grown."

"Did anyone else see them on the plane?"

"Of course they did. They were just too scared to admit it. I told the stewardess when the lights came back on and she said she'd handle it. Hah! You call this handling it? Maybe I'll sue them for letting the bastards loose in my apartment. Must've snuck through in my luggage. Big as rats, they are."

"What about the lights?" Bane probed.

"What lights?"

"The ones on the plane."

"They went off for a few seconds."

"And that's when you first saw the bugs?"

"Yes." Confusion claimed Renshaw's face. "How did I see them if it was dark?"

Bane realized the man was being faced with his own delusion, dangerous potentially for someone in

201

Renshaw's state. "Because the emergency lights must have snapped on," he said quickly.

"Of course," Renshaw agreed, relaxing. "That's it."

"You say the lights were only off for a few seconds?"

"Long enough for the bugs to come."

Bane was going to ask Renshaw if he'd noticed any of the other passengers behaving strangely but thought better of it. There was no way he could expect a coherent answer at this point.

"Oh God, oh God," Renshaw muttered. "Don't move! Do you hear me! Don't move! . . ."

With that, the madman raised the magnum's barrel and leveled it direct for Bane's groin. He cocked the hammer, closed one eye to steady his aim.

"Hold still," Renshaw whispered. "If you value your balls, don't move a muscle."

Bane strained his eyes to see if any shells were present in the chambers. No way to be sure. He gauged the distance between himself and Renshaw and decided chancing a leap against a potentially loaded gun was even more ludicrous than waiting for the madman to fire it.

"Steady," Renshaw whispered and Bane held his breath. "Steady . . ."

The trigger started back.

Bane flinched.

Click.

"Bang! Got the sucker! Saved your balls, I did, saved your balls. Big as a rat, it was, big as a rat."

Bane stood up. "I'd better go downstairs and get my equipment."

Renshaw rose and a smile stretched from ear to ear. "I'd go and help you bring it up, but the bastards would overrun the place while I was gone. That's what they're waiting for you know. For me to leave or fall asleep."

"I'll be right back up."

Renshaw regarded him thoughtfully on the way to the door. "Maybe you should call in more men. Big as rats, they are, big as rats."

Bane closed the door behind him.

He had a friend at Bellevue he could call about Renshaw. Though it might prove a mistake from a security standpoint, there was no way he could stomach leaving the poor man up there, a captive of his mad delusions. He now knew two of the passengers who had traveled on Flight 22. One had developed psychic powers and the other had gone totally mad. Interesting contrast.

Bane couldn't wait to learn what else might lie ahead of him. As it turned out, though, there wasn't much in the next hour and a half. Of the next five names on his list, three were not home, a fourth claimed to have slept through the whole flight, and the wife of a fifth assured Bane that her husband showed no ill or unusual effects from Flight 22, certainly ruling out madness or psychic powers.

Bane then decided to give the COBRA cars following him a treat by leading them into Westchester County. There were seven names on the manifest that resided here and Bane elected to start with a woman named Gladys Baker, a widow from Scarsdale. Mrs. Baker was sixty-four and lived on Carthage Road, surrounded by yards that later in the afternoon would be dominated by children out to challenge the early spring cold. Her house was the simplest on the block, a two-story colonial with a flagstone walk. Strangely, Bane found himself teetering on the slabs, avoiding the grass at all costs. Once again a feeling of discomfort, of intruding, gripped his insides. It reached its peak after he rang the bell, when Gladys Baker opened the door and faced him from the other side of a screen.

"Yes?"

She was a gray-haired woman who looked more than her age. The glasses propped up on her nose were strung to a chain that would allow her to dangle them at her chest.

Bane flashed an ID card that made him a Federal Aviation Administration investigator. "I wonder if I might have a word with you, Mrs. Baker."

"What about?" she asked nervously.

"It would be easier if we talked inside."

Gladys Baker checked the I.D. more closely. "Joshua Bane . . . That sounds like a biblical name."

"My mother was religious."

She opened the door for him, her eyes thankful. "I'm so glad you've come. You don't know what a load it is off my mind to see that someone else realized something was wrong with that flight."

Bane felt his stomach flutter with anticipation.

"That is what you've come about, Mr. Bane, isn't it?"

Bane followed her in and caught the familiar drone of soap opera music. "As a matter of fact, yes."

"I was just relaxing a bit," Mrs. Baker told him.

"This won't take long."

"Let it take as long as it must. What a release it'll be to talk about this finally. You'd like a cup of coffee or tea perhaps?"

"Well . . ."

"Please. It would be my pleasure. I was just about to make some for myself anyway."

"In that case, thank you very much."

He moved with her into the kitchen, feeling much more at ease and eager to hear the old woman's story. She set the water boiling. Bane waited for her to sit down before he took a chair across from her at the kitchen table.

"I'm investigating some complaints we've had about the flight you took from San Diego back to New York six days ago," he said.

Gladys Baker's face whitened. She tucked her fingers under the table so Bane wouldn't notice their trembling.

"Thank God," she sighed, "it wasn't just me who felt there was something wrong with the flight. But I didn't say anything. Since my husband passed on I've had some . . . problems. Adjusting and all, you understand. I've spent some time in therapy. I have relatives who'd like nothing better than to make it permanent . . . from my husband's side, of course. He left me everything, you see. So I couldn't tell anyone about the flight, I just couldn't."

"You can now."

"And you'll take what I say in confidence?"

"So far as I can."

Gladys Baker sighed again. Behind her, the teakettle started to hiss. "There's not much to tell really. I'm not a very good flier and without Dramamine I'm generally a nervous wreck. I thought I had one left but it wasn't until we were in the air that I realized I didn't. Stupid of me really. I thought I'd have to ride the whole way with my heart in my mouth but I was doing fine until a few minutes before we landed when . . ." Gladys Baker brought her trembling hands up over her face.

"Please go on, Mrs. Baker, I'm here to listen."

"Well, right before we landed I started seeing double, two of everything. Then I got very dizzy, ter-

205

rible spins, and I thought, 'Well, after six smooth hours here I am about to blow it.' So I started taking deep breaths, but it didn't help. The double vision didn't go away and the dizziness got worse. Everything in the plane was going crazy, turning and floating, even the people. I couldn't find the stewardess so I turned to the nice young couple next to me—I was sitting on the aisle, you see." Mrs. Baker took a deep breath. "They weren't there."

"You mean they had changed seats?"

"I mean they had disappeared."

A shudder crept up Bane's spine.

"A few seconds before the spell came on," Mrs. Baker continued, "I was looking right at them. They never walked by me. They just weren't there anymore."

"Might you have passed out?"

Mrs. Baker shook her head. "I was too sick. I couldn't even close my eyes without feeling like I was about to fall out of a roller coaster. Besides, a few seconds later they were there again."

"The couple?"

The old woman nodded, ignoring the kettle which had begun to whistle its readiness. "Mr. Bane, does this all seem a bit much to you?"

"Not at all," he said unhesitantly, glad he could be of some comfort.

"There's more."

"I'd like to hear it."

"They didn't come back all at once—the couple, I mean. They came back a little at a time, like when you focus a camera and the picture slowly takes shape. First there was just an outline. Then it started to fill in but you still couldn't see all of them. Then they were back. About that time I realized the dizziness had subsided so I asked them if they were all right. They looked at me strangely and said 'Of course,' as if nothing was wrong, as if nothing had happened. But it did happen, Mr. Bane, I know it did."

The kettle was screaming now. Gladys Baker rose, pushing herself up by pressing her palms against the smooth finish of the table. She lifted the kettle from the range and uneasily poured out two cups of boiling water, neglecting to stir up the coffee. The cups trembled in her hands and would have slipped to the floor had not Bane relieved her of the burden halfway back to the table.

"I'm not usually this nervous," she apologized. "I haven't been in three years since my husband passed on. But I'm scared now, Mr. Bane, and it all started with that flight." She was sitting down again, trying to raise the cup of coffee to her lips. Her fingers betrayed her and the scalding liquid dripped over the rim in small waves. She gave up, returning the cup to its saucer. She looked at Bane desperately. "I need help but I'm afraid to seek it. If those relatives learn the state I'm in, they'll start proceedings again and I'll lose everything I have, even my home. I haven't been sleeping well, Mr. Bane. Every day I go through long periods of depression, worse even than right after my husband passed on. Then suddenly they go away and I find myself remarkably giddy for no reason at all. The periods rotate in cycles and waves, and I'm not sure which one I dread the most. I was never like this before, Mr. Bane, you've got to believe that. I was never like this before in my life until that flight home. I've tried to pass it all off to forgetting my Dramamine, but somehow I know it was something else." Again she tried the coffee cup, failing this time to even raise it off the saucer. "Am I going crazy, Mr. Bane? Am I cracking up?"

Bane could only look at her sympathetically, his untouched coffee steaming toward his nostrils. She had just described textbook symptoms of manic depression, symptoms she claimed had come on as a direct result of Flight 22. Davey Phelps, Renshaw, and now this.

"There's something else I feel I should tell you, Mr. Bane," Gladys Baker continued softly, "something else that was strange about the flight, but I didn't pay much attention to it because of everything else. It was my watch."

"Your watch?"

"I checked it against a clock in the terminal after we landed and found it was running forty minutes slow."

A shudder grabbed Bane's spine. "The spell you had, Mrs. Baker, you say it came on just before landing?"

Gladys Baker nodded.

"And it only seemed to last a few seconds after which the plane touched down?"

"That's right."

Bane looked down at his cup of coffee, stirred it thoughtlessly. Flight 22 had landed forty minutes after Jake Del Gennio reported it missing. Gladys Baker's spell coincided with the moment Jake saw the jet vanish and her watch lost forty minutes somewhere in the air, a missing forty minutes which apparently had never passed inside Flight 22. What had happened to them?

"And I'll tell you one other thing," Mrs. Baker was saying, "it's not just me. At least, I don't think it is. You see, I knew a girl who was on the plane. Well, actually I know her mother, but I recognized her and said hello on board. They're from over in New Jersey. Hillsdale, I'm pretty sure, a beautiful neighborhood. I've tried to call her a few times this week but every time I mention the flight to her mother, she hangs up on me and I haven't talked to the girl yet. I know something happened to her too. I can just feel it." Tears welled in Gladys Baker's eyes. "You do believe me, Mr. Bane, don't you?"

"Yes," Bane said, and that helped Gladys Baker relax just enough to bring the cup of coffee to her lips.

The girl's name, Bane had learned before departing, was Ginny Peretz, and she lived in a house at least twice the size of Gladys Baker's on Mountain View Terrace in the fashionable New Jersey suburb of Hillsdale. The maid who answered the door, though, seemed determined to keep Bane outside. He persisted and she finally disappeared in search of the lady of the house.

"My lawyer's on the way," Mrs. Peretz, a well-groomed lady nearing fifty with only the few gray hairs that had sprung up since her last trip to the salon, said by way of introduction.

"That's not necessary," Bane told her.

"We don't want any trouble."

"I'm not here to cause any. I gave your maid my credentials."

Mrs. Peretz scoffed. "Those mean nothing to me. My husband's a man of considerable influence. A few phone calls by him and you will regret this day."

A bluff, clearly. If that were so, Bane reckoned, there would have been no reason to call the lawyer. Aware the woman was lying, he seized the advantage.

"I want to see your daughter, Mrs. Peretz," he demanded.

She glanced out behind him. "Do keep your voice

down. There are neighbors to consider, you know."
She let him step far enough inside the door to let it
close over the marble floor in the foyer. "Damn busy-
bodies. All they do is talk. I've had to have the doctors
use the rear entrance. They say it'll pass, just temporary surely. They aren't sure what caused it, not
precisely anyway."

Bane didn't want to seem too eager. "Caused
what?" The now familiar prickling was back at his
neck hairs.

"My daughter is unable to see you," Mrs. Peretz
retreated.

"It won't take long. Only a few questions."

Mrs. Peretz was shaking her head. Her eyes had
become moist. "You damn fool, don't you understand?"

Bane's silence confirmed he didn't.

"She can't answer any of your damned questions
about that damned plane because since she got off it,
she hasn't spoken one word!" Mrs. Peretz screeched.
"Not one damn word! She just sits in her room and
stares out the window. She doesn't move now unless
we move her. She doesn't eat unless we feed her."
Mrs. Peretz suddenly looked old. She rubbed the
black sleeve of her dress against her face, lowering her
voice as well as her eyes. "The doctors say she experienced a severe trauma or shock. They say she's totally
withdrawn into herself as a result of it. But they're
wrong, all of them!" She was almost shouting again.
"A sudden severe trauma or shock, they say. But she
was fine when she boarded that plane—I checked
with the close friends who dropped her at the airport.
Then six hours later she stumbled off white as a ghost
and hasn't uttered a word since, so I suppose the doctors would have me believe the shock occurred in the
jet. Hah! Can you tell me what kind of traumatic
experience could happen in midair?"

Chapter Nineteen

Bane lost his tail on the way to Janie Finlaw's apartment, for naught as it turned out because as he pulled into the parking garage he spotted an obvious COBRA team in a sedan just down the street. He was meeting Janie here for dinner and he was glad now he'd invited Harry the Bat along. Harry's presence would have kept the men at bay if they'd had plans to do more than watch prior to Bane's arrival.

He rode the elevator to the twelfth floor and rang Janie's bell.

"What's the password?" Harry's voice called from the inside.

"Open the door, you son of a bitch."

A chain rattled. "Got it right on the first shot." Harry swung the door open.

"How'd you know it was me?" Bane asked, closing it.

"Saw you drive into the garage."

"Then you've no doubt noticed our friends."

"The fuckers have been parked across the street for the past hour. Be a lot easier if we just invited them in for coffee."

Janie appeared from the kitchen. "You boys plan on talking shop all night?"

"Not if you tell me what you dug up on the com-

211

puter," Bane said.

"I focused on what you asked me to, Josh," she reported after they sat down in the living room, "and I think I latched on to something." She consulted her notes. "To begin with, Colonel Chilgers relies primarily on two men for the day-to-day functioning of COBRA: Dr. Benjamin Teke and Professor Lewis Metzencroy. I've got pictures of both of them, in addition to one of Chilgers for you to look at later. Anyway, Teke's the more well rounded of the two but holds no real expertise in any scientific field. He's more or less become COBRA's chief administrator as well as Chilgers' confidant. Metzencroy's another matter entirely, an absolute genius in the fields of physics and astrophysics. His work for COBRA is confined to the laboratory and their Confidential Projects section and he almost never mixes with politics. According to his title, he fills the vague position of chief of new weapons research and development. But I doubt he even goes near anything but the big stuff, top secret all the way—nothing you'll ever read about in the paper."

Harry the Bat sighed. "That computer tell you how much he makes a year?"

"No, but it did have something to say about seven scientists hired by Metzencroy and COBRA over the last three years, and they've all got one thing in common: Einstein."

"Einstein?" Bane wondered, and drew a nod from Janie.

"All strict disciples of the master who have followed his words virtually to the letter throughout their careers."

"I assume the same holds true for Metzencroy."

"Even more so. Metzencroy's somewhere in his mid-sixties which would put him roughly in his mid-thirties when Einstein died in 'fifty-five. His entire career has been a continuous attempt to expand on some of his mentor's theories and complete the rest."

"What do you mean complete?" Bane wondered.

"I'm no expert," Janie said, "but it's fairly common knowledge that Einstein died with a number of theories incomplete and untested. $E=mc^2$, some say, was child's play compared to what he worked out later. So potentially he was onto forces in the world even greater than nuclear fission. And assuming Metzencroy has picked up his work—"

"—COBRA might be developing it right now," Bane finished. "With the help of seven additional experts Metzencroy has chosen just for the job. I think we're on to something here."

"Except that's about as far as we can go without additional information," Janie explained. "COBRA's computer lines are sealed in San Diego so there's no way Harry or I can tap in. The only thing we seem to have gained is the possibility that Metzencroy is developing one of Einstein's uncompleted theories."

"I'd say it's more than just a possibility," Bane noted. "It's not just Davey Phelps who's been affected by Flight 22; the whole damn plane was cursed." And he went on to relate the essence of his meetings that day; with a madman, the mother of a catatonic, and a manic depressive who swore she saw two passengers vanish on board only to reappear.

"Sounds to me like COBRA zapped that plane," Harry the Bat concluded.

"And whatever they zapped it with," Bane followed, "went to work on the minds of the passengers. Every one of them was affected differently, and a few—as many as half I'd guess—were affected at levels too small to notice . . . yet."

"'Yet'?"

Bane nodded. "The effects appear to be cumulative. They grow, worsen instead of dissipating. Davey Phelps's powers have gotten progressively stronger. Gladys Baker claims her manic depression is getting worse, and Mrs. Peretz insists that her daughter withdraws more and more every day. It's possible, then, that those who haven't noticed any effect from the flight will before too much longer."

"The next question, I guess," Janie said, "is what happened to them? What did COBRA do?"

"Lord fuck a duck," Harry muttered, "they must've loaded the food with some contaminant about to be let loose on Russia."

"Or a new weapon maybe," Janie added, "that attacks the nerve centers of the brain and causes the symptoms Josh has been summarizing. A mad version of psychological warfare."

"Einstein never had anything to do with psychological warfare," Bane pointed out.

"Not directly," Janie admitted. "But he might have left the door open for it somewhere. The kind of weapon we're talking about is terrifying. Developed sufficiently, it could destroy an entire nation from the inside, assuming proper methods of dispersal were worked out."

"And that," picked up Harry the Bat immediately, snapping his fingers, "could've been exactly what Flight 22 was all about."

"Could've been," Bane noted, "but wasn't."

"And I was just starting to get rolling. . . ."

"You see," Bane went on, "we're forgetting something here, perhaps the most important part of the puzzle: Jake Del Gennio. This whole thing started for us because he claimed the *whole plane* disappeared."

"So what's the point?"

"Focus on what they did to the plane itself, not the people. All passengers I've spoken to who exhibit symptoms recall a brief period on board when they felt dizzy, lightheaded, or passed out altogether. The period seems to correspond with the time Jake Del Gennio claimed the jet vanished. Except the passengers claim the spell only lasted for a few seconds, minutes at the outside, and yet Flight 22 didn't land until *forty minutes* later."

"You're saying their spells actually lasted that long," Harry surmised.

"Now we come to the real problem, because according to Gladys Baker's watch those forty minutes didn't exist."

"You've lost me, Winter Man."

Bane hesitated. "The plane didn't just disappear, it ceased to exist, went into some kind of time warp or something. Forty minutes went by but for the passengers only seconds had passed."

"Wow," from Harry.

"Remember, there was no radio contact at all with the cockpit during the missing period. The people came back and so did the plane. But whatever happened in the interim cost Jake Del Gennio his life and maybe sixty people their minds."

"And you're saying whatever COBRA did had nothing to do with people in a direct sense," Janie put forth.

"I can't be sure of that," Bane told her. "I just believe the extreme effects the passengers suffered weren't planned for or expected. Things got out of control."

"You figure that had anything to do with Flight 22 having engine trouble along the way?" Harry wondered.

"Possibly. But there's no way of being sure at this point whether that was a cause or an effect."

"Well Lord fuck a duck, then we're right back where we started," the Bat moaned.

"Not really," said Bane. "We've got the Einstein connection now, and if we plug that in with what we already know, we might be able to uncover what COBRA's up to with all this, at least get a general idea of what they're working on."

"Not necessarily," Janie interjected. "If this operation was still in the research stage, no one outside of San Diego would have to know about its existence and that includes the White House and the Pentagon, so you can forget about learning anything there."

"Terrific . . ."

"Relax, Harry," Bane soothed. "The pieces of this puzzle are starting to fall together."

"As long as we don't go down with them," from the Bat.

Colonel Chilgers closed the bulky file on Joshua Bane. He had been analyzing it for six hours until he'd found what he was looking for. He contacted Scalia.

"An interesting assignment, Colonel," Scalia told him plainly over the phone.

"The logistics promise to be difficult."

"I look at them as challenging . . . and expensive."

"Your price will be met." Chilgers hesitated. "You'll be working with Trench."

"I work alone."

"I feel the logistics would be better served by the two of you."

216

Chilgers could feel the coldness coming over the line.

"It's your money," Scalia said finally. "But I don't trust Trench. He thinks too much. He's played the Game on too many sides."

"And you?"

"Money has no side, Colonel."

"Tomorrow's timing is certain to be very delicate. The two of you together should assure against any slip-ups."

"A quick hit on Bane would seem more logical."

"Matters have progressed way beyond that."

"As you wish." Then, "You're certain about the information in Bane's file?"

Chilgers toyed with the edges of the manila folder. "Absolutely."

"We'll talk tomorrow, Colonel."

Scalia hung up. First.

Chilgers hated him and was content that they'd never have to meet. The colonel did not relish the sensation of being controlled, of having this killer's upper hand waved in his face. Scalia was nothing but a repairman, called in when something had gone wrong. He fixed the problem, collected his fee, and went on his way. So banal. So trite. And yet he had spoken to Chilgers in a demeaning and sententious manner. Chilgers steamed, smiled finally at the thought of sending Trench after Scalia when this was over, then quickly changed his mind. Crossing Scalia could cost him much and gain him little.

A knock sounded on the door of his spacious, wood-lined office.

Chilgers lit his pipe and puffed it. "Come in, Teke."

The doctor entered and took a chair directly before Chilgers' desk.

"I called you here, Doctor, to ask you a few questions. I want your answers to be honest and accurate, wholly so on both counts."

Teke nodded, his bald dome showing a day's growth of stubble on its sides.

Chilgers pulled the pipe from his mouth. "Has Project Placebo reached a point where Professor Metzencroy's contributions are no longer required?"

Teke didn't hesitate. "Absolutely."

"Then am I to assume, Doctor, that the professor is now superfluous to the ultimate completion of Vortex, that the operation *can* be completed without him?"

"Most certainly." Again, no hesitation.

"In your answers you have laid personal feelings aside, Teke?"

"My answers are strictly professional, Colonel."

Chilgers smiled and forgot all about Scalia. Wordlessly, he reached for the phone.

The colonel elected to remain at the base all evening. It was hardly an unheard-of practice for him, so no undue attention would be aroused because of it. The risk would have been worthwhile in any case; he wanted to be here when news of Metzencroy's death reached the complex. The matter had to be handled tactfully in a way that would cause not even the slightest repercussions. Chilgers could afford nothing less at this stage.

There would be questions, of course, but these would be easily answered. He had arranged that the professor's medical report be revised to indicate a history of heart trouble. That way the final attack which would soon claim his life would arouse a bare minimum of suspicion, perhaps none at all. The drug used was very fine, only a small amount being required to do the job, and it was undetectable after two hours under even the closest autopsy. Chilgers knew all about it.

The drug had been developed at COBRA.

The colonel slept not one wink all evening. There were plans to revise, details to revamp. Metzencroy was a brilliant man, and there was no doubt he would be missed in certain quarters. Hell, Chilgers reflected, if not for the professor there never would have been a Vortex or a Project Placebo. Twenty years of patient research and testing had placed the United States on the verge of unchallenged global domination, thanks to a man who would not be alive to see it.

Chilgers did feel some compunction over the necessity of the professor's passing, though he did not let it show on his features. Metzencroy had clearly proven himself to be too much of a threat. It would not be easy replacing him, but it would have been even harder to have his every move monitored. If allowed to continue working at COBRA, Metzencroy might, conceivably, have resorted to sabotage or, worse, exposure, thereby destroying Vortex and erasing all his brilliant work.

Chilgers spent the night running all this through his head, further convincing himself of the necessity for his decision. Murder was nothing new to him. A man who couldn't stomach it certainly didn't belong in his position, or in any position of power for that matter.

Strangely, the only thing that didn't occur to him as the dark hours gave way to light was the possibility that Metzencroy's suspicions, his fears, might have been correct. Chilgers' vision was clear, but narrow. He could not consider the professor's final reports as anything but absurdity because the consequences they posed were too awful to contemplate.

Metzencroy had threatened Vortex.

All threats to Vortex had to be put aside at all costs, at any costs.

Five levels above him, the sun had come up when Chilgers' phone rang at almost the precise minute he expected it to. The voice was that of a COBRA security guard sent to gather Professor Metzencroy at his home for an emergency meeting.

"I'm afraid I have some bad news for you, sir. . . ."

The Fifth Day:

PURSUITS

Doctor Heckyll works late at the laborat'ry
Where things are not as they seem
Doctor Heckyll wishes nothing more desp'rately
Than to fulfill his dreams
Letting loose with a scream in the dead of night
As he's breaking new ground
Try'n' his best to unlock all the secrets
But he's not sure what he found . . .
Whoa, it's off to work he goes
In the name of science and all its wonders.

—Men at Work

Chapter Twenty

"The death of Professor Metzencroy came as a shock to all of us. Please accept our regrets, Colonel," the President offered from Washington over the high security conference line.

Chilgers was glad for this method of meeting. It spared him the necessity of keeping his features as composed as his voice. "Your thoughts are most appreciated, Mr. President," he said humbly.

"Then please accept our concerns in the same light. Mr. Brandenberg, Mr. Jorgenson, and I are curious as to how the professor's unfortunate passing affects Project Placebo?"

"Not in the least, sir," the colonel reported confidently. "Please understand that the professor has been sick for some time. He had more or less removed himself from the project actively as of six weeks ago. His participation from that point became advisory or instructional in nature. So he will not be missed on this project in any tangible sense, though with him, sadly, has passed the kind of intangible contribution to the field of science that is not easily replaced."

"I understand," said the President.

The deep voice of Secretary of Defense George Brandenberg, filled the room. "But the point now is that Project Placebo can go on as scheduled."

"I can say yes in all confidence."

"That's good," said the President, "because after going over your report we've decided to accept your proposal verbatim, including activating Project Placebo's final stage, a full-scale Red Flag alert, to coincide with delivery of the doctored missiles from COBRA."

"Thank you, Mr. President."

"Don't thank me yet, Colonel. If anything goes wrong here, there'll be hell to pay. The Senate Armed Services Committee will want to put somebody's ass in their witness chair and, excuse my frankness, but it's not going to be mine."

"I understand fully."

"See that you do, Colonel. When are the doctored missiles scheduled to arrive at Bunker 17?"

"Sunday afternoon, sir."

"Then following your scenario we should bring the base to Yellow Flag some hours before then. You understand, of course, that all-alert status signaling will be handled from our end. We control the pace and can choose to abort the exercise at any time."

"Certainly, Mr. President. That's precisely what I proposed. Technically, I know of no other way it can be handled."

There it was, Chilgers thought as he hung up the phone minutes later; he had done it. Project Placebo would go into effect sometime tomorrow and from that point it would be unstoppable. Vortex, too, would be unstoppable. Everything had worked out even better than he had let himself hope.

Metzencroy was out of the way and within the next few hours all the remaining holes would be filled.

Chilgers clamped his hands triumphantly together and smiled.

* * *

Bane had visited four more of the passengers from Flight 22 with no further results when the feeling struck him. A dread fear crept up his spine and he knew immediately something was wrong. He had lost his COBRA tails one hour into the morning, sick of worrying about them. Now he found himself missing their presence and their actions at any given time as a barometer for the opposition's intentions.

He had to get to a phone.

"Josh, thank God you called!" The Bat had answered his phone before the first ring had ended.

"Harry, what's wrong?"

"The King called a few minutes ago, talking crazy and swearing his head off."

The fear tightened around Bane's spine. "What about?"

"He wouldn't tell me, but he wants you to call him as soon as you can."

"Thanks, Harry."

Bane plunged another dime down the slot and pressed out the number of the King's gym.

"Josh boy?" the King rose tentatively. He did not bother to say hello.

"It's me, King."

"I lost him, Josh boy, I lost the kid."

King Cong unlocked the door to his gym twenty minutes later just long enough for Bane to enter.

"It was crazy, Josh boy," the King explained, following Bane toward the back room where Davey had been staying. "All of a sudden all the lights went out. I was movin' toward the fuse box when I felt somebody real close by. Shit, he musta been in the same league as you and me—maybe better. Anyways, I got a fix on his outline and was movin' for him when somethin' that looked like white smoke shot into my

225

face and the next thing I know I'm wakin' up with a head twice normal size."

Bane caught the scent of a faint odor in the air. "Panodine," he announced. "Highly toxic poison, especially in a gaseous state. Fatal even in small inhalations."

"I'm still breathin'."

"You wouldn't be if you were six inches shorter and a hundred pounds lighter."

They had reached the entrance to the back room. The King fumbled for the right key.

"Soon as I come to," he continued, finally finding it, "I checked back here where two of my boys were handlin' the baby-sittin' chores." The King swung the door open. "Somebody blew their heads off."

Bane stepped inside and saw for himself. The two fullback-size blacks lay face down in a pool of blood and brains, the rear of their skulls blown totally away. He couldn't help but shudder.

"Who coulda done this, Josh boy? Who coulda pulled it off?"

Bane was asking himself that same question. A single devastator bullet in the back of the head was Scalia's trademark as a killer. Could this be Scalia's work?

Bane shuddered again and at once knew it was.

Scalia was in New York and now he had Davey!

But the boy wasn't dead. Otherwise, his body would be lying here with the others. He'd be on his way to COBRA by now. Worse, Trench and Scalia were both in the city, both working for the opposition.

"How long, King? How long ago did this happen?"

"I don't know for sure, Josh boy. I was out maybe a half hour so figure 'bout twice that or a little more."

King Cong took a deep breath. "I let you down, Josh boy, I let you down real bad."

"My fault, King. I should've known they'd link you to me."

The King looked at him with sorrowful eyes. "Yeah, well the dude they sent iced two men like they weren't even there, Josh boy. And when he came at me I could tell he was quick, quick like a cat."

Bane started from the back room, froze in his tracks. Suddenly COBRA's strategy was clear to him. With hard, cold fear he realized the next stage of their plan: the boy was theirs; it was time to clean up the rest of their tracks.

Bane rushed into the gym office and grabbed the phone. He dialed the Center's number. It started ringing.

Come on, come on! Answer! Somebody answer!

No one did. The receiver slipped from Bane's fingers and he charged past the King toward the exit.

Trench watched the passenger door open and the tall man slide in. He had only met Scalia once previous to this day and that occasion had found them on different sides, each resolutely trying to kill the other. Now they were working together and their eyes revealed the knowledge that this time any lapse would mean death.

"I've taken care of the phones. The people are yours."

"How many?" Scalia asked, his eyes on the Center's brownstone.

"Three since noon, just as the colonel informed us."

"The girl?"

Trench nodded, reluctantly.

Scalia pulled back the sleeve of his overcoat. "Quarter past. I'd better get moving before the others dribble back from lunch. Don't want to run up the colonel's bill now, do I?"

He pulled an Ingram machine pistol, a close cousin to the Uzi only more powerful, from the back seat and fit it snugly under his overcoat. Scalia was thin to the point of being gaunt. His straight combed hair was black, as were his eyes. His body was taut and coiled, prepared at an instant's notice to spring into violent action. He wore tight leather gloves over his hands, perfect for the unusual cold snap, but Trench knew they would have been there even on the hottest summer day.

Scalia looked over at him, turning his mouth into a twisted smile. "You don't like this work much, do you?"

"I don't see the point."

"You don't get paid to look."

Trench hesitated. "The girl, Scalia."

"Yes?"

"You'll make it fast for her, of course."

Scalia smiled one last time and climbed out of the car, moving toward the Center.

Charlie, the security guard, heard the bell ring and looked up from his magazine at the TV monitor which showed a sleek, well-dressed man at the front door. He depressed the intercom button.

"Yes, what can I do for you?"

No response. The man just stood there in the cold, hands tucked in his pockets.

"I said, what can I do for you?"

Still no response.

Damn thing must be on the fritz again, Charlie

thought, and he hit the access buzzer atop his panel and waddled over to greet the visitor in the anteroom.

"Now, what can I do for you?" Charlie asked, swinging the inner door open so it was still held by the heavy chain.

He saw the black, perforated cylinder jamming toward him but was powerless to do anything but gape. It wedged through the slim opening and a burst burned into his stomach, killing him before he struck the floor.

Scalia tossed his strength behind a thrust at the chained door and sent it reeling inward. Millie the receptionist had just grabbed the phone when Scalia fired a silent volley through her head, blowing her backward.

His primary target was on the third floor. Scalia took the carpeted steps quickly, soundlessly.

Janie heard something downstairs. Immediately, she felt unsettled, but she pushed aside the knobs of fear forming in her stomach. She picked up the phone and buzzed Millie. No answer. She buzzed twice more, then decided a call to the police was in order.

"Put it down."

The voice came from the doorway. Janie looked up to see a tall man in a dark overcoat standing before her, a small automatic rifle in his hands. A thick tubular extension projected from its barrel. A silencer, she realized. Oh God . . .

"What do you want?" she managed, knowing.

"Move away from the desk," Scalia told her.

She did as she was told, clinging to whatever hope she could muster.

Scalia switched the Ingram from automatic to semi.

Janie caught the motion, watched his eyes narrow,

and opened her mouth for a scream that never emerged.

The two bullets pounded her stomach. A pair of kicks to her belly, then hot raging pain spreading inside her. She felt herself crumbling but never felt the floor. The agony was everywhere, was everything.

Scalia watched her body twist and writhe, fingers clawing the floor, blood pooling underneath her. Then there was another silenced spit and her head rocked sideways, split open. Her eyes locked, dead.

"I told you to make it quick," Trench said with restrained anger, gun still pointed at Janie's head.

Scalia looked at the pistol smoking in Trench's hand and raised his Ingram enough to make sure Trench saw it.

"You're a butcher," Trench said. "I ought to kill you now."

Scalia raised the Ingram. "Go ahead."

Trench flirted briefly with chancing a shot. It would take only one but there was the hair-trigger Ingram to consider. Scalia could fire the whole clip with a simple touch even a head shot wouldn't preclude. So it was a stalemate and both of them knew it.

Trench backed away slowly, wordlessly, eyes speaking for him. He reached the stairs and started down, never shifting his gaze from Scalia, pistol tilted up. Scalia was out of sight by the second level but Trench was still leery, hoping for an attack now and disappointed when it hadn't come by the time he'd moved outside and walked away from the Center.

Despite it all, Bane held his calm.

His response was programmed, a reflex reaction.

He double-parked his car, dashing across the street with no regard for traffic. Horns honked. Brakes squealed. Tire rubber jammed against concrete, bumpers rammed each other.

He knew he was too late even before he found the door was open.

Bane saw Charlie first, a heap of bleeding flesh, head and shoulders held upright by the wall, eyes gazing down emptily at the unloaded gun he wouldn't have had time to draw anyway.

Bane turned toward the reception area but didn't go in. The blood-streaked walls informed him of Millie's fate. His eyes moved to the stairs, knowing what lay up there for him. It was lunch hour. Scalia would have had the Center's operating schedule and personnel duties down pat. Bane climbed the steps, his stomach fighting its way up his throat.

Janie's blood had reached the doorway to her office. She lay on her side, face twisted up, eyes still open and gazing at him accusingly.

It's your fault I'm dead. . . .

Bane leaned over and closed her eyes, though not to hide their accusation because he knew it was justified. This *was* his fault, all of it. She was dead because of him, because he had involved her and left her alone unprotected.

He made an instinctive mental note of her wounds and felt tears forming in his eyes. Two shots in the stomach would account for just about all the blood, the one to the head—different caliber maybe—had been the killing shot. The first two, by themselves, would have made her linger in agony indefinitely, her death inevitable but slow in coming. What kind of bastard would—

Bane cut off his thoughts because he already knew: Scalia.

He wanted to take Janie's head in his lap and cradle it but held back. He hated himself for not loving her fully or enough, an empty, bitter feeling spreading in the pit of his stomach. But it was rage that swelled with it more than grief, a rage he recognized from the murder of his father over twenty years before. Again the thirst for vengeance rose in him. People would pay now as they had paid then. He would make them pay.

For now, though, it was time to follow procedure. He was alone, yet he wasn't alone. He had the whole United States government on his side against the forces of one corporation. The problem all along had been how to convince them COBRA was up to no good. Now that problem was taken care of, three murders at the Center forming the proof he needed.

Bane retraced his steps, heading out of the building now, Browning drawn and ready in case Scalia had left someone in the vicinity. A phone was his first need, a clean line in a booth or box. He moved back outside and down the Center's steps, his eyes scanning about him. He held the Browning at hip level, just under the flap of his sports jacket to keep it from view; an old, established trick.

He found a pay phone close enough to a building to make him feel safe from that side. It was the box variety instead of a booth which was good because Bane planned on avoiding cramped, difficultly maneuvered spaces at all costs now.

The dime rang through and he pressed out a number locked in his mind from the past.

"Central dispatch," a voice droned.

"Bane. Disposals."

"Hold please."

Then another voice came on. "Disposals."

"This is Bane. The—"

"What is your designation?"

"Winter Man, dammit!"

A brief pause. "I'm sorry. I have no such designation. If—"

"Search under inactive," Bane broke in.

A longer pause. "I have you, Winter Man."

"Then stow the bullshit and listen to me. The Center's been hit."

"Level?"

"Three. All dead."

"Survivors?"

Bane figured rapidly and the bile bubbled against his stomach linings. "Five. Imminent return expected. You've got to act fast, and I want an immediate patch-through to Arthur Jorgenson, director of Clandestine Operations, designation—Hercules." He could trust Jorgenson, his former boss at DCO. Jorgenson would understand.

"Negative, Winter Man. Time limit on this line has elapsed. Surface again in thirty minutes and call Relays. Patch-through will be effected then. Jorgenson will be waiting. Clear?"

"Clear."

"Signing off."

Bane hung up the receiver, scanned the area more routinely. If Scalia had left someone to take him out, the attempt would have come during the phone call while he was reasonably distracted. Feeling safer, he started to move from the phone, swung swiftly back. Harry the Bat! COBRA was filling in the holes: Davey, the Center. They would know about Harry too. He'd be next on the list! Bane dialed the Bat's number and felt his heart thunder more with each ring. Five passed and still no Harry.

Come on! . . . Come on!

"You've got the Bat. I'm all ears."

"Thank God . . ."

"Josh? That you? What the hell's going on? What did the King want?"

"The boy's gone, Harry."

"Shit! They didn't . . . ice him?"

"No, just made him disappear."

"Well, at least—"

"Harry, they hit the Center."

"They *what*? Janie?"

Bane's silence answered for him.

"Lord fuck a duck, Josh," Harry moaned, "we got us some scores to settle on this one."

"I've got a call into Jorgenson. He'll bring us in. We can't—"

"Hold it, Josh," Harry whispered. "There's someone outside the door."

"Stay away from it, Harry. Scalia might still be lurking about."

"Scalia? No shit! Hold it, they're working on the knob now. Just hang on there, Winter Man."

Bane heard the receiver meet the wood of the Bat's coffee table.

"Harry? . . . Harry! . . . *Harry!*"

The blast was muffled by the phone line, still clear enough for Bane to figure it came from a twelve-gauge shotgun. Then silence.

"Harry! . . . Harry!"

No response. Bane felt frustration and helplessness claw at his spine. They had shot Harry. The poor guy was lying dead or close to it and all Bane could do was listen. He let the receiver drop from his fingers and bolted toward the street. Half a minute passed before a taxi answered his whistle, and he gave the driver the Bat's address along with a crisp twenty and instructions to make it fast.

The driver made it in eight minutes and Bane was

upstairs on Harry's floor in just over one more. He snapped the Browning from its holster and pressed his back tight against the wall, sidestepping quickly toward Harry's apartment.

Then he saw the door, what was left of it anyway. The shotgun had torn an irregular splotch big enough for a basketball to squeeze through from the wood. The still strong smell of sulphur and cordite burned his nostrils. Double-aught buck for sure. Trench maybe. Or Scalia.

He poked his head in through the hole and saw Harry's wheelchair lying on its side with the top wheel still spinning. Somewhere nearby, he reasoned, the Bat lay blown to pieces. Only there was no blood Bane could see, a fact that had just struck him as strange when the distinctive click of a pistol hammer froze him stiff.

"One move and I'll—Jesus Christ! It's you, Josh! Lord fuck a duck . . ."

Bane turned to the right and saw Harry propped up against the wall, magnum in hand and bleeding rather badly from the forehead.

"Sorry I can't get the door for you," Harry said.

Bane pushed his way in. "How bad, Harry?"

The Bat dabbed at his forehead and scalp with a handkerchief. "This? Nothing. Damn splinters got me more than anything else, 'cept maybe the fall."

"Splinters?"

"I got lucky, Josh. The killer must've fired when he caught my shadow under the door. Only he fired at where my head should've been instead of where it was. Lord fuck a duck, there are times when having your head only four feet off the floor is a plus."

"Apparently."

"He must've looked in just long enough to see me sprawled against the wall and figured I'd bought it.

235

He wouldn't have wanted to stick around too long under the circumstances."

"You see him?"

"Nah. I was out cold. Must have a hundred wood chips stuck in my head. I crawled over here soon as I came to. Knew you'd be coming. Figured if it was somebody else I'd be able to take them by surprise."

"You certainly did that," Bane said and helped the Bat back into his wheelchair. He wheeled him into the living room and swabbed his forehead and scalp with alcohol pulled from the medicine cabinet.

"Ouch! Be a lot easier if I just drank that stuff."

"Get me a tweezers and I'll get to work on the splinters."

"Fat chance, Josh. I'd rather chance the buckshot again." The Bat bit his lip. "Sorry about Janie. I spoke to her just a couple hours ago. She called to tell me that COBRA's Professor Metzencroy died of a heart attack last night. . . . Why her, Josh, why?"

"She knew . . . too much. I dragged her in."

The Bat's fingers clenched into fists. "You really figure it was Scalia who hit the Center and King's?"

"Along with Trench maybe," Bane nodded.

"Lord fuck a duck, if those two are working together, the worst is on its way."

"The worst ended at your door fifteen minutes ago, Harry. It's time to let the big boys bring us in."

"Jorgenson," the Bat muttered. "You trust him?"

"I don't have a choice. But he's always played clean with me and this whole mess is right up DCO's alley."

"Yeah, except you haven't seen the man in five years," the Bat moaned.

"Relax, Harry, I'll have Jorgenson order up a couple medals for us as soon as I reach him."

"To pin on our chests, Winter Man, or our coffins?"

Chapter Twenty-One

Five minutes later Bane called central dispatch from the Bat's apartment and was channeled immediately to Arthur Jorgenson.

"Josh," the DCO chief's voice began, sounding strangely familiar after all the years, "I'm on my way to the White House right now. I've got a pretty clear picture of what happened but not why."

"You send a removal team to the Center?"

"Just got their initial report. Three dead, just as you told central. We rerouted the rest of the personnel when they returned from lunch. Whoever was behind this had things timed perfectly. They knew the workings of the Center inside and out."

Right up Chilgers' alley, Bane thought. "Anything else?" he asked.

"I'm afraid not. It looks clean, Josh, strictly professional all the way. I'm just having trouble figuring why someone would hit a bureaucratic branch of the government."

"Bring me in and we can discuss it over dinner tonight."

"You read my mind, Josh, but it might turn into a late supper. Picking you up is going to take a while to set up and I don't want to take any chances. We've got to hit every angle. Choose a spot."

"Penn Station. I like crowds."

"So do I." Bane heard papers shuffling on the other end. "Now follow me closely, Josh. The Metroliner leaves New York for Washington from Track 10 at 4:45. We'll pick you up there."

"How many men?"

"Four's still the standard. Let's keep it at that to eliminate confusion. Should be strictly routine from here."

"How will I know them?"

"Newspapers under the arms too mundane?"

"Too easy to spot and too common at five o'clock in the afternoon, Arthur. Have your men dress in business suits with their shirt fronts out. White shirt fronts."

"I like it. Makes spotting them from a distance a bit easier for you."

"My point exactly."

Jorgenson sighed. "I'm almost at the White House, Josh. If you listen hard enough you'll be able to hear the wind ruffling the marines' dress uniforms. I need to give the President more than we've already got. Why was the Center hit, Josh?"

"The people behind it have a long reach, Arthur. This line may be untraceable but that doesn't mean somebody's not listening."

Jorgenson hesitated. "I understand. I'll cover for you with the White House until we bring you home."

"The President's been informed?"

"The Watergate age is long over. He's the first to learn everything now. You called the right people."

"I hope so."

"It's just past one-thirty. We'll talk as soon as my men pick you up at Penn Station."

"Shirt front out."

"Right. Stay on your toes, Josh."

"Count on it, Arthur."

There was no reason for Bane to arrive at Penn Station too early. In fact, doing that might prove the worst security measure possible because it would give the COBRA forces more time to spot him. A shootout between Jorgenson's men and Chilgers' was not what he had in mind. So he waited until four-fifteen to leave the Bat's, allowing an extra fifteen minutes for rush-hour traffic and not worried about Harry because he had the best camouflage possible: the opposition thought he was dead.

As it turned out, Bane's timing was perfect. He cut a sharp, direct route through Penn Station, relieved to be in the presence of thousands of commuters. It would be impossible to spot one face in the crowd, even his. He reached the entrance to Track 10 just as the red light flashed its boarding signal and a moderate throng of people began to descend a staircase into the bowels of Penn and the tracks that ran through them like intestines.

He quickened his pace slightly to join the crowd at its center, sneaking past the man checking the Metroliner tickets and already scanning for men with their shirt fronts out.

Two of them were mingling with the passengers at the bottom of the steps, businessmen in no particular rush to board the train after an extremely hectic day that had left them unkempt and not concerned about it, nor too eager to make a three-hour journey to Washington at speeds exceeding one hundred miles per hour. The men were good, nonchalant enough to make Bane wonder if perhaps he had chosen the wrong signal. How many other men about to board the Metroliner might have lost track of their shirt fronts as the day drew to a close? Bane stopped himself from considering the question further.

He noticed a third man with a freed shirt front conversing with the conductor. That still left one, probably behind him now guarding his rear. Jorgenson wouldn't have left anything to chance.

Bane passed the two DCO men at the bottom of the steps without exchanging so much as a glance. Contact was up to them at this point, everything routine. He was home free. Washington might not be able to find out precisely what Metzencroy had been up to, but they could certainly put a stop to it. Chilgers' operation, whatever it was, would be finished by tomorrow.

Bane neared the train. Still no contact from the DCO escorts. Should he risk boarding it? No. That would represent a deviation from the stated plan, at least an addition to it, and all DCO operatives worked within a narrow rule plan. Bane slowed his pace.

His eyes met those of a man standing by the entrance to one of the cars, saw a professional spark in them he recognized immediately. Surely this was the fourth operative, except he didn't have his shirt front out which made no sense unless he didn't want Bane to pick him out. The man looked away, his eyes darting back toward the two men standing at the bottom of the main stairway.

Bane sensed the message in them and swung at the instant the two operatives by the steps were drawing their guns. By the time their pistols were ready to fire, Bane's already had. Twice. The men were tossed backward, the bullets tearing half their chests away.

The shots sent panicked passengers scurrying everywhere. One woman darted across the path of the fourth man whose eyes had betrayed him. She took a bullet in the throat that otherwise would have found Bane. Confused, the man lost sight of his target at the same instant the last of the exposed shirt fronts ripped an Uzi machine pistol from under his coat and sprayed the area where Bane had been.

In fact, Bane was still there, but hugging the cement now, smelling hot tracks and the terrible stink of fear as the Uzi spit its fury and bodies fell writhing near him.

Bane's next bullet carved a neat hole in the butcher's forehead and roared from the back of his skull carrying fragments of brain with it.

The fourth team member had turned to flee by this time. Bane's bullet was off the mark, a bit low, hitting the hamstring area and pitching the man sideways, feet flying, down onto the tracks where a combination of live juice and an oncoming train finished Bane's job for him.

The screaming had intensified as he pushed himself to his feet. People trampled over each other as they rushed for the stairs, clawing at whatever their fingers could find. Others clung to the cement platform, frozen by fear, not even feeling the feet that stumbled over them.

Bane joined the chaos, forced himself to moan, to tremble, to waver. He pressed up against a hesitant group to better cover the holstering of his Browning, then joined the mad rush up the stairs past city and transit police, screaming with the crowd, pushing back when he was pushed. His calm had not deserted him, but he knew that nothing stands out more in a panicked crowd than one calm face. Bane forced fear onto his features, uncertainty.

And a measure of it at least was genuine. Either Jorgenson had betrayed him or the men he'd sent had been given a kill order by someone else. Bane didn't particularly like the prospects of either alternative. In both cases, escape from the city would now be a difficult task, more so because he wasn't sure he had anywhere safe to go.

Penn Station felt hot and steamy to him, not unlike the bug-infested jungles he had spent ten years of his life in, and suddenly he felt at home. They were on his turf now, and he welcomed any attempt at taking him out. Just let them try. Bane fingered the two spare clips within his jacket. It had all come back to him, not just the rage but the sharp senses and ice-cold thinking that fueled his desire. Word of the shootings had preceded him up the stairs and an already hectic Penn Station was now heading toward utter chaos. Only the track announcer's booming voice coming from a booth well removed from the violence and terror remained as a calm and routine counterpoint. Everything else was bedlam.

Bane steered clear of it, down a less congested corridor and past a natural-snack booth, starting to relax.

A tall man sprang out in his path, gun leveled.

Bane knew it was Scalia, had barely touched his own pistol when the shot came, just a spit to the ear, and it was over just like that. I'm dead, he thought, looking up one last time at his killer.

Crimson painted Scalia's face red, running from a hole in his forehead. The killer wavered, a drunk devoid of balance, and then dropped facedown to the Penn Station floor.

A hand grasped Bane's shoulder. He turned and found himself staring into the liquid gray eyes of Trench, silenced pistol still smoking by his side.

"Let's get out of here," Trench whispered.

Chapter Twenty-Two

"My car is just around the corner, Winter Man," Trench told him when they had made it outside.

"You saved my life," Bane managed lamely, not fully believing this was the same man who had killed Jake Del Gennio and who had wanted to kill Davey.

"We're even. You spared mine in the hotel room two nights ago."

They had reached Trench's car, a maroon Cutlass. Seconds later they were in traffic, both breathing easier.

"Who were the men at the station working for?" Bane asked.

"Chilgers."

"COBRA . . ."

"Chilgers is COBRA, Winter Man. One does not exist without the other."

"Then Scalia was working for him too."

"As well as myself. Until today, that is."

"You changed sides."

"I don't keep sides, Winter Man. I work for who pays me until they reach their limit or I reach mine."

"Which is it in this case?"

"Both. Chilgers has gone too far. He must be stopped."

"And who's paying you to do it?"

243

Trench tensed as two taxis pulled up on either side of him. They sped away as soon as the traffic light turned green. "I'm working for myself on this one, Winter Man. If I don't get Chilgers, he's sure to get me now that I've disrupted his plans. It's a question of survival."

Bane's eyes grew cold. "What was it a question of when you paid a visit to Jake Del Gennio?"

Trench looked over briefly. "I had no choice. You should understand that better than anyone."

Bane shook his head. "I've been through with this kind of life for a long time now," he said trying to mean it. Hadn't his return to the Game cost Janie her life? Weren't Nadine and Peter dead now because he had made a similar return five years ago?

"Yes," Trench responded, "because the damned Americans decided you couldn't hack it anymore."

That brought Bane's eyebrows up. Trench's phrasing had just eliminated America as one possible point of his origin. Bane had always been curious about the killer's roots. This was hardly the time to probe further, though.

"I made that decision on my own," he said instead.

"And now circumstances have forced you back into the Game, the same circumstances which have forced me to become independent."

"COBRA and Chilgers . . ."

"The important thing now is that they must be stopped. It won't be easy. Of all the men I've worked for over the years, I consider Chilgers to be the most dangerous, the most ruthless. He's not about to let anything stand in his way."

"You seem to know an awful lot about him, Trench, including no doubt what he's been working on."

"Not necessarily. I was a soldier to him, called in

244

only when a soldier's duty was required. I never concerned myself with the scientific aspects of what was going on around me. But there were bits and pieces concerning Vortex I couldn't help picking up."

"Vortex?"

Trench turned another corner. "The operation which cost your friend Del Gennio his life, Winter Man. It's centered around making objects disappear and then appear again. Other than that, I'm afraid I know nothing."

"But you've finally confirmed that Flight 22 really did disappear. Jake was right."

"But there were complications, beginning with engine trouble, that threw the timing of the experiment off. And then that boy escaped and gradually revealed the newfound powers he'd acquired on his ride on that plane. At that point, it became a soldier's problem. After Del Gennio, I was assigned to bring the boy in."

"But you elected to try to kill him instead."

"An independent action on my part," Trench explained. "My parting with Chilgers was already inevitable and I couldn't tolerate him controlling the kind of power the boy possessed. Besides, I had no intention of allowing the boy to use his abilities on me. I know my limitations, Winter Man, and whatever this boy has well exceeds them. Killing him was the only alternative."

"Except now Chilgers has him, thanks to Scalia."

"All the more reason for us to work fast. Chilgers will be after us both when he learns of his failure at Penn Station. Together, we might just prove a match for his army, though it might not be a bad idea for you to contact your old friends again."

Bane frowned. "Only I have no idea who I can trust anymore, Arthur Jorgenson included."

"Jorgenson had nothing to do with what happened this afternoon."

"But one way or another, those were his people who tried to take me out. And by your own admission, Trench, you were never aware of everything afoot at COBRA. Jorgenson, the entire government even, could have been in on this from the beginning."

The car became stuck in traffic. Trench tensed again. Horns blared maddeningly around him.

"No," he insisted, "Chilgers planned to activate Vortex without government knowledge. He has controlled this operation on his own. For twenty years, he has personally supervised Professor Metzencroy's work."

"Metzencroy's dead."

Trench's eyebrows fluttered briefly. "I'm not surprised. Chilgers' displeasure with Metzencroy's attitude had become obvious of late. And with Chilgers, displeasure often leads to elimination."

"You're saying he had Metzencroy killed."

"Almost certainly." Trench hesitated, squeezed the wheel tighter. "There's something else you should know, Winter Man."

"I'm listening."

"In Berlin, five years ago, my target was supposed to be you."

"I know. Someone else went in my place."

"You don't understand. I was hired by . . . certain elements of your government to do the job."

"*What?*"

"After all these years, I thought you would have suspected."

The shock hit Bane like a kick in the stomach. "Who?" he asked bitterly. "Who gave the order, Trench?"

246

"Such men have no faces, Winter Man. Someone high up wanted you killed or neutralized, taken out of the Game. You insisted on returning to the field. The risk of that was too great. You knew too much if captured."

"Jorgenson," Bane muttered.

"No. It would be someone considerably higher in the government, beyond Jorgenson's level, buried too deep, perhaps, after all these years to uncover. But there's always a chance. Perhaps Jorgenson can even help you. He can still be trusted more than the others. All the more reason to see him," Trench said in an almost fatherly tone, and the difference in age between them made it acceptable.

"How have you done it?" Bane asked him. "How have you stayed in the field so long?"

Trench started to chuckle but gave way to a sigh. "I never align myself with countries or causes. Politics are good for nothing but developing a conscience, and a conscience in our business is an ill-afforded burden. You were the best, Winter Man, but you let it get to you. You played for only one side because you genuinely cared and eventually that ate you up. East, West; Communism, democracy—they're all the same. See them all or don't bother to see any. Either way, morality for me never enters in. As soon as it does, emotion takes over. You hesitate, doubt, think too much. Times don't change, only politics do. Eliminate politics and you become ageless. The demand for our kind of work is always present if one does not choose his employers on conscience."

"Was it conscience that made you save my life back at Penn Station?"

"Perhaps. Or maybe it was the same thing that stopped you from killing me in the hotel room. We provide each other with scale. Each of us justifies the

247

other's existence. We're different yet the same, both anachronisms who've lived far beyond our allotted time. We're the best but the best craves competition, rivalry."

"We're not rivals anymore."

"You have a place to regroup, of course."

Bane nodded. "The best kind. A dead man lives there."

"There's one problem," Bane said when they reached the Bat's apartment building. "The man putting us up is the man you made a cripple in Berlin."

"Harry Bannister?"

"That's right. Someone tried to take him out today but the job was botched. The shooter didn't know the Bat lived out of a wheelchair."

"He's not still in the field, is he?"

"No, he's moved on to computers which means he might be able to help us learn more of what Vortex is all about."

Harry the Bat regarded Trench with vague recognition as he followed Bane into the apartment. Then his eyes bulged and his head snapped back against the wheelchair's rest. His hand grasped his magnum.

"Jesus Christ . . ."

Bane was upon him before he could get the gun from his lap, pinning his hand where it was. "Listen to me, Harry, he's on our side now."

"Yours maybe, not mine!" And the Bat's left hand was moving toward another of his pistols.

Bane pinned that one too. "He saved my life today, Harry."

"And fucked up mine five years ago. You expect me to forget that?"

"Not any more than I expect you to forget that Janie was killed today and Davey was kidnapped, and Trench can help us get the people behind it."

The Bat's eyes filled with tears. "That fuckin' son of a bitch killed my legs, Josh. I've got to nail him. You've got to let me nail the fucker!"

Bane kept the Bat's arms pinned. "Listen to me, Harry, and listen good. They tried to take me out at Penn Station today and they came damn close. I'm only alive now because this man put a bullet between Scalia's eyes. Do you hear me, Harry? He saved my life! That's what we're down to now, life and death. Real bullets and real bodies. The stakes are different and I don't plan on losing. The only people I care about right now are the ones who can help me stay alive and that makes you . . . and him . . . the only two. Don't force me to make a choice."

Bane felt a hand on his shoulder and then a gentle tugging as Trench pulled him away. "Leave him his guns, Winter Man, let him to do what he must."

Harry raised his magnum in a trembling, sweat-soaked hand and aimed at Trench's head.

The killer held his ground, looked down at him distantly.

The Bat cocked the magnum.

Trench kept looking.

The Bat dropped the pistol back onto his lap, covering his face with his hands.

"That fucker killed my legs," he moaned. *"My legs!"* And he slapped his thighs as if they were to blame.

Then Trench gave him his dignity. "I was wrong in the car, Winter Man," he said, holding his gaze on Harry. "There are still three of our kind left, not two."

Harry looked up, eyes sharper.

"I did what I had to do," Trench told him. "I will not offer insulting apologies. Instead, I'll only remind you that men like ourselves judge everything in the context of the moment. In the context of this one, we need each other."

"And when it's over, I'll put a bullet through your brain," Harry said with grim coldness.

Trench smiled, apparently satisfied. "It will not be so easy the next time. You've had your chance. Next time we start out even."

"Fine by me, you fucker," the Bat snapped.

"I believe we have arrived at a truce," Trench told Bane. "For now at least."

"Good," Bane retorted, "because we're going to need Harry's computer."

"I'm dead, remember?"

"I-Com-Tech has a service entrance and you're cleared for weekend and evening duty."

"What do you need?" the Bat asked, glad for the attention. His eyes never left Trench for more than a second.

"There's got to be some connection here we're missing. A link somewhere, a common denominator between Einstein and Metzencroy that will tell us precisely what COBRA's up to with Vortex."

"Vortex?" Harry quizzed.

"Project name for the operation Jake Del Gennio led us into. Meanwhile, I think a call to Arthur Jorgenson is in order. It's time to go home."

Jorgenson was on the other end of the line two minutes later. "Josh, where are you?"

"Do you really expect me to tell you?"

"Not if you don't want to."

"It's been a long time, Art."

"Should've been less, Josh. I'm sorry for what happened at Penn Station."

"You were almost apologizing to my corpse."

"It won't happen again, you have my word. I'll handle things personally next time."

"How do you know there'll be a next time?"

"Because we've known each other too long for there not to be."

"We never knew each other."

"Don't go philosophical on me, Josh. We're running out of time. I've got to know what you've uncovered."

"One hell of a mess."

"I know. Just name your terms for coming in and I'll meet them."

"You, Art, I want you face-to-face."

"I already offered. Name the place and time and I'm yours."

"The Washington Bullets have a game at the Capital Center in Landover tomorrow night. I'll leave a ticket for you at the box office, a couple for your bodyguards as well near our section. If they try anything, they'll be dead before they finish. You know that, Art."

"Yes, I know."

"You'll also be interested to learn that I'm working with Trench now and we've developed a mutual insurance policy. If I don't walk out of the Capital Center tomorrow night, my newest friend will take you out."

"Can't we meet sooner?"

"It's been a long day, Art, lots of people dropping dead all around me. I need to collapse for a while and tomorrow I don't plan on taking a direct route to the capital."

"Nobody wants you to make it safely here more than I do, Josh."

"Let's hope so."

Chapter Twenty-Three

"Bane just called in," Jorgenson reported, closing the Oval Office door behind him and moving to his chair.

"Did you trace the call?" the President wondered.

Jorgenson shook his head. "Couldn't. He routed it through a sterile emergency exchange again."

"Damn! . . . What the hell happened up there, Art?"

"It's just as I expected when the initial reports arrived. Bane killed the four men I sent to bring him in because they tried to take him out."

"*Your* men?"

"Strictly speaking, they're not mine. DCO, CIA, NSA, DIA—none of us are permitted to run domestic operations but sometimes necessity forces our hand. Like this afternoon. On those rare occasions, we choose agents from a free-lance pool. Getting a DCO team together and briefed and on their way would have taken an extra five hours or so and we couldn't spare the time, which left us with the pool. I never even met the men assigned to bring Bane in."

"You making excuses, Art?"

"Just explanations; for Bane, not myself."

"What does he want now?"

"A little more insurance that we're not the ones who are out to kill him. Specifically, he wants me."

"You?"

Jorgenson nodded. "He's set up a meeting for tomorrow night on his own terms. He worked under me for seven years after Nam, so I guess he figures I'm still his best bet."

"He gave you no idea of what he's latched on to, I assume."

"None whatsoever. Bane doesn't trust phone lines, no matter how sterile they're supposed to be. The only thing we can safely conclude is that the forces behind the hit on the Center have access to the same free-lance agent pool we do and rearranged things a bit this afternoon."

"Only a government branch or department would have that kind of access," the President pointed out.

Jorgenson looked at him grimly.

"You're saying someone in Washington wants Bane dead."

"At least someone with powerful connections in Washington. The question is who? And why?"

"There's another possibility," began George Brandenberg from his chair. "Bane could be behind all of this himself."

"That's ridiculous!" charged Jorgenson.

"Is it?" the secretary of defense challenged. "Consider first that we have no evidence that the Center was actually on to something, no evidence at all, other than Bane's unsubstantiated word in the wake of the massacre."

"That's good enough for me."

"I don't see how it could be. I've been going over Bane's file for the past two hours. His personality was listed as unstable five years ago and his psychological profile lists the possibility of 'neurotic or manic behavior' in addition to 'repressed violent tendencies.'"

"There was never anything 'repressed' about his

253

violent tendencies," Jorgenson noted.

"Not until he withdrew from the field perhaps. What about after?"

"What are you getting at?"

"That Bane might have taken out his escorts without provocation. That we might be dealing here with a homicidal maniac."

"I suppose you'd also like to suggest he was behind the Center hit as well."

Brandenberg raised his eyebrows. "You said it, Art, I didn't."

"Bullshit!"

"I'm not so sure."

"You'll need more to support such a conclusion than you've put forth, George," cut in the President.

"And I believe I have it. I've analyzed hundreds of these psychological profiles over the years and it's not hard to see from Bane's what we have here is a power keg waiting for its fuse to be lit, for something to set it off. *Anything*, perhaps. We've seen what the sudden and total loss of combat can do to a man like Bane over the long term. The effect comes slowly, building up over time. Then one day he cracks."

"He didn't crack," Jorgenson argued.

"We don't know that, do we? We're talking about a man who, in essence, developed a second personality he used for killing, a persona partially separate from his own. I ask you now who is loose in New York, Joshua Bane or the Winter Man?"

"They're the same person, George."

"Don't be naïve, Arthur. For more than ten years Bane's only job was to kill. Period. He did it better than anyone else we ever had, and he also did it longer. Most men like Bane run out of luck long before they find a different line of work. They're not expected to live past thirty, not by any of the rules of the Game. Bane should have died in Vietnam. Our mistake was bringing him home in the first place."

"My God," Jorgenson hissed, "listen to what you're saying."

"Just consider the kind of values he would have had to develop to play the Game successfully for as long as he did. Consider in a general sense the kind of man he would have had to become. Now what happens to that man when Bane quits? Does he simply fade away and disappear? Or does he live under the surface waiting for his chance to rise up again?"

"As long as you're talking about Bane's past," Jorgenson countered, "you'd better keep in mind that he might be the greatest soldier America has ever had. Oh, there were plenty through the years who could have matched or exceeded him physically. Bane's edge was in his mind, wholly psychological. He understood what he had to do and he may have enjoyed it because that was the only way he could keep going. But if he was going to crack, the split would have been obvious a long time ago. Bane survived the Game as long as he did because of mental, not physical, strength. Clandestine Operations puts me near hundreds of *men*, not just files— men like Bane—and psychologically he's the toughest of any I've ever dealt with."

"This bickering isn't about to get us anywhere," the President interjected firmly. "There's a point here you both seem to be missing: an installation of *this government* was butchered today, and quite possibly another installation was behind it. Three people who drew treasury paychecks are dead and I can't buy madness as the motivation. And the implications of the episode at Penn Station have got me scared as hell. Whoever was behind it must want

255

Bane out of the way pretty badly, which makes it imperative for us to find out why, if we're ever going to get to the bottom of all this."

"That means bringing Bane in," concluded Jorgenson.

"At a level of risk I find unacceptable," argued Brandenberg. "We're talking about Arthur's safety here."

Jorgenson was unmoved. "That's a chance I'm willing to take."

Davey Phelps woke up cold, yet in a sweat. Everything was dark around him and he was conscious of motion. But when he tried to move his arms, he found the way blocked in all directions. His feet probed about and found similar walls, then Davey had the sensation of being trapped in a coffin en route to burial.

His mind slowly sharpened and he guessed his eyes did as well, though there was no way to tell in the blackness. Blackness . . . That was how it had started. He remembered being in the back room of King Cong's place with two guards. He was fiddling with the radio in the corner when all the lights went out. One of the guards told him not to move, but then The Vibes went crazy, telling him someone cold and evil had entered the room. He pushed for The Chill but without the use of his eyes he had no way to aim it. Davey heard two soft spits and then a blindingly bright light flashed in his eyes, taking his mind from The Chill for a second. A second must have been all it took for the tall figure he'd glimpsed to shoot a dart into his arm and strip his consciousness away.

And now he was here. It didn't matter where because the sense of motion told him he was on his way somewhere else. He could have been traveling by plane, train, car—anything. It didn't matter. Escape was the issue now.

Davey cleared his mind, fought to relax. He grabbed his cool in the blackness and took a series of deep breaths, focusing his mind on the dead-smelling box they had put him in. He saw it hinged, locked, chained. He saw himself breaking out of it.

Davey reached for The Chill.

The box creaked.

Davey pushed harder.

Metal stretched outside, scraping against wood.

Davey felt the sledgehammer switch on in his head.

The chains were beginning to give. Davey reached back for everything he had, tried to pull the locks apart.

The box trembled and he sensed it was almost ready to burst apart at the joints. He squeezed his eyes closed, fighting back the awful pain racking his head, and pushed for all The Chill could give him.

The box was really shaking now, rubbing against the floor and rattling the chains. Then there was a bright flash before his eyes and it all stopped. Davey felt nauseous. The agony in his head came and went like the ticking of a clock.

He took another series of deep breaths, trying to steady his stomach against the horrible outcome of puking in his miniature prison. He tried not to think about it. He was getting colder now, and he tightened his arms across his body, wrapped them round himself and wondered where his leather jacket was. The inside of the box was dank, and he caught the faint odor of the sweat The Chill had brought to his flesh. Finally he relaxed.

He tried for The Vibes hoping they could tell him where he was, where he was going. But he couldn't find them, so he squeezed himself tighter and turned his thoughts toward Josh. Josh had saved him once. He wouldn't let him down now.

Davey wondered if he made The Chill hard enough, pushed for it super hard, whether maybe he could grab Josh's mind and tell him where he was. Except even if he could, he wouldn't know what to say. He was in a box heading . . . somewhere. That was all. And just thinking about The Chill brought the pounding back to his head.

He tried for The Vibes again but only flashes of the ones he'd felt before came—some the horrible ones that had made him tell Josh something awful was coming. Again he saw destruction, death, darkness. Everything had been blown away. There were craters instead of buildings and flesh pools where people had been standing. The whole world seemed hot, smoldering, steam-baked.

Davey wanted to sleep but couldn't. He found himself rubbing a sore spot on his right arm, where he figured the dart had jabbed home. The drug it carried had worn off, and now he was doomed to spend the rest of the journey awake.

Josh . . . Come and save me, Josh! . . .

Davey knew Bane couldn't hear the words, but saying them in his head made him feel better and took his mind off the black box which enclosed him.

I know you'll come, Josh. I know you will. . . .

The Sixth Day:

ISOLATION

He's gotten so lost
He's been double-crossed
By a change in the wind.
He's gone solo again
And he can't slow down now
To pick up a friend.

—Dan Fogelberg

Chapter Twenty-Four

The second showing in twelve hours of *The Road Warrior* was just about over in the meeting room of Bunker 17. Since the installation's two shifts seldom corresponded with traditional "daylight" time, one showing had been held at midnight and the second began at noon Saturday.

Maj. Christian Teare had watched them both.

"Now that, Cap," he told Heath who was sitting next to him as the credits rolled by, "was a real movie. Wish like hell we could get more like it. Enough blood and guts for ya?"

"Plenty."

"Hey, Cap, you ever think much about what it would be like if it all came true like in the movie? You know, the world's over and all that's left are scattered pockets of people who might be better off as fertilizer for a garden somewhere."

"I try not to, Major."

"So do I but sometimes you rightly can't help it." Teare tugged at his bushy beard. "And you know what gets my gourd the most? A couple things really. First, that we're the ones who'll be right in the middle of a shootin' war and second that, well"—Teare groped for words—". . . that more'n likely we're gonna watch the world end seventy feet under all the shit that's goin' down. Give me a machine gun and a belt with a million rounds and I'd be an awful lot happier." Teare paused and Heath hoped he was finished. He wasn't. "Hey, Cap, you ever think 'bout how the final big one'll start?"

Heath had started to answer when all the lights in the compound switched to yellow, signaling a rise to the second highest level of alert status.

"What the fuck? . . ."

"A drill, Major?" Heath asked hopefully.

"Not on my authorization it ain't. Who's duty officer on the con?"

Heath consulted his ever-present clipboard. "Parkinson."

They were in the corridor now, moving fast.

"Old Willie B.?" Teare exclaimed. "Shit, that dumb fuck probably misread the code. I'll have his ass for this, Cap. You don't fuck with the dynamite we're packin' here."

Teare and Heath hurried through the circular corridors that would continue to be bathed in yellow light for the next two minutes, after which only status boards located in all Bunker 17 rooms would maintain the color. Around them, installation personnel scurried to their Yellow Flag positions, all somehow conscious that this wasn't a standard drill. It was quite unlikely that a Red Flag alert would come unless Yellow was triggered first and now that unthinkable progression had begun, breaking the malaise and routine of the base.

"This better be good," Teare told Heath.

"As long as it's not real," the captain muttered in return.

Command Central was located halfway across the installation from the Disco for security reasons. Once the launch sequence began, the missiles could either be fired or aborted from here in the event that the Disco was hit and the computers channeled the switch in time. Teare stuck his ID into the Com-center slot, waited for the green light code, then pulled it out. The door slid open.

Command Central was far more mundane in appearance than its name indicated. Besides a series of computer lights and gauges coating the walls monitoring every function of the installation, the only piece of equipment of note was a single ordinary console right in the center. The console was connected on-line to NORAD headquarters, and in the event of an emergency the only orders to be regarded were the ones that came over it. A joint numerical-alphabetical sequence flashed across the screen every fifteen minutes, usually decoding into something akin to maintenance of standard proce-dure.

Willie B. Parkinson sat behind the console punching in his third confirmation request code. Parkinson's con duty had forced him to miss both showings of *The Road Warrior* but he had quickly forgotten his disappointment when the latest se-quence had been decoded.

"It's Yellow Flag for sure, Major," he told Teare as the major crept behind him to check the board. "I don't believe it but it is."

"What you believe, Willie B., don't mean shit here. Let me double-check."

Parkinson shrugged and gave up his seat to Teare, whose rapid check confirmed Parkinson's original reading.

"Jesus H. Christ . . . It's Yellow Flag all right, Cap. Somethin' must really be cookin' up top."

The SAFE Interceptor, a device no bigger than a shoe box hidden within the Com-center console, was

263

now in control of the base.

"It could be a drill," Heath groped.

"Not without informin' the base commander first, it ain't. Such things just ain't done."

"Then what are we facing here?"

"Well Cap, in the *en*-tire history of NORAD and its predecessors, a genuine Yellow Flag has only occurred three times. The first was the Cuban Missile Crisis, the second was back in nineteen seventy-two when someone in the Mideast farted and Nixon smelled shit, and the third was in nineteen seventy-nine when somebody in Washington inserted the wrong message tape and damn near started World War III."

"I guess this makes four," Heath lamented.

Christian Teare frowned, looking more like a hairy bear than usual. "Somethin' don't smell right to me." Then, "Let's head down to the Disco and see how things are shakin'."

"We're still a long way from the launch order, right, Major?" Heath asked as their pace picked up to a trot.

"Need Red Flag for that, Cap, and now that can only be triggered through the SAFE system. We can get confirmation a million times but if those red lights start flashin', there ain't no way in hell we can shut them off. That means we got our launch order. Direct to Command Central through the Interceptor. In effect, Cap, they shut me out like a screen does flies. I can't even issue an override order."

Heath nodded knowingly. "That sucks."

"Yeah, well flies eat shit when they can't get in for dinner."

Captain Heath nodded as though he understood.

They had reached the Disco, and Teare repeated the access procedure that had gained him entry just forty-eight hours before. Inside, things were proceeding smoothly. A yellow alert was more psychological than anything else. The whole concept of a missile base was that it maintained a constant state of readiness. Yellow Flag honed this to a sharp edge to ensure that all systems were constantly being checked and updated and all personnel were on call.

Nonetheless, the tension in the Disco was thick and Teare could feel it as plainly as the beard on his face. The men and the one woman inside knew this wasn't a drill and were going about their duties with extra precision and sweaty brows instead of light smiles, in the backs of their minds the awareness that any second could bring the Red Flag order and the missiles would be on their way. Worse, with Yellow Flag procedures underway, the base was now sealed off. There would be no entries or exits and it would take an entire armored division to crack ground level security. The people of Bunker 17, in other words, had been totally shut off from the world beyond. What hurt the most was that they all knew something must have happened above them and they quite possibly would die here without ever knowing what. It was a helpless sort of feeling there was no way to prepare for in practice drills.

Teare scanned the Disco and noticed the king for the day was a man he had only moderate faith in. The major checked his watch. Just twenty minutes more until this shift expired and the man would be replaced, Teare hoped by Kate Tullman. Woman or not, she was the best Bunker 17 had. Teare found her in front of one of the six tangent monitoring consoles.

"Kate T.," he said, stepping up behind her. "What's the T stand for?"

"Trouble," Kate Tullman replied, cracking a

slight smile.

"How'd you like to be Disco queen until further notice? Could you handle two staggered nine-hour shifts?"

"Just keep the coffee coming, Major, and I'll do fine."

"That's what I wanted to hear," Teare said and he moved back toward Heath.

"I still don't get it, Cap. Somethin' ain't right here."

"All routine as far as I can see."

"I mean with Yellow Flag comin' out of nowhere."

"Isn't that where you would expect it to come from?"

"Maybe. I guess I never figured we'd ever face a real shootin' war."

"Who says we are? It's only Yellow Flag now. Somebody in the Mideast might have farted again."

"Not with this president. He don't screw around."

"All the same, Major, if a shooting war ever did happen, don't you think this is just the scenario it would start with?"

Teare tugged at the knots in his beard, unconvinced. "Then why didn't they program us to Red Flag right away?"

Heath thought for a moment. "Preparation, psychological and otherwise like the book says."

"I don't give a shit about the book. In a shootin' war there wouldn't be time for all that crap. Unless . . ."

Heath felt suddenly queasy. "Major, you're not suggesting—"

"A first strike, Cap. Maybe that's what they're gettin' us ready for. Somethin' none of our drills really take much note of."

"But Bunker 17 is defensive in nature."

"There ain't much defensive 'bout thirty-six MX missiles totin' ten warheads each."

Heath shrugged.

"All systems got flaws, Cap. A smart man can figure how to scratch his ass even in a strait jacket. You know what the most popular movie in the whole NORAD system is, Cap? *Dr. Strangelove*, where one man goes crazy and destroys the world."

"The system's been built to prevent that, Major."

"Flaws, Cap, flaws." Teare nodded to himself. "I'm not about to disregard orders, Cap, and if we get to Red Flag I'll plant my ass on the button if that's what it takes to launch. I just wanna be sure we ain't gettin' sideswindled here."

"How?"

"To begin with, I want you to rig me somethin' through the main feed lines that'll let me spend some time monitorin' civilian broadcasts to see if there's somethin' goin' on up top we should know about."

"That's against the rules, Major."

"Rules ain't gonna mean shit, Cap, when farm dirt in Pawtawnee County, Georgia, catches fire."

Heath shrugged. "Let's hope there's nothing unusual on the civilian bands then."

"In which case, Cap, I'd be obliged if somebody told me what the hell we're doin' at Yellow Flag."

Chapter Twenty-Five

Arthur Jorgenson sat impatiently, high in the upper level of Landover, Maryland's Capital Center. Below on the court, the New York Knicks were soundly trouncing the Washington Bullets in a game that held no interest for the chief of Clandestine Operations. He had picked up the ticket Bane had left for him and found his seat well before the game got underway. He had expected something closer to courtside with more people in the area. As it was, he and Bane had virtually the whole section to themselves which, now that he thought about it, would be exactly what the Winter Man wanted.

Jorgenson was a nonpartisan department head who handled projects beyond the scope of the traditional intelligence community. Clandestine Operations was composed of soldiers mostly, field men whose assignments were aimed at tilting the balance of power toward the U.S. or at the very least maintaining it where it was. Sabotage, espionage, assassination, terror tactics—all were known to the men of DCO, while DCO was known to only a handful. It was the last organization to operate under a veil of secrecy, though its days there were severely numbered, which had made Jorgenson increasingly nervous well before this particular mess had begun.

He had been ready to retire five years ago but hadn't because no other man could run DCO at the standard he had created. The powers of the job defied conscience, and Jorgenson knew that power abused was power lost. He preached moderation at DCO, while he knew other men would use the organization's vast resources and blanket charter to meddle where they had no right to, and would create conditions of international strife where otherwise none would have existed. So he had stayed on at DCO and probably would until his death at which time he hoped the organization would be disbanded, having fulfilled its purpose.

"Enjoying the game, Art?"

Jorgenson turned to see Bane taking the seat beside him. He thrust an open bag toward him.

"Peanut, Art?"

Down on the court, half time was approaching.

"You're late."

Bane cracked a shell and popped its contents into his mouth. "Hardly. I've been here long enough to see you arrive. Just playing it safe. Besides, I saw nothing wrong in making you sweat a little. It's not so bad once you get used to it." Bane's voice tightened. "Like in New York yesterday."

"If anything that should show you how important it is that we work together."

"What do you know about COBRA, Art?"

Jorgenson felt a slight tremor of fear pass through him. "What do they have to do with this?"

"Everything. It was Colonel Chilgers who tried to have me taken out yesterday."

"Chilgers? Why?"

"Because I stumbled upon his prize operation. Because a friend of mine saw a 727 disappear thanks to his technological magic, and my friend ended up dead a few days later.''

"Josh, you've got to slow down," Jorgenson said anxiously. "None of this makes any sense to me." He pushed back the fear rising in him again. Somehow Project Placebo was connected here; he knew it was.

"Of course it doesn't make sense. One giant corporation with enough power to activate its operations without government sanction or even knowledge. Nope, no sense there."

"Josh, what are you talking about?"

"Vortex."

"Vortex?"

The buzzer sounded ending the first half down below. Bane and Jorgenson sat silent while the few fans seated in their section moved into the aisle toward the refreshment stands.

"You've never heard that term before?" Bane wondered.

"Not that I recall. What's it all about?"

"Something to do with making objects disappear and then reappear. My involvement began with a Flight 22 into Kennedy eight days ago. . . ." And Bane went on to tell him about Jake Del Gennio's vanishing 727 and the events of the subsequent days. Putting all the facts together at once made the story seem ludicrous. If he wasn't telling it himself, he never would have believed it.

Jorgenson's eyes were bulging as he finished. "That's incredible."

"There's more," Bane told him, "all centered around a fifteen-year-old boy who has apparently developed psychic powers as a result of Flight 22." And then he told Jorgenson about Davey Phelps, everything he knew right up to the point when Scalia nabbed him from King Cong.

"Oh my God," Jorgenson muttered. "It's out of

270

control. COBRA has this boy now?"

"His body would have been with the others otherwise, and if he'd escaped, he would have found me. He's in San Diego by now."

Jorgenson nodded. "Chilgers will see this power he's developed as a potential weapon to be uncovered and exploited. But you say not all the passengers were affected."

"The ones with no outward symptoms might have been in a neglible way or one that hasn't shown up yet, I'm not sure. The common denominator with the advanced cases like Davey is the mind. During the period that the jet dematerialized, the missing forty minutes, different parts of the brain went haywire causing depression, catatonia, madness, and in the boy's case telekinesis in the most advanced form I've ever heard of."

Jorgenson shook his head, ran his hands over his face. "You've got to believe me, Josh, this is the first I've heard of any of this. Chilgers has broken off, he's gone mad. Only that doesn't tell us what in hell he's discovered."

"We believe it has something to do with Einstein."

"Einstein?"

Bane nodded. "Metzencroy's background dictates that, as does the latest batch of scientists COBRA has retained."

"Metzencroy died last night."

"Chilgers had him killed."

"Good God . . . Why?"

"To begin with, Trench told me Chilgers was disenchanted with his behavior in recent days. Trench seems to think that Metzencroy was trying to make Chilgers abandon Vortex or postpone it. The professor must have discovered something and it all goes

271

back to Flight 22. Vortex, whatever it is, didn't work exactly as it was supposed to. I'm betting that Metzencroy found out why, so Chilgers snuffed him *and* what he uncovered. The colonel will go to any and all lengths to prevent his plans from being disrupted. He won't tolerate delays or any man who suggests them."

"You seem to have quite a handle on him."

"He's the enemy, Arthur. It's no different from Nam. You live or die by your knowledge of the enemy, intuitive and otherwise."

"Nam's a long way gone, Josh."

"Maybe not."

Jorgenson found himself unable to meet Bane's stare. "Let's go back to yesterday. You're saying Chilgers had the Center hit?"

Bane nodded painfully. "Everything was coming together for him. He had a line on the boy and Metzencroy was out of the way, meaning Vortex has to be all but ready for activation. Janie, Harry Bannister, and I were the last people who could hurt him but he only got one of us. I'm betting his plan all along was to take me out after I made contact with you, using Scalia as a backup. What's been bothering me about all this is the timing. Things have been happening too fast. Chilgers seems to be in a rush. There's got to be a factor here I'm not considering."

Jorgenson's mouth dropped. Gooseflesh prickled his skin.

"Art?"

The DCO chief stared vacantly ahead. "You can't consider it because you're not aware of it. Oh my God, I should have known, I shouldn't have let them agree to it." Fear swam in his voice and eyes. "Let me give you a brief scenario, Josh, and tell me the first thing that comes to your mind. Let us assume that

Chilgers has sold the President on something he calls Project Placebo, an experiment designed to monitor one missile installation's reaction to stress up to, during, and after launch."

"*After?*"

Jorgenson nodded slowly. "All similar previous tests have stopped at the crucial button pushing moment, potentially the most important period of all. But Chilgers has gotten around that. He's fitted a new shipment of MX missiles headed for a bunker with dummy warheads that will defuse as soon as they hit three thousand feet."

Bane's palms felt cold with sweat.

"What's the first thing that comes to your mind?" Jorgenson asked him.

"Flight 22. Like I said, everything comes back to it. Jake Del Gennio was vehement about the fact that the jet didn't just vanish from sight, it vanished from the radar screen as well."

"Precisely . . ."

"So if Chilgers can make a 727 disappear, he can do the same with those missiles. He'd be able to slip all thirty-six of them by our fail-safe and abort systems. They'd be on their way to Russia, the end result being a first strike on our part leading directly to World War III." Bane paused deliberately. "The only thing that doesn't fit into the scenario is Metzencroy. Everything's set and ready to go when, according to Trench, all of a sudden he uncovers something and gets cold feet."

"And then dies conveniently before he can pass the information on to anyone else. . . ."

"We—" Bane stopped when two men squeezed by on the way back to their seats. "We can be reasonably sure of a few things anyway. To begin with, Metzencroy has been working on Vortex probably for as long as COBRA's been paying his salary. It was under his guidance, then, that this whole operation was developed and activated. So whatever spooked him must've been something awfully big."

"Flight 22 again," Jorgenson concluded.

"As I said before, that's the indication."

Jorgenson thought briefly. "What it did to the people, perhaps. What exposure to the forces of Vortex did to their minds."

"Doubtful. People have nothing to do with launching MX missiles for Project Placebo. No, the people were just an offshoot, a tangent at best. It was something else."

"Any ideas?"

"None. But Metzencroy thought enough of it to throw away twenty years of work in addition to his life."

"It doesn't matter anyway, Josh, because I've got enough to take to the President and lay on the line for him."

"Will he listen?"

"He'll postpone Project Placebo which will give us the edge we need to turn the rest of Vortex up and deal with Chilgers." Jorgenson seemed to shiver. "Project Placebo went into its first stage this afternoon, Josh, and after tomorrow afternoon we could be looking World War III right in the eye."

"Why tomorrow?" Bane wondered.

"Because that's when the shipment of MX missiles, loaded with God knows what, are scheduled to arrive at Bunker 17." Jorgenson watched Bane's eyebrows flicker. "That of any interest to you?"

"Tell me more about Bunker 17."

Jorgenson did.

Down below the Bullets returned to the court, pro-

274

voking a chorus of boos in the sparsely populated arena.

"Hell of an arsenal," Bane commented when the DCO chief was finished.

"And that arsenal might be responsible for starting World War III."

Something nagged at Bane. "Except that would have been a potential, even expected, ramification of Vortex from the beginning," he noted. "Whatever Metzencroy uncovered must be worse."

"Worse than nuclear war?"

"He'd still be alive otherwise."

Jorgenson sat there blankly. "We've got to see the President now, Josh, immediately. I want him to hear all this firsthand from you."

"As a matter of fact I've got a few things on my mind I'd like to ask him about."

"You wouldn't mention them if you didn't want to talk."

Bane's stare went cold. "Who put the kill order out on me five years ago, Art?"

Jorgenson's mouth dropped. "What?"

"Don't play dumb with me."

"I swear, Josh, this is the first time I've heard of it."

"Then you deny it."

"I can't deny it any more than I can affirm it. Five years is a long time in government, Josh, a whole era. There were different people running things then."

"Different from you, I suppose."

"No better, no worse. You do what you have to."

Bane's eyes narrowed into somber slits of fury. "I want to know who put the kill order out, Art."

"It may be buried."

"Dig it up."

"If the information still exists, I'll find it. You

have my word on that."

Bane briefly swung his eyes around him. "You left your bodyguards in the lobby, Art. You took quite a chance."

Jorgenson swallowed hard. "They'd only have gotten in the way. I trust you, Josh, and besides, if you wanted to kill me badly enough, a hundred of them wouldn't have made a difference."

"True."

The DCO chief started to stand up. "Then let's go see the President, Josh. It's time to—"

Jorgenson's head snapped backward. He collapsed back into his chair.

"Art!" Bane screamed, grabbing him.

Jorgenson's head slumped to his chest, his eyes open and sightless. A neat hole the size of a nickel had been carved in his forehead. There was little blood but Jorgenson was dead, hit by a sniper's bullet.

Bane eased his hands away, found they were trembling slightly. The sniper might have his sights turned on him now. Keeping his body low, Bane moved into the aisle, slipping behind a pair of men descending toward the refreshment stands. He was covered now. The sniper, if he hadn't fled after killing Jorgenson, had no view of him. Bane ducked when he came to the archway, sped in front of the two men and rushed down the ramp toward the upper level concession stands, considering his next step. He could move toward the lobby, find Jorgenson's men, and tell them what had happened. But that would mean exposing himself unnecessarily. The sniper could be part of a larger team and in trying to find Jorgenson's men, he might end up being found himself. The risk was too great. Jorgenson was dead and the bodyguards weren't about to change it. Bane would have to make contact another way from

276

another place. He started for the stairs marked Exit, struck by a sudden surge of desperation.

The only man in Washington he could trust was dead. A man who had always been there when he needed him would be buried in two days' time because Bane had insisted on taking precautions which had proven unnecessary. He felt distinctly alone, and the feeling bothered him more than it ever had before. Jorgenson had supplied him with a number of the missing pieces to the Vortex puzzle but he still lacked enough to put it together.

Thirty-six missiles packing ten warheads each . . .

Something awful's gonna happen, Davey had said, and whatever it was would make World War III pale by comparison.

Bane found he was trembling as he stepped out of the arena into the night.

Chapter Twenty-Six

"Are you ready to begin, Doctor?"

"I was only waiting for you, Colonel," Teke said, rising from his desk chair. "Please come in."

Chilgers entered Teke's office. These had been in many ways two difficult days for the colonel. Things hadn't gone as planned, unsuspected factors having entered in. How could he know Trench would cross him? The bastard had, though, and Bane had remained alive because of it. A new strategy had been called for, and Chilgers had chosen one that would allow him to deal with two problems at once. Now Jorgenson was dead and Bane had disappeared. Chilgers felt better, able to look forward to tonight's experiment with a clear head. All other matters seemed trivial when measured against the potential of Davey Phelps. The time had come to test how far that potential stretched.

"Thank you, Doctor," Chilgers said and took a chair, feeling immediately uncomfortable within the steel walls and tile floors of Teke's sterile domain, missing the walnut paneling and thick carpet of his office.

"I'd better explain a few things first," Teke began, his bald head shimmering beneath the white fluorescent lighting. "Our initial scans of the boy's brain have found nothing unusual other than a bit of unconscious flux that reads higher than it should. This lack of findings is nothing to worry about, though, because the boy has just now begun to regain full consciousness. We've kept him sedated the entire time since he arrived here to avoid any harmful reactions before or during our preliminary testing. Precautions, you understand, against what we suspect the boy might be capable of."

"I understand."

"In any case, we are slowly bringing him around from the sedation for observation of his . . . abilities when in a conscious state."

"You have a means to control him in such a situation?"

Teke shrugged, bulky shoulders cramping his thick neck. "Not quite. I've got a few ideas but nothing I'm totally comfortable with. It's a catchy situation. We must allow the boy to be fully conscious before testing his powers. But if these powers are what we suspect them to be, we may be placing ourselves in a somewhat risky predicament. The boy's power seems to be greatest when he is threatened, which the incidents in New York more than testify to. Once he is allowed to fully awaken and realizes what's happened, I dare say we might be treated to a more thorough demonstration than we had planned on."

"There are ways around that surely."

"Yes," Teke acknowledged, "but all of them involve the direct use of some kind of sedative. No matter what the level, though, strong or mild, a sedative will undermine his powers and make it impossible for us to accurately test their level. What's more, including the time it took to deliver him, he has now been under to some degree for nearly forty hours. The possibility of permanent nerve *and* brain damage now begins to enter in."

"We can't have that," Chilgers said flatly.

"No, we can't. The problem then becomes how to control the boy once we withdraw the sedative and begin stage one."

"Ah, so you've already developed an agenda," Chilgers said satisfied, smoothing the corners of his suit jacket.

"You would have expected something different, Colonel?" Teke cracked a small smile which vanished quickly. "I've broken this particular operation into three stages: gauging the general extent of the boy's power, isolating its location in the brain— point of origin, that is—and finally learning what caused it, our goal being the eventual recreation of the effect in our own subjects."

"Splendid," Chilgers beamed genuinely. "Let's take them by the numbers."

Teke glanced at his notes. "Stage one is in many ways the easiest but similarly the most crucial. Our preliminary testing has already confirmed that whatever psychic powers the boy now possesses are directly related to his ability to generate an extremely strong energy concentration of alpha waves. The waves are channeled from his brain outward not unlike the way a television signal is beamed from satellite to living room or, even simpler, the way electricity moves from socket through cord to create live juice. In this instance, the 'juice' originates in the boy's head and is jettisoned outward in an amazingly high energy burst which can be measured with some modifications on our standard monitoring equipment."

"You have something specific to monitor, I assume."

Teke nodded. "Just as electricity has its limits, fuse overloads and such, the unstable energy at the core of the boy's power must as well. Across the hall in the laboratory, I have arranged for six eight-foot-square slabs of six-inch, lead-reenforced steel to be placed along with a similar number of extra-thick window panes. Simply stated, Colonel, we will gauge the boy's power by finding out precisely how much lead-steel it takes to negate his energy waves. It's my guess he uses only what he has to in a given situation and calls on vast reserves when the task proves greater, as your men witnessed in New York. Stage one will allow us to see how deep these reserves go and what energy levels the boy exerts in summoning them."

"Good," Chilgers nodded. "And stage two?"

"A bit more involved, I'm afraid. We cannot isolate the exact location of the boy's power until we've fully gauged it. And then to achieve complete accuracy, we *must* have a constant exertion and single focal point. Based on preliminary testing, this will entail utilizing a human subject."

"A human subject?"

Teke nodded again. "It is here where the boy's powers, his energy waves, are most focused and thus most easily traced to their precise point of origin in his brain. The exact procedures on our part will be almost identical to those of stage one, with a few mechanical variations, of course. The difference lies in making the boy change his target from inanimate matter to a living being who can resist his power."

"Target," echoed Chilgers.

"In stage two, we ask Davey Phelps to repeat for us the power he exerted on Trench's man in New York. That should give us the precise origin of his alpha waves. Of course, we'll have to come up with a way to have the subject threaten Davey. Otherwise, his energy resources will never become fully active."

Chilgers seemed unperturbed by the implications of what Teke was suggesting. "And then?"

"Stage three: we determine how to recreate the effect of the boy's alpha waves, how to medically implant other living beings with such an energy field. It might be as simple as magnetizing a microscopic portion of the brain or so complicated it is like putting a jigsaw puzzle together with only half the pieces."

"Which proves considerably easier when you know what the final picture is supposed to look like."

"But not where to find it necessarily," Teke explained. "Davey Phelps could be a one-in-a-billion shot. Remember, what we did to that jet affected only him in this way. It could take us years to determine precisely what sparked the surge of these alpha waves and the development of the boy's personal energy field."

"Something makes him different," Chilgers reflected. "Something sets him apart. Find it and you'll have your answer."

Teke hesitated. "That may mean stage four."

"You said there were only three."

"I held the fourth one back because it is to be used only as a last resort, a last chance because once we resign ourselves to it there can be nothing else after." Teke held the colonel's stare. "Stage four is the removal and subsequent microscopic dissection of the boy's brain to search for cellular irregularities and possible alterations."

"See that it doesn't come to that, Teke."

"I told you it would be used only as a last resort once we've exhausted all other options."

"We have plenty of time, Teke. Vortex will give us

all the time we need."

Teke checked his watch. "In that case, let me inform you that the boy is due to be given another sedative in fifteen minutes time which will necessitate a four-hour delay in the activation of stage one . . . unless we find a way to control him without needles."

"I think I have an idea," Chilgers said smiling.

Davey Phelps awoke slowly, realizing first that he wasn't in the bed where he had spent the last day and second that he wasn't even in the same room. His vision cleared and the smell of alcohol burned his nostrils. He was in a large white room filled with gadgets, gauges, machines, and the sound of computer tapes whirling in the cool air. He was turning behind him toward most of the noise when something tugged at his head.

"You'll find this much easier if you stay still," said a voice he couldn't place among the ones he was familiar with here, wherever he was.

Davey turned slowly to his right and faced the owner of the voice, a medium-sized gray-haired man wearing a three-piece suit. Then he realized for the first time there were others in the room, a dozen maybe, but they were all dressed in white lab coats. And Davey sensed there were even more manning the mindless machines behind him.

Consciousness snapped all the way back home, and he found his arms and head were covered with probes attached to wires running to the various machines, especially on his skull. There must have been fifty wires running in a crown from his forehead, down his temples to his chin, and then around back and up, finishing eventually at the machines to his rear.

"Please don't jar the wires," came another voice from beside him, one that Davey recognized.

He turned ever so cautiously to find the stocky, bald man who had spent so much time hovering over him in the room they had put him in. The nameless bald man stuck his hands in the pockets of his white lab coat.

"Ready whenever you are, Colonel," he said to the one in the three-piece suit who, Davey saw, was holding a small black box about the size of a transistor radio in his hand.

His mind cleared further and a picture of Joshua Bane filled it.

Help, Josh, help! . . .

"Power surge just registered," from a voice behind him.

"Vitals fluctuating," from another.

Davey watched the one called Colonel smile slightly and move his thumb just a bit. The boy then felt a jolt to his groin that nearly lifted him off the chair, as if someone was yanking him by the balls. His teeth smacked together and his breath left him in a rush. He felt his legs shaking and couldn't stop them; then he tasted blood and realized a few of his front teeth must have pierced his tongue. The horribly corrosive smell of burnt plastic reached his nostrils, and he noticed for the first time a pair of thick wires running from under his white hospital nightshirt. He shifted his unsteady legs just a bit, felt a slight pull in his groin, and knew then where the wires were attached.

"Pain is a great persuader, boy," said the man holding the box. "It provides control."

Davey narrowed his eyes at the one called Colonel, feeling that hate surge through him and spill over.

The man's face was still fixed in a slight smile, the black box an extension of his fingers. Well, Davey could show him.

He started to push for The Chill.

"All levels rising," a voice sounded.

"Extreme power surge registered," from another right after.

Chilgers' head for a brief instant felt as though someone had stuck it in a vise. He found the red button just in time.

Davey Phelps's body jerked spasmodically, his face turning purple. A trickle of urine ran down his leg.

Chilgers felt the pressure subside, steadied himself, waited for the boy to recover from the shock fully before speaking.

"We know about your abilities," the colonel said. "In point of fact, boy, that's why we brought you here." His right hand made a twisting motion. Davey flinched involuntarily, tightening his features. "Relax, boy, I'm not going to press the red button and I won't again unless you give me reason to. However, I have raised the shock level to three times that of what you just felt. As you've certainly figured out, we've attached the electrodes to an extremely sensitive area of your body. But you need feel no more pain. Cooperate with us, do as we say, and we will spare you further agony. Is that understood? Don't speak, just nod."

Davey did, glancing down at a white-jacketed figure wiping up the warm piss that had soaked his leg.

"What we are going to ask of you is quite simple," Chilgers continued, "and you have no good reason not to follow the instructions you are given." Chilgers held the black box out toward him. "This contains unspeakable agony that can drive you to hell

285

and back again in a single instant. I hold it in my hand now only as a reminder. Beside you stands Dr. Teke, a far more mellow sort than I, who is about to give you your instructions. If you do not do precisely as he says, I will be forced to use the box again, and each time I shall increase its potency threefold. Is that understood, boy?"

Davey nodded again.

"Good. Proceed if you will, Dr. Teke."

Davey felt a cold hand grasp his shoulder in a façade of warmth. The hand squeezed his flesh tenderly, sickening him, making him bite his lip to force The Chill down because he feared the horrible promised pain in his groin. The wires felt tighter around his balls and the cooling piss still soaked his leg. He'd do whatever they told him.

"Davey," the bald one said, fondling his shoulder. "I want you to listen carefully." He nodded at someone to his right. "I'm going to ask you to do something for me, quite simple really and it won't hurt. Understand?"

Davey nodded, watching two men wheel a huge slab of shiny steel six feet before him. Then something else was stationed behind it but Davey couldn't tell what.

"I'm going to ask you to use your power in a moment, Davey," Teke said, finally taking the terrible hand away, "but before I do I must warn you to focus it only as I instruct. Otherwise the colonel will be forced to use the black box again and I'm sure we don't want that, do we? You will limit the concentration of your power to the boundaries I give you. Understood?"

Davey nodded again.

"Good. Then let's begin." Teke backed up slightly, beyond Davey's peripheral vision. "Placed behind the steel slab is a window pane of very thick glass. I want you to destroy it. I want you to focus your power directly through the steel and shatter it."

Davey glanced quickly at him.

"Delays, boy, will prove costly," said the one called Colonel, sliding his index finger over the red button.

"The power, Davey, use the power," said Teke.

Davey looked at the steel slab and through it. The window pane locked onto his consciousness.

He tried to make The Chill.

Nothing happened.

His features tensed, eyes squinting. He tried harder.

Still nothing.

"I am growing impatient, boy," the colonel snapped and his index finger started to move.

Davey made The Chill, hard and sure. His spine quivered with the icy touch.

Behind the slab of steel, the window pane shattered in a sudden blast. Men in white coats lurched back, trying to avoid flying slivers. Davey noticed a number of others writing things down feverishly on clipboards.

"What was the level?" Teke asked.

"Seven-point-two," came the answer.

"My God," Teke muttered. "That's bare minimum." Then he moved toward Chilgers and started whispering. "The boy's power, as I speculated, is apparently most effective when he is threatened. You were going to jolt him again, yes?"

"My finger was on its way," the Colonel acknowledged.

"The boy sensed your intention. That's what brought the power out."

"Your conclusion?"

"That the boy's power originates at the subcon-

287

scious level. It was at this level he sensed your intentions and activated his alpha waves."

Davey felt a dull pounding in his head. He hoped the men were through with him but he knew they weren't.

"We're going to try it a second time, Davey," the bald one told him gently, "this time with two steel slabs. I will give you ten seconds to use the power. If after that period you haven't . . ." Teke turned his gaze toward Chilgers and the black box.

Davey watched the lab assistants slide a second steel slab behind the first, then another window pane was wheeled into place.

"Okay, Davey, shatter the glass again."

Davey concentrated hard. The Chill eluded him.

"Only five seconds left, boy," warned the colonel.

That was all he needed to hear. Davey made The Chill.

The glass shattered, breaking along lines identical with the first pane.

"Incredible," muttered Teke, as men in white coats feverishly recorded information on their clipboards again. "Levels?"

"Seven-point-five," came a voice from behind Davey.

"Good God! Barely no change at all."

"What's that mean?" Chilgers wondered.

"That we haven't even begun to tap into his power level yet. This is absolutely fantastic. The concentration of energy waves this boy is able to call upon defies belief. I've never seen anything like it."

The dull pounding had grown to a throb in Davey's head. A snake tightened around his neck muscles and his back seemed to lock out. The worst of the pain rotated from one temple to the other. He wanted to make them stop, tell them he couldn't go

288

on anymore. But when he opened his mouth, there were no words.

"Are you all right, Davey?" the bald doctor asked him softly.

Davey swallowed some air. "My head. It hurts."

"Just a little more. I promise, we'll be done in just a few minutes."

"Please . . ."

"Two more slabs this time," Teke instructed his assistants, and Davey found himself staring at a row of steel two-feet thick.

"Do you think you can manage it, Davey?"

"Later. Please, later."

"Now," came the colonel's resounding voice. "Now or you'll feel the fury of the box, boy." And his finger crept onto the red.

"No! . . ."

The two lab men were just easing the dolly holding the window pane into position when Davey made The Chill. The glass ruptured over them, digging into the exposed flesh of their arms and face, the larger slivers jabbing through their clothing. They dropped to the floor writhing in agony.

"I didn't mean it!" Davey screamed. "I didn't mean it!"

"I know, Davey, I know," comforted the bald doctor, patting him on the shoulder again. "Get those men to the infirmary on the double. You two, move up here and replace them." Then, to the monitors at Davey's rear, "What was the level of that one?"

"Eight flat."

"Effortless," muttered Teke. "What about the energy concentration ratio?"

Another of the technicians consulted his clipboard. "Ninety-two-five. Up from eighty-six flat."

Teke's eyes bulged. "There must be some mistake.

That's impossible."

"That's what the gauges read, Doctor."

"Why is it impossible, Teke?" Chilgers asked.

"Because on an energy scale equivalent, the power it should take to shatter these panes is comparable to that used by a jet plane to take off. But the amount of energy expended by the boy remains under ten—the amount it would take you or me to tie our shoes."

Chilgers smiled faintly. "Let's try it with all six slabs then, shall we?"

"No," Davey moaned.

"Rather feel the black box, boy?"

Davey tried to shake his head.

Teke moved back toward the boy. "Give me input on the vitals."

"Blood pressure up forty percent and climbing."

"Pulse rate up same."

"Blood pressure stabilizing, beginning to drop. . . ."

"It doesn't make sense," Teke said to himself. "Low energy expenditure and distinct rise in metabolic rates. Stress factor?" he called behind him.

"Settling down," a voice returned. "Needle has yet to enter the red."

"I want to know immediately if it does."

"Let's get on with it," Chilgers ordered.

"No, don't make me!" Davey pleaded. "I can't! . . ."

Teke thought briefly. "Colonel, it may be best to call it here until tomorrow."

"Concerned for the boy, Teke?"

"No, for the experiment. We've entered a new realm here. The figures aren't as I expected them to be. Too many inconsistencies. I need time to evaluate the data."

"Now you're talking like Metzencroy," Chilgers charged.

Teke noticed the boy was still trembling. "Colonel,

I must suggest we hold off on any further testing until tomorrow."

"We finish the experiment, Doctor, with or *without* you."

Teke leaned over toward Davey. "Just one more time and it'll be over."

"My head," the boy muttered. "Feels like it's coming apart. Don't make me. I can't."

But the two new lab assistants were already wheeling the final two slabs in place. Then the window pane was moved behind them.

"Just one more time," Teke assured.

"No," Davey moaned. *"I can't. . . ."*

"The clock's ticking," Chilgers snapped and Davey watched his finger crawl over the red button. "Ten seconds."

Davey tried for The Chill and his head seemed to split.

"I can't!"

"Five seconds."

"Levels rising, sir," a lab technician shouted to Teke. "Eight-four, eight-five, eight-six . . ."

"Four," said Chilgers, "three . . ."

"Stress needles into the red!"

"STOP! . . ."

"Two . . ." Chilgers' finger settled on the button.

"Energy concentration ratio one hundred, one-oh-one . . ."

"Power levels at eight-eight, eight-nine, nine-flat. Still climbing."

"NOOOOOOOOO!"

"Time's up," said Chilgers and he pressed the red button.

"Ahhhhhhhhhh . . ."

Davey's scream punctured the room. The window pane didn't shatter, it melted into nothing, just wasn't there anymore.

The gauges popped, cracked, glass shattering over needles suspended forever in the red. Smoke rose from the machines' backs. Red and green indicator bulbs exploded.,

"Sedate him! Sedate him!" Teke screamed and two lab technicians rushed forward only to be blown back as if struck by a hundred-knot gale. The syringe dropped by Davey's feet. Teke crawled for it.

Chilgers tried to work the red button but he too had been blown backward against a row of knobs and dials which struck his spine low and hard, tearing his breath away. He slid slowly down, a grimace stretched across his face.

Teke reached out for the needle.

The fluorescent ceiling lights blew out, the sound like machine-gun fire. They showered hot sharp glass down on the technicians who had dived for cover or been dropped as they stood.

Teke grasped the syringe in a trembling hand. He was queasy and unsure of motion. Glass and broken equipment had clogged the air vent, turning the lab into a steam bath with practically no oxygen. Teke started to raise the needle toward the boy's arm.

Davey just sat there, wires still running from his head but attached to nothing now. His eyes bulged, unblinking, though his stare remained vacant. He gazed ahead seeing nothing, unbothered by the destruction wreaked about him.

Teke touched the syringe to his arm.

Davey swung toward him. Their eyes met and Teke felt his skin scorch, starting to melt. He screamed horribly because of the terrible pounding of his own heart and jammed the needle home.

The boy's eyes dimmed and his head slumped forward to his chest. Teke grabbed his wrist and checked his pulse, finding it incredibly near normal. Then the doctor struggled to his feet and moved toward Chilgers, who through it all had never lost consciousness.

"We pushed him too far," Teke said, helping the colonel rise and then supporting him.

"No," Chilgers countered between labored breaths. "We pushed him just far enough."

Chapter Twenty-Seven

"Anything new, George?"

Secretary of Defense Brandenberg reentered the Oval Office to find the President with his face smothered in his hands. The early morning darkness was broken only by a single lamp on the chief executive's desk. Its light cast thin shadows in the room and made it seem smaller.

"We've received confirmation that Arthur was killed by a sniper shooting from the other side of the arena in a section of seats closed for repairs," Brandenberg reported.

"That's it?"

"That's it."

"Art and I went back a long time, George."

"I know."

The President gazed up emptily. "What the hell happened there?"

Brandenberg sat down. "There's only one man who can tell us that."

"Bane . . ."

"And he's disappeared again, with good reason I'm afraid."

"What are you implying?"

"Nothing. I'm merely continuing a theory I set forth yesterday afternoon. Let's say Bane blamed

Arthur for the fiasco at Penn Station. Tonight's meeting then becomes an elaborate setup for him to gain revenge."

"He was sitting right next to Arthur when the sniper fired."

"I believe Bane hired the sniper. Why else wouldn't he have been taken out as well? Besides, the idea of using someone else to kill Arthur furthers my theory that two distinct personalities are alive within Bane. One honestly and desperately believes it's on to something catastrophic. The other has created the illusion of this coming catastrophe and has been behind everything, from the hit on the Center to Arthur's murder, to reenforce it and justify the emergence of the Winter Man again."

"In which case we'd have an extremely dangerous man on our hands, George."

"In more ways than one. Bane's got enough information stored in his head to make Watergate look like back-page news. If he talks, he could bring this entire government down, send it whirling out of control."

"A perfect time for the Russians to force the issue," the President reflected.

"My point exactly."

"Then you don't think we should even try to bring Bane in."

Brandenberg shook his head. "The risk would be too great. Let him live and sooner or later he'll talk to someone. We can't live with that over our heads. Bane's unsalvageable."

"How I hate that term. . . ."

"It's accurate in this case, I'm afraid. Bane's too dangerous to bring in, sir. We wouldn't be able to control him. He honestly believes the shadows he's boxing are real. Destroy that illusion and he becomes a hundred times more dangerous."

"So instead we destroy him."

Brandenberg wet his lips. "We declare him unsalvageable, sir. The rest will take care of itself."

"Don't hide behind words, George," the President snapped, his features springing suddenly to life. "You want me to sanction a man's death which amounts to the same thing as holding a gun against his head and pulling the trigger. The fancy terms don't mean a damn thing to me. They didn't when I ran for this office and they sure as hell don't now. I've got a conscience to think of."

"And a country."

"I hesitate to think what the country has come to if men must die without due process to preserve it."

"Bane's become a liability to that same preservation."

The President rose and leaned over his desk. "And what if we're wrong about all this? What if Bane went to Arthur with something so big that somebody had to kill the chief of Clandestine Operations to keep it quiet? If we just assume for one moment that it wasn't Bane who took Jorgenson out, then who did? What did Art learn that mandated his elimination?"

Brandenberg said nothing.

"Maybe we're thinking just what our *real* opposition wants us to," the President continued. "They've isolated Bane, set him up as a scarecrow in a cornfield and we're buying the outfit. That might explain why his body wasn't left next to Art's tonight. If they had killed Bane, that would have confirmed he was on to something. Instead, they want to leave us with a red herring. If we kill Bane our troubles will be over, right? But maybe they'll just be beginning."

"We can't leave him out there, sir. If he talks, he could bring this whole government down."

The President held his eyes closed for a long moment. "Then we'll do it your way, George. But God help you if you're wrong. . . . God help us all."

"You've got the Bat," Harry's voice greeted.

"Harry, it's—"

"Josh, where the hell are you? What the hell went down tonight?"

From his room in the Hotel Washington, Bane sensed the Bat's panic. He started to speak but Harry's words drowned him out.

"You've been declared unsalvageable."

"*What?*"

"I was digging up some more info on that Einstein connection when word came in over the intelligence channel of the computer. I eavesdropped. Almost shit my pants when I ran the code through." Harry paused. "It's open season on you, Josh. Every hitter in the book's got a free shot and you can bet they'll take it. Better get back to Jorgenson and have him get you off the hook."

"Jorgenson's dead."

"Oh shit . . ."

"A sniper took him out at the Capital Center. Somebody's got me pinned for the hit," Bane realized.

"Terrific."

The sweat forming on Bane's hand glued the receiver to his flesh. "It gets worse. Jorgenson put it all together for me tonight. COBRA's planning to start World War III and that's just for starters. Now I can't even get the information to the White House because every schmuck with a .38 will be in the streets by breakfast."

"Sounds like it's time to make it back to the city

that never sleeps, buddy boy, and I might have something to make the trip worth your while. I took your advice about looking for a link between Einstein and Metzencroy," the Bat explained, "and I found one: they both worked for the Navy Office of Scientific Research in the early forties. Metzencroy's career was just starting out while Einstein's was drawing to a close. Then I did some cross-checking and found a *third* name in the group: Dr. Otto Von Goss. Einstein, Metzencroy, and Von Goss must've been pretty chummy but their direct association ends on all records as of the middle of 1943 with something called the Philadelphia Experiment."

"What the hell is that?"

"According to the Navy lines I broke into, it doesn't even exist. I found it mentioned in passing on all three dossiers circa 1943. It's the only link between our three scientists."

Bane thought briefly. "One thing's pretty obvious: Einstein wouldn't have been working for the Navy in World War II on Tinkertoys. They must have retained him for weapons research."

"I smell a connection with whatever COBRA's come up with that makes jets pull a disappearing act."

"Good for your nose, Harry. But we won't know for sure until we find out what the Philadelphia Experiment was."

"We're stonewalled from my computer end. But it just so happens that Dr. Otto Von Goss is still very much alive. He's a professor over at Princeton. Dropped out of active research after a lab accident, something to do with his hand."

"Maybe I should make Princeton my next stop."

"Don't rush. Von Goss disappeared yesterday."

"COBRA?"

"No, it was orderly. Witnesses saw him packing up his car. Looked like he planned to stay away awhile."

"Sounds like he's hiding out, Harry. He's afraid what happened to Metzencroy will happen to him too, which means he must share at least some of the late professor's knowledge, possibly lots. You've got to find him, Harry."

"Way ahead of ya, Josh. I've already put Trench onto it." The Bat chuckled but there was no trace of amusement in the sound. "You know, Josh, I still hate that fucker for what he did to me, but I trust him. I trust a goddamn killer who blew my legs to hell and I don't even trust my own government. Lord fuck a duck, what does that mean?"

Bane didn't have an answer.

The Seventh Day:

THE PHILADELPHIA EXPERIMENT

Why do we never get an answer
When we're knocking at the door?
There's a thousand million questions
About hate and death and war.
'Cause when we stop and look around us,
There is nothing that we need
In a world of persecution that is burning
   in its greed.

—The Moody Blues

Chapter Twenty-Eight

"Are we ready for stage two, Doctor?" Chilgers asked Teke from behind his mahogany desk. His back still ached from smashing up against the console yesterday, but painkillers were out of the question because he needed a clear head.

"Quite, I should say," responded Teke. "I've analyzed the data from stage one and have found few surprises on top of the unexpected inconsistencies. As I suspected, the boy's power works best when he is threatened. The reason for this, I've now confirmed, is that it is activated by his subconscious mind. This explains why the boy's pulse and blood pressure readings increased while his conscious level of spent energy remained incredibly low."

"Are you saying he has no control of his power?"

"Not entirely. The line between the conscious and unconscious minds is a narrow one, Colonel, and one that is difficult to define. We resort to defense mechanisms without consciously meaning to. There are conscious forces which trigger the unconscious responses of tears and laughter. The boy's power isn't all that different from such responses or from a standard defense mechanism. He activates it when he needs it, when there is no real alternative or that alternative is pain."

"He used his power to purchase a jacket in New York," Chilgers reminded. "Quite consciously."

"And the effort required to do so was infinitesimal for him, easily accomplished at the conscious level."

"Unlike yesterday."

"We went too far with him yesterday," Teke explained. "The pain came from within himself and when we wouldn't let him ease up, we lost control. We're all lucky to be alive, considering the splintering glass and the escape of toxic gases from those fluorescent lights. The boy nearly killed us."

"Consciously?"

"It doesn't matter. The point is that he, too, lost control. The pain was too much for him."

"From the shock prods?"

"More from his own head. It appears that extended use of his power causes increased pressure to the region of the brain where it originates. The result is something akin to migraine headaches that grow in intensity the deeper he reaches for his power."

Chilgers rose tentatively. He tried to stretch his back muscles out but the motion proved too painful. "Any lasting effects?"

"Difficult to say. I'll know better after stage two today. I plan to do a brain scan on him during the next experiment, to pin down the origin of his power and show us if any damage has been done by past use."

"We'll also have to come up with a surer way of controlling him. We can't have any repeat performance of the havoc yesterday."

"Your electroshock rigging is superb for negative conditioning, especially in view of the way the boy responds to pain. Today we add to that an i.v. needle placed in his arm with the flow of sedative pinched off in the middle by one of my assistants. If he releases

304

the pressure, or circumstances force him to, the sedative will automatically enter the boy's arm and knock him out."

"That should do nicely," complimented Chilgers. "What have you done about securing a subject?"

Teke leaned forward. "I've retained one of our human guinea pigs at twice the usual price with the usual security precautions observed. Of course, he has no way of knowing that his participation in the experiment will quite likely result in his death." Teke hesitated. "What the boy did yesterday was truly amazing but virtually all of it was focused on inanimate matter. To fully gauge his powers, isolate and learn how to control them, we must push them to their ultimate extreme. How well the boy fares in that situation will tell us how far that extreme stretches. Mechanically everything will be about the same with the addition of the computer-enhanced brain scan which will provide us with a motion picture of his mind's activity during a more demanding experiment. That will give us what we need to move on to stage three: control."

Chilgers smiled. "You've done well, Teke. I haven't missed the late Professor Metzencroy's presence at all."

"Then I assume Project Placebo is proceeding on schedule."

"Our shipment of missiles will be arriving at Bunker 17 this afternoon as planned."

"And yet your enthusiasm for it has waned in favor of the boy."

"Vortex represents only the present, Teke. Davey Phelps is the future."

Davey woke up disoriented, in darkness. He

twisted about in bed and found, much to his surprise, he had freedom of movement. When he tried to swing his legs off the bed, though, his muscles resisted, balking at the simple commands, and Davey realized that part of the drug they'd been giving him hadn't worn off yet.

He closed his eyes and pushed for The Chill to help himself, but he couldn't focus; the drugs were still dimming his mind. He tried to remember everything that had happened the day before, found that was foggy too. The Chill had been strong then, too strong. It had nearly split his head in two. But still they made him keep using it. Didn't they understand? They wanted him to control it for them when he couldn't control it even for himself. And then those horrible jolts to his balls which shook all his insides apart and made him piss on himself. They had embarrassed him, made him feel weak. He hated them all, and he wasn't weak anyway.

Davey heard keys being turned in the locks outside the door which opened slowly, permitting two large men in white coats to enter. They lifted him into a wheelchair manned by another while a fourth waited in the corridor holding a hypodermic. Davey didn't resist, didn't even move. Maybe if he played dumb, they'd lay off the drugs and he'd get The Chill back to use against them.

He let his head slump to his chest but raised his eyes to follow the wheelchair's path, realizing with a start they were heading back in the direction of the laboratory. They passed the one he remembered from yesterday and stopped at another just down the hall. One of the men opened the door.

"The sedative should be wearing off right about now," came the familiar voice of the bald doctor as Davey was wheeled in.

Then they were easing him into a chair that had arms this time. Two of the men held his wrists and latched leather straps across his flesh, fastening him tight to the chair.

"It's just to keep you still, Davey," the bald one told him. "We'll be needing more precise readings this time and we'll be scanning your brain throughout the experiment."

"No pain," Davey muttered.

"Not if you cooperate," Teke said, but his eyes avoided Davey's.

The doctor proceeded to supervise the attachment of wires to Davey's arms, face, and head. The final set probably contained a hundred at least, all strung onto a round cap the size of a beanie. Teke fitted it personally over the dome of Davey's skull until it was snug, squeezing his thick hair down tight.

"This apparatus will allow us to visually monitor the functions of your brain. It causes no pain whatsoever," the doctor promised. "However, it will be necessary to inject you with fluid of a slightly radioactive nature—for the microbes to pick up for monitoring." Here, a lab assistant held a tray out to Teke and he removed a single syringe from it. "Please don't move." He dabbed at a vein at the base of Davey's skull with an alcohol swab and then gently plunged the needle in. It stung only briefly. "That could be the worst of it for today."

But Davey knew he was lying. He felt his neck being strapped to the back of the chair to hold his head in place, after which his ankles were laced to the heavy chair's legs as well. He could barely move a muscle. Even a deep breath would have been impossible. Out of the corner of his eye, he saw a technician fastening a plastic tube with a needle on its end atop his arm. Then the needle worked its way into the vein at the top of his forearm and stayed there, the technician backing up to inspect his handiwork. He moved away, leaving the needle as it was and wheeling a tray closer to Davey's side. Then he was doing something with the tube Davey couldn't quite see.

"Ready, Doctor?"

The voice of the man called colonel sent fear up Davey's spine. The holder of the horrible black box was back. . . .

"Not quite. Just a little longer."

Davey tried to move his eyes to find the colonel, but couldn't until the man stood directly before him, grinning.

"How we feeling today, boy?"

Davey said nothing.

"Electrodes all check," the bald doctor reported and Davey realized with horror that the hot wires from yesterday were being led up his nightshirt to be twisted about his balls again. There was a slight tugging and Davey felt them being wrapped tight.

"These should do the trick," the doctor said, pulling his hands out and looking at the colonel.

"They'd better." A brief pause. "Let's try the lights, shall we?"

Somewhere Davey heard a switch being flicked and a small compartment twenty feet away in the room's center was suddenly lit up. He picked up the trail of wires leading from his groin and followed them to the compartment's front wall which was dominated by a large window starting a yard off the floor and stretching to within a foot of the compartment's roof.

"Check systems," Teke instructed.

"All monitors working," came one response.

"All gauges working," from another technician.

"All connections in place," from a third.

"Do we have a brain picture yet?" Teke asked a

technician standing just beyond Davey's line of vision in the room's front.

"Getting one now. Sharpening...Sharpening... I'm adjusting the focus. We've got it in clear."

"Begin recording now," Teke told him. "Tie the computer into all gauges this time." The doctor turned toward the colonel. "We're ready, sir."

Davey heard another switch being flipped, louder this time, and suddenly the inside of the room's enclosed cubicle became visible. Davey saw a man sitting in a chair, a big man, almost as big as Josh. He couldn't make out all his features clearly but he did pick out an object he held in his hand.

The black box with the awful red button!

Davey shivered just looking at it, his groin tingling in fearful anticipation. Then he noticed the wires running from the box were indeed the ones spliced into the cubicle from his groin. His balls tingled again.

Who was this man? Why was he holding the black box?

"Davey," the bald doctor began, "the man in the compartment cannot hear or see you. It's soundproof and the window is made of one-way glass. He thinks it's a standard mirror. He's oblivious to whatever goes on in this room. Do you understand?"

Davey nodded. He noticed the colonel enter his field of vision again and move directly toward the compartment. He pressed a button and spoke into what looked like an intercom attached to its front.

"Can you hear me?"

"Yes." The man inside had been told only he was going to participate in an experiment to judge the levels of human endurance to pain and tolerance of both the victim and the controller. He had been told his was the controller's role and the black box in his

309

hand seemed to confirm this. He didn't give it much thought really, having done a number of strange things for COBRA in the past always at a fair price.

"Turn the knob located near the top to the third position and hold your thumb over the red button." Chilgers' eyes sought out Davey's. "Prepare to press it on my signal."

"No!" Davey screamed but the word came out muffled.

"Kill the man in the booth, Davey," the bald doctor instructed. "Kill him with your power before he has a chance to hurt you."

"I . . . can't. You're making him! It's you who want to hurt me! . . ."

"Press it," Chilgers said into the intercom.

Davey's head lurched back as far as it could, straining his muscles. His buttocks tried to lift off his chair, stretching the straps. He felt a spasm in his bladder and the terrible warmth of urine trickled down his leg again.

"Turn the knob to the fourth position," Chilgers told the man in the booth.

"No!" Davey tried to scream again but this time no sound emerged at all.

"Use your power," the doctor was telling him, "it's the only thing that can save you from the pain. Aim it at the man in the booth. It's him that's hurting you. It's *his* thumb on the button."

Davey bit his lip, thought of aiming The Chill at the colonel but knew it would get him nothing but more pain.

"Slight vibration in energy levels."

"Alpha waves just popped up. Readings normal again."

"Vitals on the rise."

Chilgers found Davey's eyes again. "Get ready to

press," he said into the intercom.

"Energy levels in state of flux."

"Alpha waves approaching the red."

"Energy concentration ratio at eighty-three, eighty-four, eighty-five . . ."

"Vitals climbing, climbing . . ."

"Press it," said Chilgers.

This time Davey's buttocks succeeded in leaving the chair, yanking the leather restraining his body with them and tearing his breath away with a horrible kick. His groin was in a vise that somebody was tightening. He tried to breathe but all he felt was a racked set of misplaced muscles. There was another brief jolt, like an aftershock, and Davey felt his bowels go loose on him and was barely able to control their contents. The bald doctor leaned over and dabbed a towel to his mouth, wiping away the saliva and dribbling blood. He spit some more out and the doctor wiped that away too. His breath came back, but he couldn't get enough to satisfy his starved lungs, so the room darkened briefly and something fluttered inside his ears.

"Turn the knob to the fifth position," he heard Chilgers say into the intercom.

"Stop!" Davey pleaded to the doctor, seeing only half of him. "Help me, please! . . ."

"I can't help you, Davey," Teke said. "Only you can help yourself. Use the power. Stop that man from hurting you."

"Get ready to press on my signal," Chilgers went on.

"He wants to hurt you, Davey," the bald doctor was telling him. "The black box has another seven levels to go and each is much worse than the one before. He'll go all the way if you let him. Stop him, Davey. Stop him!"

311

Davey's eyes bulged. The Chill rose in him.

"Energy levels passing seven."

"Alpha waves reading all in the red."

"Vitals rising dangerously fast."

"Press on my signal," Chilgers repeated into the intercom.

"Energy concentration ratio at ninety . . . ninety-one . . . ninety-two, ninety—"

"Energy levels at seven-point-five . . ."

"—three . . . ninety-five . . . ninety-seven . . ."

Teke faced the man behind a separate console in the room's front. "What have you got on brain scan?"

"Significant activity and it's increasing."

Inside the booth, the man had begun to shake. Every muscle and joint in his body was affected. His tongue vibrated in and out of his mouth. His eyes bulged wide, locked unblinking.

"Energy levels just passing eight. . . ."

"Energy concentration ratio 100 . . . 101 . . . 102 . . ."

Blood frothed at the corners of the man's mouth, began to seep from his ears. His feet pounded the floor and then kicked hopelessly before him. His hands clawed the air, like a drowning man's struggling for the surface of the sea. His features went beyond scarlet to purple, his blood seeming to boil.

Davey Phelps stared straight ahead, feeling and hearing nothing, intent on his target. His eyes held a calm, yet intense, glare.

"Energy levels approaching nine . . ."

"ECR at 105 . . . 106 . . . 107 . . ."

Chilgers moved his finger from the intercom. "Press it," was all he said.

Davey Phelps's eyes jumped.

The black box in the booth ruptured, seeming to explode. The glass of the compartment's window cracked but didn't shatter, saving the lab's occupants from seeing what happened next.

The man's insides broke apart, lifting him to his feet in a twisted, shriveled way. His flesh contracted, withdrew. Ribs poked at the surface, then jammed their way through skin and clothes as his entire body fought to turn itself inside out. His head exploded and a stream of blood erupted from the top of his skull, painting the remnants of the window and filling the cracks with spent flesh. What was left of the body hung on its feet still writhing for several seconds before tumbling forward to the floor in a misshapen heap.

"Oh my God," muttered Teke.

Chilgers backed away and, much to his own surprise, covered his eyes.

Davey Phelps felt the pain coming and tried to shut his eyes to it. But it racked him anyway. He felt as if somebody were sticking needles into the backs of his eyeballs, only worse because the pain was everywhere and he couldn't even raise his hands for futile comfort. His toes twitched, fingers spasmed.

Teke loosened his assistant's hold on the plastic tube and the emergency dose of the sedative rushed into the boy's veins.

The pain had become too much. Davey felt his breath going and his life following after. It was over; he knew that, accepted it, welcomed it. Anything to be rid of the pain. Then he felt calm and sure, suddenly relaxed. Breathing easily and drifting away toward oblivion.

Chapter Twenty-Nine

"What?" Christian Teare leaned closer to the intercom in his private quarters. "That's crazy, Cap."

"It's the message, Major. I've checked it three times myself."

"What about confirmation?"

"Got it."

"From base?"

"Direct from Com-con at NORAD."

"It's still crazy."

"You better get up here."

"On my way. Teare out."

Teare stretched. His powerful muscles, sorely in need of exercise, spasmed and he slowly brought his hands back to his sides to ease the strain. He had almost fallen asleep for the first time in more than a day when a shrill buzz signaling a page from Bunker 17's Command Center shook him from his cot.

Teare's pace moved from a trot to an all-out sprint and he covered the distance from his quarters to Com-center in record time. Captain Heath was waiting inside, face drawn into lines indicating confusion. He handed over the decoded message.

"I just reconfirmed."

Teare read it four times. "Jesus H. Christ . . ." His

eyes came up from the paper. "Okay, Cap, let's put this thing together. Twenty-four hours ago we get kicked up to a Yellow Flag alert. Now we get instructions through the SAFE Interceptor to raise all defenses at thirteen hundred hours today to accept shipment of thirty-six MX missiles for immediate loading into silos. You get the feelin' someone in Washington's fuckin' with our minds?"

"Those missiles have been scheduled to arrive from COBRA on this date for over a month now."

"But under Yellow Flag they'd be frozen in San Diego."

"Unless Com-link has reason to believe we may need them."

"I can buy that. But it still doesn't explain why we've been ordered to load them immediately into the silos."

"Maximum efficiency probably," Heath proposed. "These Track Ones are the latest thing off the drawing board. Their accuracy is unparalleled."

"Which practically implies we're gonna be usin' them 'fore much longer," Teare theorized, tugging at his scraggly beard. "And I been monitorin' civilian frequencies for a solid day now and as far as I can tell there ain't nothin' goin' on out there out of the ordinary."

"They could be keeping it secret from the press."

"Come on, Cap," Teare scoffed, "there's enough leaks in Washington to bring Noah back for a return engagement. This whole mess stinks to high heaven." Teare stroked his beard and thought briefly. "No way I can talk to the President direct, is there?"

"Negative, Major, not under Yellow Flag."

"Yeah? Well, back in farm country stand down-wind and you can smell shit all day. I think I got me a whiff of it now, Cap."

A buzzer began to sound and a red light flashed on the perimeter defense board located on the far left wall of Com-center.

"Jesus H. Christ, what the hell's that about?"

"A caravan of heavy vehicles headed our way, Major," reported one of the technicians. "Just passing checkpoint two now."

Heath moved to the left half of the control room and flipped on the master switch activating six closed circuit TV monitors. Six black and white perspectives of the ground above Bunker 17 appeared immediately. Two clearly showed a parade of green missile transports under heavy armed guard approaching the installation.

"That'll be our delivery from COBRA," Heath said.

"Should I activate base defenses, sir?" asked the man behind the main console.

"No," Teare told him. "We got our orders. Let's get this done with. I want them outta here inside of an hour. Record time, Cap, record time." Then, to the man behind the console, "Signal temporary halt to Yellow Flag procedures. All personnel stand ready."

"Yes, sir."

Teare turned back to Heath. "Cap, let's you and me head for the elevator. I want us to meet these sons of bitches personally."

They started for the door.

"And, Cap?"

"Yes, Major?"

"We're gonna watch these assholes like a horny John at a whore's peephole. And I'll tell ya something else; I want the fail-safe mechanisms on those missiles checked a dozen times to make sure all systems are functional."

316

"You really think there's something wrong here?"

"Does a bear shit in the woods?"

Bane hit East Sixty-ninth Street and headed for Harry the Bat's apartment. After a generally sleepless night at the hotel, he had left Washington early in the morning and followed a haphazard route back to New York, making use of both trains and planes, the latter having forced him to discard his Browning. He had gotten used to carrying the gun these past few days and being without it, especially now, had him feeling vulnerable and insecure. Hands were fine, but not against an army of killers called up by an unsalvageable order.

Bane had used the trip to put his thoughts together and plan his next steps as best he could. There would be no help coming from the government; Jorgenson had been his last hope there. It was up to him now along with Trench and Harry, to finish fitting the puzzle together with the help, hopefully, of Otto Von Goss, the third man in the Navy trinity with Einstein and Metzencroy. Somehow Bane felt the Philadelphia Experiment which linked them together was the key to everything, the link to Vortex and its ultimate destruction. He could only hope that Trench had had sufficient time to track Dr. Von Goss down.

Bane neared the building's entrance.

"Keep moving, Winter Man, and don't turn around."

Bane recognized Trench's voice, coming from about a yard behind him, immediately.

"They took your friend away, Winter Man, and they're waiting upstairs for you. He put up quite a fight but fortunately was taken without harm. At the next corner, I'm going to turn right. You keep going.

There's a room reserved for you at the Diplomat Hotel on Park Avenue South in the name of Summers. I'll meet you there in half an hour."

They reached the corner. Trench veered away. Bane kept on straight, heading farther into the madness.

"You're sure Harry's all right?" Bane asked as soon as Trench had closed the door to the hotel room behind him.

"For now," Trench said. "I was across the street when they took him. He was all right enough to be giving them a mouthful."

"Then they were official types."

Trench nodded. "The kind who sometimes wear ID's pinned to their lapels. It was all very legitimate. Your government works in strange ways, Winter Man. I'm surprised you're still alive."

"And I'm surprised you're still here, everything considered."

Trench pulled a gun from his jacket. "The Americans have been trying to locate me with an assignment to kill you." Bane's eyes locked on the gun. He didn't move. "I'm sure they'd pay quite well for the death of the Winter Man but"—Trench swung the pistol's butt toward Bane, offering it to him—". . . I turned them down."

Bane allowed himself a sigh of relief and took the pistol.

"A Browning," Trench told him. "I figured you might have mislaid yours somwhere along the way."

"So what's our next step?" Bane asked, giving him the lead.

"Your friend Harry passed on to me what he learned of Von Goss. The professor disappeared from

Princeton three days ago."

"About the same time Metzencroy was eliminated. Harry told me."

"Proceeding on the assumption that Von Goss fled willingly into hiding, I did some checking and learned that a close associate of the professor owns a cabin in the Pocono Mountains of Pennsylvania. Von Goss has been known to use it from time to time. Further questioning revealed the cabin is actually a house built into the side of a mountain, accessible only from one side: the front. A fortress, Winter Man."

"Then Von Goss is there."

"I've been trying the phone number all day long. Twenty-one times, no answer; once, a busy signal."

"Could have been a misdial."

"More likely, Von Goss is not answering his phone unless some sort of code is used with the rings, but he is making a few occasional calls to check on the home front."

"If he's that scared, chances are he's got some idea of what Metzencroy was on to."

Trench nodded. "My own experience with scientists has shown me they are great talkers—but only with each other. They love to consult, to trade information. Now let us assume, Winter Man, that Metzencroy and Von Goss were two of Einstein's greatest direct disciples, and that after his death each chose to continue their mentor's work in his own way: Metzencroy at COBRA and Von Goss at Princeton. It seems logical to assume that they would never be long out of contact with each other. The bonds made over forty years ago would easily have lasted this long with something like Vortex to consider."

"Except Von Goss dropped out of active research and turned totally to teaching after an accident."

"Something to do with his hand," Trench explained. "It happened in the late sixties when he was on the verge of making a major scientific breakthrough."

"Any idea what this breakthrough concerned?"

"Unfortunately, not a clue."

"But I suppose you've obtained precise directions to this house in the Poconos."

"Of course."

Bane regarded Trench's liquid gray eyes which suddenly didn't look so cold. "You could walk away clean from this, Trench, and no one would be the wiser. You could hide yourself so none of them could find you, even Chilgers. Your stake in this could be over."

"And what of you, Winter Man? If I abandon you, what chance would you have against the army of amateur killers falling all over each other on your trail? I resisted Chilgers' original order to eliminate you because I couldn't bear to see the only other true professional left killed for no reason. I can't walk away now because of that same concern."

Bane smiled hesitantly. "I was just thinking of something Harry said about not knowing who your real friends are. I guess people change."

"Not really. It's times that do. People like you and me, Winter Man, stay as we are, clinging to our special world which offers clarity above all else." Trench paused reflectively. "But I suppose you're right. Another time, another place we might've been associates, friends even. For now all we have is Chilgers and Vortex to hold us together."

"That's plenty." Bane checked his watch. "We've got a long drive ahead of us, Trench. We should reach the Poconos a little after nightfall if we leave right away."

"I've got a car downstairs."

It took Harry Bannister a few seconds to adjust to the light after his blindfold was pulled off. One of the men who had lifted him from his apartment untied his wrists and stripped the tape off his mouth.

"You fuckers are gonna pay for this," he charged the three men standing before his wheelchair in the scantily furnished single room. "Boy, are you gonna pay. . . ."

The three men were silent.

"I suppose you got a good reason for dragging me here, you know like a warrant or something. How 'bout a dime so I can make my one phone call?" Harry licked the tape's residue from his lips.

The three men stayed silent.

"Well, if any of you fuckers had a mind I could tell you a whale of a story that looks like it's gonna have a pretty rotten ending 'cause the assholes you work for can't tell the good guys from the bad guys." The Bat looked them in the eye one at a time. "Hey, any of you got a tongue? How 'bout a good pair of ears? . . . Nope, I didn't think so."

"I'll listen, Mr. Bannister, if you think you've got something to say."

The voice came from the area near the door through which a big man had just entered. Big as Josh easy, Harry figured.

"And who the fuck are you?"

The man stepped farther into the room. "The name's Wentworth, Phillip Wentworth." Wentworth motioned the other three men out of the room and closed the door behind them, looking back at the Bat. "You were saying, Mr. Bannister."

"I don't suppose you're gonna tell me which group you work for."

"Throw any three letters of the alphabet together and you're bound to hit one of them."

"Lord fuck a duck, aren't you a big-fuckin'-shot." Then Harry thought of something. "Big enough to get the ears of the President are you, Wentworth?"

"Depends on the reason."

"How about the fact that he's trying to kill the wrong guy. It's not Joshua Bane who's gone mad, it's a guy named Chilgers out in San Diego, and if something's not done fast, it's the whole fuckin' world that's gonna end up unsalvageable. Do you read me, Wentworth?"

Wentworth's expression was unchanged. "Let me tell you something, Mr. Bannister. About fifteen years ago I was taken to the same training camp Joshua Bane got taken to and we were the last two left. He ended up with the job and deserved it because he was the best I ever saw. I've got more respect for him than any man I've met in my life. So when that unsalvageable order came down last night, I figured something screwy was up and if you can tell me what, you can be damn sure I'll bring it to the President if I have to use some of the Winter Man's tricks to break into his office."

"Pull up a chair," said Harry.

Chapter Thirty

A black, moonless night had fallen over the sky by the time Bane turned the Ford off route 81 in Scranton and onto 380 for the final stretch leading to Otto Von Goss's mountain retreat in the Poconos of Pennsylvania.

"We still can't be sure he'll see us," he repeated to Trench who sat silent but alert in the passenger seat.

"I believe our chances are good. Consider first that Von Goss went into hiding the same day Professor Metzencroy's death was reported. He went to the mountains in fear, Winter Man, because he must possess the same information Metzencroy did, and he believes they'll be coming for him now too."

"He hasn't been active in research since the accident which crippled his hand fifteen years ago," Bane reminded Trench.

"If he ran, he knows. Our primary task will be to convince him we're on the same side."

"First we'll have to convince his guards. Under the circumstances, he wouldn't have run to the Poconos without taking an army with him."

"They won't be expecting an attack to come from a single car approaching at night with its lights marking its path."

"All the more reason to raise their suspicions,

Trench, and their rifles."

The car filled with silence as the road wound on. The air outside grew colder and colder, slipping gradually below the freezing mark. Bane flipped the heater on and slid the temperature control all the way to the right. Finally, he saw signs directing him toward route 423 and the last stretch of road leading toward the Poconos.

"You know this area well, Winter Man?" Trench asked him.

Bane tapped his high beams on. "Well enough. Most of the Poconos are jammed full of resorts. But this is the off-season and Von Goss's retreat lies on the western perimeter. Hunting and fishing area mostly and virtually all undeveloped save for a few lodges."

"And one fortress."

Bane nodded.

Another few miles and he swung onto route 423. The heart of the resort community came a little after in soft light and amber signs, then faded just as quickly. The road darkened and narrowed. The high beams barely made a dent ahead. Bane took a right onto a mountain road that wound circularly on a slight rise. Two more roads came and went before he turned onto one made of gravel instead of tar, lit only by the rising moon and wide enough for only one car. Bane cut his speed to fifteen miles per hour but even that seemed too fast against the ominous looming of the mountain's edge. Almost imperceptibly, they had climbed to a point halfway up the steepest mountain in the Pocono chain and thus unattractive to tourists. This mountain was a favorite only of diehards, locals mostly or people whose families had owned property here for generations. It was probably quite beautiful, Bane figured, though a cold mist rising in the night

324

obscured everything including the road, which led to several very anxious moments as the drive continued.

"Von Goss chose well," Trench said softly. "An attack from the air seems the only way to reach him. Helicopters perhaps."

"Not likely. The tree cover's too high even at this elevation."

"Good point."

Up ahead, Bane thought he caught a flutter of movement and then a reflection flickering. He turned toward Trench, noticed his focused eyes.

"You saw it too," he advanced.

"A lookout, I should guess. It appears, Winter Man, we've been made."

"Good. Saves us the trouble of an unexpected arrival, so long as we're not greeted with bullets."

"They probably think we're lost vacationers," Trench proposed.

"Desperate men like Von Goss often act rashly."

"Quite close to what we're doing right now."

Bane slowed the Ford to a crawl as the ledge turns became maddeningly close. It seemed at times that part of their car actually passed over the black edge, teetering on oblivion before the wheel drew it back.

"They'll want our weapons, Winter Man," he said suddenly.

"Then we'll give them over."

"Of course, we haven't even considered the possibility that Von Goss may be in with COBRA and that we could be walking straight into a trap set for us by Chilgers."

"If so, it's about to spring so we might as well have at the cheese."

Bane swung the car slowly around still another corner and jammed the brakes hard. Light had poured into his eyes, blinding him. White, hot light that singed his pupils beneath his lids.

"Stay where you are!" a voice commanded, echoing in the misty mountain air. "Do not leave your car! Repeat, do not leave your car!"

The light stayed locked on his eyes, and Bane finally adjusted to it at about the same time his ears picked up the crunching of gravel—coming for them fast, four sets of footsteps by the sound of it. Then two large shapes were hovering in front of the Ford's hood, blocking the piercing light out. Each held an automatic rifle tight at waist level, focused on the windshield. Bane killed the engine, heard the latch on his door being pulled.

"You are trespassing on private property," the same commanding voice told him. "You will leave immediately."

Bane glanced quickly at Trench. "We've come to see Professor Von Goss."

The barrel of another automatic rifle jabbed him in the ribs. "I'm going to pull the trigger unless you give me an awfully good reason not to," the cold voice snapped.

Bane turned slowly and met a face just as cold. "And if you do Professor Von Goss will remain a prisoner of fear on this mountain for the rest of his life. We've come here . . . to help him and to seek his help."

"I don't know what you're talking about," the man said.

"The Professor—we're on the same side. We're his only hope as he is ours. You can kill the two of us now as we sit but when Von Goss finds out who we are and where we came from, he'll have your head."

The man hesitated and Bane knew the tide had turned.

"Well?" he prodded.

"Who should I say is here?" the man asked finally.

"Tell him Joshua Bane. Tell him I'm here about Vortex and I know what they did to Metzencroy. Tell him—"

"I'll relay your message," the man said impatiently.

He turned away and crunched more gravel under his heavy step. Bane's vision had adjusted to the light enough to make out a pair of jeeps squeezed together on the narrow road, just to the right of a small cut in the mountain's side that allowed for turning around. This had hardly been a random setting for seizure. It was perfect for the action.

Bane caught a walkie-talkie's crackle and then a muffled voice. More crackle and silence. He looked at Trench. The killer's fingers had crept under his overcoat, ready to whip out his pistol at an instant's notice. Gravel crunched back toward them. A good sign.

"I'm instructed to lead you up," the man at his window said.

"Thank you."

The man eyed him, gave a warped snicker. "I'll take your weapons here."

Bane handed his over and Trench followed.

"Any more?" the man demanded.

"Two rifles in the trunk," Trench answered.

"You'll be searched before we let you see the professor. If you're lying, you'll die." A pause. "And those orders came from Von Goss himself."

A few hundred yards up the pass, the road leveled off and a thick slice in the dense forest rose to greet them. Bane saw lights flickering between the trees as they swung to the left and the break in the mountain's rise. The gravel road turned to a stone-laden driveway, circular in construction, weaving toward the origin of the lights and then cutting a U around a private forest between the house and the road. The sound of the tires rolling over the stones reminded Bane of a rattlesnake's trademark and he could only hope they hadn't been lured into the den of one. He checked the silent Trench and found him impassive and expressionless.

Before them, a surprisingly large, wood-colored house sprang from the mountain as it broke to rise again. The house was built right into the side, built on stilts and cinderblocks instead of a foundation. Bane made out sun decks on either end of the structure, an armed guard watching alertly from each. The house was long but narrow, and drenched in floodlights as was the surrounding area. He noticed most of the shades were drawn, a few windows even shuttered as a precaution against snipers, and he couldn't help but be amazed by Von Goss's precautions. Calling this a fortress was an understatement. Tree cover made it totally inaccessible by air, and the mountain at its rear made ground defense a relatively simple matter with the number of forces undoubtedly present. Add to this the narrow, precarious approach road and attack bordered on suicide. It would take an army. Armed guards patrolled the house's front in regular patterns. The two men on the outdoor decks swept portable spotlights about the trees, illuminating the night in long, thin patches.

Otto Von Goss was certainly safe.

Bane pulled the Ford to a halt when he saw the lead jeep's brake lights flash on and heard the whine of the jeep behind him doing the same. He and Trench exchanged nods and waited to be led from the cars before climbing out. Their submission was total; weaponless, they really had no other choice.

"Inside," the man from the road told them, hanging back beyond the range of any attack they might have mustered. A professional surely, probably a mercenary and a damn good one with battle experience. Von Goss was sparing no expense.

A large wooden door opened before them and they climbed a set of steep steps toward it. Bane and Trench passed through, with a half-dozen men right behind, to find themselves in a spacious hall warmed by a fire from a central hearth. It smelled old, clean, and rustic, had wood-paneled walls and a floor of parquet. The hall was a genuine masterpiece of construction.

The man with the cold voice moved in front of them and opened the door to an equally spacious living room filled with rich leather furniture which played perfectly off the wood around it.

"We're going to search you in here," he said, locking onto Bane's eyes, then Trench's. "If we find anything, it will be as far as you get."

Bane held the man's stare a bit longer, lingering even when he looked away. He was a professional, all right, who had killed often and well before.

Bane and Trench submitted to a thorough, expert search which turned up nothing. This procedure comforted them more than anything because it significantly reduced the odds of this being a clever trap laid by Chilgers. Of course, he could be playing the ruse out to its fullest to ascertain everything they knew and to find out what information they'd passed on—and to whom. Bane doubted that, though. That wasn't the colonel's style at all judging by recent experience. Too subtle.

After the search, Bane and Trench were led to a polished stairway that climbed steeply to the second floor.

"I'll leave the talking to you, Winter Man," Trench whispered as they ascended side by side. "Less confusion for our friend Von Goss if he has only one of us to concern himself with. I'll remain your silent partner." They had reached the top of the stairs. "And a watchful one."

The head mercenary led them down a narrow hallway toward a door in the middle.

"Show them in," a voice from inside instructed after the mercenary knocked.

The man ushered Bane and Trench in, preparing to close the door with himself still between them.

"Leave us," came the voice from the room's rear. "I'll signal if I need you."

The mercenary shrugged, eyed Bane one last time, and took his leave.

"I've been expecting you, Mr. Bane."

Dr. Otto Von Goss stepped out of the shadows. The room was lit, save for a single sixty-watt bulb, by a roaring fire he had been tending. It cast an eerie radiance, flames crackling and dancing about, tossing their shapes against the walls.

"In fact," Von Goss proceeded, "I thought you'd be here earlier."

The professor stepped further into the half-light, giving Bane his first good look at him. Von Goss was tall and painfully gaunt with a thin, angular face topped by thinning gray hair collected in bunches, one of which fell over his forehead and flirted with his eyebrows. He was wearing thick, steel-rimmed glasses which exaggerated all the more the sickly, gray pallor of his flesh. Otto Von Goss looked like a dying man, or at least one who had resigned himself

330

to death, perhaps even looked forward to its coming. Bane looked down for the first time and saw the black glove which covered the professor's left hand. He approached Bane with it dragging lifelessly by his side, almost as though he had forgotten it was there.

"We have much to talk about," Von Goss said, extending his good hand forward.

"Then you know why we've come," Bane responded, taking the hand and finding the professor's grip dry and weak.

"My sources have informed me of your pursuits these past few days, the questions you've been asking and what you seek." Von Goss noticed Bane's wandering eyes. "You seem impressed with my security measures. I've been expecting a time like this to come for years. I've been prepared for it, ready to move always at a moment's notice."

"And Metzencroy's death became that moment."

"Yes," Von Goss said softly. He glanced briefly at Trench who had retreated to a darkened corner. Then his eyes moved back to Bane. "Professor Metzencroy had stayed in contact with me religiously since the time he'd joined COBRA. Sometimes he sought my opinions with the company's permission, other times without it. We established a whole system of relays and codes for those other times. We scientists are strange people. We can only talk seriously with our fellows and for Metzencroy and myself that left only each other, regardless of what COBRA ordered otherwise. Nonetheless, Metzencroy's final report came to me three days ago without benefit of code or courier. He violated our own security because he was scared and because he knew it didn't matter anymore. He knew he was finished at COBRA. He knew their plans for him, but he didn't seem to mind. In his final report he wasn't seeking confirmation, you see,

331

just release for his conscience. When I learned of Metzencroy's death I feared the worst and came here. I'm still frightened, Mr. Bane, because the professor was absolutely sure of his findings, absolutely certain that the world as we know it was about to come to an end."

Bane's mouth felt dry. He had been wondering for some time what could be worse than World War III. Now he knew.

"As I said, we have much to talk about," Von Goss continued. His eyes tilted toward the fireplace. "It's warmer over there. Let's make ourselves comfortable in the chairs. It's time you learned about Vortex."

Chapter Thirty-One

Trench remained set in the corner as they took chairs facing each other in front of the fire. Bane watched the flames' shadows dance across Von Goss's pallid face, seeming to consume him.

The professor pulled his lifeless left hand into his lap and stroked it. "I can't feel anything under this glove, Mr. Bane. My hand is dead," he muttered, and Bane realized it wasn't covered by a glove at all but more of a mitten that masked the fingers in a bunch instead of individually. "I killed it myself. I killed it because I went too far. I searched for knowledge man was not meant to possess and was not ready for. Metzencroy felt differently. He joined COBRA and continued the experiments that had turned me into a freak. He ignored my warnings, just as I ignored the last warnings of Einstein."

"Einstein?"

Von Goss leaned forward until his whole face was splashed with light and nodded. "The origins of Vortex, Mr. Bane. How much do you know about Einstein?"

"Not much beyond $E=mc^2$."

"Hah! His most simple and pedantic principle. Taught in elementary schools now, would you believe it? The theory Einstein is most recognized for and yet the least startling of all his major works. The most startling is a theory he never completed: the Unified Field Theory." Flames crackled in the hearth. "The basis of Vortex."

"I've never heard of it."

"Not many people outside the field of physics have, which is just the way Einstein wanted it."

"But it was his theory."

"And he damned himself for it in the end. Einstein hated war, Mr. Bane. The first World War was a horrible shock to his sensibility because he saw the kind of weapon $E=mc^2$ was leading to and vowed never to work on any project that might lead to a basis for weapons again. Then the Nazis came along and he grew to fear their menace more than war itself. War, he decided, was morally justifiable if it meant wiping out Hitler's army and cause. So he went back to the drawing board, back to a theory he had abandoned in the twenties."

"Unified Fields . . ."

"Exactly. He had given it up in the twenties because he realized man was not yet and might never be ready for it. Then Hitler came along, and by 1938 he had changed his mind and set about completing it. Metzencroy and I joined him a few years later when he linked up with the Navy."

"Yes, the Scientific Research Department."

"Actually, it was the Bureau of Ordnance. Mere semantics, though, and not worth dwelling on. The real essence is that Einstein was petrified that the Nazis were onto the bomb too and would have theirs fully operational before ours. So he searched for another kind of weapon that would make the atomic bomb obsolete before it was ever used and his search took him back to the Unified Field Theory. How is your knowledge of science, Mr. Bane?"

"Not very deep, I'm afraid."

"Then I'll explain as best I can in layman's terms. The Unified Field Theory has as its basis the fact that the universe is constructed, made up, of four fields: gravity, electromagnetic waves, a strong force, and a weak force. The strong force binds particles known as quarks together to form protons and electrons. The weak force rules the subatomic world and causes radioactive decay. Electromagnetism holds together atoms, molecules, all objects in general. And gravity is the feeblest of the four but the most pervasive, its effects being felt and influenced by all forms of matter and energy. Einstein's work in Unified Fields set up the possibility that all four fields were governed by the same rule, that in fact this one rule governed the *entire* universe."

"You're losing me, Professor."

"I'm coming to the primary point now. If fields are in fact unified, tied implicitly together by nature, Einstein went on to speculate that matter was actually a product of energy, startling a scientific community that had always accepted them as two separate entities. This has more recently been proposed as part of the Inflationary Universe Theory—more confirmation of what Einstein suspected all along. But I'm getting off the track. Einstein's next contention was that physical matter, that which we can see and touch, is actually only a local phenomenon controlled by gravity. The ramifications of this are staggering, Mr. Bane."

"Why?"

Von Goss's stare became distant and withdrawn. His eyes glanced furtively at his covered hand. "Because simply put the theory postulated that the same rules that apply for energy waves do likewise for tangible matter. And, since electromagnetism

335

holds an object together, if you could demagnetize it the object would . . . no longer exist in a physical plane and could consequently be manipulated in the same ways energy can."

"Jake Del Gennio's disappearing 727 . . ."

Von Goss nodded slowly. "Consider, Mr. Bane, how easily we can control the movement of sound, light, and electronic waves. Then imagine that you could similarly control the motions of matter and objects by applying a similar set of rules as set forth by the Unified Field Theory. For Einstein everything jelled during the Philadelphia Experiment."

Bane felt a rising in his stomach. His lips quivered slightly.

"The term is familiar to you?" Von Goss wondered.

"It turned up in my research as the link which brought you, Metzencroy and Einstein together," Bane said, sensing the crucial answers were soon in coming now.

"Indeed, and then it served to drive us all apart: Einstein into isolation, Metzencroy to COBRA, and me . . ."—Von Goss held his eyes on his lifeless hand—". . . into my own private hell."

"So all evidence of the experiment ever having taken place was wiped off the books."

"More than that, out of it all rumors began to spread that Einstein had burned his notes. No, he was far too clever for that. Instead, he altered his notes and equations to purposely throw others off and lead them down fruitless, and thus safe, avenues. I didn't understand why at the time and all these years it's remained a mystery to me . . . until I received Metzencroy's final correspondence. Apparently he stumbled upon the same information Einstein discovered during the Philadelphia Experiment but never made us privy to."

"What was the Philadelphia Experiment?"

Von Goss took a deep breath. "The degeneration of a destroyer escort ship called the *Eldridge*. We made it disappear."

"Like the 727 ten days ago . . ."

"Now you're on the right track but our methods more than forty years ago—the experiment took place in 1943—were much cruder. Following his theories on the connections between matter and energy, Einstein found a way to drastically increase magnetic resonance, thereby transferring matter back to its base form as energy in keeping with the principles of Unified Fields. This is all given added substance today by the proven existence of tacheons which apparently form as base energy in the atom, then immediately disappear as energy, or gravity particles, again. In any case, drastically increasing the magnetic resonance in 1943 allowed us to create pulsating energy fields that warped space into which our object was sent. Simply stated, we demagnetized the *Eldridge* and transported it into another dimension."

Bane thought briefly. He was sweating now, only partly due to the fire's heat. "Something obviously went wrong."

"Oh, quite a few things actually, not the least of which was the effect the experiment had on the crew. A few went totally crazy and within a year all had been discharged for being mentally unfit. The symptoms were often immediate and drastic."

Bane's flesh tingled. "Like those experienced by the passengers on the 727."

"And a cover-up resulted in both cases; by the Navy in 1943 and by COBRA ten days ago. With good reason, I might add. The world wasn't ready for the

337

results in either case." Von Goss hesitated. "Einstein was present at the Philadelphia Navy Yard on the day of the experiment, Mr. Bane. He monitored all the controls and gauges and studied all aftereffects."

"Including the crew?"

"Yes, but it wasn't their erratic behavior that led him to change his notes. It was something else, something he uncovered while reviewing the dematerialization segment of the experiment, something that wasn't clear to me until I read Metzencroy's report. Behind all this, Mr. Bane, was the wonder of invisibility. What if we could dematerialize our ships from both sight *and* radar? They could be right on top of the enemy and the enemy wouldn't know it. The prospects were awesome. But Einstein wasn't about to proceed with the experiment and the Navy didn't argue much in view of what happened to the men exposed to the Vortex fields on the *Eldridge*. It was deep-sixed, buried forever. Einstein took himself out of scientific research and turned to academia, claiming he lacked the mathematics needed to complete the Unified Field Theory when in reality nothing could be further from the truth."

"And now it has been completed for him."

Von Goss's face became drawn. His voice grew bitter. "It wasn't enough for Metzencroy and myself to follow our mentor's lead. We broke away from him and set about continuing work on the principles of the Philadelphia Experiment and the prospects of invisibility on our own." An intense pause. "Now Metzencroy had paid with his life and I with my . . ." Von Goss held his eyes on the dead hand resting in his lap. "I learned my lesson. Metzencroy did not until it was too late."

"He continued with Einstein's experiments," Bane concluded.

"And expanded on them. Forty-two years ago, in the preatomic age, Einstein lacked the ability to check his most advanced, drawing board equations for accuracy. Something was missing."

"Computers . . ."

"Exactly. And with the giant mechanical brains available to COBRA, all limitations were removed. All the barriers that had been in Einstein's way were chopped down. Still, it took Metzencroy twenty years to even approach the level our mentor was at when he died—a testament to Einstein's incredible genius. What he lacked in brilliance, though, Metzencroy more than made up in technology. We have machines now, Mr. Bane, capable of exerting unbelievable concentrations of energy and electromagnetics. These machines allowed Metzencroy to eventually go Einstein one better: he took the master's energy-matter thesis and actually discovered a way, a formula, by which to apply the rules of one to the other."

"More invisibility?"

"And far beyond. Again I'll try to be brief and untechnical. An object causes space to bend, Mr. Bane, to buckle in accordance with its shape and mass, thus accounting for the presence of gravity. What Metzencroy discovered was a means of electromagnetically distorting gravity. Remember now that gravity according to Einstein was the ultimate force in the universe. Metzencroy's electromagnetic change in gravity allowed him to change space locally in the path of an object, to fold space back on itself so that the object was transposed onto the other side . . . in another dimension.

"He created a vortex, Mr. Bane, and the object could be made to disappear into it. In effect, it would cease to exist. It would not only be invisible to the naked eye, but also to radar. It would still be there, traveling in its path on the other side of space. But if you reached out to touch it you would feel nothing. It could be regenerated after a certain period of time or once it encountered a certain sequence of conditions. But until then, it wouldn't be there . . . or anywhere."

"The missing forty minutes," Bane muttered.

"What?"

"The period the 727 was . . . gone felt like seconds to the passengers but it was actually forty minutes."

"Once inside the vortex, Mr. Bane, time ceases to have meaning. It's an entirely different continuum. Time becomes warped. You might say everything happens between the beats of a heart and ticks of a watch."

"That's incredible," was all Bane could say.

"And Chilgers, of course, saw all this as a means to develop the ultimate weapon. The very phrase 'arms race' is a misnomer, Mr. Bane, because there is really no such thing. The superpowers are not racing to keep up with each other, they are both struggling to find a means to end the race forever. Nuclear arms will never be used in their uttermost form because one side knows no matter what it does the other will still have retaliatory capabilities. Satellites tell us— and them—as soon as a launch occurs, after which comes a twenty-minute lag before impact. An eternity. Under these circumstances, striking first will at best gain one power an advantage of two or three minutes; hardly worth the effort. The idea has always been to find a first-strike attack that would take the enemy totally by surprise. Without those precious twenty minutes, his retaliatory capabilities would be effectively neutralized. The advantage would belong clearly and irrevocably to the party

340

which launched first."

"Project Placebo," Bane said slowly. "Metzencroy discovered a means to send thirty-six MX missiles whirling into the vortex. The Russians would never know what hit them."

Von Goss nodded. "Now we come to the real problem. Metzencroy uncovered the same flaw in the theory that Einstein did, though by a different route."

"And it all comes back to the disappearing 727."

"Just as Einstein's problems began with the *Eldridge*. The business with the 727 was a tangent phase of Vortex, wholly unnecessary really, but Chilgers wanted a detailed study of exposure to Metzencroy's version of energy fields in contrast to Einstein's regarding the effects on people. Something went wrong with an engine in midflight, though, and the Vortex timing mechanism was thrown off, so when the jet disappeared, it was in full view of the runway. This turned into a disaster because it ultimately drew you into the operation but it had nothing to do with the flaw Metzencroy uncovered. That was based first on a flutter, a bubble—a discontinuity—in space."

"A bubble?"

Von Goss nodded again. "A bubble which followed the same principle as the kind you're more familiar with, only this bubble occurred within the gravitational line where space folded over itself, actually within *the fold* itself. It was slight in size and virtually nominal in duration but it bothered Metzencroy and he checked into it. What he found led him to plead with Chilgers to call off Project Placebo and Vortex, and when he failed he contacted me." Von Goss's voice became distant. "Einstein said that the Unified Field Theory was better left alone, that man

341

wasn't ready for the potential it offered and probably never would be. After twenty years of work, all Metzencroy could do was prove him right."

"What did he find out?" Bane asked, finding himself dreading an answer he had sought for almost a week now.

"It all came back to the bubble. On a wider scale, a larger one, when burst, would carry the potential to rip a hole in the fold, creating a tear in the fabric of space."

"Like a Black Hole?"

"Worse because potentially it would be in motion, creating an open seam right across the universe. Metzencroy ran some tests and determined that the bubble had appeared when the second jet engine—the one that had failed temporarily—kicked back on as the pilot started his descent and your friend in the tower made brief visual contact." Von Goss leaned as far forward as he could without slipping off his chair. The fire was dancing madly about his face now, its crackling accentuating the twisted rhythm with his words. "Follow me closely now, Mr. Bane, because we're coming to the end of our scenario and none of it is pleasant. The sudden starting of a jet engine is not unlike a mininuclear explosion, though the release of energy is only one-billionth that of a fusion bomb. However, we will be facing three hundred and sixty such bombs in Project Placebo, ten per missile. Now, add the same factor to that scenario that Metzencroy did."

"Space folds back on itself allowing all thirty-six missiles to disappear and be transposed onto the other side of space in another dimension."

"Go on."

"The Russians would never know they were on the way and all standard abort and fail-safe features

342

would be rendered useless because the missiles wouldn't be anywhere where the procedures could reach them. The three hundred and sixty warheads would reappear over their targets, thus taking the Russians totally by surprise in the ultimate first strike and . . ." Bane felt himself gripped suddenly by a shudder. The sensation was akin to vertigo. He felt as though he were falling from his chair, dug into the arms for support. The sight in his mind clouded his eyes, brought first mist and then wet tears of shock he was afraid to wipe away for fear of losing his grip altogether. "Oh my God . . ."

Von Goss looked at him, nodded. "I think you've hit on the essence of our problem, Mr. Bane. The three hundred and sixty warheads, each traveling in its own fold, will have to return back to the other side of space before triggering, except the folds will not have time to close completely prior to detonation. Sort of like a door that stays open just a crack. But a crack is more than sufficient. The detonation of three hundred and sixty hydrogen warheads in the megaton range will cause a monstrous tear in the fabric of our universe, actually a series of three hundred and sixty individual tears that will eventually link up. But only one would be needed to start a process that might conceivably feed off itself until the dimensions converged on each other with nothing left to separate them. Understand I'm speaking purely theoretically here, but we could end up with the Big Bang theory in reverse . . . and the total obliteration of our world."

Bane just sat there.

"At the very least," Von Goss continued, "all the Earth's precious gravity will slip through the tear in the dimensional fabric. All air would naturally follow it through. The waters of every lake and ocean would rise toward the sky. Buildings would be ripped from their foundations, people popped like balloons. A vortex would be created in which our entire world would be turned inside out." Von Goss paused. "The other, far less dramatic possibility is that gravity will pour through from the other side of space, crushing the Earth to a gravity point source, a singularity, an infinitely small point."

Bane felt his body drift backward against the chair. Von Goss was describing what The Vibes had shown Davey: the future, the world coming to a sudden and violent end. But coud it be changed?

"He saw it," Bane muttered, "he saw it all. . . ."

"Who did?" Von Goss wondered. "What are you talking about?"

"There was a boy on Flight 22. He came back able to see things . . . and do things." Bane went on to relate a capsulized version of the events experienced by Davey Phelps and the other passengers from Flight 22.

"Lord in heaven," Von Goss said distantly when he had finished, "it's even worse than I thought."

"What did the flight do to him . . . and the others?"

"Basically, exposure to the Vortex fields switched on new parts of their brains and/or switched off others, the effects in this boy's case being rather extreme." Von Goss smiled ironically. "But under a controlled situation, not as extreme as we may think. You see, with Vortex, Metzencroy has merely scratched the topmost surface of this area of physics, first grade math compared to calculus. With Project Placebo, we are witnessing the most infantile of applications. Do you realize, Mr. Bane, that in an advanced stage the vortex principle could solve the problem of space travel? Pack your bags, step into warped space, and you could be on the moon, Mars, or anywhere else in the universe. Vortex reduces the distance from light-years to inches. We could actually colonize other solar systems as easily as walking through a door, not to mention the wonders of the mind Vortex might unlock." Von Goss's brow was sweating. "But all that is not to be. The base stubbornness of the military has kept science from advancing in geometric bounds rather than arithmetic ones. In the end Metzencroy even suggested to Chilgers that waiting two or three minutes to detonate the warheads after regeneration would alleviate the problem by allowing the vortex energy fields to dissipate, thus sealing the door to the other universe. The colonel refused to bend even that much out of fear that superior Russian ground detection systems and beam weapons could not be given more than fifteen seconds."

Von Goss stood up, the fire's light barely reaching his trembling lips. "We have tampered with forces in the cosmos I suppose we were never meant to discover." His right hand had moved across to his left, begun tugging at the black leather mitten to free it from the flesh. "Allow me one more lecture, Mr. Bane. All amino acids are asymetrical, either left or right. Since the ultraviolet light we are exposed to every day destroys the right-handed proteins, our bodies are composed of left-handed proteins. The universe where the *Eldridge* went in 1943 and where the 727 went ten days ago is right-handed to conserve parity."

Von Goss had the mitten off now. He began to raise his naked left hand alongside his right toward the fire's orange glow. "Yes, Mr. Bane, I can move this dead hand; I just can't feel it and can never expose it to light. I haven't felt it since a day fifteen years ago when I artificially created a Vortex field and couldn't resist reaching over to feel the other side. I reached over, Mr. Bane, into a world I had no business invading."

Von Goss stretched his palms upward till all ten of his fingers scraped at the fiery embers reaching out from the hearth. Bane watched the tips quiver and realized in one horrible instant what he was seeing.

Dr. Otto Von Goss had two right hands.

Chapter Thirty-Two

Bane aimed the Ford through the misty night, driving faster than he should have around the tight corners.

The end of the world . . .

"You say something, Winter Man?" Trench asked him.

"Just thinking out loud."

The mist thickened and Bane tried his high beams without success. The curves came suddenly and blindly; if not for the desperate lack of time he might have opted to stay at the mountain fortress overnight. As it was, though, Von Goss said Project Placebo was scheduled to begin in less than thirty-six hours, probably. Time wasted now was time never to be made up.

"Where to?" Trench wondered.

"Ultimately San Diego."

"To take on COBRA by ourselves?"

"I don't see much choice."

"And I'm sure that's the same way Chilgers sees it. He'll be expecting us, Winter Man."

Bane braked the Ford around a corner, sticking as close to the mountainside as he dared. The curve angled sharply and he felt his bumper scrape up against rock.

"There isn't any choice, Trench. We're the only ones who know enough to stop Vortex."

"There's desperation in your voice, fostered by Von Goss's conclusions no doubt."

"The whole world's desperate, Trench, but we're the only ones who realize just how much."

"So we strive to save a world that has declared you unsalvageable to live in it."

"Before Von Goss I could have almost turned my back and walked away from the whole mess," Bane lied. San Diego had been in his plans all along because Chilgers had Davey. The whole world might end tomorrow but Bane felt worse about the boy. Thoughts of rescuing him fueled his emotional desires, and promised to keep Bane going long after he stopped caring about saving a cold, impersonal world that had turned both of them into freaks. "We'll head for New York first," Bane went on. "I've got a friend there who can help us get to the West Coast."

Trench smiled faintly. "We could almost pull this off given enough time."

"We don't have—"

The light blinded Bane as he swung around the corner. He braked the Ford to a sliding halt, barely holding it on the road.

A towering yellow dragon thundered forward.

"A goddamn bulldozer!" he shouted, jamming the Ford into reverse and taking the mountain road backward.

Trench yanked out the pistol Von Goss's guards had returned to him and squeezed off five shots in rapid succession, succeeding in knocking out one of the dragon's eyes. The next four bullets slammed harmlessly off its tempered steel flesh.

"I'm out," he reported.

Bane struggled to free his pistol from his belt and tossed it over.

The yellow dragon roared up the hill.

Bane didn't see it, his eyes were locked on the back window. He fishtailed into turns, fighting to judge angles from his impossible perspective. It had been hard enough taking the corners going forward. Backward made his flesh crawl. His tires spit gravel. The Ford's gears screamed in protest.

The yellow dragon leveled its mouth in line with the car's hood.

Bane misjudged a corner and his back end slammed hard into the rocky mountainside. He fought down panic and floored the accelerator. The car lurched backward, leaving a fender behind which the roaring monster crunched in its path.

The gap closed still further.

Bane jammed the pedal down again, trying to put as much distance between the Ford and the dragon as possible. The effort proved futile. The monster took the curves effortlessly, swallowing Trench's bullets as it went.

Bane felt the pedal give a little, then come back.

"Gas tank's going!" he shouted. "We're almost out!"

Trench said nothing, just held the gun at nothing in particular. The Ford started to sputter, creeping up the straightaway.

The dragon roared at them, engine growling.

Suddenly Bane saw what they had to do.

"Get ready to jump!" he told Trench.

The dragon lunged down the straightaway, picking up speed.

Bane slammed the Ford's brakes, felt its rear tires teeter halfway over the edge, and jammed the car from reverse into drive before its skid was complete.

The tires tore holes in the gravel and then pushed the car forward with its last breath of gas, finding purchase and hurtling it out toward the dragon.

"Jump!" Bane screamed.

Trench already had his door open. Bane tumbled out his side an instant after him and an instant before the Ford climbed into the dragon's mouth.

The monster coughed, spit it out up and over its head. The rear tires it used for feet dug deeper as its smaller front ones were parted from the ground. The dragon reared up on its hind legs, seeming to hover there for a moment before the weight of its massive shovel arm forced it to tumble over, metal screeching against hard gravel and forming a death scream as the metal creature slipped over the side, mouth first. Flames jumped up in its path.

Bane struggled to his feet, then limped over to Trench. Trench's arms had been torn by the rocky surface, and his hands were reduced to mangled slabs of meat. His fingers trembled as he returned Bane's gun.

"You'll need it," he said, his eyes pointing toward a convoy of lights, narrowly spaced like those of jeeps, climbing the mountainside.

An army was approaching, coming for Von Goss no doubt.

Bane saw Trench's spent gun protruding from his belt. "I've still got two clips. That leaves one for each of us."

And he was handing one to Trench even as they scampered toward a rock ledge leading to a plateau. Trench snapped it home, started clawing for purchase in the stone above him.

The parade of jeeps was almost upon them.

They climbed quickly, dragging hand over hand

and squeezing fingers against stone until the tips of their fingers bled raw. The jeeps' headlights slid against them as they reached the top and they dropped low, hugging the ground and holding onto the hope that they hadn't been spotted until bullets pounded the ledge just below them.

Trench started to go for his gun, resigned to making their stand from right here.

"No," Bane said, grasping his arm. He glanced around. The plateau they had reached boasted only a slight rise. Through the darkness, he could make out breaks in the dense forest. Trails . . . "Over there," he showed Trench.

And they set out down the first one they saw. Bane bit his lip against the locking pain in his legs. His knees had suffered the brunt of the dive from the car, leaving his motions unsteady. Trench was not much better. His left leg was virtually useless and had to be dragged behind him like a chain, not to mention the horrible wounds on his hands. But with a trail to follow now they could make it. They could—

Bullets sliced the air in the path to their rear. Bane glanced quickly back and caught only the flicker of dark motion. No sense in wasting a shot; he'd need every bullet he had. Bane made out four sets of footsteps twenty yards behind them and another half dozen or so closing rapidly from the opposite side of the woods. The opposition had obviously found another route to the plateau and was exploiting the advantage to its fullest.

"We can't outrun them," he told Trench.

"Or outfight them at this point. Unless . . ."

Their eyes had locked on the same target simultaneously: an old, weather-beaten log cabin. Someone's hunting refuge, no doubt left abandoned for years, standing in a clearing some fifty yards ahead to the right. Bane lit out toward it, helping Trench along.

Trench crashed through the door, but Bane didn't follow. He swung abruptly back as he felt the shapes rushing in from the rear enter his sure-killing range. His move took them totally by surprise and by the time they had slid to a halt and readied their rifles, Bane had snapped off four shots, three of them kills and one just as good.

"I bought us some time," he said, as Trench closed the heavy door behind him.

"For all the good it will do."

Bane shrugged. He knew it was hopeless now, knew it was over. But it was not in his nature to give up. More than anything else that was what his training had taught him and more than anything else that was what he retained. Hopelessness had never existed for him. There were always alternatives, the problem being to find them.

The two side windows of the cabin shattered in a hail of automatic fire. Bane and Trench dove to the floor, instinctively toward opposite sides. Bullets thundered over them and more glass coated their backs. Each crept toward a window, palming the pistols which felt like toys against the powerful weapons of their attackers.

Bane chanced a volley, firing three shots at shadows in the dark, aiming only at motion. Two figures lurched backward. Trench fared even better. Four of the attackers chanced a rush in his direction and three ended up piled in a bloody heap, scarlet pumping from their neatly ruptured hearts.

Silence reigned outside, evidence of their attackers changing their strategy. The fact that taking them wouldn't be a simple task was obvious now and the opposition would stop looking for a clean kill and try for something else.

The first grenade shattered the brief stillness of the night and the second followed immediately. Both were direct hits on the roof and sent a measure of the ceiling showering down, exposing Trench and Bane to the black air. A third grenade pounded the front door while another made it through a break in the roof only to be caught miraculously in midair by Trench who proceeded to hurl it back out the window with half a second to spare. The blast took out five more of the opposition, but Trench had exposed himself and he now felt a rapid series of spits cough into his abdomen and spine. He went down hard, holding tight to his pistol, then crawling back to his perch by the window and holding on there as death reached out for him.

Bane was about to move across to him when the next grenade blast tore a hole in the floor. Bane followed Trench's dying eyes toward it. The hole was deeper than it should have been and Bane quickly realized why. It was a tunnel! This wasn't a hunting retreat at all, but a hideout for someone who needed an escape route available at all times. The Poconos were full of such cabins, in past years used as hideaways for criminals on the run, and they had stumbled upon one.

Bane looked over at Trench.

"Go," he grimaced. "Get out while you still can."

For some reason Bane hesitated, as bullets singed the air around him.

"You're the best, Winter Man, you always were. Go and save your world. I'll . . ."—Trench struggled for breath and coughed blood—". . . hold them back

353

as long as I can."

Bane nodded and slid his pistol across the floor toward Trench. He wanted to say something, do something more for a man who for so long had been his rival and would now die his friend. His hand reached out as if to grasp Trench, the gesture precluded by the distance between them, and Trench smiled slightly, motioning him to go.

Bane plunged into the hole. The tunnel was totally black but darkness had been a friend to him longer than it had been an enemy. He visualized himself back in the city twenty years before under the King's careful tutelage. It was like having the blindfold on all over again. A training exercise, nothing more.

Bane snailed on through the narrow, blackened corridor on his hands and knees. The dirt was cold but firm, solid on all sides of him. Above, he could still hear muffled shots and explosions. Trench would not let them take him with merely bullets. He'd make them bring the whole cabin down on top of him, sealing the truth of Bane's escape long enough for it to become complete.

The dirt ceiling lowered and Bane dropped all the way to his stomach, clawing his way forward against the cold dirt on his elbows the same way he had during fire fights in Nam. There was a blast from somewhere above him and Bane felt a shower of dirt rain down coating his back. Trench had made the opposition blow the cabin up, thus hiding the tunnel and Bane's escape from them. His rival turned friend had done what he had to, and now Bane would do the same. He shook his head free of dirt and pushed his way forward, oblivious to the pain and the red rawness of his forearms.

He might still have miles to go but it didn't matter. The slow rising of the tunnel's roof told him the end was coming and he could almost smell fresh air. Soon a ray of light would break the darkness he had grown to welcome and he would be out. From there nothing would stop him.

Because he was the Winter Man and he had promises to keep.

Chapter Thirty-Three

"I hope you understand our position," the President told Colonel Chilgers over the phone two hours after receiving Phillip Wentworth's report. "We're not canceling Project Placebo, just postponing it for the time being until we find the leak."

"No, Mr. President, I'm afraid I don't understand your position," Chilgers snapped. "Months of planning have gone into this. We may never have a similar opportunity again."

"We'll make one."

"That's not the point. Hesitance, Mr. President, will eventually be the death of us all." Chilgers' voice was rising, quickening. "Our enemies act while we consider acting. It has been that way for nearly forty years and I suppose things won't change until it's too late to matter. Yours and previous administrations have been characterized by total indecisiveness, an utterly reprehensible refusal to push forward. Project Placebo would have revealed, clearly and undeniably, how our defensive systems would perform in a crisis. I believe that is something you really don't want to be aware of, sir. If you don't know, you can't be blamed."

"The matter is closed, Colonel."

"Only for now, Mr. President, only for now."

Chilgers slammed the phone in his office down, letting his smile grow into a laugh.

"Do you think he bought it, George?" the President asked Secretary of Defense Brandenberg.

"It doesn't matter whether he did or not. We've canceled Placebo, stripped all his control away. Whatever he was planning is finished, neutralized."

"I suppose." The President's eyes wandered. "The cancel order was given *after* the thirty-six MX missiles with dummy warheads were delivered to Bunker 17, correct?"

"Yes."

"Something bothers me about that. Have we got Bunker 17 back on line?"

"They never went off it."

"Then I want you to make sure personally that they've removed the dummy missiles from the silos. As long as they're in place, COBRA still might have something going."

"The order to return active missiles to the silos went out at the instant of termination one hour ago. Beyond that, I don't see what we have to worry about from Chilgers. The base is back on general status. Yellow Flag is over."

The President frowned. "Have NORAD keep a line open to them constantly. I'm just not comfortable with this and won't be until we get Chilgers' ass in a witness chair before the Senate Armed Services Committee. I want him out."

Brandenberg's eyebrows flickered. "That will mean admitting our giving the go-ahead to Placebo without Congressional approval. Our dealings with Bane might come out as well."

"I'm well aware of that. Right now I'm more concerned about bringing Bane in safely."

Brandenberg looked away uneasily.

"George?"

Brandenberg shrank back in his chair. "I've withdrawn the unsalvageable order but it will take a while to filter down into the field."

"You're trying to tell me that we might still end up killing Bane, is that it?"

Brandenberg nodded slowly.

"Then let me make myself clear on this. I don't care if you have to go into the field yourself to pull every man back, I want him brought in alive because if there's any merit to the information Wentworth forwarded us, then Bane's the only one who knows what the hell Chilgers is up to."

"Whatever it is, we've put a stop to it by canceling Placebo," Brandenberg insisted.

"Let's hope so."

The bulk of Bane's journey back to New York was made in a car stolen from the first resort lot he came upon in his descent through the Poconos. His clothes and flesh were filthy but their smell reassured him, brought him back to Nam when everything had been so simple and his indestructibility was a given.

He abandoned the car near Penn Station and washed himself as best he could in one of the bathrooms. It was late enough at night for the station to be quiet, so anyone attempting to follow him from it on a haphazard trip through the subways would have his work cut out for him.

Even before Bane had surrendered to instinct, his destination had been determined. There was only one safe place for him in New York; where he could rest, regroup, and prepare the next segment of his strategy. He headed toward Harlem, toward the King, where the Winter Man had learned his most important skills. He leaned his head against the glass of the subway-car window, feeling fatigue sweep over him, but he was jolted awake every time his eyes dared close for an instant.

He had to get to San Diego. Vortex was centered there at COBRA. The entire operation would be controlled by machines and machines could be destroyed. Even a computer can't function once you pull the plug. He would destroy Vortex by himself.

Why, though, should he bother?

His own people had tried to kill him once five years ago, and now they had declared him unsalvageable, while he was doing his best to salvage the world. Where was the sense in his going on?

Survival . . . Bane's prime directive all along, the very essence of the Winter Man. Overcome all obstacles. Survive at all costs. The mission had to be completed. Abandoning it was no easier than holding his own breath until he died. The mission gave the Winter Man substance from shadow.

Then there was Davey. Somewhere deep within Bane, thoughts of the boy stirred. He, too, was in San Diego, a toy for Chilgers to play with. Bane wanted the boy, needed him. Somehow Davey had come to mean very much to him, the one feature both sides of his personality had in common and the thread that held them together. Without the boy he'd become a machine as he had been years before, a machine little different from the ones he would have to destroy if the world was to survive.

Bane found himself climbing up from the subway at a stop five blocks from the King's place. The Harlem streets were deserted, silent save for an occasional beat of music coming from an open apartment window. Bane kept himself pressed tight against buildings, stayed off the main streets, his route longer but safer.

A nest of tired brick apartment buildings rose on his right, lamps at their front doors nipping at the darkness. Bane had passed the second one when he sensed someone following him. Whoever it was stepped when he stepped, stopped when he stopped. The man, if it was a man, was good.

Bane kept moving, locking his eyes forward.

Behind him, his pursuer closed the gap.

Bane steadied his pace, felt reflexively for the pistol he'd given to Trench. Guns weren't much good at night anyway really, not much more than noisemakers even for the best shot. That thought comforted him only slightly. His pursuer would have a gun, an advantage no matter how you looked at it.

Bane swerved around a corner and felt the steps behind him quicken just a bit. Soft and graceful, the movements of a professional. But this was his turf, his game. The King had taught him to fight blindfolded and once you got over the initial fear, it wasn't so bad really. The thing that got you killed was hesitation.

Bane didn't hesitate. He kept walking, keenly aware that the gap between him and his pursuer was narrowing with each break in the sidewalk. The man—he could tell that much from the steps now—was choosing his moment to strike. Bane would have to choose it for him. He swung down an alley that ran between two battered apartment buildings and connected two parallel streets.

"King?" he called softly, just loud enough for his pursuer to hear. "King, where the hell are you?"

He moved forward a good distance into the alley,

then suddenly reversed his field, moving quick and sure back toward the entrance.

His pursuer was caught totally by surprise.

Bane reached the alley front just as a dark shape crossed into the blackness, drawing back too late for it to matter. Bane went for his wrist first because that was where the gun, a CIA standard-issue Browning, was, and the weapon more than anything else had to be neutralized. But he managed only a glancing blow as the man holding the gun pulled back, and when Bane tried again a fist slammed into his throat, just missing his windpipe.

The CIA man tried to free the gun and Bane let him, throwing all his force forward till his assailant was rammed against the jagged brick of the nearest building.

The man winced and lost his breath, but he still had the pistol and jerked the barrel for Bane's head. Bane jabbed his whole body upward and slammed a knee into the man's groin. A bullet exploded but the shot went wide. The CIA man twisted his body out and around, pulling from Bane's grasp; went for the trigger again and found a second finger stuck there, wedging it in place.

Bane felt the sharp back of the trigger bite into his finger, chewing his skin. The CIA man pulled back hard and Bane lost his balance long enough for the man to smash his testicles with a vicious kick. He was dimly aware of the awful pain and of the bile rising in his throat when the CIA man's free elbow pummeled his thorax.

Bane started to slip down. His assailant towered over him, Bane having misjudged both his size and strength. The man struggled to rip the gun free, yanked for it hard instead of trying to finish Bane with his hand.

A costly mistake.

Bane tightened his hand into a square and lashed upward with his palm, not for a killing strike because that the CIA man probably would have been able to fend off easily, but just for the front of the nose. The man's timing was thrown out of sync, a batter fooled by a fastball pitcher's change-up. Cartilage seemed to crack on impact. Blood started steadily out.

For a brief instant, the CIA man was blinded. Bane seized his chance.

There was still the gun to contend with, but he had too much of an advantage now to bother with that. His left hand kept it pinned low, the flesh of his finger still tearing, while his right hardened into a fist and went for the bone just beneath the man's nostrils.

There was a sickening crunch and Bane felt he could have driven his fist right through the CIA man's head with a bit more thrust. His grip on the pistol slackened and Bane closed his left hand around it and pulled, screaming from the agony of his torn finger.

The gun came free from both their grasps and sailed into the street.

The man tried for Bane's eyes with a clawlike hand. But the move was slow, awkward, poorly timed. Bane caught the fingers out of midair and bent them backward until they snapped.

The man's scream lasted only until Bane's hand clamped over his mouth and drove his head back against the brick, to come away matted with thick blood as the CIA man slumped slowly down leaving a trail of scarlet ooze behind him.

King Cong stepped out of the alley.

"How many others?" Bane asked him.

"Three."

"You take care of them?"

The King just smiled. "I knew there'd be action just as soon as you called from Penn Station. Had the itch."

"Scratch it enough?"

"Fuck, no! Never can scratch this kinda itch 'nough."

Bane realized for the first time how much his finger was hurting. "That's good because we got a lot more ahead of us."

"Now, you're talkin'!"

"Ever been to San Diego?"

"Not 'til tonight, Josh boy. You figure it'll be safe for you to travel?"

"Safe enough," Bane said, as they started down the street.

"Yeah, well if we meet up with any more of 'em 'long the way they gonna have to go through the both of us and the odds of that ain't too good." The King hesitated. "I lost that kid of yours, Josh boy. I owe ya for that."

"Then let's go get him back."

Chapter Thirty-Four

"The news is rather disturbing, Colonel."

Teke stepped into Chilgers' office lugging a load of computer print-outs and notebooks. Chilgers looked up calmly, unmoved. With Trench and Bane both buried under a mountain of rubble in Pennsylvania, he could stomach a little bad news.

"Something to do with Davey Phelps no doubt," he advanced.

Teke nodded. "I've spent the last eight hours collating and analyzing the results of our stage-two experiment."

"A splendid success, I thought."

"On the surface, yes. The full extent of the boy's power was finally revealed to us. However, the machines monitoring him have uncovered some rather severe drawbacks."

"Specifically . . ."

"The drop-off points of the boy's energy exertion level and energy concentration ratio were much sharper this time."

"Explain."

"He was forced to call upon more energy reserves to generate sufficient force, to a point where there were no more reserves to call upon. The task required of him was far greater in this instance than it was in

364

stage one which accounts for a measure of the change. But the variation was present even at the outset. Simply put, the boy was substantially weaker than demonstrated in our first test and the energy he was able to summon did not maintain levels as high as long. He's depleted."

"For good?"

Teke shook his head. "No. Run a car battery down and it will recharge itself after a while, though to a substantially weaker level. And each time the process is repeated, the weakening continues until there is no juice left at all. That basically is what's happening to the boy. You recall his complaints of headaches during the course of the experiments?"

Chilgers nodded, watched Teke finally sit down.

"His use of 'The Chill,' as he calls it, forces a massive concentration of blood to the area of the brain we believe his power is emanating from. The blood vessels have weakened substantially, raising the very real possibility of the formation of blood clots. Simply stated, Colonel, the boy suffers a stroke every time he uses The Chill. Oh, it's nothing serious enough to impair bodily function immediately. But it does place a tremendous amount of pressure on all vital organs, which seem to be deteriorating from the strain, especially the blood vessels supplying the brain itself. The process is irreversible now. We're looking at the possibility of a massive cerebral hemorrhage at anytime. The boy is dying."

"All this because of our experiments?"

"They certainly accelerated the process, but it had been started even before. The mind, Colonel, is an infinite mechanism while the body is not. What's happened to Davey Phelps is not a supernatural phenomenon, but merely an exceptional reaction to an outside stimulus in the form of Flight 22. The telekinetic power he generates, which his mind is a funnel for, proceeds at a rate far in excess of his body's capacity to deal with it. The boy himself, then, is of no further use to us." Teke paused, just long enough. "But his brain is another matter entirely."

Chilgers looked closely at him.

"I want to remove it for close study before tissue damage destroys the nerve center of the boy's power."

Chilgers fingered his chin. "You have an end in mind, I assume."

"Of course," Teke acknowledged, leaning forward over his knees and squeezing the wad of computer print-outs. "Our experiments on the boy, while intensifying the deterioration process, have pinpointed for us almost the precise area of the brain where his power originates—in other words, the point directly affected by his experience on Flight 22. What we need to find out now is precisely how it has been affected, specifically what nerve centers and cells have been altered and restructured to account for his . . . capabilities. If we are successful, it's possible that we'll be able to synthesize chemically the same response to those nerve centers and cells to produce Davey Phelps's abilities in human subjects of our choosing."

Chilgers nodded reflectively, a faint smile drawn over his lips. "You're talking about an army with the boy's powers."

"It's possible. . . ."

"An army that could turn an enemy's mind against itself; could assassinate, terrorize, execute, infiltrate, destroy without use of guns or bombs." His eyes sharpened and met Teke's. "Doctor you could be talking about a weapon far more advanced than Vortex. Destroying our enemies entirely from the inside. Making them turn their missiles on them-

366

selves, kill their own leaders, pass their greatest secrets on to us. Why a single Davey Phelps in the Kremlin could—'' Chilgers stopped suddenly. ''Wait, by your own admission this power is killing the boy. Our agents wouldn't exactly have very long, effective life spans.''

''Not necessarily,'' said Teke. ''Once we learn the roots of the boy's cellular dysfunction, we should be able to take steps to compensate. Keep in mind that everything which has happened to Davey Phelps was sudden and unexpected. Our subjects would be under total control. Their power could be refined, developed, nurtured. Drugs might be used to diminish or neutralize the potential adverse side effects. You'd have your army, Colonel, for as long as you needed them.''

Chilgers' smile broke free. ''And to think that even you, Teke, urged against the tangent phase of Vortex, against Flight 22. You told me there was nothing to gain from it at this stage, that we'd be risking too much. There are always risks, Doctor, but in this case they were well worth it. I'm stepping up the Vortex schema slightly. The bombs will be on their way in twenty-four hours.'' Chilgers rose and moved from the desk, clasping his hands behind his back. ''Yes, twenty-four hours from now the balance of power will tilt almost totally in our direction. But for how long, Teke? How long will it last? There will always be enemies, rising forces which challenge our own. The power of this country must remain supreme and *un*challenged. Yes, there were risks involved in Flight 22 but the gains more than justify them as I always felt they would. An army with the power of Davey Phelps would eliminate the need for bombs and overtly aggressive tactics. Our approach could be subtle while at the same time becoming infinitely more effective."

"Isolating and testing the precise factors involved might take considerable time," Teke warned.

"Years, Doctor? A decade perhaps? Vortex took an entire generation to bring to the eve of activation but my commitment never wavered. Even through the failures and disappointments I refused to give up because I knew we were on the verge of something fantastic, just as I know we're on the verge now of something even more fantastic. My entire career at COBRA has been dedicated to creating a totally secure America. Not just from bombs and missiles, but from oil shortages, embargoes and the threats that go with them. In twenty-four hours, Russia will be devastated and the first half of my goal will be virtually complete. Following through on your present plan successfully will complete the second half. Vortex will buy us the time we need. America's voice will emerge as the *only* voice. The word foreign will cease to exist. It will all be ours, the entire world." Chilgers gazed across at the wall, imagining the coming shape of what lay beyond it.

Teke cleared his throat. "We're getting ahead of ourselves here, Colonel. Beyond Vortex, everything depends on the boy's brain. And removing it, not to mention sustaining its vital existence apart from the body, is no easy task. I've taken the liberty of sending for a team of expert brain and neurosurgeons, tops in their fields and all security cleared, who will be arriving at various times tomorrow. But still there are no guarantees. Success rates in all types of brain operations have never been very high, never mind the type we'll be attempting."

"Make it work, Teke. Whatever it takes, make it work."

"Time is the key element. Every moment we wait,

every moment we allow the boy's condition to worsen in the slightest, reduces our chances for success."

"There's no way you could perform the operation immediately with base personnel?"

"Not within an acceptable level of risk."

"Then I suppose we have to wait. How long did you say it'll be before you can begin?"

"Close to twenty-four hours when you consider briefing the team on exactly what has to be done and developing a strategy for the operation."

"Twenty-four hours, then." And that brought another smile to the colonel's face. "The missiles might just be heading on their way as you start, Doctor. Fitting, I suppose. The world is going to be a vastly different place when we wake up two mornings from now." Chilgers paused. "And we might not even recognize it."

The Last Day:

THE WINTER MAN

How can you be so sure?
How do you know what the earth will endure?
How can you be so sure
That the wonders you've made in your life
Will be seen
By the millions who'll follow to visit the site
Of your dream?

—The Alan Parsons Project

Chapter Thirty-Five

"It ain't right, Cap. All diddley shit, if you ask me."

Maj. Christian Teare eyed Heath from the double-mattressed bunk bed in his private quarters. Night had fallen in the world beyond. Bunker 17's Yellow Flag alert now stretched into its third day.

"Everything checks out," Heath offered.

Teare frowned, unsatisfied, curling his fingers through his beard. "This thing's gonna burst soon and I got an ache in my gut that tells me the spill's all wrong. The timin' of that MX shipment's delivery still bothers the hell outta me."

"If Red Flag's coming, they'd want those missiles to be the first out of the gate."

"Well, Cap, I'd be obliged if somebody would tell me just who 'they' are."

"Major?"

"I mean, we always talk about 'they' this and 'they' that but who are 'they'? All we rightly know is that they got a master computer somewhere that fucks ours with a cable when we go into alert status."

"Somewhere in Washington . . ."

"Yeah, Cap, tell me all about it. 'Cept then I'd like ya to tell me why we can't even confirm that much during Yellow Flag."

"That's the system."

"Then the system blows horse cock. We got thirty-six MX missiles sittin' in our silos, and the only thing between us and a launch is a coded sequence on the board in Com-center. Back in Surry Gulch we used to say that manure stinks the least when you're standin' knee-deep in it."

"So?" Heath posed tentatively.

Teare pushed himself up from the bed and stretched. "So, Cap, you're a communications expert. I want you to spend some time in the computer communications room. I want all incomings monitored. I want to know where the fuck they're originating from."

"That'll take an awful lot of rewiring. Folks in Washington won't be too pleased."

"Tough shit."

"It'll still take time to pin the transmission down once it comes in." Heath hesitated. "What happens if it doesn't come from Washington or NORAD in Colorado?"

"Then they can stick their Yellow Flag up their ass."

"That's COBRA," Bane said, handing the binoculars to King Cong.

They sat hidden in a grove of trees on a hill overlooking the complex. It was four P.M. San Diego time and it had taken a full sixteen sleepless hours to arrive here after obtaining some necessary equipment.

"Jesus shit," the King muttered. "They got a fuckin' army down there."

The steel, barbed wire-topped fence which enclosed the complex of interconnected buildings was patrolled by men holding dogs, weapons or both. They were dressed in green combat fatigues and Special Forces caps.

"That is the army, King," Bane told him. "COBRA officially qualifies as a defense installation so the government takes responsibility for perimeter security."

"Terrific . . ." The King turned his binoculars toward the front gate where a limousine was pulling up. "Better take a look at this, Josh boy."

Bane refocused the binoculars.

"Make anything?" Cong wondered.

"Two men in the back seat. I can only see their silhouettes."

The gate guard spoke briefly to the limousine's driver and then signaled him through. The gate had not even closed entirely when another limousine pulled up.

"Must be havin' a fuckin' convention in there," mumbled the King.

"Something like that," agreed Bane. "Just one man in the back seat of this one."

The gate opened and allowed the second limousine to follow the first. Bane swept his binoculars in a wide arc across the spacious grassy grounds between the fence and the main COBRA entrance where both limousines were pulling up.

"A lot of ground to cover in the open," he said as much to himself as to the King.

"In the daytime anyway. Night's different."

"Not for the dogs."

The King winked. "Then we'll have to think us up a way around them. You figure the fence is electrified?"

Bane shook his head. "Not the kind of image COBRA wants to present to its neighbors. We passed

375

a little league field about a half-mile back. The problem is that getting inside the complex is only half the fun. I've also got to get into the maximum security levels underneath."

"We could just kill that shit Chilgers."

"That won't help us find the machines that will be controlling the paths of the missiles."

"You mean makes 'em invisible?"

Bane nodded.

"So if we destroy these machines, they'll become visible again, right?"

Bane shrugged. "I guess."

"And then the Russians'll sure as shit know they're comin'. They ain't gonna be too happy 'bout that, Josh boy. We might be lookin' down the mouth of another world war that even the Winter Man couldn't win."

Bane recalled Von Goss's description of the alternative. "At least there'll still be a world."

"You ever figure that maybe lettin' it blow up might be a ways better?"

"Not for long."

The King cracked a smile. "Me neither." The smile vanished as his eyes sought out a black knapsack resting against the tree behind him. "Ain't gonna be enough to just flip the off switches on them machines, Josh boy."

"That's why you're here."

The King's eyes held Bane's as his head twisted back toward the knapsack. "Been a long time since I messed with that kinda stuff. It's changed a whole lot since Korea."

"Only for the better. More stability and ten times the power easily."

"Yeah, yeah. Next thing you're gonna tell me is that settin' the charges is like fuckin': once you get

376

the hang of it, you got it for life."

"As a matter of fact . . ." Bane tried for humor but it eluded him. "You've helped me get this far, King. Nobody says you have to—"

"Bullshit, Josh boy!" The King's eyes flamed. "I ain't felt alive now for ten years. The world's changed, even Harlem, and there ain't much room for my kind no more. Know somethin', Josh boy? I hated Korea while I was over there but I never felt more alive. Last night brought all that back to me, and I'm not much inclined to let it slip through my fuckin' fingers."

"We can live without blowing up the whole complex, King."

"Is that a fact, Josh boy? And how you fixin' to get by all that genuine government security without the kinda diversion we got stored in that knapsack? I don't give much of a shit 'bout the world and even less 'bout COBRA. But if you think I'm gonna let you fry alone in there, you're fuckin' crazy."

"If I wasn't crazy, I wouldn't be doing this."

The King steadied his breathing. The massive forearms that could break a man's spine in two relaxed. "How much of this has to do with that kid I lost?"

"I don't know for sure," Bane said reflectively. "A lot I think. I spent over ten years of my life saving little parts of the world, so fighting to save the whole thing at once really isn't that new. But there's something about the kid I can't get out of my mind. I haven't gone an hour without thinking about him since I pulled him out of that hotel room. I don't know what it is."

"I do," said the King. "The two of you is the same. The kid and you both got powers nobody else got that make you feel all alone. And you both been runnin' too. People used you for your power for all those years like you just said, and now you see 'em doin' the same to the kid. The kid tried to run, but they caught him. You tried to run, Josh boy, but there was no place to hide."

Bane simply shrugged.

"You'll get him outta there, Josh boy, and I'll be 'round to help ya." The King fixed his gaze on the COBRA complex. "I'll be goin' in at night. Night's my time; always has been. 'Cept the way you been talkin', you gotta get in before I make my move or you'll have no time to stop 'em. Any ideas how to crash this party?"

Bane watched a third limousine pull up to the gate. "Just one."

Teke found Chilgers walking through the red-marked COBRA corridors, briefcase in hand. Red lines punctuated the walls in three of the five below-ground levels, signaling access was allowed for only those with top-level security clearances.

"The members of the surgical team have all arrived," the doctor reported.

"When will you be ready to start?" Chilgers asked, still walking.

"Within six hours, maybe five."

"So long?"

"They must be briefed on the particulars of the operation. The requirements and procedures promise to be rather . . . extraordinary."

"How much will you have to tell them?"

"Just enough to emphasize the importance of the surgery they are about to perform. All members of the team are cleared at the highest levels. They know when to stop asking questions."

Chilgers stopped. They had reached the private

underground garage which allowed him to pass in and out of COBRA's most secure operations level without ever seeing what lay above. He pushed a button and part of the wall rose, revealing his black limousine with his driver/bodyguard poised to open the door for him.

"I'll be back in time to watch the operation from the observation area."

Teke regarded him with shock. "You're leaving the complex—"

"Business as usual, Doctor, the front must be kept up at all times. There's a dinner in the city I committed myself to attend months ago and my absence would raise too many eyebrows, *political* eyebrows. We can't have that, especially tonight."

Teke moved with Chilgers toward the car. "We won't start until you return."

The colonel seemed not to hear him. "A glorious night, Teke, a glorious night. The dawn of a new age. The greatest weapon presently known to man is about to alter the balance of power, while we stand on the threshold of discovering an even greater weapon that will preserve the new balance. I won't activate the final stage of Vortex until the operation is underway. There's a symbolism there I rather fancy."

Chilgers climbed into the limousine's back seat and let his chauffeur close the door. Teke stepped back off the steel section of the floor on which the car rested and watched the platform begin its rise toward ground level.

Chapter Thirty-Six

Chilgers' watch ticked past ten P.M. as his limousine returned to the front gate of the COBRA complex. This was to be the greatest day in his professional career, yet he showed no signs of excitement or anxiety. All told, he had never felt calmer or more in control. He leaned back, with a sigh he smothered and a smile he didn't, reviewing the elements of his strategy which had made Vortex possible from the beginning.

Government minds were too fickle to rely on for the completion of Project Placebo; he'd known that all along. The key was completing delivery of the thirty-six MX missiles with the Vortex generators installed. While one half of the delivery team was fitting the missiles into the silos, the other half was putting into place a series of devices that, together, would jam all computer signals coming into Bunker 17 from Washington and Colorado. The signals into the SAFE interceptor were replaced by those emanating from a COBRA transmitting station here on the base. Coming up with the correct binary code to trigger Red Flag seemed a mathematical impossibility until COBRA's responsibility for implementing the SAFE system to begin with was considered. Chilgers - had had the system designed with a built-in back door which would allow him to enter and gain control, knowing someday that might be necessary. It had been a tall order, taking nearly three years to perfect. But Vortex had taken over twenty. The key was patience.

The end result was to place Chilgers in total command of Bunker 17. When Washington made contact to confirm status, they spoke with COBRA personnel on a signal beamed first to Montana, and they had no reason to believe it was anything but legitimate. The officers at the Bunker, meanwhile, had no call to suspect that the continuance of their Yellow Flag status was a product of anything other than a world-crisis situation or elaborate drill. Either way, they would obey their orders without question because that was what they were trained to do. And when Chilgers bumped the status up from Yellow to Red Flag, the buttons would be pressed and the missiles hurled irrevocably at their targets inside Russia.

NORAD headquarters and monitoring boards all over the nation would be aware of the launch. Before any abort or destruct systems could be triggered, however, Vortex would become operational and the missiles wouldn't be there anymore. A hundred-billion-dollar fail-safe system would be rendered useless. Confusion would result. Men would grope and struggle for answers. Their search would end after twenty-one minutes when the 360 individual warheads detonated over their Soviet targets, catching the Russians utterly by surprise and effectively wiping out both their attack and retaliatory capabilities.

Chilgers allowed his smile to broaden as his limousine wound down the COBRA drive and into the private bay that would lower five stories underground to the complex's most secure level. Bunker 17 was his. There had been a number of confirmation requests from the base commander over the past twenty-four hours, and since voice contact was technologically impossible, he had no choice but to abide by the computer signals he received in return because they were precisely what they should have been. Bunker 17 was powerless. Washington was powerless. The national-defense war room at NORAD in Colorado was powerless.

The power was all his.

But Vortex was just the beginning, Chilgers thought. A great axiom of weapons research was that a new weapon was obsolete the first time it was used. No matter. Work would be beginning momentarily on the brain of Davey Phelps, and a newer and greater weapon would soon belong to him.

The elevator-car bay came to rest on underground level five. Chilgers checked his watch again. The operation would be underway within a half hour surely. He would contact Teke once inside the complex and find out if there were any new developments. He would watch the operation, a portion anyway, and then retire to his office where the activation button of Red Flag at Bunker 17 had been rigged. He had insisted it be set up that way so that his ultimate moment of control could be enjoyed in total solitude. His vision had been solitary and so, too, would be his success.

His chauffeur pulled open the door and Chilgers climbed out wordlessly. When he hit the blue button on the side wall, the front section slid up, not unlike the simple opening of a garage door. Funny thing about technology, Chilgers reckoned, it was often adapted but seldom changed.

With a taut smile on his lips, the colonel made his

way down the red-lined COBRA corridor, hearing the door to his private bay seal closed behind him.

When Bane heard the large door close from his cramped position in the trunk, he knew Chilgers had entered the COBRA complex. Then an extra opening and closing of the driver's door of the limousine told him the large, muscular chauffeur was staying put, making him Bane's last obstacle to overcome before entering the top secret underground level.

He went to work on the trunk latch.

Bane's original plan had been to head off one of the arriving limousines before it reached COBRA and somehow change places with the man in the back seat with the King taking the wheel. Then when a different model limousine left COBRA with a man he recognized from Janie's picture as Colonel Chilgers in the back, he knew a different strategy was called for.

He followed Chilgers' car all the way into downtown San Diego, to a Hilton Hotel where some sort of civic function was being held. At that point he toyed briefly with the notion of incapacitating the chauffeur and taking his place behind the wheel. From there, he could kill Chilgers at will but that wasn't the answer. After all, he had no way of knowing if the colonel was the only one able to trigger the final stage of Vortex. Perhaps there were numerous fallback measures in place. If so, by killing Chilgers Bane would, first, lose his ticket into COBRA and, second, strip himself of a known *single* quarry.

So when the chauffeur went across the street and into a drug store, Bane chose that moment to work the trunk open, climb in, and wait. The waiting was over now. It was time to enter the complex.

The latch came free. He had only to raise the trunk lid to exit the limousine.

Bane checked his watch: 10:10. If the King was able to gain access to COBRA, and Bane had no doubt he would, his explosive charges would begin at midnight sharp. Bane would have to time everything with that in mind.

His thoughts turned to Davey. Getting himself out of the complex when all hell broke loose would ordinarily be something he'd consider only when his mission was completed. Escape was tangent to success and until such success had been achieved, considering it was more a diversion than anything else. Not this time, though. With Davey to think of, escape had to be regarded as a primary objective and not taken for granted.

Bane started to raise the trunk lid slowly, not worried about sight so much as sound. If the chauffeur picked up a squeak or a metallic tang, his eyes would be alerted and he would catch Bane at a most vulnerable time. As it was, Bane could hear the shuffling of thin pages, evidence the chauffeur was reading the newspaper he had bought at the drug store, its contents hopefully distracting enough to shield Bane's exit.

Bane continued to push, even more slowly at the end when the danger of vibrations and sounds was greatest. Then came the most difficult part of all: lifting his 200-pound frame from the trunk without causing the car to sway and lean. Bane angled his body to the side and eased his right leg out first as a balance point. It was badly cramped, and as he stretched it down pain exploded through every tendon. He swallowed the agony with a grimace and finally found relief when his foot reached the floor. He shifted his weight a pound at a time, feeling the back of the car rise ever so slightly as more of his bulk left the trunk.

The chauffeur kept flipping the pages of his newspaper.

Finally Bane's left foot joined his right on the floor and he was already sliding toward the driver's side of the car and peering around the flank to find the chauffeur going to work on the second section.

Bane shuffled slowly toward the driver's door, his shoes grazing the cement but never quite leaving it, seeming almost to float. Using the .45 the King had provided without a silencer was unthinkable, leaving him only his hands which was just fine. He would have to be fast, though. He couldn't risk the attention a lengthy scuffle might bring.

Bane coiled his fingers, saw the chauffeur's window was open. He was almost to the door. The man looked up at the instant Bane's fingers jumped at him, too late to maneuver from his confined position. Bane's hands locked on either side of his head, pulled and twisted. He felt the chauffeur's neck snap, his head go limp and slump from Bane's grasp. Bane opened the door and leaned further in to drag the chauffeur's corpse out.

Then he saw the briefcase. it rested on the leather upholstery of the back seat bearing Colonel Chilgers' initials. A plan came to Bane's mind. His main problem all along had been how to infiltrate COBRA without drawing attention and without utilizing assault-type maneuvers. Chilgers had to be outwitted, not outgunned. But how? The briefcase gave him the answer.

He and the chauffeur were about the same size, and from a distance or at a passing glance he might be taken for the man, especially if Bane tipped the chauffer's black cap low over his forehead. He would carry the briefcase noticeably before him, his intention obviously being to return it to the colonel who had left it behind in the car.

Wasting no further time, Bane pulled the dead chauffeur's clothes from his body and stripped off his own. In three minutes he was dressed just as the dead man had been right up to the knot in his tie. The clothes made a surprisingly good fit, except for the pants which dragged a bit over his heels. After stowing the chauffeur's body in the trunk, Bane tightened the black cap on his head and tilted it low; then he retrieved the briefcase from the back seat. He tucked his .45 beyond his left hip and jammed a pair of extra clips into one of the jacket's pockets. Then he steadied himself with as deep a breath as he could manage and pressed the button on the side wall he guessed would provide him access into the complex.

The sliding part of the wall came up without so much as a creak, revealing a pair of long, wide corridors jutting out at right angles from each other. Sudden exposure to the fluorescent lighting stung Bane's eyes but he ignored that and, holding the briefcase tightly, stepped out of the private garage bay to press the button just beyond the break in the wall. The door began its descent. His eyes adjusted to the brightness.

Bane had made it into COBRA.

He noticed the thick red lines painted across the walls like boundary markers and realized immediately he was in the high security section. All the better. Whatever he sought was contained somewhere down here. Still holding the briefcase clearly in front of him, Bane started to walk, toward the left because it felt correct. He saw a trio of white-coated scientific personnel moving toward him. Too late to do anything but keep going, not letting himself flinch or hesitate. He kept his feet steady, eyes straight; filling his mind with one thought:

I belong here. . . .

Tentativeness and hesitation were dead give-aways, the absolute worst enemies of an infiltrator. Bane recalled stories of a man who made a hobby out of mixing with celebrities at media events even though he had no right or reason to be there. The man just pretended that he belonged, believed it so strongly that no one ever challenged him.

The white-coated figures were almost upon him, two men with a woman between them. Bane maintained his pace, swung the briefcase forward and back just a bit faster to draw their eyes to it. He passed them with no problem at all, fighting down a deadly urge to turn around and look behind to see if they were still watching him.

Bane continued on down the corridor as it swung to the right. Immediately he found himself amidst more congestion, and he noticed for the first time, that all personnel wore red badges pinned to their lapels. He had the briefcase with Chilgers' initials showcased, which was just as good; but for how much longer? Sooner or later someone would challenge him. The resulting confrontation might forfeit everything. Still, he had to press on.

Then Bane saw a man dressed in a green surgical outfit coming toward him, the man vaguely familiar. Bane felt a slight swell of panic as their eyes met and the man veered away into a room. Bane realized this was one of the men who had arrived in limousines that afternoon, and he ducked into the room which bordered the one the man had entered.

The room smelled heavily of alcohol, which made Bane realize at once that the corridors on this level bore no smell whatsoever other than the perfume or cologne of the workers he had passed. He glanced around him and realized he was in some sort of surgical scrub room; complete with lime green uniforms, piles of surgical masks, and at least five different kinds of soap. Trays of sterile instruments lined the counter that made up the left wall. Bane could see steam rising from a few of them which meant they had been prepared recently for an operation still to take place. Bane moved to the right wall which bordered the room the man from the limousine had entered. He quickly caught muffled voices and pressed his ear closer, focusing in.

"Then we're all agreed on the procedure?" asked the first clear voice.

"So long as we can keep on schedule every step of the way," answered another. "Frankly, I'm skeptical. My experience in brain surgery bears out that very seldom do operations finish without unexpected hitches popping up along the way."

"We can deal with them," the first voice came back.

"How old did you say the boy was?" A third voice.

"Fifteen," answered the first.

"Well, his inner cranial development and temporal lobes shouldn't prove much of a problem. And his x-rays show an extremely fit organ. Much of the time in brain surgery you have to deal with lots of swelling and that's what slows you down."

"Actually, I'm not expecting any hitches at all," commented a fourth voice. "Gentlemen, all of us are experts at repairing damaged brains. Extracting a healthy one should prove child's play."

"Not when we have to keep it alive," countered the second voice, "and that means not denying it oxygen for more than fifteen seconds."

"Indeed," added the first voice, "we can afford no

cellular damage at all."

"Where's the anesthesiologist?"

"Prepping the boy now," replied the first voice. "Hopefully shaving that bushy hair of his to get it out of our way." Muffled laughter followed.

Bane felt himself go cold. He was suddenly aware that his hands were digging into the cabinet's handles. The men in the next room, surgeons obviously, were discussing Davey Phelps. They were going to remove his brain for some hideous experiment! Bane's rationality deserted him briefly. His hands came away from the cabinet clenched into fists. It was all he could do to restrain himself from charging into the adjoining room and killing the members of the surgical team. And he could do it, rather easily in fact. But he held back, letting the Winter Man guide him again. Killing the surgical team would accomplish nothing except to alert COBRA security to the presence of an intruder. Chilgers would know the complex had been infiltrated and Bane could never stop Vortex if the colonel was waiting for him. He had to keep surprise on his side.

In the adjoining room, the conversation droned on in terminology Bane didn't understand.

He felt himself grow calm. His thinking became more precise. The surgery might turn out to be a blessing in one way: he couldn't have asked for a better distraction to allow him free run of COBRA's highest security areas. He might even be able to confront Chilgers on his own terms or perhaps find the center of Vortex and destroy it without so much as seeing the colonel. Yes . . .

Something in his mind balked, pulled back. He couldn't risk sacrificing Davey to the emotionless men in the next room. There had to be a way to save

389

the boy and destroy Vortex. Davey was as important to him as the world, and without one the other could not exist in his head. Again Bane's mind roared ahead, impelling him to reach for a set of green surgical garb. He stripped off the chauffeur's black suit and climbed into the greens, stuffing the discarded clothes into a pop-up wastebasket. He tied a lime cap over his head and tightened the surgical mask behind his ears. Inspecting himself in the mirror over the sink, he found that his face was virtually obscured. As a final touch he strapped the .45 to his calf with white adhesive tape. No place to store the extra clips, though. Twelve shots were all he was going to get.

His plan was simple: find the boy and move him to another room; a closet, a linen shed—anything. With luck, COBRA would be thrown into an atypical state of confusion and disarray which would allow him even more freedom of movement. A little more luck and the surgery would be delayed long enough for Bane to finish his business with Chilgers and then rescue Davey when the King's plastic explosives provided the final diversion.

Bane stepped back into the corridor sure of his stride and purpose. His next task was to find Davey's room or everything else would be superfluous. Asking someone would raise too many eyebrows and suspicions. Attention would be drawn to him and that he could afford least of all. He decided to use the process of elimination, first crossing off the entire corridor he had bypassed in favor of the one that had led him here. Yes, this was the biological experimentation wing of this complex where sensitive weapons of the gaseous or liquid variety were developed. If major surgery was to be performed, this section was already equipped for it. It made sense to Bane that

Davey was very close by—but where?

Davey's eyes twitched in his sleep. In the dream he'd seen Josh very near and strained to reach out to him.

Josh, I'm here! Help me! I'm here!

Bane felt himself being pulled down the corridor toward the last room on the right. His heart was pounding as he opened the door without hesitation to find two armed COBRA security men and one startled green-garbed doctor, the anesthesiologist obviously, staring at him from their positions over a bed. The security men had their hands on their guns. The anesthesiologist held a straight razor.

"Is he stable?" Bane asked, mask down, not bothering to regard anyone but the doctor as he strode forward into the room closing the door behind him.

The doctor moved the razor away from Davey's head. The boy's shaggy curls had already been snipped neatly off, exposing his forehead and ears. The razor would finish the job.

"Vitals are strong," the doctor replied, eyeing him cautiously.

"Sedation?" Bane asked, grabbing the offensive.

"I was about to administer the final i.v. dose as soon as I finished the shaving," the doctor responded more easily.

Since the surgical team was apparently composed of strangers, Bane knew the anesthesiologist had no reason to challenge his presence in the room.

Bane moved directly to Davey's bedside and glanced at his closed eyes. "He's looking good."

"I've maintained sedation as low as possible to keep him strong."

"Excellent," Bane complimented.

The anesthesiologist looked away, was moving the

razor back toward Davey's head when Bane acted, ramming his elbow into the doctor's solar plexus and then up against the underside of his chin, in the same instant smashing down hard on the arm holding the razor. It clanged to the floor. The first security guard was still fumbling for his pistol when Bane grabbed a syringe from a tray near Davey's bed and jabbed it right into his windpipe, pressing the plunger. The man's eyeballs bulged as his hands groped for the needle, finding it only after consciousness had been stripped from him with death soon to follow.

The second guard wasted no time going for his gun. He went for Bane instead. Bane felt a set of powerful arms wrap about his head and neck in a Green Beret hold that brought sure, quick death. Bane twisted sideways and kept the second guard moving, stopping his grasp from becoming firm. The guard's timing was thrown off and he toppled headlong over Bane's shoulder, crashing hard against the floor yet lunging, meanwhile, toward the panic button at the bedside, and thereby exposing his entire neck at a strange angle. Bane reached his head before he reached the button. Bane threw all of his force into the blow, jamming the second guard's head down so his throat mashed against the bed frame's lowest railing. Bane felt the cartilage crack and give way, and then the neck went totally limp and became puttylike in his hands. He rolled the man over and glanced into a pair of eyes that would never close again.

Bane pulled himself to his feet, using the handrail for support, and found his eyes meeting Davey's which had suddenly opened full and sure. They widened briefly, looking behind Bane's shoulder, when something crashed into the back of Bane's skull.

There were two more blasts to the back of his head before he felt himself slipping toward the floor. Out of the corner of his eye he saw the anesthesiologist he had neglected to finish off sweeping something from the tile. Bane realized it was the razor in time to deflect the first blow and redirect the second so that it whipped across the doctor's throat, splitting it in two. The man's fingers clawed the air as he crumbled backward, making a gagging sound.

Bane rose again to face Davey. The boy's eyes struggled to stay open, fighting off the sedation Bane figured had been employed to neutralize his power. He found Davey's hand and squeezed it.

"Can you hear me?"

The boy managed the semblance of a nod.

"I'm going to get you out of here. Just hang on."

The boy nodded again, this time forming the shadow of a grateful smile with his lips.

Bane went to work. First the three bodies had to be disposed of, hidden for the time being, starting with the anesthesiologist's because the blood from the slash in his throat was just reaching the floor. Bane dragged him by the shoulders into the bathroom and managed to stuff one of the guards in there as well. The second guard he jammed into the room's only closet. That they would be discovered after it became known the boy was missing was inevitable. Chilgers would then know beyond any doubt that COBRA had been infiltrated. For now, though, Bane needed to steal all the time he could. The hope of avoiding violence was gone, so Bane directed his thoughts toward the next step.

The problem at this point was to get Davey out of the room, to somewhere that would serve as a hiding place while Bane completed his other appointed task. Then he would return and collect the boy, timing his escape to coincide with the King's explosive diversion and the confusion that resulted. Wasting no time, Bane unhitched the bed railings and let the wings down, pulling the dolly the anesthesiologist must have brought in up close to move Davey onto it. The boy's eyes flashed a bit brighter. If only he could come round fully, if only he could use the power . . .

Bane realized he was looking at the boy as a potential weapon just as Chilgers must have, instead of the victim that he was. He shook off the lapse and squeezed the boy's hand again, tighter as if to apologize for his thoughts.

Davey's eyes found his and seemed to say he understood.

The stare brought a shudder to Bane's gut.

He looked at me and he knew, knew every-thing. . . .

Bane pushed the thought aside. Gradually he eased the boy's body off the bed and onto the white sheet lining of the dolly, its wheels now locked into place to prevent motion. An extra surgical cap lay on the bedside tray and Bane tucked it tight around Davey's head to hide what remained of his hair. He would steer the dolly through the corridor, pretending to be on his way to the operating room. Before anyone could question him, Davey would be hidden and Bane would be on to the next stage of his plan: destroying Vortex.

He had unhitched the wheels and started to swing the dolly around when the door opened suddenly.

"What happened to the guards?" asked Dr. Teke.

Chapter Thirty-Seven

Bane pushed back his fear an instant before it showed on his features. He recognized the bald man standing in the doorway, surgical mask dangling around his throat, clearly from Janie's picture.

"I sent them for another dolly," he said, not hesitating, realizing that Teke assumed he was the anesthesiologist.

"Well, this one will have to do. The colonel wants us to get started immediately."

"In that case . . ."

"Is the boy under?"

Bane knew he couldn't hedge in the slightest if his deception, born of fortune, was to last. He recalled the dead anesthesiologist's intentions.

"I've just administered the final i.v. dose," he said.

"The gas is ready in the O.R.?"

Bane just nodded.

Teke regarded him only briefly as he moved across the room, raising his surgical mask. Two orderlies followed in his wake, finishing the job of swinging the dolly for the door. Davey's eyes sought out Bane's briefly and then surrendered as the orderlies started to wheel him from the room.

Bane felt Teke draw up even with him, his bulbous head dripping rivulets of sweat. Only the dim light was saving him from recognition, Bane reckoned, but what would he do under the bright fluorescent lighting promised in the operating room? He had to take the risk that Teke, the only one present who might recognize him, would keep his attention focused on Davey. It would be to his great advantage that the surgeons who had arrived in the limousines were all relative strangers to each other and would have little way of knowing which faces belonged and which didn't, especially beneath surgical masks. Bane considered making his move now, before they reached the operating room, but only briefly. The corridors were crowded, with staff and security personnel. His only hope lay in going along with the charade, even into the O.R. Except the charade at best could last only until one of the surgeons removed Davey's lime surgical cap and saw his head still layered with hair. Bane had no way of knowing how far into the procedure that would happen.

Then, as he turned with Teke to follow the dolly out of the room, Bane noticed the black shoe of one of the dead security guards sticking out from the closet.

Teke's eyes swept in that direction.

"I had a little trouble with the monitoring equipment in the O.R.," Bane said suddenly, hoping the words sounded both professional and legitimate.

Teke's eyes turned toward him, away from the closet. "Remedied, I trust."

Bane shrugged, smothered a sigh of relief. "I'll make do," he said, setting up possible delays in the O.R.

He followed Teke out of the room, moving in two steps behind the dolly. He felt his heart flutter. His whole plan was finished, ruined. They had the boy and, worse, they had him. He was a prisoner of his own deception.

However, even as Bane moved down the corridor, a new plan was forming in his mind. He would have to time things perfectly and take full advantage of where the eyes of the others in the room were expected to be, but that was nothing new for the Winter Man. As anesthesiologist he was responsible for putting the boy out . . . or not putting him out. The levels of the anesthetic were his to control. He could see Davey's eyes coming slowly back to life. If he held back more sedation long enough, the boy would regain his senses and with them would come his power. But would it be in time?

Suddenly the thought of using the boy as a weapon didn't bother Bane.

He moved with the dolly in Teke's shadow down the corridor toward the O.R. The rooms and people he passed became a blur. He followed Teke into the scrub room where they joined the rest of the team for a final washing.

"Are we ready, Doctor?"

Bane turned from his sink toward the man raising the question from the doorway and found himself looking directly into the cold cat's eyes of Col. Walter Chilgers. His surgical mask was in place, but for a horrifying instant he thought Chilgers was looking at him with more than passive interest before he realized the colonel's stare was fixed on Teke who stood just to Bane's right.

"Right on schedule, Colonel."

"Splendid. Then I'll expect no complications."

"There shouldn't be any. Our surgical team has studied the case from all possible angles. Every step we're about to perform has been planned to the letter."

"I'll watch as much of the process as I can from the viewing gallery."

"We'll try to give you a good show."

Teke dried his hands. Bane did likewise, fearful of committing any action anomalous to standard surgical procedures. Just observe and follow, he told himself, observe and follow. . . .

The next half hour of final prepping under the white hot lights of the operating room became a blur for him, one minute running into the next. He kept his eyes from meeting those of the others involved for fear the uncertainty he felt might betray him. His knowledge of this kind of medicine was limited to watching medics in the field and the emergency procedures he had learned himself. Nothing in his past even came close to preparing him to play the role of a full-fledged anesthesiologist in a sensitive brain operation. His only choice was to continue going through as many of the motions as possible. Past observation had shown him that no member of the surgical team ever watched the actions of the anesthesiologist closely during an operation. The more complex the surgery, the less they watched. They would, though, regularly ask for a reading on vitals, which meant Bane had to familiarize himself with the digital and wave levels curving all about the machines surrounding him. With any luck, the word "stable" was all he'd have to use until he grasped the complexities of the machines.

Bane's chair was located on Davey's right side, even with the boy's forearm. Ordinarily, the anesthesiologist sat directly behind the patient, but in brain operations that was clearly the domain of the surgeons. He went through the motions of aiding the lab technicians to attach the wires that would monitor the boy's vital signs and then set about studying the red, green, or white read-outs which flashed across an array of screens in constant motion behind his shoulder. It all looked like a bizarre electronic dance to Bane, and if he had still possessed the capacity he might have smiled beneath his surgical mask.

He stole a quick glance above him and caught a glimpse of Colonel Chilgers in the observation gallery, a semicircle lined with chairs and enclosed by thick, soundproof glass. Sensitive microphones poked out from its two near corners making the colonel and everyone else up there privy to any discussion the surgeons might have.

Thoughts of Chilgers made Bane's right hand shift involuntarily down to his left calf where the .45 was strapped. The possibility that the slight bulge might be spotted never occurred to him. Nor did the possibility that the three bodies he had hidden in Davey's room might be discovered soon. There was too much going on inside COBRA at this point for eyes to notice either.

Of more concern to him was how to go about creating the illusion he was continuously feeding Davey anesthetic when, in reality, he was doing his utmost to revive him. Bane had virtually no idea how vital signs were specifically affected by sedation. The wrong signs would be a dead giveaway to the surgical team that something was wrong.

Stable . . .

The word returned to him. The purpose of anesthesia was to guard against any unwarranted flux in bodily functions. All Bane had to do was keep Davey's read-outs just as they were now, perhaps a bit lower, anything but the rise that would come as the boy slowly regained full consciousness of the scene around him. But how?

Bane's fingers touched Davey's forearm.

Stay calm, he thought as hard as he could, *stay*

totally calm.

For a brief instant, noticeable only to Bane, the pulse and heartbeat waves rose into the highest grids on their screens. Davey had heard his thoughts, understood. All his vital signs stabilized with almost chilling suddenness. Then one of the lab technicians was handing Bane the black rubber mask that would pump anesthetic gas from the tank into the boy's lungs. Bane fastened it around the back of Davey's neck.

Don't react, he thought even harder than before. *Stay calm.*

The needles, waves, and numbers wavered not at all.

"Should I start him at two?" the technician was asking him.

Bane realized that the operation was finally about to begin. A terrifying combination of precise surgical equipment and tools that might have come from a carpenter's box was wheeled over on a cart to the surgeon who would perform the initial incisions and removed the skull bone enclosing the boy's brain. To keep the skull area sterile, Bane concluded, the flesh would not be exposed until the last moments before that initial incision was made, thus securing the deception Davey's hair would otherwise have given away and perhaps buying Bane the time he needed.

"Ready to begin gas flow at level two on your mark," the lab technician was saying to him.

Bane held the thick rubber tubing which ran from the tank under the table, testing its strength. He tried to pinch it together, hoping to close off most of the flow, but found it was too strong to hold in any worthwhile position for very long without being noticed. He thought of readjusting the mask so that the anesthetic would be steered away from Davey's nose and mouth, but he couldn't think of a way to make such an obvious medical error without attracting immediate attention. How, then, was he going to keep the boy from losing consciousness again?

The answer lay before him, at eye level on the surgeon's tray.

"You have my mark," Bane told the lab technician.

And in the fleeting instant all eyes were drawn to the vitals indicators above his shoulder, he swept a scalpel off the tray, moving it immediately toward the tubing still grasped beneath the operating table.

The surgeon seated directly behind Davey pulled a similar scalpel from the tray and tested its weight. Bane figured he was going to use it for cutting back the scalp prior to removing the skull dome.

"Let me know when he's under," he said to Bane and Bane knew at once the deception would have to end shortly one way or another because the surgeon's hands had gone to Davey's lime cap.

Bane made a quick, neat slice in the rubber tubing, spilling the anesthetic gas into the room's air and wondering if its effects or smell would be immediately noticeable. He took in several deep breaths, found no trace of gas in the air.

From the observation area, a motion that seemed somehow out of place brought Colonel Chilgers to his feet. He wasn't sure exactly what it was, only the general direction from which it came: the anesthesiologist's chair.

The surgeon behind Davey was ready to strip off the boy's cap and start in with his scalpel, awaiting word from Bane that the boy was under and his flesh could be sliced. Davey was starting to come round; Bane could feel it. In spite of the fact that he must have known where he was now and what was about to happen to him, the levels of his vitals remained stable. Still, Bane was waiting too long. The patience of the surgical team was starting to wane. Soon they'd know something was wrong. Bane started to reach slowly for his pistol.

I won't let you down, Davey, I won't let you down . . .

Chilgers' eyes were locked on the anesthesiologist. Something about the man seemed all wrong, out of place. He saw the man's hand sneaking toward his ankle and knew then this was a stranger, an intruder. He smothered thoughts of how the man had gotten in until later.

"He's under," Bane told the surgeon, who steadied himself with a deep breath and started peeling Davey's surgical cap back, feeling knots of hair beneath it.

"What the hell? . . ."

The boy's vitals began to fluctuate, red lines dancing crazily on the monitoring grids.

Chilgers moved his lips to the intercom which connected him with the four guards on duty outside the O.R. door.

"The anesthesiologist!" he screamed. "Take him! Take him!" Then, into another speaker to the O.R. "Stop the operation! Stop the operation!"

The guards started through the door.

Bane ripped the .45 free of his leg. His first three shots took out the largest of the overhead lights, casting the room in a dull, shadow-dominated haze. The four guards had drawn their guns quickly and surely as they stormed into the room, but the haze made them hesitate. All the green-garbed figures scurrying away or reeling back from the table in fearful confusion looked the same. Which was the anesthesiologist?

For Bane, the situation was far simpler. There were only four uniforms to consider and he dropped each one with a single bullet. Then, as reinforcements rushed for the doorway, he shot out the rest of the room's lights and pulled Davey from the table, stripping the tubes and wires from him.

"Don't shoot!" Chilgers screamed into the intercom connecting him with the blackened room below. "I need the boy alive! I need the boy alive!" His fingers scraped against the tile walls for the switch that would activate the emergency lighting. To allow for optimum viewing of the operation, all lights had been left off in the gallery and now the resulting darkness slowed Chilgers' progress, obscured the familiar surroundings.

Below, chaos reigned in the O.R. as more guards swept in and green-garbed surgical team members scurried for the door in panic. Bane pulled Davey tighter to him, resigned to his failure and pondering the pain he could save the boy by killing him mercifully now. The boy hadn't awakened enough to use his power, so there would be two bullets: one for Davey and one for himself.

Chilgers located the button, pressed it. A measure of the operating room's lighting came back, certainly enough for the guards to locate the two figures huddled beneath the table. Bane steadied the .45, closed his eyes to the horrible necessity of firing it two more times.

Davey made The Chill.

Bane felt something, a blast of cold on a hot summer's day. The hair on his arms pricked up, stood on edge, whipped about as gooseflesh sprouted outuard.

Oh my God, he thought, *it's happening. . . .*

The thick glass in front of the observation area shattered outward, huge shards and slivers becoming deadly projectiles that rained down with blinding force. Bane shut his eyes to the carnage as the bodies of guards and members of the operating team became

403

bloody pincushions, barely resembling the beings they had been just seconds before. Severed limbs and heads blasted against the walls with sickening force. The fury spared no one. Over in ten seconds at most, it left behind a scarlet pool which dripped, ran, spread everywhere.

Davey wasn't finished yet.

He pushed for The Chill again and all of COBRA was plunged into total darkness, broken after three seconds by the sparsely located battery-powered emergency lights. An ear-piercing alarm began to sound every other second, adding to the chaos.

In the naked light of the operating room, Bane saw Davey's eyes squint, his temples throb. He reached over to pull him from under the table and found the touch of his flesh to be that of a live, exposed wire. He yanked his fingers away convinced they were singed, imagining almost he could smell his own burnt, smoldering flesh.

Bane shook himself from the spell, grabbed Davey again and yanked hard. The boy gave way, clung to him with one arm. There was a laundry chute in the far right corner and together they crawled through the blood toward it. More guards would be coming soon and Chilgers would certainly give a kill order now, meaning no time could be wasted.

Bane pushed Davey into the chute, then plunged in after him, the drop seeming to last forever.

The impact from the blast had thrown Chilgers off his feet into the back wall of the observation gallery. He had felt the sudden energy surge stand his neck hairs on end an instant before the glass disintegrated and knew in that same instant he had been a fool not to have had the boy killed at the first sign of danger.

Chilgers knew now the invader was Bane, knew

somehow he had escaped from the army sent after him to the Poconos. The Winter Man was the only one capable of damaging his plans so thoroughly . . . but not completely. Even the Winter Man couldn't stop him from triggering the final stage of Vortex at this point.

The regular screeching wail of the alarm kept Chilgers from blacking out into an oblivion that would have doomed Vortex to failure. He was dazed all right and the back of his neck was numb with pain. But he still found the reserve strength to push himself from the floor and, using the wall for support at the start, to find his way into the corridor.

No ordinary man could pose a threat to the vast power of COBRA. Bane, however, was no ordinary man, and now he had the boy with him who was anything but ordinary as well. All told, Chilgers felt threatened for the first time in longer than he cared to remember. His whole professional life had been built around avoiding moments like this, moments when the cold grip of failure fights to grab hold as you writhe and squirm to twist away from it.

The corridors looked like a darkened, fuzzy labyrinth to Chilgers' throbbing eyes. He knew he had to get to the console in his office to trigger a Red Flag alert at Bunker 17 and change the face of civilization. He'd had the equipment set up there and rigged through the main computer banks on underground level four so the moment of this supreme accomplishment could take place in the same solitude in which all the great moments of his life had occurred.

Chilgers was still a soldier, not as physically capable as he'd been years before but mentally as strong as ever. He fought to clear his mind. The corridors became sharp again, his sense of direction was restored. Breathing heavily, he stepped up his pace and focused his thoughts on the button he would be pressing in a matter of minutes.

Bane felt Davey cling to him as they moved away from the laundry chute. The boy sobbed and moaned alternately, wrapping his arms tightly around Bane's shoulders.

"I had to do it! I didn't mean to hurt them so much but I can't control it! *I can't control it!*"

Davey smothered his head against Bane's chest and the Winter Man held him, held him like he'd never let go. His green surgical outfit was caked with drying blood, as were the baggy white pants and shirt the boy was dressed in. Bane was glad Davey had collapsed against him because it prevented the boy from seeing the horror still in his eyes. Bane recalled the sensation of watching the boy "make" the Twin Bear turn his knife on himself in the New York hotel room. That had been eerie, frightening. What he had witnessed in the O.R. just minutes before was a hundred times more potent, a power stretching beyond the scope of human comprehension.

The emergency alarm continued to wail.

Chilgers had wanted Davey's brain as a weapon, perhaps to create a thousand more like him. Now Bane could understand why.

The boy hugged him tighter.

"It hurts!" Davey's feet started to slip. "My head! Oh God, my head! They made me use The Chill when I didn't want to. They hurt me when I wouldn't. It hurt me bad, so bad, but they didn't care. They just kept making me use The Chill." The boy pulled away, then looked up, eyes wide with fear and uncertainty. "I didn't mean to kill all those people. I didn't!"

"I know," Bane said.

"The pain won't stop! *Why won't the pain stop!*"

Bane placed one arm across Davey's shoulders. "Let go, Davey, let go. It's all right now. Just let go."

The boy went limp against him. The emergency alarm stopped screaming. The regular overhead lighting snapped back on. At the end of the corridor, Bane saw an elevator, a second elevator in fact because one also rested directly in front of the laundry chute.

Strange, Bane thought, but maybe not so strange. Yes, in the event of an emergency Chilgers would want potential escape routes both up . . . and down. The second elevator must be a direct route to and from his office where the final activating device of Vortex had to be located! There would be a way to get back to ground level from here somehow, a hidden stairwell or something. But Bane cared nothing for that. The elevator was all he needed.

"Come on," he said to Davey, already leading him toward it.

The boy's feet squeaked against the linoleum floor, Bane realizing for the first time they were bare. Bane reached the elevator and pressed the button. Gears ground above.

Come on! Come on!

"What I saw," Davey said suddenly, "all the death The Vibes showed me. It's gonna happen. We can't stop it, can we?"

Bane couldn't find an answer for him, couldn't find any words at all. He heard the elevator floating down, locking into place. Slowly its doors slid open.

Chilgers reached his office and locked the door behind him. That Bane was nearby and closing, he didn't doubt for an instant. But time was on the colonel's side now. One quick motion with his wrist was all that remained to set the final stage of Vortex into operation.

Chilgers hurried over to what looked like an unstocked dry bar in the corner of his office, aware suddenly that his private elevator was in motion. He knew it was Bane but didn't care; there was nothing the Winter Man could do to stop him now.

Chilgers flipped a swtich on the side of the dry bar. The top gave way to a square console no larger than a portable typewriter and decorated with a series of lights and buttons, all surrounding a large red button the size of a silver dollar in the center.

Chilgers hit five switches below the red buton and five above it, waited.

The elevator's gears whined to a halt.

The lights on the console flashed green.

The elevator's doors started to open.

Chilgers moved his finger deliberately for the red button in the console's center.

Bane had the .45 out and aimed in the same motion. The gun's roar reverberated in the small compartment and stung his ears.

Chilgers' finger had made contact with the trigger button at the instant the bullet grazed his wrist and spun him around. His balance was gone and he was falling but the red button was still there and he reached for it, as the floor was pulled out from under him and a second bullet whizzed past his ear.

The hammer of the .45 clicked on an empty chamber. Bane rushed across the room and tackled Chilgers low, then looked back at the console and saw the red button in the center was . . . gone.

No, not gone. Just pushed down, depressed.

Bane lunged toward the console, tried to unjam the button as if that would somehow erase the signal already sent to a missile complex in Montana where the end of the world was about to begin.

Chapter Thirty-Eight

Maj. Christian Teare was maintaining his vigil in Bunker 17's Command Center when the signal for Red Flag alert came through.

"Well, Jesus H. Christ . . ."

The terminal operator was too caught up in the frenzied pattern of computer signals flashing across his screen to hear him. Automatically, all lights in the bunker changed to a dull red, triggered by the SAFE interceptor. A chiming alarm sounded for five seconds, then stopped.

"Get me confirmation from base," Teare ordered the nervous operator, knowing the command was futile.

The man punched out a series of instructions on his keyboard and waited for a response. When it came, he turned slowly to Teare.

"Confirmation established, sir."

"In a rat's ass," Teare muttered, waiting for Heath to arrive from the Com-link center where he was hopefully tracing the origin of the signal order down.

Out of frustration, Teare reached over his shoulder and grabbed the black receiver that would, under normal conditions, have connected him directly with NORAD, lifting it to his ear slowly as though to pray for a tone.

"Shit!" he bellowed when none came.

On the board which made up Com-center's entire rear wall, all monitored systems of Bunker 17 flashed from red to yellow and finally to green. Final missile launching checks were being made. The Disco was now shut off from the entire world. Twenty-eight seconds had passed since the triggering of Red Flag.

"Launching sequence will commence in one minute," droned the computer-keyed monotone voice. "Fifty-five seconds . . ."

Looks like we're gonna break our own record, Teare reflected ironically.

Captain Heath rushed through the Command Center's sliding doors, sweat caking his face and eyes bulging. Teare grabbed him at the shoulders when he was halfway across the room.

"The signal!" Heath managed, struggling for breath. "It came from San Diego! *Red Flag was triggered from San Diego!*"

"COBRA!" Teare screamed. "Jesus shit, it was COBRA all along!" Then, "There's got to be some goddamned way to call this thing off! It didn't come from Colorado or Washington! It ain't legitimate!"

"Except the computers don't know the difference," Heath said rapidly. "The SAFE system overrides all manual orders. The Disco's sealed. We won't have enough time to break through. Red Flag means *total* commitment." Heath paused. "World War III."

"Launching sequence will commence in thirty-five seconds. . . ."

"We'll see about that. . . ."

Teare sped out of Command Center with Heath on his heels.

"There's nothing you can do!" the captain insisted.

"There's plenty," Teare shot back, pulling a square-shaped key from around his neck.

"What the—"

"*Launching sequence will commence in thirty seconds. . . .*"

"NORAD don't exactly trust their machines one hundred percent, Cap. This key'll give me access into the Disco and allow me to override all previous launch procedures right up to the final button," Teare said, rounding another corner.

"Then why didn't you use it before?" Heath shouted from just behind him.

"Red Flag had to be in effect. Don't work before."

"*Launching sequence will commence in twenty-five seconds. . . .*"

In the Disco, Kate T. sat in the center console as the queen. At the twenty-second-to-launch mark, she removed a key exactly like Christian Teare's from her neck. The men sitting on either side of her followed suit. Behind her she knew twelve wide-eyed men and women were monitoring the Missile Status boards, two on each to ensure against error. She could not look at them because at this point her eyes had to stay locked forward on her console. Years of training had taught her the board was the only thing that mattered now, her entire life. But the years of training could do nothing about the fluttering of her heart. She still clung to the hope that this was another drill, though somewhere down not so deep she knew it wasn't. There were thirty-six MX missiles in the silos and ultimately it would be her key that fired them. No escaping that.

"*Launching sequence will commence in fifteen seconds. . . .*"

"We have commencement of primary ignition," reported the man on Kate T.'s right.

Before her, on the main terminal board which charted the progress of the missiles once they were fired, thirty-six lights flashed white in a perfect circle like a birthday cake's candles.

"Board shows all systems go, all lights green," announced the man on her left.

"Terminal shows all systems go, all lights green," followed his counterpart on the right.

The six voices from behind her were quick to pick up the act.

"Silos one to six, all systems check."

"Silos seven to twelve, all systems check."

"Silos thirteen to eighteen, all systems check."

"Silos nineteen to twenty-four, all systems check."

"Silos twenty-five to thirty, all systems check."

"Silos thirty-one to thirty-six, all systems check."

"Launching sequence will commence in ten seconds, nine, eight, seven. . . ."

Maj. Christian Teare reached the heavy Disco door with his key in one hand and his ID in the other. He shoved the plastic card into the slot tailored for it and counted the long instant it took for a key lock to pop out from the adjacent wall.

"Come on, come on," he urged, jamming his key home finally with a trembling hand.

"Launching sequence commences now."

Kate T. spoke with her breath hot in her throat, eyes locked to her console. "Computer attack sequence Plan D for David, A for Adam, D for Daniel."

"Confirmed," from her right.

"Confirmed," from her left.

"Commence final launch procedures."

The two men followed her lead by jamming their keys into their console activators and then waited for system activation while the Disco queen punched in

412

the personal code for the hour. The red trigger button on the center of her console popped up. The light above it flashed green.

In the silos, thirty-six MX missiles roared and shook from the strain of being held back, like eager race horses at the starting gate. Exhaust fumes poured out of their bottoms with increasing force until the observation glass of each was heated to temperatures exceeding a thousand degrees. The on-duty personnel donned their protective goggles which would protect them until the blast screens lowered automatically at launch.

Maj. Christian Teare turned his key from left to right and the Disco door, four feet of solid steel, slid open.

Kate Tullman's finger had hesitated for an instant on the trigger button. But then training had taken over, superseded reason, and determined her action.

"No!" Christian Teare screamed, the only word he had time for before Kate Tullman pressed the button.

Bunker 17 trembled ever so sightly with the vibrations as thirty-six missiles, each packing ten warheads, exploded from their silos and rocketed into the sky, white blurs climbing for the clouds.

Christian Teare didn't feel that sensation or any other. His eyes darted feverishly from Kate T.'s console to the main board which now projected the thirty-six white lights beginning their outward path.

"Trigger emergency override system," he ordered Kate Tullman.

She looked at him awkwardly, afraid she had made a horrible mistake and wondering how it could be her fault. This was totally against procedure. The commander didn't belong in here, no one did. But the same feeling that had prevented the on-duty armed guards from shooting the apparent intruder

413

now made Kate Tullman respond to him.

"Missiles already out of range for override, Commander."

"Tie in primary fail-safe system."

Kate T. hit a flashing button. The white lights on the main terminal board kept rising.

"Negative response, Commander. Primary fail-safe system inoperative." Then she looked up at him. "The signal's been jammed."

Major Teare leaned over Kate's right shoulder. "Then we'll just have to blast those fuckers outta the sky." He turned briefly toward Heath. "What's a safe destruct distance, Cap?"

"Six thousand feet, Major."

Teare jammed his square key into a hidden slot underneath the center console table and turned it until a black button popped up beside the red one the Disco queen had pressed to launch the missiles.

"Fuck you, COBRA," he whispered. "NORAD don't tell you all its secrets." He cocked his head to the rear. "Give me a distance update on those missiles and keep 'em coming, son."

"Three thousand five hundred," came a voice from behind him. "Course steady. Four thousand feet. . . ."

Teare moved his massive index finger to the black destruct button, his eyes fixed on the board displaying the missiles' track. "I think I'm gonna pay me a personal visit to those bastards in San Diego. . . ."

"Four thousand five hundred . . . five thousand."

Teare got ready to push.

"Five thousand five hundred feet . . ."

Teare's finger started to move, eyes locked on the display board.

"Six thou—"

"What the blue blazin' fuck? . . ."

The white lights on the main terminal board, all thirty-six of them, went out before Teare could press the destruct button. The major did a double take, blinked rapidly, checked around the Disco to make sure he wasn't losing his mind and found a host of faces as dumbstruck as his own watching the impossible in silence.

Thirty-six MX missiles had simply disappeared.

The triggering of the emergency alarm had brought the NORAD commander down to the main operations room in the Cheyenne Mountains of Colorado with his uniform jacket only half buttoned.

"We've detected a launch, sir," the shift chief yelled to him as he descended the stairs, eyes searching about the eight screens on the massive blackened wall before him.

"The Russians? Oh Christ, what grid?"

The shift chief hesitated. "Not the Russians, sir, it was . . . us. Our launch, that is."

"What?"

"Our MX installation in Montana."

"Bunker 17? That's impossible. The drill was canceled. I'm sure that—" The NORAD commander's eyes finally found the screen monitoring the flight of the thirty-six missiles. "My God . . . Did we get confirmation on this?"

"Negative. All communications with the installation have shut down. But confidence of the launch is high. In fact—"

The shift chief's words were broken off by a collective lost breath spreading through the operations room. On the center board, the computer-enhanced lines following the missiles' path weren't there anymore, which meant the missiles weren't either.

But the commander's eyes stayed on the board as if they were. "Better get me the President on the blower, Chief."

The receiver felt extremely heavy in Secretary of Defense Brandenberg's hand. The President's call on the red line had awakened him from a sound sleep. He could only hope he was still dreaming.

"Disappeared?" he wondered.

"That's the word from NORAD," the President told him.

"Computer foul-up perhaps."

"The only foul-up was on our part for not realizing Chilgers had something up his sleeve with Project Placebo. Those missiles launched all right."

"What does Bunker 17 say?"

"Nothing. We've been unable to raise the base. Total communications blackout."

"But I spoke with them this afternoon. . . . Good God, they must have been infiltrated!"

"Not infiltrated, George, fooled by Chilgers just as we were." The President paused, collected his thoughts, "Wentworth's report said this whole thing started with a disappearing 727."

"Which later came back."

"And so will those missiles when they reach their detonation points . . . over Russia."

"Have the Soviets contacted us?"

The President nodded. "They wanted to check on the nature of a suspected launch their satellites picked up and then lost. We told them we had a blowout in some of our silos. I think they bought it. They'll know the truth in twenty minutes anyway. We all will."

"World War III," muttered Brandenberg. "Or worse."

The sudden return to normal lighting stung King Cong's eyes. He finished setting the tenth timing device and moved on to place the final five charges.

For the past fifteen minutes, he'd moved about the lower and upper levels of COBRA as if he belonged and in all the confusion no one had challenged him. Strangely, his biggest problem hadn't been subduing the guards after cutting his way through the fence into the compound, but finding one large enough. As it was, the guard whose uniform he appropriated was still four inches shorter in the legs. The dogs hadn't been a problem either; they'd just made a lot of noise he had quickly silenced with ease.

He set the small, but extremely potent, explosives at the weakest structural points of the building. The King had done lots of demolition work behind North Korean lines years before, and although the technical particulars eluded him, he had gained an instinctive awareness of the best places to blow if you wanted to bring a structure down. Not that he possessed any illusions that fifteen charges could do that to COBRA. If properly placed, though, they could virtually shut the complex down, wreaking havoc everywhere and creating a diversion for Josh's escape.

The return of the lights would bring a return to relative normalcy. Take away their hundred-watt bulbs and the bastards were basically helpless. The King loved the dark and working in it once again had been a pleasure. Now he would have to work faster and keep on the move. Five more to go and then he'd be on his way out of the building to watch the fireworks from the nearby hill. And, hell, if Josh didn't come out, then he'd go in after him.

The King snaked down the corridors as if they were the streets of Harlem. People were passing him from both directions now and he just acted as if he were doing what he was supposed to. Of course, if any of them ventured too close he was ready for that too, even hoped for it—but not until the final charges were set.

He felt more alive than he had in years. Death and destruction were in his blood. Take them away for too long and a kind of anemia resulted. The King knew his veins were pumped full again.

He placed the twelfth charge and set the timer for five seconds after the last. All the explosives had been placed, the first timed to go off at midnight sharp, twenty minutes away.

Long time, the King figured.

Chapter Thirty-Nine

"I should kill you right now."

Chilgers looked up at Bane from behind his desk, clutching his still numb wrist.

"Go ahead, Mr. Bane," he said. "My work is done. In twenty minutes the world will move on to a new and brighter course."

"In twenty minutes the world is gonna break up all around us."

Chilgers glanced away from him, back toward the elevator where Davey stood trembling slightly. "You destroyed the next stage of my operation. Pity really. A total waste."

Bane lunged over the desk, grabbed Chilgers by the lapels. "Bring those missiles back, you bastard! Don't you understand what's about to happen, what you're about to cause?"

The colonel remained totally calm. "Fully, Mr. Bane."

Bane tossed him back into his chair.

"There's no way those missiles can be recalled now," Chilgers went on. "Why, for all intents and purposes they don't even exist anymore. You spoke to Von Goss and I'm sure your able mind has filled in any holes he might have left."

"And what's going to fill the hole left when the

Earth gets scrambled into cosmic dust?"

"There will be no such holes, Mr. Bane. Instead there will be three hundred and sixty considerably smaller ones all centered in the Soviet Union. I dare say their retaliatory capabilities will be rendered utterly helpless. With no hope of regaining their advantage, I'm expecting an unconditional surrender."

"If there's anyone left to surrender to . . ."

Chilgers frowned. "More of that? I must say, you disappoint me, Mr. Bane. You must think me a total fool to proceed with an operation that would, to use your words, 'scramble the Earth.' I didn't ignore Metzencroy's report, nor did I disregard it. Other scientists on my staff totally refuted his theory."

"You didn't speak to Von Goss."

"Ah, the old recluse who spent his last day in a research lab fifteen years ago. Of course, I had to have him eliminated as well. He became a nuisance."

"A nuisance who understood the forces you're unleashing."

"I weighed the opinions of Metzencroy—and accordingly Von Goss—against the considered opinions of half a dozen other experts, all of whom insisted their theory was completely out of hand."

Bane leaned forward over the desk. "But none of them worked directly with Einstein forty years ago. None of them possessed the kind of intuitive insight that could only be gained from that kind of direct experience."

Chilgers checked his watch. "Eighteen minutes, Mr. Bane, eighteen minutes until a new balance of power is set forth in the world. And even if I could recall the missiles, I hardly think this intuitive insight you speak of would be reason to do so. You're not a scientist, Mr. Bane, and even allowing for your

420

newfound knowledge, can you honestly tell me that you know beyond a shadow of doubt that Vortex will end in the obliteration of our planet?"

Bane said nothing.

"Of course you can't, because you don't know. Nobody knows. Certainly the possibility exists but in the realm we have entered, *all* possibilities exist. You see, scientists know absolutely nothing. They merely perceive and make deductions, feed data if you will for the rest of us to base our decisions on. Scientists are totally incapable of activating anything. Given the responsibility, they would argue forever about the right approach and the *potential* ramifications. Science is too important to be left to the scientists, Mr. Bane. Decisions must be left to the military, men who have built their lives around making them. Science is a tool for us, nothing more."

"Speaking for the Pentagon now, Chilgers?"

"Their thoughts, not their words."

"You're really willing to risk destroying the world, aren't you?"

"If the risk present is at an acceptable level, absolutely. And in this case it is. You see, Mr. Bane, we don't know at all whether Metzencroy's theories are correct but we do know that the Russians' particle beam weapon will be completed within the month." Chilgers noted Bane's surprise and then proceeded. "Sixteen minutes, Winter Man, I have no reason to lie at this point. Yes, the weapon our . . . scientists claimed was an impossibility is about to be activated by our greatest adversary. Only ground based, mind you, but the beam will still be capable of picking up and totally eviscerating any missiles we launch before they even get close to striking distance. Do you know what that means, Mr. Bane, do you have any idea? The Russians will have won. They'll be able to institute a first strike fully aware that they can brush aside any retaliation we mount with barely an effort. So I took matters into my own hands to save this country from its own disastrous future. For years the Russians have thrown all their scientific energies into developing their beam weapon, believing it to be the ultimate force in the universe. They're in for quite a surprise. Even if the beam were operational today, and it may well be, it would be helpless to do anything about the thirty-six missiles now irrevocably on their way. You can't hit what you can't see, Mr. Bane, and by the time the warheads become visible they'll be over their targets."

Now it was Chilgers who leaned forward. "You see, we're talking about risk here all right, *acceptable* risk. To me the very real risk of a working Soviet beam weapon is far less acceptable than the risk presented by a crazed scientist."

"It really is that simple for you, isn't it?" Bane charged. "All you can see are war plans and casualty figures presented on green print-out paper by some monster computer and you look at people the same way. Look a little closer, Colonel. Einstein discovered a power so frightening he spent the last of his years far away from the laboratory. Only two men had any idea what this power might be. One ended up with a pair of right hands because of it, while the other rediscovered it only to realize the same thing Einstein did forty years ago: that it represents Armageddon, Colonel, the Big Bang theory in reverse. Think about it, Colonel, for once just *think!*"

"Thirteen minutes, Mr. Bane. And I should imagine the guards will be coming to check on me well before then." Chilgers paused, eyed Davey in the rear of the room. "Of course there's an alternative to execution for you. You could join us, in a high-level position too. All I would ask in return is that you . . . help us with the boy. The Russians don't have Vortex and they also don't have Davey Phelps. His power needs to be developed, controlled. Help us do so."

Bane snapped. All the reason in him gave way to impulse. He was across the side of Chilgers' desk in an instant, the tip of a letter opener pressed firmly against the colonel's jugular.

"There's got to be a way to stop those missiles, Colonel. Tell me or all you'll see in the next thirteen minutes is your blood spilling on the desk." And he pressed the point a fraction closer.

"Twelve, Mr. Bane," Chilgers corrected, not even flinching. "My idea of surgery to remove the boy's brain was rushed, wrong," he managed through a contracted throat. "Of course with you around to help control and coax him, such rash action will no longer be necessary. You have my word."

It was the final statement that nearly triggered Bane's hand into a tearing motion, but then something occurred to him. Chilgers had struck a chord in his mind. He'd had the means to obtain the information he needed all along. How negligent he had been. He could only hope it wasn't too late.

"Come over here, Davey," was all he said.

The boy drew up even with the desk, locking his eyes trustingly with Bane's.

Bane moved the letter opener from the colonel's throat. "Use The Chill on him, Davey. Make him obey us. Make him do as I say."

Davey nodded, turned toward Chilgers. The colonel glanced at Bane, then Davey, and finally away. His expression remained fixed for a moment but suddenly it flashed fear.

Davey looked into his mind and through it. He called upon memories of the wires strapped to his

423

balls, of stinking in his own urine, and of the horrible agony he'd felt when the colonel pushed the button, to fuel a hate which rose from deep within him, awakening The Chill. He felt it coming strong and sure, felt it first as a dull throb in his temples and then as a racking in his whole head.

Bane felt it too, as if the air in the room had been split into a billion separate fibers standing on edge, heating up, charging with electricity. Something forced him to move away from Chilgers.

The colonel's fingers started to tremble, soon his arms too. His teeth clamped together, separated, clamped again. His mouth dropped finally, his eyes bulging open, unblinking. The trembling in his fingers worsened, and now Bane could see the veins near his temples pulsating wildly.

"Is there a way to stop the missiles?" Bane asked him, knowing he had just over ten minutes left to do so.

Bane could see Chilgers straining to resist. Davey pushed harder. He was master of The Chill this time, finding it surprisingly simple to control its level with so narrow a field of focus. The feeling pleased him.

Chilgers succumbed. "Yes."

"How?" Bane demanded. "How can we stop the missiles?"

Chilgers resisted again. Bane glanced at Davey, saw the boy's eyes had narrowed into tiny focused slits blazing at their target. He felt that if he passed his palm before them, a pair of holes would be burned in his skin.

Chilgers' teeth ground together, every pore of his facial flesh vibrating enough to blur his features. A trickle of blood started from one of his nostrils. His mouth pulsed open, wider with each beat.

"Whole plan," he muttered toward no one, unable

to hold the words back any longer. They came reluctantly, as if his own voice had turned on him. "Whole plan was to have missiles and later warheads travel within individual folds in space long enough to get them to their detonation points. Space would then fold back to normal to allow them access back to our side where they would become visible"—Chilgers mounted another attempt at resistance; blood trickled from his other nostril—"and tangible again. Detonating missiles on reverse side of space would serve no purpose, would—"

"But how can they be stopped?" Bane cut in, knowing the nine-minute mark was fast approaching.

No resistance this time. "Each warhead is equipped with its own gravity-demagnetizing device, but all are controlled from the main computer. The computer can be reprogramed to . . . reprogramed to . . . *Ahhhhhhhhhhhhhhh*! . . ."

Chilgers started to collapse. Davey pushed harder. Sitting half bent over, the colonel resumed.

"Computer can be reprogramed to reduce the fold openings to an infinitely small degree so that the warheads would be unable to pass back through them, effectively trapping them on the other side for infinity."

Chilgers slumped. Bane jerked him back up by the hair.

"Loop would continue forever on other side of fold. Warheads for all intents and purposes would cease to exist in our dimension."

"That's it!" Bane screamed. "Where is this computer?"

"Upstairs. Control console in private room in main terminal area."

"How can we get there?"

425

"Main terminal area accessible by private elevator."

"Take us there," Bane told him and Chilgers fidgeted in his chair only briefly before rising dazedly.

Davey's eyes stayed locked on him, maintaining their intensity. Bane looked at him and saw the hate, felt it, was afraid to move any closer to the boy. Something occurred to him suddenly.

"Do you keep any guns in your office, Colonel?"

Chilgers' face twitched horribly. Bane realized he'd have to wipe away the blood dribbling from his nose before they reached the computer area.

"Cabinet in closet," the colonel told him.

Bane opened it and chose an Uzi from a wide assortment of automatic weapons. Time was the only concern now; only eight minutes remained before the 360 MX warheads would reenter through the folds in space and detonate over their targets. He led Chilgers to the elevator, careful not to come between him and Davey. The computer terminal room was located on the floor directly above them. Bane pushed number *4* and slid back the Uzi's bolt as the compartment began its agonizingly slow climb. Davey positioned himself behind Chilgers, focusing on the colonel's neck. Its thin flesh began pulsing. Bane couldn't believe what he was seeing, what he was feeling. The boy had actually taken over the bastard's mind. But for how long could he maintain control? Bane saw the strain was telling on him already; his breath was coming in rapid heaves and his eyes were squinting in what might have been pain.

Just seven more minutes, Davey. Hold on for just seven more minutes. . . .

Davey wasn't sure if Josh spoke the words or just thought them. Either way, they came in loud and clear and he wanted to tell him he could control Chilgers forever. He had never been able to hold onto The Chill this long before without pain splitting his head, but never before had he been able to concern himself with the *single* target of a man he truly hated. His escapes in New York, the experiments, the destruction of the operating room—all had required infinitely greater expenditures of energy on his part. Oh, the pain was there all right, but it was holding at a dull throb and that much he could take.

The elevator doors began to slide open.

"You go first, Colonel," Bane said. "Walk directly to the console room that controls Vortex." Bane stepped closer, hid the Uzi between his and Chilgers' sides. Davey was still directly behind the colonel.

The doors finished their slide. Chilgers stepped out first.

The Vortex console was located in the far right-hand corner of a mammoth room filled with computer banks, consoles, and terminals. It was contained by a newly built structure that looked like a bank vault. The eyes of the on-duty COBRA personnel followed them as they approached the Vortex center. Since Chilgers was apparently in the lead, though, none took any steps to intervene. A dozen guards stood poised outside the main entrance to the computer center, committed to denying access from that point as ordered. The only other means of entry was through Chilgers' private elevator and that did not pose a security risk. The men maintained their vigil.

"Open the door, Colonel," Bane instructed when they had reached the Vortex vault. "Open it now."

Again Chilgers resisted. Again Davey pushed harder. Chilgers dug his shoes into the tile floor. The blood started from his nostrils again. His face grew ghastly purple, as if he were holding his breath. Finally, he swung violently toward the vault door, moving his fingers toward it as though invisible hands were controlling his actions.

A number of the on-duty personnel who had been observing began to approach, sensing something was wrong, a few noticing the blood on Bane's and Davey's clothes and moving in for a closer look.

Chilgers extended a key toward a slot with a trembling hand that balked at the motion. Finally the key slid home, turned, allowing a plate to rise revealing a block of numbers three in each row.

Two COBRA computer operators caught a glimpse of the Uzi hidden against Chilgers' side and sprinted for the door to alert security.

Chilgers punched in the proper nine-number sequence, his index finger trembling briefly over the code's final digit.

A troop of security guards rushed through the main entrance. Bane sent a volley of bullets toward the door, felling the first ones through.

The vault door swung electronically open.

Bane fired another burst, grabbed Davey, and pulled him through the opening, shoving Chilgers as he went. Bullets chimed off the steel. One struck the area where Bane's hands struggled to force the door closed again. He lost feeling in his right palm and thumb, kept the door moving anyway. It sealed shut. Bane swung around.

Chilgers stood in the middle of the small room, features still purple, bulging eyes furious, enraged now. He made no effort to wipe the blood from his nostrils, all his inner strength turned to regaining control.

The computer terminal sat in the vault's center, innocuous enough save for a clock resting on top of it flashing the countdown in bright red letters.

2:59 . . .

Less than three minutes and the MX missile warheads would reenter space over their targets. Vortex would be complete.

"Reprogram the computer, Colonel," Bane instructed clearly. "Reduce the folds in space to an infinitely small degree."

Chilgers started toward the console, lurched back, a puppet being pulled in two directions. Finally he stood over the terminal and switched it on. His teeth sliced through his tongue. Blood started from his ears now.

Davey moved a little closer, tightened his stare as much as he could. His head was starting to pound now, the familiar pain returning. But he wouldn't give in to it. He'd hold on to The Chill for as long as Josh needed him to. He gritted his teeth, pushed harder.

2:45 . . .

Chilgers' fingers quivered over the keyboard, then descended upon it. He hit a series of numbers and letters, and a geometrical pattern appeared on the screen representing the points in space where each warhead would make its reentry, the vortexes themselves. Though there were 360 separate vortexes now, this one model represented all of them. It was cone-like in design, stretching across the screen with the illusion of motion and three dimensions, its insides filled with honeycomb, oblong shapes. Bane guessed there were 360 of the shapes, one for each warhead.

2:15 . . .

Outside, Bane could hear them working on the vault door.

Chilgers had stopped typing. His eyes sought out Davey's. The boy didn't so much as flinch. The colonel went back to the terminal, started punching in instructions again. Figures and letters, random-looking to Bane, started appearing under and over the Vortex cone. Chilgers' fingers were flying now and the machine responded instantly. The honeycomb shapes began disappearing from the inside of the cone. When all were gone, Bane knew the folds would have been made infinitesimally small. So long as one honeycomb remained, however, one or more of the missiles would still be able to slip through. The door Von Goss had described would remain open far enough for the end of the world, as The Vibes had shown it to Davey, to come to pass.

1:30 . . .

Only two more of the honeycomb shapes remained, one last button for Chilgers to press. The colonel's finger rose over the center of the keyboard, moving for the row of numbers. It shook horribly. His last bit of resolve halted his progress. A generation of work was about to be lost forever, destroyed; and Davey could not erase the part of his mind which remembered that fact. The boy squeezed his eyes shut and pushed as hard as he could. Chilgers' mouth dropped for a scream that wouldn't come. Then his finger started moving again.

It was almost to the row of numbers, hovering over the middle, when a sudden explosion cracked the vault door open wide enough for one machine-gun barrel to sneak through and spray a series of random shells into the vault. Davey lurched backward, blood stitching a jagged design on the wall behind his torn shoulder. He slumped down, eyes dimming.

Chilgers collapsed, dazed but freed.

Bane made it to the door as the crack started to widen. He jabbed the Uzi through the opening and fired a burst. The guards beyond jumped back. Bane dropped the Uzi and slammed his body into the vault door, grabbing the blown latch with both hands to try to lock it back in place. A ragged, six-inch shard of steel came off in his fingers, slicing his flesh. Bane screamed and the shard went flying across the room into the computer console's side.

:59 . . .

Ignoring the pain, Bane snapped what was left of the latch into place again and swung around in time to see Chilgers pounding a shoulder into his midsection, jamming him against the vault door. Then the colonel was squeezing his throat in a viselike grip born of rage and pain. Bane managed to break the hold but Chilgers went for his groin with a series of kicks and thrusts, enough finding their mark to stagger Bane and partially double him over. Then Chilgers interlaced his fingers and pounded the back of the Winter Man's neck.

:45 . . .

Physically he was hardly a match for Bane and certainly would not be able to keep this pace up for long. But he didn't have to. Seconds kept passing on the red clock, drawing the final moment of Vortex closer, and the vault door might be breached even before that.

Chilgers went for Bane's eyes but the Winter Man caught the colonel's wrist and pulled, depriving Chilgers of balance. The colonel compensated too much and Bane forced him backward. Chilgers tottered, eyes grasping the red digits ticking ever downward.

:35 . . .

He swung away from Bane and started for the Uzi but the Winter Man tripped him up and kicked the gun aside. Chilgers struggled back to his feet, never quite making it as Bane slammed a knee under his

431

chin, blasting him hard against the wall. His head hit first and he crumpled to the floor.

Bane rushed to the console. Chilgers had been moving his finger toward the middle of the keyboard's row of numbers—*6* perhaps, or *5* or *7*. Even *4* or *8* conceivably.

He heard the sound of metal scraping against tile and swung just as Chilgers was raising the Uzi. In an instant, Bane's professional instincts provided him with a response. He grabbed the shard of steel from the blasted door latch that rested on the console table.

The colonel went for the trigger.

Bane was already airborne, into a headlong dive with the ragged weapon held taut and sure. He landed just as Chilgers' finger had started to close, forcing the Uzi away and plunging the steel shard down toward the colonel's midsection.

The Uzi fired a harmless volley into the wall.

Chilgers gasped, his mouth dropping wide for a scream lost in the rush of air up his throat. His eyes bulged, then grew glazed and distant, locking open, his grasp on life relinquished far more easily than his control of Vortex had been.

Bane pushed himself up off the corpse and rushed to the console, aware the vault door was almost certain to be blown open any second.

:15 . . .

His own death—and the boy's—were inevitable now. No getting around that. It would be mercifully quick and at least his mission still stood a chance of success before the moment came.

:10 . . .

Bane narrowed his choice of numbers to *5, 6, or 7*. Pick the right one and Vortex would be finished, the final folds in space closed forever. Pick the wrong one and the machine would register an inconsistency, an error of syntax Bane would be helpless to correct in time. One chance, one chance only.

:07 . . .

He moved his finger forward, relying on the instincts that had saved his life so often in the past and now had to be called upon to save the entire world. One chance in three . . . He'd faced far worse odds than that and won.

The Winter Man's finger plunged down and he didn't realize it was the six he'd chosen until his eyes followed.

The final honeycombs disappeared. The outline of the cone faded from the screen.

The folds in space had all closed. Vortex had been destroyed.

The red digits locked at :03.

But Bane wasn't taking any chances. He fired the remainder of the Uzi's clip into the console until it smoked, flamed, and popped. His eyes moved to the vault door, knowing it would be blasted open before the next minute was out and caring more than he thought he would.

Bane knelt next to Davey and cradled the boy's head in his arms. Davey's blood soaked through his green surgical outfit and Bane had to force down his tears.

"I'm here, Davey, I'm here."

He couldn't tell how serious the boy's wound was and didn't bother to check. He was not even sure Davey could hear him. It was over; nothing could change that now. The Winter Man was out of miracles. He cradled the boy closer.

"We did it, Josh," he murmured, "didn't we?"

Before Bane could answer, a blast came from outside and the vault door swung all the way open. Bane sat there waiting for the bullets to come from the guns of the rushing guards.

They stormed the door, rifles ready. Bane found himself rising, unable to stem the instinct for survival that had controlled him for so long. But the move this time was pure reflex, nothing more.

And then the explosions started.

The first came with a force sufficient to slam the vault door back on the two guards who were not quite all the way inside, crushing them between steel with thousands of pounds of pressure. The next explosion sounded and it seemed to Bane that the whole building was collapsing, and in fact, fragments of the false ceiling did shower down on the swarm of guards waiting beyond the vault. The entire COBRA underground structure rumbled, pulsed.

The King! The wondrous, glorious King! The explosions had come from his charges!

Where a moment before there had been no hope, Bane saw a flicker and seized it. The vault door was swinging open again, allowing the two crushed guards to tumble to the floor and revealing stun grenades on each of their belts. Bane grabbed a pair along with a fallen rifle; then swooping up the half-conscious Davey in his free arm, he roared into the main computer area to be greeted by another blast which seemed to come from directly above. Bane lobbed one of the stun grenades to the left and one to the right. The blasts were deafening. The rest of the guards staggered, their shots which otherwise would have been straight going well wide of their targets and allowing Bane the instant he needed to make it through them.

His forward motion toward the door was constant, keeping his and Davey's frames low all the way. Thick gray electrical smoke from a host of shattered computer terminals and wires filled the room, turning all shapes into shadows that further shielded his escape. Then the main lighting died yet again, obscuring him even more.

He raced into the corridor at the moment a fourth riveting blast pounded the walls. Holding his balance, he slung the M-16 over his shoulder and grasped Davey in both arms for the flight down the corridor. Bane's bearings had returned to him. He was one floor up from the garage where Chilgers' limousine was stored—right now his only sure means of escape.

He noticed that the bullet had penetrated Davey's right shoulder and passed straight through. The boy was losing a lot of blood, and in his already weakened state the strain of the wound would prove fatal unless Bane reached help fast.

The limousine . . . It was his only hope.

Bane found a stairwell and descended it effortlessly, aware for the first time that the emergency alarm was wailing again, although buried at regular intervals by the King's explosions. COBRA was out of control, the system of command broken, no one sure precisely what was going on. Everywhere people rushed to find answers, save equipment, flee. Smoke from damaged wires poured through the stairwells and corridors. Sprinkler systems randomly switched on, adding to the confusion.

You outdid yourself this time, King.

Bane blended perfectly with the havoc. He bolted down the fifth underground level's corridors with Davey clutched in his arms, unchallenged by COBRA personnel. He swung round the last corner and made out the vague outline of the hidden garage panel in the half light. He rushed to the control button against the wall, pressing it twice without success and realizing the system had shorted out. Footsteps rushed about him, pounding the floor. Orders were screamed. Bane had to take a chance.

Since there was no way to operate the door electronically, he'd have to lift it manually. The panel itself, though, was nothing more than a slice of wall—no place to gain purchase—and he doubted that he'd be able to lift it alone anyway.

Three men in white coats charged forward, oblivious to his presence.

"Quick! Help me!"

They took a look at his green surgical outfit, still matted with blood, and then at the prone figure in white on the floor. They moved toward Bane without speaking, taking note of his rifle only when he stripped it off his shoulder and carved a series of chasms in the hidden garage panel with a single spray to serve as handgrips.

"Help me get the door up!" he screamed at the technicians, eyes raging with a surety that made the three men obey.

The door resisted at first, then gave. The men realized only then that something was very wrong. After all, this was the colonel's car, the colonel himself!

Bane leveled the M-16 at them. "Get your asses the hell out of here!"

The men scampered away. Bane had no more time to waste. Security would certainly be on his trail now if they weren't already. Worse, they'd know his precise location and plan, and he couldn't count on any more miracles from King Cong to help him get out of the building. He lifted Davey gingerly but quickly and hurried toward the black limousine, stretching the semiconscious boy out on the back seat.

"Josh," he muttered. "Josh . . ."

"Over there! Over there!" Bane heard someone scream as he slammed the front door behind him, lunging behind the wheel to find the keys still in the ignition. He hadn't even bothered to consider the very real possibility they were in the pocket of the uniform he had appropriated from the dead chauffeur.

Bane gunned the engine and then hit a switch on the dashboard he prayed would activate the hydraulic lifts under the bay.

Nothing happened. He clicked it again. Nothing still.

Something cold gripped Bane's insides. To have come this far to find the lift mechanism shorted out . . . No, it couldn't be. Chilgers would have covered all angles to provide for his own escape in an emergency. The lift would operate off a separate power line and generator. The problem was the switch; where was it?

Bane's fingers probed about the dashboard and discovered the correct switch on a separate panel under the glove compartment. The lift began to rise, the squealing sound it made the most beautiful he had ever heard. A throng of green-uniformed COBRA security men reached the bay when the lift was halfway to the fourth level. Bane ducked under the steering wheel as a rapid burst of fire tore into the windshield on the passenger side. He heard bullets clanging up into the car's front grill and could only hope penetration hadn't been deep enough to do any severe damage.

The engine grumbled briefly, but stayed on. Bane gunned it, looking back over his right shoulder and preparing to tear out as soon as the bay opened on ground level.

The lift sighed to a halt. Bane hit the button which

had done him no good the first time and incredibly the hidden ground-level door began to slide upward.

A jeep—no, two of them—screeched to a halt just as the door's rise was completed, trying to cut off possible escape routes for the car, trapping it in the bay. Bane didn't hesitate. As the jeeps' spotlights flooded the limousine's interior, he shoved the big car into reverse and floored the gas pedal. Its tires spun furiously, grabbed hold. The big car lunged backward, Bane spinning its wheel to angle its rear bumper against the front of both jeeps. Impact shook him, smashing his teeth together and wrenching his neck. He held his breath, conscious of the effect on Davey.

The grinding sound of the collision was still fresh in his ears when he drove the car backward again, spinning the wheel quickly away and jamming the limo into drive. The guards inside the wrecked jeeps fought to aim their weapons, but their shots angled harmlessly into the trees as the big car roared toward the front gate.

Bane never slowed down. His speed had passed fifty when the heavy steel gate came into view and he hoped it would be enough to crash him through. A pair of spotlights from the guard tower grabbed him as he sped forward, into the final stretch now. Bane knew what was coming next. He threw his whole body under cover of the dashboard an instant before a barrage of bullets shattered the remains of the windshield, covering him with splinters of glass. A ricocheting slug burned into his side, a graze only but enough to make him lurch reflexively up so that a second bullet slammed into his shoulder and sent his senses whirling. He felt his lips trembling and struggled with the car, holding tight to the wheel with his one good hand.

Another burst of fire blew out the rear window, and Bane could tell by the angle of the shots that the car was almost upon the gate. He couldn't raise his eyes enough to check but felt confident he had kept the wheel straight and steady under fire. He felt warm blood soaking through his surgical top and fought down the urge to comfort his wounded areas, knowing he had no hand to spare for the act.

Bane caught the flash of the fence's top as the limo smashed through it with little resistance. The impact, though, sent the big car careening wildly, out of control; spinning, screeching, its tires making smoke and churning up dust. Only then did Bane raise his head above the dashboard, neck tense against a possible burst from the tower. The car was heading off the road, directly for a tree. He righted it, too much so, in fact, and the tires sank momentarily into the soft shoulder on the other side. He fed the gas just enough to prevent the car from digging itself in and then tore down the open road toward the freedom promised by the lights of San Diego. Miles ahead, he caught glimpses of lights moving in military convoy fashion toward COBRA, their presence a late but welcomed assurance that Washington had finally bought his story, though he didn't bother considering how.

Bane felt dazed, dizzy with pain. A hospital wouldn't be a bad idea for him either. His eyelids fluttered. The car flirted with the center line, crossed it. How could he make it all the way to a hospital?

Fire engines screamed by en route to the chaos he had left behind, forcing him alert again. Bane allowed himself a smile, imagining for an instant he could see all of COBRA burning in the rear-view mirror.

What he didn't expect to see when he moved his

eyes back to what had been the windshield was a man in a COBRA security uniform standing in the center of the road. Armed, no doubt, and it was too late—Bane was too sluggish to take evasive maneuvers.

He aimed the limo right at the man, hoping desperately to blind him in the spill of his high beams. The lights caught a huge grinning face instead of a rifle barrel, and Bane screeched to a halt just to the right of the massive figure it belonged to.

"Goin' my way?" wondered the King.

EPILOGUE

Bane met the President on a frigid April afternoon two days later. It was cold enough for snow to be in the forecast even in Washington, which made Bane's wounds throb all the more.

"The doctors tell me you can expect a full recovery, Mr. Bane," the President said, facing him from behind his desk in the Oval Office.

Bane shifted his right arm in its sling. His left side, damaged more than he had originally suspected, was tied tight with tape to restrict movement. He grimaced as he crossed his legs.

"And the boy, did they tell you about him as well?"

The President hesitated. "A flesh wound. Nothing that time and patience won't heal."

"And the rest?"

The President's mouth dropped. He said nothing.

"Come now, sir, you didn't really expect they'd keep it from me, did you? I can be a most persuasive man when the spirit moves me." Bane grimaced again. "He's dying, Mr. President. Part of his brain's ruined. Oh, his life will be normal all right for a week, a month, at most a year. But then one day a few blood vessels will go and the boy will simply collapse. So you see Davey Phelps hasn't got much time and I haven't got much patience."

"If you'll let me, Mr. Bane, I'd like to make amends for all that's happened."

Bane slowly uncrossed his legs.

The President's eyes moved to the empty chair next to his. "That belonged to Arthur Jorgenson. It's yours if you want it."

"You're offering me the directorship of DCO?"

The President rose and held Bane's stare while he moved toward the window. "Mr. Bane, I don't have to tell you about the trying times we live in. COBRA is finished. It will be rebuilt, both structurally and personnelwise, but without Chilgers the level of its contributions promises to be substantially reduced. For all his faults, the colonel was primarily responsible for maintaining our technological edge against the Soviets. I fear we've lost that edge now, Mr. Bane, and I don't want to lose any others." The President pointed at the empty chair. "I'm offering you that chair or whatever else you want because you represent one of those other edges and I don't want to lose you. You're the best, Mr. Bane."

"I wouldn't be very helpful from a chair."

"You could do with the job whatever you saw fit."

Bane shook his head. "I don't think so, Mr. President."

"Name your terms. Anything." A pause. "We need you."

Bane considered the offer. "I want a name."

"A name?"

"I want to know who put the kill order out on me five years ago."

"Kill order? I don't know what you're talking about. I wasn't even in office then."

"The information's available to you, sir, probably closer than you think."

"What do you mean?"

"You didn't put that unsalvageable order out on me on your own. Someone else, maybe more than one person, convinced you to. I've thought the whole thing out. Someone knew I was getting close and had to save his ass. Someone blew it five years ago, blew it because I didn't die. It's someone close to you, Mr. President, that's the way I've got it figured."

Brandenberg, thought the President. Brandenberg had been top intelligence man in the Pentagon five years back.

"A name, Mr. President."

"I haven't got one for you."

"But you'll look."

"I'll . . . look. Am I to understand then, Mr. Bane, that if I furnish you with this name, you will come back to work for us?"

Bane held his stare coldly. "What you are to understand, Mr. President, is that if you don't come up with a name I might come after you instead."

"You're threatening me, Mr. Bane."

"Just a warning, sir. I plan to do a lot of thinking in the next few months. I'll have nothing but time, because I plan to take Davey Phelps to see some of the world, a lot of it in fact. He deserves that much."

The President returned to his seat. "I might have a name for you by the time you return."

"I believe you will have, sir, but I'm not sure right now I'll be coming back, because every time I see Davey I realize how out of control our world has become. We almost destroyed ourselves two days ago and we're certain to try it again before too much longer. I'm not sure I want to be a part of that scenario."

"Having you on our side might help prevent it."

Bane shook his head. "The words sound good, but that's all they are. You can't control technology with

such words any more than you can control the
Soviets with them. Davey Phelps is an example of
how far we can go to get nowhere. Vortex is finished
and Chilgers is dead, but there'll be others, probably
are already. I think maybe the best thing to do is to see
it out on a deserted island somewhere."

Bane struggled up from his chair. The President
rose to join him.

"I'll be in touch when you return, Mr. Bane."

Bane nodded and left the room.

"Car's over there, Josh," Harry Bannister said
when Bane returned to the freezing air in the White
House parking lot. The Bat had insisted on making
the trip to Washington with him, if for no other
reason than to act as his driver. He even found an
agency which provided special vehicles for the
handicapped. Now he wheeled himself alongside
Bane toward the station wagon he had rented. "We
heading back to New York?"

"Yeah."

"Worried about the kid?"

"Not at all. The King moved into his hospital
room. He's not about to lose him twice."

"For sure." The Bat cocked his head back toward
the White House. "How'd it go inside?"

"Well, I don't think they're about to let me quit
again."

"Can't say I blame them. The President make you
an offer?"

Bane nodded. "Which I promptly turned down. I
told him I was finished."

They had reached the car. Harry eased himself into
the specially designed driver's seat while Bane stowed
the wheelchair in the wagon's tailgate section and

then slid gingerly into the passenger side.

"And are you finished?" the Bat wondered.

Bane just looked at him.

And suddenly Harry knew. "You're playing hard to get, you bastard. That's what this meeting was all about, for you to set the ground rules so you can have things on your own terms. And when you get back from taking the kid on vacation, what then, Winter Man? A return to the Game maybe?"

"Why, Harry," Bane said with a wink, "you know me better than that."

"Yeah? Well if you go back in just remember to take the Bat with you, you son of a bitch."

Thick, wet snow flakes had begun to fall from the sky when Harry started the engine.

"Shit, will you look at that," he moaned, as the windshield wipers swiped at them, squeaking against the glass. The Bat gunned the heater and blew into his hands.

Winter had returned.

AUTHOR'S NOTE

The Safe Interceptor, Project Placebo, and Bunker 17 are products of my imagination. The Philadelphia Experiment, though, has been arguably documented in the superb investigative study by William Moore and Charles Berlitz, which provided the impetus for this novel.*

Einstein's Unified Field Theory, meanwhile, remains a baffling and controversial concept. My special thanks to scientist Emery Pineo for making sense of it for me and theorizing on ways it might be employed to create the ultimate weapon. Thanks also go to Scott Siegel, scientist John Signore, and Dr. Morty Korn, whose brilliant career as a cardiologist is rivaled only by his expertise as a critic of my early drafts.

The principles and effects of the Vortex fields lie not only within the realm of credibility, but also within the reach of contemporary technology. Sometimes fiction seeks to imitate truth. Sometimes they are very much the same thing.

*Charles Berlitz and William L. Moore, *The Philadelphia Experiment: Project Invisibility*, Fawcett Crest, 1979.

THE BEST IN ADVENTURES FROM ZEBRA

GUNSHIPS #2: FIRE FORCE   (1159, $2.50)
by Jack Hamilton Teed
A few G.I.s, driven crazy by the war-torn hell of Vietnam, had banded into brutal killing squads who didn't care whom they shot at. Colonel John Hardin, tapped for the job of wiping out these squads, had to first forge his own command of misfits into a fighting FIRE FORCE!

GUNSHIPS #3: COBRA KILL   (1462, $2.50)
by Jack Hamilton Teed
Having taken something from the wreckage of the downed Cobra gunship, the Cong force melted back into the jungle. Colonel John Hardin was going to find out what the Cong had taken — even if it killed him!

THE BLACK EAGLES #3:
NIGHTMARE IN LAOS   (1341, $2.50)
by John Lansing
There's a hot rumor that Russians in Laos are secretly building a nuclear reactor. And the American command isn't overreacting when they order it knocked out — quietly — and fast!

THE BLACK EAGLES #4: PUNGI PATROL   (1389, $2.50)
by John Lansing
A team of specially trained East German agents — disguised as U.S. soldiers — is slaughtering helpless Vietnamese villagers to discredit America. The Black Eagles, the elite jungle fighters, have been ordered to stop the butchers before our own allies turn against us!

THE BLACK EAGLES #5:
SAIGON SLAUGTHER   (1476, $2.50)
Pulled off active operations after having been decimated by the NVA, the Eagles fight their own private war of survival in the streets of Saigon — battling the enemy assassins who've been sent to finish them off!

Available wherever paperbacks are sold, or order direct from the Publisher. Send cover price plus 50¢ per copy for mailing and handling to Zebra Books, 475 Park Avenue South, New York, N.Y. 10016. DO NOT SEND CASH.

THE SURVIVALIST SERIES
by Jerry Ahern